BLADE OF BROKEN SCALES

Blade of Broken Scales

Playlist

Here's a playlist of songs I listened to while writing Blade of Broken Scales. Enjoy!

Pronunciation Guide

Falrin .... Fahl-rin

Calum .... Kal-um

Amira .... Ah-meer-ah

Cydinth .... Sigh-dinth

Aurelius...................... Are-ehl-ee-us

Raegorath .... Rag-or-rath

Drakmoor .... Drak-moorh

King Thorian .... Thor-ee-an

Synacthdris.....................Syn-ock-dris

Seraphina ....Seh-rah-FEE-nah

Adeline Ambrose .... Add-ah-line

Roman Drache .... ROH-muhn Dra-ck-ee

Trigger Warnings

Blade of Broken Scales is a fantasy romance
based in a fictional realm – and while it may be
fun, this story includes content that some
readers may not find suitable;
Explicit sexual content, profanity,
kidnapping (of an adult), blood, death,
death of a minor (on page),
non-consensual kissing, and violence.

If anything on this list bothers you, please put
yourself first; your mental health matters to
me!

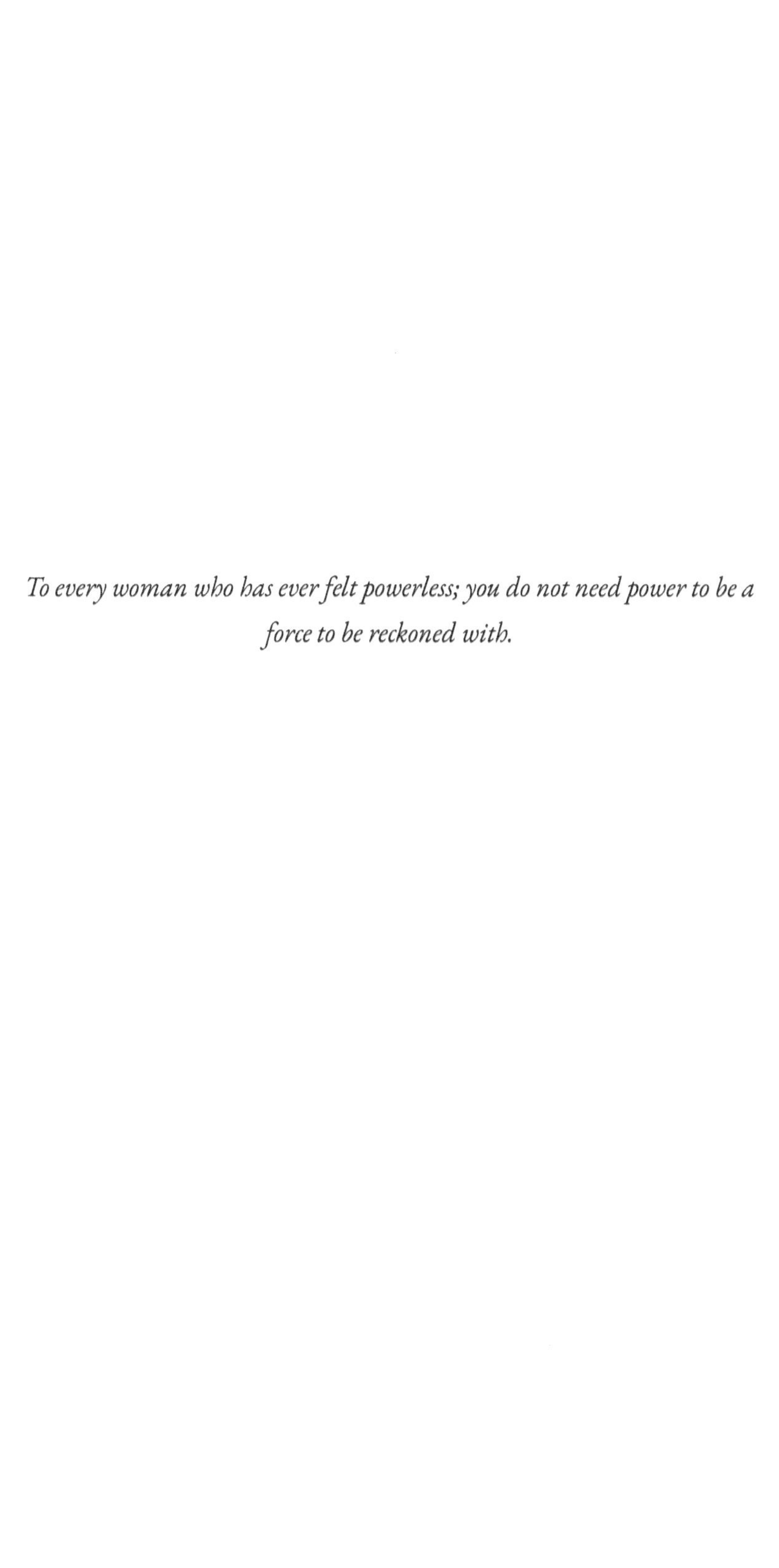

To every woman who has ever felt powerless; you do not need power to be a force to be reckoned with.

PROLOGUE

ONE HUNDRED AND FIFTY YEARS BEFORE

THE BLADE OF DEEP obsidian pierced midnight-black scales. Amira bit back tears and threw every ounce of her strength into landing the final blow; the killing blow. She tightened her fingers around the dagger's long, slender hilt, ensuring her hold on the weapon was firm, precise; it would be detrimental to lose her grip. She stretched, testing her body's limits and ignoring the searing pain that roared to life in her muscles to ensure the blow landed. With an ear-splitting roar, the black dragon bucked, furious. It took every ounce of Amira's focus to release her hold on the creature at just the right moment to leap from the dragon's neck to the forest floor below. She tucked her head, folding her whole body in on itself as she rolled into the fall, coming up on wobbling legs, but solidly planted feet. In mere moments, the forest around her shook with fervor as the dragon collapsed into a massive heap on the moss covered earth, shaking the dirt beneath her faded leather boots. Wiping away the tears gathering in her bright green eyes, Amira laid a gentle hand on the dragon's head, running her calloused fingers over the ridges of its scales, a final act of comfort to the now lifeless creature before her. Raising her left hand, she brought her middle and pointer fingers to her mouth, pressing her lips to them in a gentle kiss before placing them on the jet-black scales just above the dragon's snout, a sign of respect to his lost life.

Dragons used to be something Amira believed to be of great danger, the very thing that made up the fairy tales told to the children who lived in her quaint little village. Parents would run their hands through their little ones's hair and speak of creatures of great protection and grace as a soothing lullaby. Amira's mother had been fascinated with all the dragons stood for, and had instilled that passion and tender love for the curious beings in her daughter. Amira's mother described dragons as beautiful creatures of loyalty and immense power. They were not to be feared, but idolized. That is, until they weren't.

No one knows quite what happened or where the dragons came from, but Amira personally believed that they had always been there, living peacefully in the surrounding lush green forests until they were provoked. Maybe it was some overly curious adolescents with a need to prove themselves, poking around caves they shouldn't have ventured into. Maybe the dragons simply grew tired of watching humans destroy their land, chopping down the towering trees that made up their home to build villages where they weren't welcome.

One day, they just *snapped*. Dozens of villages nestled in the heart of what used to be an endless expanse of forest were reduced to ruins of ash and dust. The Scorching had begun, and humanity quickly lost all hope.

People were killed, some indistinguishable from the ashes of the village itself, others skewered by the incomprehensibly sharp talons at the ends of the dragon's feet.

Communities attempted to rebuild after the initial attacks, having assumed that was it, only to be leveled into fiery pits weeks later. Riddled with terror and still not certain what the catalyst of such anger had been in the first place, humans had no choice but to face the fury of the creatures. Even among the fear, villages were rebuilt time and time again—a symbol of hope in the midst of such tragedy.

Not a single kingdom was left untouched by the dragon's wrath; people had no place to flee to, nowhere to run. Yet, the villagers refused to give in to the torment and pain fate handed to them, and they continued to rise again.

Years went by like this, and people grew tired of the loss and hurt they faced. Their desperation grew until they believed the only thing that could be done to protect their beloved land and families from further attacks was to slaughter the dragons themselves. Considering that dragons are much larger than even the tallest person, towering over all humans in a looming threat, they were difficult to conquer.

Due to the impossibility of the task at hand, there was no quick solution. It took villages banding together and combining their arsenals of expertly crafted crossbows, swords, and daggers. Even then, it was still not enough. Large groups could not kill a single dragon with their iron weapons as the ore was no match for the hardened scales of the beasts. Years were spent training tirelessly, honing the skills of their own makeshift armies in hopes that, eventually, it would be them who would successfully slay one of the creatures.

To this day it's a mystery how it happened, but the first slain dragon was brought down at the hands of a single, almost inconsequential, man. No one even knows his name. The Scorching halted once that first dragon was conquered, stopping just as abruptly as it had started. With a taste of retribution after years of torment, the people's war on dragons quickly boiled over into something uncontrollable. Not only were the kingdoms furious with the great beasts for the devastation and ruin they had caused, but with the first fatal blow to one of the majestic creatures came the knowledge that he who slays a dragon becomes heir to the dragon's *power.*

With this realization, people became ravenous for power, each wanting to become stronger than the other. Rationality was quickly lost to all as *everyone* physically capable set out to kill a dragon, or more than one if they were brave enough. Humans honed new weapons from the long curved claws that once decimated the people of the kingdoms. The nearly indestructible scales appeared among the more elite. Before long, dragon scales became a highly coveted item in the world, and more starving villagers trained tirelessly to annihilate dragons as a means of financial gain.

Weapons and armor crafted from dragon scales made the warriors stronger than humanly possible. Even with these great weapons of protection, many would never be successful in their endeavors. Society became overrun with warriors craving the ability to wield power not meant for the human body, but training as though it would be their destiny, creating a greater epidemic than the dragons had.

The Scorching had spanned half a century before the first dragon fell. For fifty years, the kingdoms fought to hold onto any sliver of hope that it would end soon, that they could put a life of grief and violence behind them. It was funny, almost, how quickly they became comfortable with slaughter when it was they who wielded the power.

After Amira's family faced the terrible fate of being burned alive when dragons attacked their village during the twentieth year of The Scorching, she had no one to turn to and nowhere to go. Being only five years old she had no choice but to take to the streets, and eventually, at twenty, taking up an occupation as a dragon slayer was the easiest way for her to survive; even if her heart broke a little more every time she watched one fall.

It had been twenty years since the first fallen dragon, and still Amira Drache felt nothing but sympathy for these mighty creatures. Even though she made a considerable profit selling the scales of her victories, money that she needed to survive, Amira still found herself racked with guilt as she brought down each great beast. The onyx dragon earlier today brought her up to three in her time as a dragon slayer. Meaning that she had officially slain more dragons than any recorded person. Maybe that was why she continued to don the oversized wool cloak, hood up to shield her identity from buyers, hiding her in the shadows. Although incredibly talented, Amira's shame for what she was doing made her prefer to remain anonymous to those she interacted with.

Looking down at her left arm, she realized the power transfer had begun. Raising it to eye level, Amira watched in wonder as purple smoke enveloped her limb, as if she were being swallowed by the very spirit of the dragon before her. A smile danced across her lips as she watched the tendrils grow smaller in size, absorbing into her tanned skin and curling around her fingertips as if locked in a waltz with them. It was a quick thing, the power transference, but Amira always soaked in every second of it, finding it to be an elegant display for only her to witness. Something about it called to her, almost tugging at her soul as if her and the power were long lost friends.

As the transfer ended, Amira lowered her arm back to her side, a feeling of disappointment dancing in her chest. She knew that she should be grateful for the power she had just absorbed, but again the guilt gnawed at her. These majestic, benevolent creatures deserved so much better than the fate they had been handed. Amira dreamed that one day she may be able to save the dragons, or at least help the world better understand them. But as she finished gathering as many of the deep black dragon scales as she could fit into her tattered leather pack, she couldn't help but feel as though it would never be more than that, just a dream. No matter how much hope she held onto, the reality of the world around her never failed to smother her ambition.

Just when Amira felt she might give up on the idea that dragons truly were kind creatures, only fighting to protect their own, the dragon attacks just...stopped, seemingly overnight. After more than half a century of torment and pain, their resilience won out. The Scorching just *ended*, as if it had never happened at all. Every few years, there would be the rare report of a dragon attack, though since The Scorching the creatures seemed to direct their ire at only one; the centralmost kingdom of Scalebreak.

CHAPTER ONE

S TRAIGHTENING THE SILVER TIARA atop her head, Adeline took one last look in the mirror, inspecting her reflection to ensure that not a single chestnut brown hair was out of place. She took a moment to admire her current ensemble; a beautiful blood-red ballgown with a corset bustier clung to her body, hugging her narrow hips before flowing out into waves of deep ruby silk. Tulle sleeves hung off her shoulders, resting just above the slight bulge of her biceps, drawing her eyes to the growing muscle there. Pride ignited within her at the strength her body possessed. Smiling to herself, she swayed ever so slightly from side to side, watching with admiration as her eyes caught the subtle sparkles glinting throughout the entire dress, an unexpected surprise. With her every movement, the dress came to life, twinkling as if designed from stars plucked right out of the night sky.

The tiara atop her neatly pinned hair was a gorgeous collection of silver swirling vines with tiny specks of diamonds and the perfect sprinkling of rubies throughout. Vines curled together around the large ruby centerpiece, cradling the precious stone. A shade of lipstick perfectly matching the gown she wore painted her lips, and she couldn't help but feel that the color accentuated her full pout. Adeline smoothed her hands over her considerable skirts, tapping her thumb twice over her right thigh beneath the mass of fabric, knowing the secret of what lay beneath. She met her blue eyes in the mirror, feeling almost outside of her body, looking at the girl staring back at her.

Well, here goes nothing.

Turning on her heel, she took one last deep breath as her slender fingers wrapped around the curve of her chamber doorknob, steeling herself against the growing anxiety. That moment was all she allowed herself before she finally stepped out of the safety of her bedroom and into the waiting chaos.

Just yesterday, Adeline Ambrose had turned eighteen years old, a day most normal children would look forward to with excitement. Adeline, however, was not quite a normal girl. Holding the title of Princess of Scalebreak and now being eighteen years old meant, much to her disdain, that she had just become the most eligible bachelorette in the entire kingdom.

"Adeline, there you are!" her mother fretted. "There are four suitors waiting to meet you in the throne room to win your hand and *you* are *late*!" There was nothing her mother hated more than tardiness, and Adeline sensed the anger radiating off of her as she approached.

She looked up, meeting her mother's gaze. Adeline was always taken aback by her almost celestial beauty. Queen Eloise had the same piercing blue eyes as Adeline, only hers were paired with several feet of long silver hair that was always perfectly styled around her crown of choice.

Dressed to perfection in a custom-tailored gown at all times, Eloise was the picture of regal elegance. She set an example of a poised woman for her two young daughters. What the queen had wanted most for them was to one day take her place upon the throne, becoming dignified leaders of Scalebreak in their own right. Adeline could not imagine a more suffocating fate.

She didn't even have a moment to reply to her mother's biting remark on her tardiness before Eloise grasped her arm and whisked her through the seemingly endless castle halls to the throne room.

Four thrones made a sort of centerpiece atop the dais where the Ambrose family sat; a sight to behold. King Thorian Ambrose looked as intimidating as ever, his glaring gray eyes scanning the crowd while sitting on his iron throne. His hair, chocolate brown with a dusting of gray, was neatly combed over so as not to draw attention away from the gleaming silver crown atop his head. Looking at him now, Adeline felt a familiar tug in her chest at the features they shared.

The queen took her spot on the dais to the left of the king, running her fingers over the dainty iron roses—a nod to the family name—etched among curling vines atop the back of the throne, forever frozen in bloom, before taking her seat.

Adeline's eyes momentarily caught on Briar, her younger sister, dutifully perched on the throne staggered behind their mother's. Her sister was her exact opposite both physically and in character. She was the spitting image of their mother, with the same silver locks and affinity for rules. Briar was everything Eloise wanted in a daughter. Her haunting blue eyes were the only hint at her relation to Adeline, a detail that never failed to leave her a little breathless when looking at her sister.

With a tight smile pointed at Briar, Adeline reluctantly took her seat just behind the king—a mirror to her sister's position. All of them now sitting dutifully on their iron thrones; they had the appearance of the perfect royal family that everyone believed them to be. Adeline knew better.

Adeline took a moment to calm herself against the overwhelming nerves, drawing in a deep breath. She had *never* wanted to be married, so the idea of *four* suitors awaiting her as a potential wife and life partner was enough to make her stomach churn with unease. She swallowed with an almost silent gulp, readying herself for the coming scene. Her gaze locked on the quiet scribe poised in front of the thrones. He bowed forward, but even from her seat on the dais Adeline could make out the graying flecks in his hair. She recognized him immediately as Fen, the most respected scribe among the staff.

He rose, clearing his throat.

"Sir Anthony Blake, Prince of Farhaven," he announced with gusto as a young man with pale blond hair entered the throne room. From her spot on the dais, Adeline guessed him to be around six-two in stature—a stark contrast to her measly five-six. Sir Anthony Blake had a slim sort of build that made Adeline believe him incapable of harming so much as a fly. The dusting of near-white hair on his otherwise balding head almost disappeared in the light of the throne room. Adeline bit back hard to stifle a giggle. He approached the Ambrose family, bowing as he reached the end of the crimson-colored runner, and even from several feet away Adeline could see him trembling. As he stood, she noticed that he had a squirrely look to him, his brown eyes were rimmed in red, making him appear disheveled, perhaps even slightly drunk.

Anthony Blake was only the first bachelor who had traveled here to ask her father for a chance to court her; he left Adeline little hope for the remaining suitors asking for her hand. Being a princess meant she would get no say in who would be considered and who would not, which left her visibly disinterested in the entire ordeal.

Adeline let her gaze drift through the throne room, careful to move only her eyes. Her fear of her mother's lectures on "proper respect" had long ago trained her to keep her head still.

Light spilled through arched floor-to-ceiling windows, their peaks etched with roses so fine they seemed ready to bloom despite being carved in the stone. The thrones sat before them, their regal silhouettes framed in golden rays. Above, the painted ceilings told the story of The Scorching—flames and shadows so vivid they portrayed the kind of beauty that pressed down on her lungs until every breath felt heavy. It was a delicate talent to remind all of such a tragic event in a depiction so ethereal. Adeline found that she often felt suffocated by history standing beneath the painted ceilings.

Stone arches lined the walls, each trimmed with delicate silver roses. White and gray marble tiles stretched across the floor, turning every footstep into a lingering whisper that seemed to follow you throughout the room.

Splashes of green softened the cold grandeur—ivy tumbled over railings, vines spilled from archways—but the true garden rested on the stairs to the dais. Pots brimming with lush leaves cascadeded onto the steps as if nature itself had crept in. Adeline had always liked those plants; they felt like the forest to her.

A dark red runner poured down the stairs, a river of ruby cutting through the room to the towering doors. Her eyes slid to them now, and for a heartbeat she imagined bolting—just running until the echo of her steps faded into silence.

Her attention snapped back to the prince in front of her when she heard him proclaim to be a proficient dragon slayer. Eyebrow raised, Adeline listened skeptically. She had never heard of anyone from Farhaven being involved with dragon slaying; besides, attacks in recent years were centered around Scalebreak. The very idea that the stick of a man in front of her was capable of bringing down the great beasts was laughable. Naturally, her father snapped to attention at his claim as well.

"You declare yourself to be a *dragon slayer*? *You?* With barely an ounce of muscle on your body? From a kingdom that hasn't seen a dragon attack in nearly twenty years? You *insult* my people with such claims. Get *out* of my sight this *instant*." His tone was cold and laced with venom as he spat the words at Sir Blake.

Prince Anthony Blake looked properly petrified as he rose from his bow and quickly exited the throne room, visibly trembling with every step. Adeline couldn't help but laugh to herself. A supposed dragon slayer, but the prince couldn't even stand up to her brooding father—she was quite glad to see him go.

"Lord Jared Silverdawn!" The scribe announced the second suitor immediately after the first parted, and Adeline found herself wishing time would move faster.

No kingdom was claimed in his introduction, telling Adeline he likely did not come from much. She looked at the lord, surprise passing over her features as she scanned his expensive, flashy clothing choices. Lord Jared was wearing a suit that appeared to be made entirely of bright purple silk, a bold fashion decision in itself. The gold monocle perched under his brow and matching pocket watch tucked into his right pocket somehow clashed with the violet suit jacket. Outside of his attire, his appearance was rather plain, and Adeline presumed this was why he'd chosen such over-the-top garb for the occasion.

Flaxen hair lay too flat on the top of Jared's head, the light blond color drawing the essence of life from his face, even from where Adeline sat. The man's only discernible feature was his incredibly large, very pompous nose, and even that just barely drew the attention away from his dull, uninteresting eyes.

"Oh this ought to be good," Adeline mumbled to herself, holding back a chuckle as the man approached the dais.

Lord Jared did not bow to them, instead meeting the king's eyes, which clearly upset her father, who was now glowering at him with distaste. A gasp caught in Adeline's throat as she watched Lord Silverdawn square his shoulders in a challenge. *This man must be positively stupid.*

"I would like—" he started.

But he was cut off by the king with an exasperated, "Out, NOW!" And off he went, scurrying out the doors with his head down, as if he had never been there in the first place.

With two suitors down and two to go, Adeline found herself more entertained by this ordeal than she had anticipated. What had started as a cause of great anxiety and discomfort had turned into quite the spectacle, and she took joy from watching these "regal" men make fools of themselves in front of her earnest father.

"Viscount Feron Fike of Emberfall."

The name piqued Adeline's interest, so much so that she sat up a little straighter in her chair. She had heard of Feron Fike before, which was not surprising since he was considered the most attractive bachelor in the surrounding kingdoms. Adeline remembered the many young servant girls whispering of him in hushed tones to one another, giggles chasing his name past their lips and down the castle halls. As the grand doors opened and he strutted in, Adeline smirked. Viscount Fike was nearly six-four with a muscular build that could be seen, and admired, even through his layers of clothing. A quiff of crimson red hair ignited a fire atop his head, contrasting beautifully against his sharp emerald-green eyes. His shining white smile was framed by his barely pink, plump lips. A mustache brushed over his upper lip and curled up on both ends, as if reaching toward the sky. He truly was quite the beau. So much so, Adeline didn't even realize she'd missed his entire interaction with her father until the viscount left the room, flashing a smile and a wink in her direction. Thorian wasn't yelling, so it must have gone well. Before the viscount, Adeline had begun to hope that she could walk away from this without a single match, but now all she felt was defeat burrowing into her.

It was the fourth and final suitor of the day who entered the throne room and stunned Adeline breathless. Duke Calum Windford waltzed into the room with no introduction and Adeline couldn't fight the beaming smile spreading across her face as she watched him saunter up to her father, swagger in every step.

Calum's dusty blonde hair looked somewhat less unruly than usual today, drawing her attention instead to his cerulean eyes. Normally, Calum could be found in a white linen shirt and faded trousers, but today he was wearing a suit that looked like it had been tailor made for someone of great importance. Brow quirking, Adeline found herself perplexed by the sudden effort he put into his appearance. He looked handsome, but she would never tell him out of fear it would go right to his already inflated head.

Calum and Adeline had grown up side by side since they were a mere eight years old. His parents lost their lives in a gruesome dragon attack on the kingdom ten years ago, both of them burning alive in their home and leaving the young boy an orphan. Calum's father and King Thorian had been close friends since their own childhood, making the Ambrose family's decision to take Calum in as one of their own an easy one. Since that very first day, Adeline and Calum had been inseparable. Thick as thieves, the two of them were always scheming ways to create fun in the all too stiff and serious castle. Enough so that the hired staff knew if mischief was occurring, Adeline and Calum would not be far behind. Recalling the fond memories, Adeline couldn't help but think if she had to be forced into a marriage, it might as well be with Calum. He was her best friend after all.

King Thorian rose and wrapped Calum into a bear hug, his face softening and gray eyes crinkling as he held Calum tightly against him, beaming with pride for the boy—now a man—tucked in his arms.

"Finally, a proper suitor for my daughter!" he chuckled, separating from the hug and patting him on the back with splendor. The mood in the room suddenly didn't feel so suffocating with Calum here. Adeline glanced up and met his gaze, finding that he had already been staring at her. There was something new, almost animalistic in his eyes as he absorbed her every movement. Despite everything going on around them, he seemed encapsulated and attentive only to her and, much like his sudden neat and tidy appearance, it struck her as odd.

In an attempt to ease her own discomfort, Adeline stuck her tongue out at Calum, crinkling her button nose in the process. Rather than laugh like she had expected him to, his gaze turned more adoring than before, as if he found her charming. Adeline found his behavior weird but shook it off, assuming he was just playing up the suitor act, knowing she was already embarrassed at the display.

Tuning out the lively banter around her, she shook her head ever so slightly. Even though the familiar room should be comforting, Adeline found herself detached from it all, locked once again in a far-off daydream of fleeing the throne room and the castle entirely

Chapter Two

B oots pounded against the forest floor, each thud echoing into the silent expanse of trees as Adeline pushed every ounce of her strength into propelling forward, *faster, faster, faster*. With the back of her hand, she wiped the sweat beginning to bead on her brow. She would need as much momentum as possible for what she was about to do, and even as she pushed her body to its limit, she was not entirely convinced she was capable of such a feat.

It is too late to stop now.

Faster, faster, faster.

The thoughts reverberated in her mind until finally she launched her entire body upward in a desperate leap toward the moonlit sky. For one impossible moment, with her hand extended high above her body, Adeline thought she might be able to pluck the stars from the sky if only she could reach just a little further. That daydream was quickly shattered as the beast came into view, and she pleaded with herself to stay focused. Her life depended on it. With a desperate cry, Adeline caught her open hand on the rigid scales lining the spine of the icy blue dragon towering above her. As her fingers found purchase on the creature, a disbelieving laugh slipped past her lips.

Guiding her right hand to her mouth, she made haste of sticking the hilt of her razor-edged dagger between her teeth, biting down firmly on the cool steel hilt—she would need it out of the way in order to make her ascent. No matter how many times she trained or fought, Adeline always moved in a way that ensured her dagger's safety.

The elegant weapon had been a gift from Calum, who believed her late-night trips outside the castle walls to only be a sort of training escapade, nothing of real danger. He'd had the dagger crafted for her and given it to her in secret, always careful to protect her from the king and queen discovering her late night routine. Though he may have disapproved of her hiding in the shadows of the night, he knew Adeline would never forgive him if he was the reason she lost even an ounce of her independence.

The dagger was gorgeous, arguably an art piece better suited for a museum than a battle. Silver roses decorated the midnight black hilt, so thoughtfully placed it looked as though they were sprouting from the iron. Where the hilt ended was Adeline's favorite part, silver vines twisted with one another, almost appearing to be moving on their own, intertwining to form a beautiful barrier just big enough to protect her dainty hands from damage. It was triangular in shape where it connected to the blade, the tangle of vines playfully dancing down the length of the steel until they slowly dwindled to one singular vine at the tip. Though she often found the constant inclusion of roses in everything around her to be nauseating, the fact that Calum had paid such attention to the details was endearing. Beautiful may even be an understatement for her favored blade.

Adeline bit her teeth into the dagger's hilt harder. She would not lose it; she *refused* to lose it. With her right hand now free, she stretched, pulling all of her body weight as she grabbed hold of another ridge on the dragon's back and began her ascent up the beast. Determined, she reached for one rough scale after another, hoisting herself up with each new hold she found. Her muscles protested her every movement, begging her for even just a moment of rest, but to let go now would mean a plummet to her death. She gritted her teeth, refusing to submit to the weakness creeping in on her. As Adeline reached midway up the neck of the blue beast, it let out a screech that made her heart stop; he knew she was here and he was not happy about it. *Fuck.* Adeline still had a ways to go before she reached the end of the dragon's neck, where she would deliver the final blow.

Dragons, while mighty and terrifying to face, had hidden tender spots just below their bottom jaw where their head and neck became one. This spot was one of the only known ways to slay a dragon without having to pry off several of its scales to deliver a fatal wound. Prying the scales off of a living dragon was a feat that *no one* was quite strong or brave enough to conquer. The underbelly of a dragon was also a vulnerable spot; however, no one had survived to tell the tale of felling a dragon by way of attacking the underbelly. Instead, those who tried were found days later, flattened into the very ground they had fought upon and left to be claimed by the forest itself. The soft part of the dragon's neck was the most efficient way to bring one down; you just had to get there without being scorched or eaten alive first.

Scanning her surroundings, Adeline took a moment to blow out a breath, sending the stray hairs that had fallen free from her braid away from her face. She had to get higher, and fast. As if sensing her thoughts, the glacial blue mass of scales beneath her bucked furiously. Roars of fury shook the ground of the forest around them, and the leaves on the trees trembled in a way Adeline wished she could afford to. She stopped, trying desperately to catch her breath and adjust her grip as her hands grew slick with perspiration.

"*Shit!*" she huffed out.

Not wasting another moment, she let go of the scale she was clinging to with her left hand and reached hopelessly for the dagger between her teeth. If she was going to go down, she would go down swinging. In an effort to grasp a better hand hold, she slammed the dagger down, throwing her weight behind it and praying it would find purchase somewhere. As if the Gods themselves had sent her a miracle, Adeline's dagger lodged itself between two icy blue scales, making the perfect handle for her to hoist herself up. Her hope was quickly squashed when the dragon's cries became louder, more furious, and the bucking quickly became harder to withstand. *I will make it out of here alive.*

She gripped the hilt with as much strength as she could muster, until her knuckles turned white, drained of blood from her tightening grip. Gritting her teeth, she freed her right hand and let her body swing with the aggressive motion of the dragon. Adeline used the momentum to throw her hand out to join the other on the hilt of the dagger, where it stuck out from the beast's back. The jerking motions of the dragon were harsh, but holding tight to her weapon, Adeline felt somewhat confident that she could make it out of this, even if she wasn't quite sure how yet.

One had to be equally quick with their wit as they were on their feet if they had any hope to defeat a dragon. One wrong move and the beast would conquer you instead; you'd be lucky if you had time to kiss life as you knew it goodbye. Very few people have walked away from an unsuccessful dragon slaying, let alone lived to tell the tale, a truth that Adeline tried often not to think about.

With a deep breath, she once again leaned into the bucking of the creature, letting her body move fluidly with its own below her.

One...two...three.

Swinging her body forward, she yanked the dagger out of its place beneath the cerulean scales. Time stood still for only a moment, her body suspended in midair. As she felt her stomach find a new home in her throat, signaling her descent, she tightened her hold on the dagger. Willing herself not to panic, she inhaled slowly.

Just before making contact, Adeline bent her legs beneath her, landing gracefully on the back of the beast. As she planted her feet on the dragon's back, she met its gaze. Moonlight reflected off of unblinking obsidian eyes, making them appear almost argent. The two of them stared back at one another for a second, neither of them moving. The beauty of these creatures was not lost on Adeline, though some days she wished it was—perhaps it would make this easier. While her hatred for the dragons and the tragedy they caused her kingdom ran so deep it was practically in her blood, she still found them to be majestic and artful creatures.

She snapped out of her admiration as the dragon's head, craning to peer at her on its back, suddenly lurched toward her with snapping teeth. Reeling backward and tripping over her tattered leather boots, she landed on her butt at the base of the creature's tail. Adeline did not have even a moment to gather her bearings before she was tumbling down the length of cool smooth scales, both arms desperately scrambling to grab hold of something and stop her descent. The ridges of the scales bit into her skin. Even through her thick leather armor, it felt as if she were being sliced open with each one she slid down. She flailed, trying to get a hold of something, anything to stop her fall, but regardless of her attempts, she couldn't find purchase and before she knew it, she was airborne.

It felt as though the dragon had intent behind flicking its tail up to swat her body into the ground, as if it knew she would land with more force. But that was not what Adeline focused on as her body smacked the ground, her back making contact first and knocking every molecule of air from her body. No, her focus was on getting the *hell* up as *fast* as possible.

She drew in one breath. Then another. Each one seared her lungs as pain rippled through every inch of her, sharp and unrelenting. Her legs trembled, but she shoved herself upright. Muscles screamed, bones protested, yet she forced them into motion—to run.

This would not be her end. She would not be left as another carcass pressed into the moss, bones picked clean beneath the trees. The thought struck like a battle cry, propelling her into a sprint.

Heat flared at her back, wild and merciless. She didn't need to look to know the dragon had seen her flee—that the same dragonfire that claimed so much of her kingdom, so many of its people, was now licking at her own back.

It felt as though her leathers were beginning to blister, bubbling to life on her back as she continued to push her body forward. Spotting a familiar clearing ahead, Adeline propelled herself with all the strength she could muster, tucking her head as she rolled forward toward a stone wall plagued with dangling moss. Only her body never made contact with cool rock, instead coming to a stop in a tiny cave. She lay unmoving, dead silent as she peered out through the greenery that curtained the mouth of the cave, barely able to make out the dragon through the dense vines.

Unable to look away, she watched fearfully as the dragon drew close, sniffing with fervor in an attempt to locate Adeline, its escaped assassin. She halted her breathing, holding all the air in her lungs as the dragon sniffed at the entrance of the cave. Dirt from the forest floor stirred to life with each breath the creature took, as if he was drawing life from the very woodland around them.

I've been found. This is it, Adeline thought to herself as she prepared for the fiery death she was about to face. Shock surged through her as the dragon abruptly stopped its search, jerking its head upward and craning its neck as if it could hear something approaching.

The world around them went utterly still for several heartbeats, Adeline still holding her breath and begging her body not to give her away. It felt like several minutes had passed before the dragon finally took off in the opposite direction, though it had likely only been a few seconds. Finally letting go of her held breath, Adeline drew in quick gasps of air, her chest heaving as she fought for control.

"Holy. Shit," she gasped between inhales, still in a state of shock over what had just taken place.

Never had she been so narrow in her escape from a dragon before, and it was equal parts terrifying and exhilarating. Adeline's breaths slowed as she calmed down, lowering herself onto the dirt floor of the cave. Peering around her, she took in the familiar hideout from her childhood.

Briar and Adeline had a tendency of hiding from their nursemaids in the forested areas around the castle as children. Neither of them had liked their nurses very much and found it quite funny to make them scramble to find the missing children in the endless expanses of Scalebreak's castle grounds. In their many adventures to find the best hiding place, they eventually stumbled upon this very cave tucked behind a wall of moss in the forest. The discovery had been purely accidental, as Adeline had been kicking rocks, sending them scattering across the earth as they walked, liking to watch them flee. The two girls had been awestruck when they neared the stone wall, noticing the area where the rocks did not skitter to a halt, but instead seemed to continue past the hanging moss, becoming one with the stone walls. Curiosity blooming in the young girls, they pushed back the moss and, to their delight, found the tiny shelter that would become a haven for them.

For years, Adeline and Briar would come to this spot and craft fairy tales of impossible things, using paints smuggled from the castle to bring their stories to life on the stone walls. Eventually, after he had followed them into the trees one afternoon, they invited Calum to join them in the cave, accepting him as one of their own. He too added to the painted stories that came to life only in their little space, where the three of them could barely fit pressed together. As Adeline glanced at the now fading paintings of fairies, mermaids, and griffins that seemed to dance on the walls around her, she felt safe. She was safe. Nothing could ever touch her here.

After finally regaining her composure, Adeline had decided to run most of the way back to the castle in an attempt to keep the chill away, but that meant she made it back far quicker than she would have liked. Sighing deeply, she dusted off the bits of the forest that still clung to her leathers before looping around the back of the castle; she was far less likely to be discovered sleuthing around in the gardens at the rear of the estate.

Hurrying through the endless rows of greenery and rose bushes around her, she made her way to the staff entrance of the castle—her surefire way of getting in and out unnoticed. Much of the staff was asleep at this hour, except the guards who were concerningly easy for Adeline to sneak by, making it all too simple for her as she quietly slipped inside and through the kitchens.

As she skirted her way down the halls, she was light on her feet, walking nearly on her tiptoes to ensure that her steps did not echo off the stone. She had almost made it to her bedroom when she locked eyes with Calum, standing just outside her door, and felt her heart sink in her chest.

Oh boy. Here we go again, she thought as she approached him, not wanting to hear yet another lecture on why she should not be out this late.

He took a long look at her, taking in her tousled four-strand braid, scuffed and half-melted leathers, and scraped cheek before he spoke. "Are you going to tell me what the *hell* it is you've been doing at night that has you coming home like *this*? Or am I just going to have to keep blindly covering for you?" Steam practically curled off of him as he spoke, his face heating with anger.

"Cal, you know I would tell you if I could."

Adeline nudged past him and reached for the door handle. "Please, just trust me on this," she pleaded as she stepped through the threshold of her bedroom, closing the door on her best friend. She had faced enough disappointment for one night.

CHAPTER THREE

ADELINE GROANED, ARMS STRETCHING out, as she rolled over in her comfortable blankets. The oversized four-poster bed clad in silk fabrics was fit for, well, a princess. Behind her, flowers were etched delicately into the pale wooden headboard, each one intertwining in an endless chase to the top where they bent into elegant curves before spilling down to meet the surrounding bedframe. Layers of decadent pink fabrics swooped down from above, giving her sleeping space an enchanting aura that Adeline quite enjoyed. Cracking open her eyes, she let them adjust to the stark contrast in light as golden rays of sunshine streamed in through the towering windows next to her bed.

Peering through the slits of her eyes, Adeline focused her vision on the windows. They had always been her favorite part of her bedroom. Huge arches spanned floor to ceiling, creating a nook, and ornate swirls of stained glass danced with one another so elegantly that it left onlookers a little breathless. At the base of the windows, a plush upholstered sofa was tucked expertly into the circular space. It was adorned with dainty pink throw pillows that perfectly complemented the seat's ivory hue. At any point in the day, being seated on the sofa and peering out the decorative windows would provide one with the most gorgeous view, and Adeline had always been a sucker for a good view.

That thought was all the encouragement she needed to rise from the soft linens that clung to her body, attempting to pull her back into bed with them. Gently folding the pink satin away from her, she sat up and swung her legs to the edge, eager to watch the first glimpses of morning kiss the horizon. Adeline let the sleep leave her with one final yawn as she reached her arms high above her head and stretched her muscles, waking them up from their slumber and ignoring their sleepy protests. Pushing her body forward, she let her toes meet the soft fabric of the gray rug decorated in floral motifs. She stood, feeling the fibers of the rug encompass her feet like a warm, cushioned hug from the room itself. Adeline made her way over to the elegant windows and lowered herself onto the sofa, pulling her legs up to her chest and letting her chin rest atop her knees. The white cotton nightgown she wore now clung to her skin, damp with sweat from a restless sleep, but she couldn't find it in herself to pay any mind to the way the fabric stuck to her. Instead, she turned herself toward the grand windows, hugging her knees as she peered out over the horizon.

The Scalebreak castle sat right on the bank of Emerald Lake, with water so clear you could see straight through to the lush plant life that consumed the bottom. Emerald Lake spanned over several acres of surrounding forest, claiming most of the land for itself. Its mirror-like surface made both sunrise and sunset true sights to behold when reflecting off of the still water. Adeline, however, had always harbored a preference toward sunrise, loving the way shades of pink and orange chased one another across the skyline.

As day broke over the horizon, a warm golden hue was cast across the serene lake. The water was still, absorbing every one of the vibrant colors painted across the sky—muted pinks blending effortlessly with pale oranges and hints of blue as the last whispers of night faded away. The surrounding trees stood firm, bathing in the first rays of sunlight that danced across the land, standing a little taller as the golden light touched their branches. Even inside the castle, Adeline felt the gentle, cool kiss of the morning breeze on her skin as it blew into her bedroom from the cracked balcony door. The sheer white curtains fluttered carelessly in the wind, swaying as if made alive with the morning air.

Holding her breath, Adeline listened with a careful ear and couldn't help the calm smile that spread over her lips as she heard the chirping of birds, already making use of the early hours. Right there in her bedroom, with the first hints of morning breaking gently over the kingdom, over Emerald Lake, she let herself sink into a very rare moment of tranquility. This was her peace, the quiet to the chaos that was her life.

A sharp, definite knock at her door ripped her from the serenity of the moment. Greta had arrived. Greta was known as one of the less friendly maids, which had made Adeline take an instant liking toward the woman. Her graying hair was always neatly pulled into a too-tight bun atop her head, not one hair out of place, and her muted gray dressing gown never had so much as a wrinkle on its surface. Greta meant business, always. It was almost militant the way the maid operated, and if one asked anyone in the castle, that is what they would say. But when it came to Adeline, Greta had a soft spot. Behind the closed doors of Adeline's bedroom, the two were no strangers to exchanging belly laughs and sentiments. They would gossip in hushed tones about what the castle's inhabitants had been up to while Greta readied her for yet another day spent under the suffocating expectations of her title. Time spent with Greta was always one of Adeline's favorite distractions from her fate.

Greta did not wait for an invitation before pushing her way into the room. She rushed right over to Adeline, pulling her up by her arm wordlessly and dragging her over to the vanity in the corner. Adeline took her seat dutifully, letting her mind wander as Greta made haste of brushing the unruly tangle of bedhead that was her hair and silently thanking the Gods that Greta was allowing her a moment to wake up before speaking to her. The silence enveloped them like a gentle embrace, and it wasn't long before Adeline's mind began to wander.

Last night had been a defeat, to say the least. It had been a long while since Adeline had met her match against a dragon, and to say that it had crushed her spirits would have been an understatement. Dwelling on the events of last night made her heart sink in her chest. Although there were trained soldiers who defended the villages of Scalebreak, Adeline had always felt that it was her purpose, her duty, to protect her people. She refused to sit idly by while the *men* of the kingdom handled things, even if she was strictly forbidden from it.

I mean...no one ever told me NOT to slay dragons. She held back a laugh as the thought crossed her mind.

While Greta quietly brushed Adeline's long brown waves, she couldn't help but begin planning her next excursion into the forest. It would have to wait a few days, since Calum was always far too nosey if her trips outside the castle were close together.

What is he even doing up at that hour, anyway? Adeline thought to herself.

It was quite odd that he had found her out in the first place, considering that she made sure to leave far past nightfall. The thought was both trivial and fleeting. There was no reason to waste time thinking about things like Calum and his evening escapades, whatever they were, when she could be planning her next hunt. She decided then that she would go out three nights from now, giving her just enough time to get a bit more training in.

Gods knows I need it after last time.

She was dressed casually in a floor length-gown of pale pink linen with a square neckline and elbow-length fluttering sleeves. After adding a ribbon of a barely darker pink just under the bosom and having her long brown waves braided neatly behind her, Adeline had been ushered through the heavy oak double doors by Greta. After being practically shoved into the dining room for breakfast, she stopped, realizing Greta had been strangely silent all morning. When her feet crossed the threshold, the old woman was already scurrying away.

With every inch of the wood-paneled walls painted deep royal blue and decorated with intricately crafted portraits of ancestors and previous leaders, the dining room felt rather suffocating. It was the grand crystal chandelier hanging perfectly centered over the long, solid wood table that brought the slightest glimpse of life to the space. When the sunlight peeked in through the windows just so, it reflected off of the crystal and left little rainbows scattered across the room and all of its occupants, a detail that Adeline was particularly fond of.

Seated at the oak table before her sat her whole family, a fact that caused her stomach to churn; she would have to face *all* of them today. King Thorian took the head of the table, always sure in his place of authority, and on his left sat Queen Eloise with her long silver hair braided neatly over her shoulder. Next to the queen, Briar appeared to be nearly her exact copy, down to the precise braid that sat in the curve of her shoulder.

Across from their mother, on the king's right side, sat Calum, always the right-hand man to the king. It was as if they were all simply pawns in a game of chess, the way they all so dutifully surrounded the king.

Calum, being the only boy in the family, had recently taken his place as the commander of the king's armies. Though he may have been treated like blood, his lack of true relation to the Ambrose family meant that he would not be in line for the throne as king, a fact that Thorian himself tried to avoid the topic of. Calum had trained tirelessly, honing himself into the perfect soldier and a near machine-like warrior in hopes of securing the title he now held, and ensuring he would always be ready for battle. He didn't talk about it much, but the loss of his parents weighed on him, and Greta would say his obsession with preparing for war was a coping mechanism. His endless training sessions did not go unnoticed by anyone, and even now, in his nearly sheer white linen shirt that he had rolled up to his elbows, one could not help but notice the swell of muscle at his biceps or how prominent the veins that ran from the backs of his rough, calloused hands and up his forearms had become. There was a reason Calum had become the hottest topic of conversation among the female staff throughout the castle.

Adeline took her seat in the leather high-backed chair next to Calum, mumbling greetings and good mornings as she did so. She may have been a morning person, but this crowd sure had a way of dampening her mood. As if ignoring her mind altogether, her stomach gurgled in excitement at the display of food in front of her. A bowl of steaming porridge topped with plump, ripe blueberries sat atop her plate, beckoning her to it. She wasted no time, making haste in eating the food to quiet the rumbling in her stomach, tuning into the busy conversation around her while she ate.

"Dragon attacks have been decreasing around the southern borders," King Thorian said in a hushed tone as he dragged his finger along the southern border of Scalebreak on the sun-bleached map in his hands.

"There have been no reported sightings of the nasty creatures in days," he finished.

"I suppose the lack of celebration in your tone just now means that you are thinking just as I am," Calum looked up at the king solemnly, meeting his gaze, "that this is awfully suspicious."

Fewer dragon attacks?? That hasn't happened in years...could the war between us and the dragons finally be coming to an end? Have the dragons finally given up? What could this mean for the kingdom? Adeline's thoughts roared to life as she absorbed the information.

"—And the floral arrangements have been selected and finalized," her mother finished saying to Briar, the two of them locked in their own conversation and oblivious to the weight of the news that was just shared.

"And the invitations have been sealed and should be delivered as we speak!" Briar chimed in excitedly.

"Adeline, have you selected a gown yet?" Eloise prodded.

"Ummmmmm..." Adeline drew the words out as she met her mother's steel blue glare across the table, snapping out of her own thoughts.

Shit.

"What *exactly* am I selecting a gown for again?" she questioned, awaiting the reprimand that was sure to follow.

"The *ball* in three days' time, Adeline Camille! I have told you about this event several times, and you should have selected a gown days ago!" her mother chastised her while following the king in rising from the table.

Eloise threw a piercing glower in Adeline's direction before she and Thorian left the dining room without so much as a farewell.

"*I* have already chosen the most beautiful lilac gown to wear the night of the ball," Briar followed behind them, making haste to catch up with the quickly moving couple. She always seemed so eager to please Eloise these days, which was a far cry from the Briar Adeline had grown up with. The thought made her heart pang painfully in her chest with the realization that perhaps she was not nearly as much herself as she had been when they were girls either.

Great.

Not only had she thoroughly irritated her mother, but now she had to find the courage to ask Greta to design her a dress in just three days. Greta would have her work cut out for her, but she would handle everything perfectly, as she always did. In fact, Adeline would be quite surprised if she had not already had a gown made for her, knowing that Adeline herself would not care enough about the coming event to remember. She made a mental note to ask Greta about gown options later today as she too got up from the table. The wood legs of her chair screeched in protest against the floor.

"Adeline. Wait a second," Calum pleaded, gripping her wrist possessively.

She looked down to where his hand was wrapped around her arm, almost insulted by his forward act of physical assertion. Adeline glanced up at Calum, only to realize he looked at her with desperation in his gentle ocean eyes, an unfamiliar sight that caused her to stop resisting slightly and turn to him. He dropped her arm in response.

"I—uh wanted to maybe ask you, if you—" he rubbed the back of his neck, looking away almost sheepishly, "would allow me to escort you to the ball?" he finished quickly, meeting her eyes as he awaited an answer, a blush rising to his cheeks.

Adeline snorted out a laugh that was anything but lady-like. It was a good thing her mother had already left the dining room or she would be horrified at the noise that Adeline just made. The thought made her giggle to herself quietly before she finally answered the question that still hung in the air between them.

"Calum, you have escorted me to every ball since we were like *seven*. Why are you being so formal lately? It's freaking me out." She pushed his shoulder playfully, but Calum knit his brows together in frustration at the gesture.

"Well, I just thought—with the suitors and th—so is that a yes?" he asked, stumbling over the words.

Adeline furrowed her brow at him.

"Yes, Cal, I will be your date to the ball, *like always*," the last words were heavy with sarcasm.

Calum relaxed with her answer, seeming to let go of some invisible pressure on his body. Adeline thought he was being quite strange; she had never seen Calum stumble over his words the way he just had, let alone be nervous about anything, *ever*. He was always sure of himself, calculated, as a commander should be. This behavior was beyond odd coming from him, and she did not like it.

Could it be that he—

Adeline shook the thought from her head. There must be something else causing him to act strangely, because it couldn't be her. It could *never* be her.

"Hey! While you're here, I was also meaning to invite you to train with me tomorrow night. That is, if you're not too busy sneaking off into the night like you tend to do." Calum smiled at her playfully as the words left his lips.

"SHHH! Lower your *voice*, Calum. You know that no one, not a single *soul*, can know about that," she chastised in a whisper, looking around the room to ensure none of the staff had heard his careless words.

They had been over this time and time again, yet he still poked fun at her sneaking out of the castle often. She was unsure what Calum thought she went out to do at night, but he had a tendency to mention the topic with such playfulness that she could not help but feel he found it to be a joke between the two of them, which frustrated her beyond explanation. There was nothing she disliked more than not being taken seriously. But no matter how badly she wanted to, she could never explain to him what she was actually doing going out into the forests of Scalebreak at night, *alone*. It was already a battle with Calum all those months ago to get him to agree to let her train with him, and another fight entirely when he had caught her sneaking out the first time. He would never understand, would never approve.

"But yes, I will meet you for training tomorrow night. But only if you promise to keep this, and my midnight activities, to yourself." Adeline stared daggers at him as she held up her pinky in expectation.

"I promise." He rolled his eyes at her, locking his pinky with hers.

CHAPTER FOUR

S WEAT DRIPPED OFF OF Adeline's brow as she threw a continuous flurry of punches and jabs at the combat dummy. *Whack. Whack. Whack.* The anger she had been harboring from the previous night bubbled to the surface, begging to be let free. She threw her body weight into each swing, landing them with as much force as she could muster. Adeline had always been a talented fighter, but even the most skilled warriors had to continue to hone their skills to be the best.

It had taken nearly a year of pleading to convince Calum to train her. Even after he begrudgingly agreed, he still didn't know the motivation behind her sudden and desperate desire to become more agile, more skilled with weapons, though not from lack of prodding on his part. Anytime he asked, Adeline would wave him off with nonchalant remarks about wanting to train as a way to quell her boredom, careful not to let him know the truth.

In reality, she had been eavesdropping on an important meeting of her father's, one of her favorite things to do, when she heard mutterings of nearing dragon attacks. As the reality of the hushed words sank in, Adeline had hated how helpless she felt, knowing she would be expected to hide behind her people when the attacks finally made it to Scalebreak once again. Fed up with playing her part in the castle, she had promptly run to find Calum and pleaded with him to give her lessons. When she had finally persuaded him to train her, she could have leapt with joy, though the feeling was short-lived. Adeline had considered herself to be quite a skilled warrior for a princess, but found herself quickly corrected when Calum brought her down with ease every time they practiced. With each loss, she grew more and more frustrated at her inability to defeat him, but she was nothing if not persistent. She began coming to the training gym every morning to get in some practice before she trained with Calum, pushing herself until her body pleaded for rest, muscles screaming. The training gym quickly became a second home to her.

The walls she stood within were padded with thick fabric, meant to break the impact of an opponent during a sparring match. Of course, being in a castle meant that the room was still elegant and tasteful in its design. Padded walls rose up to meet impossibly high vaulted ceilings, curling into soft arches at their peak where they gave way to the carved wooden beams. At the very center of the room, a skylight served as the main source of light above the sparring ring. Now, in the middle of the day, the room was bathed in light, golden rays dancing across the wood beams and playfully casting shadows around the edges of the room, making the mat-covered arena feel more like a stage.

Adeline allowed herself a small break, wiping the dripping sweat from her face as she stepped back from her unmoving opponent, whose rubber skin now glistened from where her sweat had dripped onto him. She kept her breathing controlled, but given the exhaustion she felt from exerting all of her energy, it still came in quick inhales. Lowering herself down onto the mat, she lay on her back and stared up at the ceiling above her, thankful for the solitude of the room. In the early afternoon, when all the castle staff were the most occupied, she could easily slip unnoticed into the gym as she had that day.

I need to make another kill. Soon. The thought was abrupt, and it ripped her from the momentary peace she had let herself fall into.

No matter how hard she tried to fight against it, the desperate need for the power that came with killing a dragon was something she craved insatiably. Not because she felt the need to use it for nefarious reasons, or even because she wanted to feel stronger than anyone. Instead, every time she went through the power transfer, it felt like a piece of her soul *clicked* into place. It was almost like there was always this missing part of her that was begging to be filled, satisfied by the power sliding under her skin, something she had never noticed was even gone until she landed her first fatal blow. The power transfer brought her to her knees, wracked with sobs at the feeling flowing through her. From that moment on, she knew she could not live like she had before, devoid of this piece of herself.

The part of her that craved the feeling the power gave was perhaps Adeline's least favorite side of herself. She knew that there were *still* families torn apart, some lost altogether, due to continued dragon attacks. She should let *that* be the reason she fought and trained as hard as she did, but she would be lying to herself if she did not give in to the little part of her that did it for the power.

Power can be a dangerous thing. The words echoed in her mind, trying to consume her entirely. The abrupt nature of the thought had her once again scrambling for a distraction.

Staring up at the ceiling, Adeline lost herself to daydreams about her favorite afternoons in the training gym, ones where she was bursting with limitless power, finally able to put it to the test without watchful eyes tracking her every move. Over her time slaying dragons, she had experienced the magic of flame, telepathy, and lightning, but the power of flame was by far her favorite to play with. Even just the thought of fire dancing on her fingertips had a smile creeping across her lips.

Adeline had spent many a morning in the gym, testing the limits of her all too temporary power. Fire was the only ability that she had encountered more than once, which meant that she had much more practice with controlling the licks of flame than any other magic. When she had first experimented with it, she had set ablaze much of the training equipment in the gym, watching in horror as it was engulfed in mere seconds. Fortunately, being the princess meant she had easy access to people who could replace the scorched items with no word of the damage they had seen, ensuring her secret was kept safe. That was one of the very few times she had been grateful for the influence her title of princess held.

After nearly burning down the entire castle, she found herself yearning for a glimpse of that same power, finding it thrilling. So, the next time she experienced the red tendrils of smoke absorbing into her skin after a kill, her heart had nearly leapt from her chest with excitement. Adeline wasted no time in getting to the training gym, itching to toy with the curious ability. Before the first glimpses of dawn had even crept into the room, she'd gained much better control over the flame. Uncontrolled bursts of fire quickly transformed into well-managed strikes. Fine-tuning her skills with the element was something that she almost immediately excelled in, never feeling like she had to work very hard to call upon it. Soon, she had been traipsing around the gym, giddily spinning around as licks of red hot fire danced around her. It had taken only a few practice sessions with the fire before she could craft whatever her mind desired out of flame, making it twirl around on her fingertips, sputtering out only when she closed her hand in on itself. It was an art form, the power of flame, and it was the one that Adeline found herself most drawn to.

She sat up and drew her knees to her chest, taking a deep breath to draw herself from the memory. The serenity that had been her lonely afternoon training session was over far too quickly, and she had to make haste in getting back to her bedroom and bathing before Greta came looking for her.

Emphasis on the bath, she thought as she caught a whiff of herself, the pungent smell tickling her nostrils.

Rising from the floor, Adeline dusted off her leathers and made her way to her bedroom. There would be long hours ahead helping her mother and Blair prepare for the coming ball before she could even *think* about losing herself in the steady rhythm of training once more.

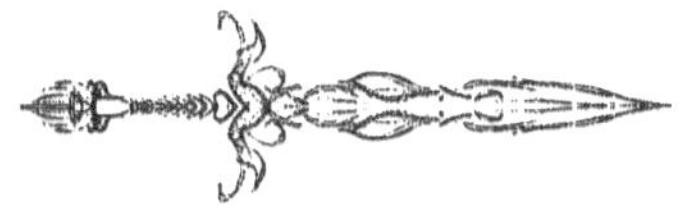

A knife whizzed by her head, slicing through the air just centimeters from her right ear. Turning her head in the direction of the attack, Adeline locked eyes with Calum, who wore a devilish grin upon his face.

Seems he's not going easy on me tonight.

She watched intently as he took several long, purposeful strides toward her; she held her breath as he drew closer. When he was only a few paces away, she finally took a long, deep breath, filling her lungs completely before she snapped her leg out, executing a sweeping kick in his direction.

Calum's blue eyes went wide with shock as his feet came out from under him and he fell toward the mat. Fortunately for him, he was quick. As his shoulders made contact with the mat beneath him, he rolled into the blow, coming back up on sturdy legs and poised for her next attack. Only a beat passed between them before Calum threw a punch toward Adeline's stomach, which she narrowly avoided in a sidestep.

What she failed to see, however, was that he was already several steps ahead of her. Sweeping his leg out as she just had, he knocked her from her stance and grabbed hold of both of her arms as he pushed both of their bodies toward the ground. They hit the mat with a *thud*, both of them taking quick, gulping breaths, chests heaving as they tried to replenish the stolen air. The force of Calum's body atop hers had robbed all the oxygen from Adeline's lungs. She lay on her back, sprawled out on the mat and completely unable to move as her lungs screamed in protest, desperate for even a sliver of oxygen.

Calum held a firm grip on both of her wrists, pinning her arms to the mat on either side of her head. He kept his knees pressed against hers, making it impossible for her to do much more than squirm. His leathers were pulled tight against his body, drawing attention to every bulge of muscle on him. Adeline wished she didn't notice. His pale blonde hair hung down slightly, with a few strands dangling just in front of his eyes. Even as she fought to regain her breath, it was hard for Adeline not to note just how handsome Calum was as he hovered over her, and frankly it frustrated her; he was her *friend,* nothing more. Looking up, she met his cerulean eyes and found him already watching her with a smirk, which just added to the irritation she felt bubbling to life within her.

He thinks he's won. It was her turn to smirk now.

Adeline stopped squirming for only a moment, making Calum loosen his hold on her ever so slightly, likely thinking that she had given up. That split second was all she had needed. Bringing one knee up, she made fast, solid contact with his groin and did not hesitate as she threw her body weight to the side, rolling them both over as she took her position where he had been only seconds prior, hovering over him. Gripping his wrists tightly, she looked down to where Calum was pinned to the mat and returned the sarcastic smirk he had given her mere moments ago.

"Just call it, Cal," she teased.

"You wish, short stuff," he grunted back as he bucked against her hold. She had always hated that nickname, and of course, her reaction to it made it his favorite to use.

Adeline reached down to her thigh, making quick work of wrapping her fingers around the steel handle of her beloved dagger and pulling it from the leather scabbard strapped there with a soft *swish*. She swung her arm forward and pressed the dagger against Calum's throat, smiling sweetly as a glimpse of fear filled his eyes. It was almost poetic, Adeline holding the beautifully crafted dagger against the neck of the man who had gifted it to her; she couldn't help but soak up the irony of the situation. Calum reached up and wrapped a calloused hand around the arm that held the dagger firmly against his neck and again, they locked gazes. A beat passed, then two, and neither of them broke the stare. Adeline's knuckles bit into the twisted silver vines of the hand guard as she tightened her grip, still not looking away. It was hard for either of them to discern what emotions passed through the tension between them, whether this was playful or truly dangerous, but that was the nature of Calum and Adeline. One could never quite tell if they held admiration or pure cunning hatred for one another when they were sparring.

Both of their chests heaved with short, almost gasping breaths, their bodies exhausted from the exertion of the fight. In just a blink, Calum's stare shifted, and no longer did it feel like he was matching the challenging stare of an opponent, but instead he seemed to be looking in adoration at Adeline, almost the same way he had watched her in the throne room three days prior. His sharp blue eyes had gone from steely to tender, loving almost. He looked at her as though she was the only thing that existed around them, the very thing he orbited.

Adeline broke the stare first, puzzled and uncomfortable by the change in his expression. Just as she opened her mouth to ask him about the strange shift, she heard the muffled sound of two taps on the mat. Calum had called the fight; she won. If she hadn't been confused before, she was now; Calum *never* forfeited. *Ever.*

Adeline rose to her feet, sheathing her dagger back at its rightful place on her leather-clad thigh. Now standing, she leaned forward, reaching an open hand to Calum and pulling him back to his feet. Even if things were strange between them it didn't mean she was going to leave him lying on the mat alone. He accepted her outstretched hand and allowed her to pull him to his feet. Neither of them made eye contact with the other, the air around them charged with tension so heavy it felt suffocating.

"You need to work on your punches, short stuff. They were rushed and sloppy," Calum finally broke the silence between them, brushing the hair away from his eyes.

"Cal, you know *you* are the one who lost...right?" She threw back at him playfully, reaching forward to punch his shoulder.

"Yeah, yeah, yeah, don't let it get to your head, Princess." The nickname made her cringe, having always detested being referred to as *princess.* She was far more than that.

"Too late."

Calum tossed her a plush towel to wipe the sweat now dripping from her face, and they moved wordlessly, working to slow their breaths as they patted themselves dry. The gym fell silent once again, save for the deep breaths passing between the two of them.

"Well, I better ge—"

"Adeline, wait. I—" He paused, scrambling to find the next words. Adeline met his gaze and felt her blood run cold when she noticed the hunger that danced in his eyes. "—Oh fuck it," Calum cut her off, taking several steps toward her.

Not allowing her a second to question him, he reached a strong hand up to cup her jaw, pushing them both backward until Adeline's body made contact with the padded wall behind her. A shiver passed over her, and she was unsure if it was due to the cold of the wall at her back or the fact that Calum now had her pressed against the wall, his mouth mere inches from her own. She didn't have time to decide before his lips crashed over hers with fervor. His kiss was demanding, taking, and for a moment she was consumed in it. Adeline parted her own lips, giving him permission to deepen the kiss and in a breath their tongues tangled in a waltz with one another. She lost herself in the familiarity of his scent as it wrapped around her. For only a moment, she let herself be distracted by the passion of their kiss. Then reality hit her, and she realized whose lips pressed against hers and how wrong it felt to be kissing *him*. Calum bit her bottom lip with a hungry moan before hastily bringing his lips back over hers and she felt herself freeze, completely unable to move.

What. The. Fuck.

Oblivious to her sudden shift, Calum moved his kisses to the corner of her mouth, slowly making his way to her jaw and down her neck. As his lips pressed against her throat, Adeline finally let out a gasp, only it was not a gasp of pleasure or want, but one of fear.

What are we doing?

"Calum I—we—I—***stop***," she finally sputtered out, pressing her palms against his chest and pushing him away from her.

His eyes met hers, confusion passing over his features at her sudden resistance. Adeline did not give either of them a moment to process the events that just occurred, instead stepping to the side, evading Calum as he reached for her and making a beeline out of the gym and to her chambers, her safe space. She was grateful that she did not hear him following her.

As the heavy wood door clicked into place behind her, Adeline slid down to the floor, her back making contact with the door the entire way down. Only here, in the safety of her bed chambers, did she allow the tears that had been gathering in her eyes to fall.

What. The. Fuck. Just. Happened.

CHAPTER FIVE

EACH STEP ADELINE TOOK was a gentle thud, her bare feet making contact with cool marble beneath them. The chill of the stone on her bare skin bit into her, making her shiver, but she invited the discomfort as a welcome distraction from her mind. She pulled her cloak—a floor-length mass of ashy gray fabric complete with a hood embroidered with tiny, delicate wildflowers—tightly around her body, blocking out the crisp morning air that whistled through the castle halls. It was nearly sunrise, but Adeline was padding throughout the corridors, lost deep in thought as she wandered through the endless maze of stone.

It had been two days since the *incident* in the training gym with Calum, and Adeline had done her best to avoid him at all costs. Mealtimes were one thing, when there were other people around, but outside of time in the dining room she had made sure to lock herself away in her bedroom where he could not get to her. Where he could not touch her. No longer did she feel safe around him.

It had only been a kiss. At least that's what she continued to tell herself, yet she could not seem to shake the grimy feeling it had left her with. Since the kiss, she had taken to spending her time endlessly scrubbing at her skin in the bathtub, crinkling her nose in disgust when the dirty feeling lingered long after she had become raw and irritated from the vigorous scrubbing.

Maybe that is just what it means to be kissed by a man, to be taken with force and left feeling eternally tarnished. The thought had her deciding that she never wanted to kiss another man again.

Today, however, she would have to leave her bed chambers and face him. The ball was tonight, and of course, Adeline had agreed to allow Calum to escort her. Her stomach churned at the thought of being alone with him, her body begging her to keep a distance between them. Something had changed in Calum over the last few weeks, and she was not enjoying this newfound sense of demand he approached her with, as if he *owned* her.

The old Calum had been kind, gentle and understanding. He was her best friend and the person she went to for comfort and laughter, but lately he was someone she no longer knew, and she hated herself for so easily giving in to his touch. Even if only for a moment.

Coming to a stop at one of the many windows scattered through the endless halls, Adeline brought her elbows to rest on the windowsill, laying her head in her palm as she gazed out over the expanse of land.

The sun was just peeking out over the snow-capped ridges of the mountains in the distance, which meant it was time for her to go back up to her room to prepare for breakfast. Knowing what the day held for her, she wished hopelessly that she could remain there, frozen in time looking out at the mountains. With a deep sigh, she lifted her head and spun on her heel, back in the direction of her bedroom.

Today is going to be hell, but I am going to face it regardless.

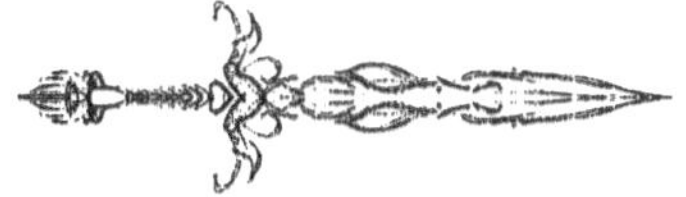

Breakfast that morning, though challenging to get through in such close proximity to both Calum and her mother, whose stress seemed to seep from her pores, had been rather uneventful. Queen Eloise and Briar had been, unsurprisingly, locked in conversation about every minute detail of the ball that night, stopping every few moments to adulate one another on their taste, earning several eye rolls from Adeline.

King Thorian was nowhere to be found at the breakfast table, likely holed away in his office to scour over battle plans, which left Calum and Adeline to sit in silence as they ate their porridge, neither sparing a glance in the other's direction. It took all of Adeline's willpower not to leap from the table as soon as she swallowed the last bite and rush to her room.

When she did finally make her escape, closing the bedroom door behind her with a slam, Adeline had all of one breath of silence before Greta was upon her.

"Addie! Where have you *been*! We are meant to be readying you for the ball!" Greta fussed as she pulled Adeline further into the room, guiding her to a seat at the vanity.

Even through her annoyance at the urgency to prepare for the very ball she had been dreading, Adeline softened at the nickname, *Addie.* Greta was the one of very few people in her life who referred to her as anything other than her proper name, and it was just one of many ways Greta felt more like a mother to Adeline than the queen tended to.

"I'm sorry Greta. I was out for a stroll."

"A stroll through the castle...so early in the morning? Are you feeling alright, my child?" Greta fussed over her, pressing the back of her hand to Adeline's forehead to check for a fever.

"I—um...yeah, I'm alright. No need to fuss over me, Greta," Adeline replied quickly, gently pushing Greta's hand away.

Greta let out a long sigh. "It's Calum, isn't it?" she prodded.

Adeline stayed silent for a moment, looking down into her lap while Greta made quick work of her chaotic tangle of brown locks. No matter how hard she tried to hide her emotions, Greta could read her like a book.

"How did you know?" she asked, gaze fixed on her hands in her lap.

"Because I myself have been increasingly frustrated with the behaviors of that boy as of late. Something has changed in him, Addie. Just...be careful with him tonight."

Adeline lifted her head to meet Greta's gaze in the mirror and found a silent warning etched upon her face as their eyes met. A pit immediately formed in Adeline's stomach. It was unusual for Greta to be so adamant about safety. A heavy silence settled around them as the old woman continued to make work of pinning the princess' hair just so, and it wasn't long before Adeline was lost in another daydream.

Her heart pounded in her ears...bum bum...bum bum...bum bum. She took a deep breath, filling her lungs with air before she raised her head. Her gaze met the hateful golden eyes of the massive beast before her. Gold dragons were a rarity these days, but Adeline knew just how dangerous they could be. She moved slowly, reaching down her thigh to free the dagger strapped there. She welcomed the frigid metal's bite against her warm skin as she wrapped her fingers around it, making sure her grip was solid. She kept her gaze pinned on the dragon before her, the beauty of the creature almost entrancing her.

Moonlight danced off the shining golden scales, and it was damn near blinding to the human eye. Adeline's heart skipped a beat as the dragon huffed, tendrils of gray tinged smoke sneaking out of its nostrils and curling into the cool night air.

Adeline blinked, and in the millisecond it took for her to open her eyes the dragon had begun tearing toward her in a frenzy. The mossy forest floor beneath her quaked with each great step taken by the dragon, the trees shaking with the force of its footfalls. Everything around them trembled with fervor, as if the very earth around them knew the power and skill carried between the two creatures about to collide. Adeline raised her blade, ready to strike once the dragon was near enough. She counted her breaths...one...two...three...and pushed through the soles of her feet as she launched herself into an extraordinary leap. She reached out a hand, ready to—

"Adeline. Did you hear me?" Greta's voice pierced through the vivid fantasy, dragging her out of it.

"Uh...yeah I...sorry...what?" Adeline blinked furiously, trying to regain a hold on her surroundings.

Her eyes focused on her reflection in the mirror before her. Greta had taken the unruly mess of brown curls she had been sporting mere hours ago and turned them into an elegant updo. Her long chocolate curls had been pulled and pinned just so, with an expertly twisted braid wrapping her head from one temple to the other. Pinned just above the nape of her neck was a beautiful bun of loosely tucked and twisted curls. Throughout the updo, Greta had left small sections of waves out to frame her face and add an elegantly mused look to the style. As Adeline took it in, her breath hitched in her throat; She looked beautiful.

"I *said* turn toward me so that I can finish your makeup," Greta replied, clearly annoyed at Adeline's lack of attention.

Rotating on her seat obediently, Adeline came to face Greta. Greta wasted no time, making quick work of swiping a coal liner on Adeline's eyelids and a mauve pink shade of lipstick on her full lips. With a few pinches to her cheeks to bring a subtle blush to the surface, Greta stepped back to admire her work, a beaming smile brightening her features as she turned Adeline back toward the mirror.

Being a princess meant that Adeline had prepared for balls before, but never had she ever felt as elegant and regal as she did now. Even still wearing her casual white linen dress, she looked beautiful; a true picture of grace. As she looked at the girl in the mirror, the regal, poised version of herself, she felt like she was looking at a stranger. When had she started to look so *mature*?

Before she could dwell on it much longer, Greta made her way toward her, carrying a giant mass of ivory fabric in her arms. *This must be the gown.* Excitement bubbled to life in her chest at the thought. Adeline couldn't help but smile to herself as Greta pulled the white petticoat carefully over her head so as not to disturb any of the curls. Getting the entire gown on without messing up her makeup or hair had been a challenge, but holding her breath while Greta laced the corset beneath the dress was another struggle entirely. With each tug of the white laces, Adeline felt the very life leaving her body, and she was sure that if the corset were any tighter she would stop being able to draw breath at all.

As if Greta heard her silent pleas, she stopped pulling the laces and tied the ends into a perfect little bow and slid her hands over Adeline's waist, smoothing down the fabric.

Adeline took a step toward the large ornate silver mirror leaning on the wall opposite the door. As she stepped into view, her breath caught in her throat, this time at the ball gown that adorned her body. Although she'd had minimal notice, Greta had come through with creating a gown for the ball, and it was utterly breathtaking.

What Adeline had believed to be white fabric was actually the palest pink she had ever seen, a detail that had a smile fighting its way to her lips. The bodice fit her like a glove; loose straps draped elegantly over her biceps before they met the beautiful sweetheart neckline framing the well of her breasts, showing off just the right amount of cleavage to be tasteful. Over the silky fabric of the dress was a subtle layer of tulle, atop which the corseted bodice hugged her, embroidered with champagne-colored roses, each one unique from the one next to it. The array of blooming flowers and thorny vines ran down the length from the neckline to the waist, dwindling in number as it drew closer to the floor. Each rose and vine was adorned with several crystals and beads of precious metal. With each sway of her hips the dress shimmered and sparkled subtly. To call this dress a work of art would simply be a disservice to its designer, and Greta deserved all the credit in the world for the gorgeous gown. Adeline looked fit to be queen.

Before she could open her mouth to compliment Greta on the exquisite work she had done on the garment, worn, wrinkled hands came over her head holding a thin silver chain between them. An oval pendant with a swirling silver border came to rest just above Adeline's breasts, the center adorned with a silver rose. She brought her hand up to touch the beautiful piece of jewelry as Greta clasped it at the nape of her neck. She turned, finding her maid's eyes heavy with tears. There were no words that would convey just how thankful Adeline was for Greta and the lovely gift, but between the two of them words were rarely needed. Holding back tears of her own, Adeline wrapped Greta in a tight hug. They embraced for a long moment, both of them letting the tears fall between them.

As they separated, Greta lifted a gentle hand to swipe the wetness from Adeline's cheeks. Even through the tender moment, she would never dare to let Adeline ruin the work she had done to make her look as breathtaking as she did.

She grabbed Adeline, gripping both of her biceps firmly as she looked up at her. "I love you endlessly, my dear girl."

"I love you too, Greta," she replied, doing her best to stop more tears from spilling over.

The tender moment was brought to an abrupt end when a sharp knock sounded on the door before echoing through the room with a sense of foreboding. Greta wiped her eyes, making her way to the door to see who was there. As she pulled the door open, Adeline glimpsed piercing blue eyes in the hallway and felt any air she'd retained while being laced into the corset leave her body; it was time to face Calum.

Fuck.

Chapter Six

A DELINE TOOK A DEEP breath to steel herself against the growing bundle of nerves in her chest as Calum stepped into her bedroom. His eyes held hers as he moved closer, his stare only leaving hers to explore the length of her body as he looked her up and down several times, his gaze hungry, just as it had been in the gym. The sight made Adeline sick to her stomach. Calum stepped forward in a bow, grabbing her hand and bringing it to his lips, pressing a quick kiss to the back before he straightened again.

"Wow, Adeline, you look...wow." He stared at her, eyes brimming with adoration.

If she had not been so on edge with his presence, perhaps she would have returned his compliment. Objectively speaking, Calum did look very handsome. Dressed in a black suit that was very clearly tailored to his muscular body, some would say handsome was an understatement. The midnight fabric swelled over his biceps; anyone with two working eyes could see the very obvious muscle definition. The bowtie around his neck was a perfect match to the champagne color of Adeline's gown and was even embroidered with the same roses found on her skirts, clearly crafted by Greta's careful hands. Even in her frustration with Calum, Greta would never allow for Adeline to attend a ball not dressed to perfection. His blond hair, usually a tousled mess to which he paid no mind, was neatly combed and styled tidily atop his head.

He does look handsome, but he will not be hearing that from me tonight. She was determined to make her disinterest in him clear, and was putting up walls she hoped he would not try to breach.

"Thank you, Calum." She supposed if she had to suffer this night with him she may as well fake being civil.

Hooking her arm in the crook of his elbow, Adeline let him lead her out into the corridor.

It had been several hours since she had left the threshold of her bedroom, but Adeline still found herself amazed at how quickly the staff was able to transform the space. Servants bustled all around them, making final preparations or adjustments to the ornate decor. On a normal day the castle was a sight to behold, each arched door and window framed with elegantly carved floral motifs; Adeline had always thought if one were to stand ever so still, the swirling patterns would appear to move and breathe with the same life as the castle itself. But on the day of a ball, the very stone of Scalebreak Castle seemed to glow as if beaming with pride at the elaborate floral arrangements and decorum placed throughout.

Carefully hanging from each railing and banister in sight were full bundles of white wisteria still on the green vines. The bright flowers hung so precisely over every archway, staircase, and windowsill in the castle. They paired perfectly with the neutral tan stone of the walls, the draping greenery adding a natural element to the already airy space. It all felt as though it were alive, so at odds with the normally cold and unwavering stone walls.

Calum cleared his throat, breaking away from Adeline to face her.

"Look, I just wanted to say I'm sorry for the other night. I never should have forced myself on you without being sure it was what you wanted, too. I mean, I definitely thought you wanted it, but clearly you didn't?" He looked up at her in question as if unsure of his own apology.

"No. Calum. I didn't *want* it. And the fact that you think that sad excuse of an apology is going to win me over is honestly pathetic," Adeline bit back, not caring who around them heard the princess speaking so callously.

"I—you're right. I'm sorry Adeline. Truly. What must I do to be forgiven? I will do anything, I just want my best friend back," Calum groveled, his eyes full of sadness.

Adeline stared at him for a moment, pondering what embarrassing thing she could dream up to make him atone for his behavior. Finally settling on a plan, she smirked up at him, taking note of the flicker of fear in his gaze.

"You want to be forgiven? Get on your knees and bow to me. Beg me to forgive you for what you have done."

"Ad—you can't be serious?" Calum stared at her, unsure.

"Serious as the Scorching. How bad do you want to be forgiven, Cal?" Adeline responded cooly, feigning indifference as she inspected her nails.

Calum stood staring back at her for several breaths, seeming to count his losses before slowly lowering to his knees in defeat. As both knees met the cold stone beneath her feet, he stared up at her in a silent plea not to make him follow through with this. Adeline stared daggers back at him, making it known he would have to bend to her wishes, and he lowered his eyes in submission before bowing his forehead to the stone, wincing as the cold bit into his skin.

Many of the staff who had been whirring through the castle had gathered near them, appearing busy by straightening a floral arrangement or a curtain as they stared curiously at the scene unfolding.

"Adeline, I beg you, please forgive me for my actions. I beg for your mercy." He groveled, sounding truly remorseful.

"Hmm, try again," Adeline spat. She felt dangerously powerful watching this six-foot-two mountain of a man bow at her feet and plead for her forgiveness; it was all too fun to toy with him.

Calum let out a deep sigh before beginning again, "Adeline, my dear, lovely—" Adeline cleared her throat, hinting at what his next words should be. "—benevolent princess, please. I beg you to absolve me of the torture that is not being near you. Please forgive me for how rash and outwardly I behaved toward you. I beg you, forgive me."

Adeline bit back the giggle that was fighting its way up her throat. "Alright. Alright. You can get up now." It was only the whispers of the staff gathered around them that had her putting an end to the spectacle. As much as she enjoyed making him beg, she would never hear the end of it if her mother caught wind of her games.

Calum rose to his feet, looking toward Adeline with a hopeful expression.

"Does this mean I am forgiven?" he asked optimistically.

"No. But I am considering granting you my forgiveness, eventually. Come, we mustn't keep our guests waiting," Adeline responded dully.

Calum's shock was written on his face for all to see, and several members of the staff let out snickers of their own as he picked his jaw up off the floor and stuck his arm out for Adeline to grab hold of again, ever the complacent pet. Adeline laced her arm through his, grabbing hold of his firm bicep and letting him lead her toward the staircase.

As their feet met the edge of the top step, a loud voice boomed through the silence, announcing the couple to the people waiting in the foyer below. Adeline immediately recognized the voice as Fen, the royal scribe, and felt her face soften with a smile.

"Princess Adeline Ambrose and Sir Calum Windford of Scalebreak!" And with that, the pair started their descent into the waiting chaos below.

The grand staircase had been properly prepared for the ball. A river of black velvet carpet spilled from the first stair and pooled out elegantly several feet from the last. The lush black runner beneath their feet contrasted, yet complemented the bright whites of the wisteria hanging on the stone railings of the staircase. Although balls were not quite her favorite scene, Adeline couldn't help but admire every delicately crafted detail of the castle around her as they made their way down the steps and into the room of people with their eyes pinned on the couple.

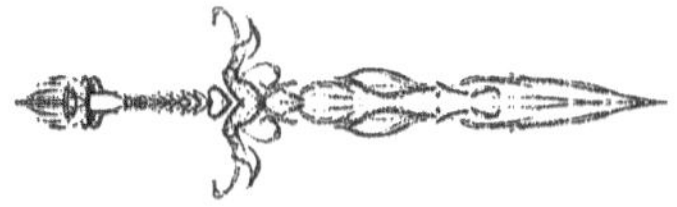

Adeline felt dizzy from the amount of dancing she had done. All of the suitors from the throne room had arrived, and they were doing their very best to steal her attention away from one another. From one waltz to another, and another, and another, and another. Adeline swore that if she was spun around one more time she would promptly empty the contents of her stomach on the shiny marble ballroom floors.

Since Calum had the honor of escorting Adeline, the other three suitors had taken to threateningly glowering at him between dances with her, and it was unclear whether they were trying to win Adeline's hand or Calum's with how much attention they were paying him.

After far too long spent suffocating under their expectant gazes, Adeline finally managed to excuse herself to get some air, stealing a moment of time alone on a second-story balcony overlooking the palace gardens, one of her favorite spots to quiet her mind. The sun had already started its descent and in doing so painted the fading sky in shades of pink and orange interrupted by flecks of purple. She leaned against the railing, letting out a relieved sigh as she took in the beauty of the sun kissing the horizon and casting the gardens in a burnt orange hue. The sky and sun made art of the earth below them, sharing a glimpse of their beauty with everything around them as they faded into the first signs of night.

The cool evening breeze gently pushed the loose brown waves from Adeline's face, making them dance in the wind and even pulling a few pieces from her tidy bun to join in. On the balcony, in the openness of the night, Adeline felt like she could finally breathe, even with the corset tightly cinching her waist.

She stood there for several minutes, relishing in these short moments to herself before someone eventually found her out here, and as she gazed down into the gardens below, she noticed several people meandering through the catacomb of greenery and florals. Many of the people she observed were split off in couples, likely young lovers trying to escape the eyes of their ever so watchful chaperones.

What really caught her attention was the man standing entirely isolated from everyone else in the center of the gardens. He stood between blooming rose bushes, staring at the fountain in front of him as if deep in thought, and though Adeline could not quite make out his expression with the quickly fading daylight, she couldn't help but feel as though he looked *pained*. She followed his gaze to the fountain in the middle of the gardens, trying to gauge what about it he found so offensive.

She had lived in the castle for the entirety of her life, and Adeline had seen the fountain countless times before, but as she took it in now, she felt as though she had never *truly* looked at it at all. The marble fountain was the centerpiece of the well-manicured gardens at the Scalebreak castle, the only thing capable of drawing the attention away from the gorgeous landscaping.

At the heart of the structure stood a mighty man, poised in battle with a greatsword in his grip. The man's figure was taut with focus, each muscle in his body etched eternally in marble. His face forever twisted in a final war cry, mouth agape and brows scrunched in strained effort. The sword in his hands came to an abrupt end deep in the serpentine scales of a dragon. The creature's full wingspan was on display as its wings jutted out from each side of its body, a beautifully tragic display of a final attempt at escape, at salvation. Forever frozen in stone, the dragon's mouth remained open in an immortalized shriek of pain and loss; the creature would not leave this battle. Cascading from the dragon's open mouth, water splashed into the pool below, lapping gently against the marble.

There was something so disastrously alluring about the work of art that Adeline found herself deep in contemplation about the event that led to that very moment carved in stone forever, immortalized in the gardens. Never having paid any mind to the fountain before, she felt an ache bloom in her chest for the tragedy hewn from the earth and put on display for all to admire.

Were we really always the heroes in history? Or are we cowering away from the shortcomings of our ancestors?

Turning her gaze back to the man who had originally drawn her attention, her breath caught in her throat as she found him staring straight up at her. In the pale light of the moon, she could not make out many of his features, but the one thing she *could* see was a jagged, silver scar cutting through the skin just above his left eyebrow. In fact, in the vague luminescence of the night, the scar seemed to almost glow as if little bits of silver had laced themselves into the damaged skin.

Adeline held his stare for a long moment, curious who this man below could be. She felt his gaze on her, piercing through the darkness settling around them, and though she could not make out his eyes, she sensed the curiosity with which he assessed her. Her fingers wrapped around the stone banister, gripping forcefully as if trying to ground herself from the sudden flush that crept over her. A blush rose to her cheeks, and she felt her body heat under the attention of this stranger, this unknown man.

"Ah, darling, there you are! I have been searching all over for you." A nasally voice cut through the intimate moment, causing Adeline to jump, startled.

"Yes. Here I am, Lord Silverdawn, I simply needed some air," she responded without turning to the man behind her, clearly disinterested in his presence.

Jared Silverdawn took this as an invitation and sauntered over to her, making himself comfortable by leaning on the hard stone railing. Adeline glanced over at him, hoping she masked the disgust she felt at his presence. Something about this man felt particularly...slimy.

"I see you have been looking upon the gardens!" he pushed a pair of gold frames up the bridge of his nose. "I would like to call your attention to the gorgeous fountain that can be found in the center of the gardens. The fountain depicts one of the greatest victories that man has ever faced, the fall of the first dragon." Lord Silverdawn spoke as if Adeline had not lived in this very castle for her entire life, but she allowed him to carry on, welcoming the excuse to look upon the mysterious man again. Adeline turned her attention back to the marble fountain below, her eyes flicking, scanning the greenery and shrubs for the now familiar silhouette of the stranger, but he was nowhere to be seen. As though he had blown away on the gentle evening breeze, the man was simply *gone*.

CHAPTER SEVEN

A FTER SEVERAL MORE HOURS spent being ushered around the stuffy ballroom overflowing with people, Adeline found herself still searching the sea of bodies for the familiar glint of a silver-tinged scar. Something about the mystery man from the gardens had encapsulated her full attention, so much so that she no longer minded being twirled in an endless waltz with the various suitors. With each spin, her eyes darted around the room hoping to locate *him*. Even though Adeline had no idea who the new object of her obsession was, she was enamoured by the idea of what he could be. After all, she found even just the idea of him much more alluring than any of the suitors who were currently fighting for her attention.

It grew late, and many of the guests had already made their leave to go back home, all except for the suitors, much to Adeline's dismay. They were finally cut off by King Thorian while Adeline was dancing her final dance with Feron Fike.

"Alright, gentlemen, I think it is time we retire for the evening," he spat at them, clearly offended by their overstayed welcome. It was mere moments before the men were scrambling toward the foyer to leave, and Adeline had to refrain from rolling her eyes in annoyance as they each said their oversaturated goodbyes.

"My lady, it was truly an honor to dance with you this evening," Lord Jared Silverdawn mumbled with a bow, his pale blond hair plastered to his forehead, wet from dancing. He kissed the back of her hand before straightening and walking off, his metallic emerald suit sparkling with every step. Adeline casually wiped his saliva from the back of her hand onto the skirts of her dress as the next suitor approached.

Sir Anthony Blake took Lord Jared's leave as his chance to steal Adeline's attention.

"Dearest, thank you for the honor of spending our evening together, just the two of us," he said with a kiss on her hand.

Just the two of us...right...

She held back a giggle as he sauntered off, the bald spot on the back of his head shining in the light, nearly blinding her. Adeline's amusement, however, was short-lived as Viscount Feron Fike stepped in front of her. Although she found his personality to be dull and overall unamusing, Adeline still felt a blush creep over her body as his attention found her; he was handsome, one had to give him that. Feron had donned a navy blue suit for the evening, which beautifully complemented his green eyes, and Adeline had a hard time looking away. Feron bowed before stepping forward to plant a kiss on her cheek. He did not speak a word, simply winking at her before parting.

What a strange, beautiful man, Adeline thought to herself before turning to take Calum's already extended elbow. The foyer was empty, everyone having made their way out of the castle by now, but she could still hear the fading click-clack of horse hooves on stone as Calum began to lead her away from the entrance, the final guests starting their journeys home.

He escorted her to the bottom of the grand staircase, stopping just at the edge of the emerald carpet and turning to her. Adeline loosened her grip on his bicep, dropping her arm to her side and eyeing him with apprehension.

"Calum, what ar—"

"Adeline, you looked absolutely stunning tonight, have I told you that yet?" He reached up and tucked a loose curl behind her ear. As he leaned toward her, Adeline could smell the liquor on his breath, and she flinched at his touch.

"Yes, you have, now can we please head up to bed?" she pleaded, sensing where this conversation was going.

"I—I uh. Adeline, I'm in love with you," he slurred. "I am so hopelessly in love with you." His words blended into each other in a garble of sounds.

Her heart hammered in her chest. Calum was *in love with her?* No, it couldn't be true. He had simply had too much to drink and wasn't coherent, didn't understand what he was saying to her.

But he leaned forward, attempting to plant another unwelcome kiss upon her lips. This time, he didn't get the chance as she gathered her skirts into her shaking fists and turned to run up the grand staircase, her pink skirts flowing in waves behind her as she made her escape. Adeline did not dare look back to see if he was following her; she wanted nothing more than to be away from him. Her heels clacked on the hard stone of the stairs, the plush runner now gone.

Thump. Thump. Thump. Her pulse quickened with each step until she finally reached the peak of the staircase, not slowing as she made her way to her bedroom door, hearing Calum's quick steps behind her now.

"Shit. Adeline! Wait! Can we talk?" Calum shouted behind her. Adeline took a final step, wrapping her fingers around the cold metal doorknob and throwing the door open. She launched herself into her chambers and slammed the door shut behind her, securing the lock with trembling fingers before sliding to the floor. Swiping away the tear running down her cheek, she took a shaky breath. *He can't get to me here; he won't.*

Calum knocked for several minutes and Adeline could hear mumblings filtering through the solid wood that she presumed were half-assed apologies. She did not dare move from her spot on the floor until the knocks ceased and his footsteps finally retreated.

Once she was sure it was safe, she stood and slipped out of her dress. There was only one thing that would take her mind off of the events of this evening, and it was a perfect night for a hunt.

Stepping out of the mass of pink fabric on the floor, Adeline attempted to catch the laces of the corset to free herself, but failed. The corset would have to stay on, as there was not enough time to free herself from it.

She slipped on her leather hunting clothes, pulling the sleeveless top over her corset before lacing up her boots. She was taking a risk leaving her arms exposed, but she couldn't bring herself to care. Adeline sheathed her dagger at her thigh and made her way to the door, silently cracking it open and peering out into the hallway to ensure that Calum had truly gone.

After making sure there was no one around to spot her, she stepped into the hall, still covered in wisteria decorations from the ball, and made her way out of the castle. She tried to take a different route out every few times she left, ensuring that no one would be able to trace her movements and follow her into the forest. Tonight, she made her way through the elaborate gardens, her favorite path to take; it was easy to shield herself within the landscape. As she slipped between blooming peonies and lush shrubbery, she let herself think again of the man she had locked eyes with earlier that evening. *Who was he?* She thought as she met the center, the fountain.

Just one moment won't hurt.

She allowed herself to pause at the base of the fountain, and although she wasn't sure what she was searching for, her eyes scanned the ground around her for *something.*

He had to have left behind something. But as she scoured the stone beneath her feet for a glimpse of a clue about the stranger who'd caught her eye, she found nothing and felt her heart sink in defeat. She had held out hope that maybe she would find a memento, or even a note left behind for her, but perhaps Adeline had not been as memorable to him. With a defeated sigh, she pushed all thoughts of him out of her head and made her way into the waiting forest.

She kept her steps light as she maneuvered through the trees. The anxiety stirring within her began to quiet. With each step deeper into the forest, she felt it embrace her, comforting her with open arms. Any ill feelings she'd had for the night dissipated under the hum of the crickets around her.

Coming to a clearing, she decided to take a moment to rest, her eyes falling on a battered oak stump that looked all too inviting to her aching feet. Though she loved wearing gowns, heels were truly her own personal hell. Telling herself she would only rest for a moment, Adeline took a seat on the stump and focused her energy on slowing her breathing, still restricted by the too-tight corset squeezing her ribs.

In...two, three, four. Out...two, three, four.

Her pulse slowed to a normal pace, the rushing in her ears quieting.

Dropping both feet to the moss-covered earth beneath her, she took another breath and felt her entire body relax; maybe she had acted rashly in coming out here tonight. Still tied in her corset, she was having a hard time even drawing breaths, let alone moving; who was she to think she could face a dragon in these conditions? At least her intent had stood true, her mind was quiet once again.

Adeline sat there for some time, the rotting wood of the stump digging into the backs of her thighs a welcome distraction from the ache in her lungs. The forest was peaceful tonight, with crickets chirping in all directions, leaves rustling in the soft breeze and glittering moonlight dancing off the forest floor, casting shadows across the earth. She would have stayed in that very spot forever if she could have, but it was beyond late, now nearing midnight; she needed to head home.

As she rose, she thought she felt a slight tremor in the earth, and her breath caught in her throat. *It can't be.*

It must just be the exhaustion setting in, she told herself, but as the ground trembled again, this time more fervently, she knew that was not the case. Fear consumed her at the reality she was about to face.

Adeline had barely enough time to undo the sheath of her dagger before the gold dragon was towering over her, staring down at her with murderous intent. She met its gaze, staring back at it with as much hate and fury as it was her. Filling her lungs as deeply as she could, she welcomed the burning pain that came with the inability to take a full breath in the corset and held the dragon's stare. Her grip on the cold iron hilt of her dagger tightened as the great creature huffed at her, tendrils of smoke curling out of its nostrils.

Great a fire bre—the scene was eerily familiar and her blood ran cold.

Before she could put further thought into it, the dragon lunged at her. Her heart thudded in her chest as she stood, waiting for the right moment. When the dragon's head was just about eye-level, she sprang forward, using the momentum to push through the balls of her feet in a leap. Her palms screamed in protest as they met cold, hard scales, and she curled her fingers, trying to solidify her hold on the dragon's back. The moon glinted off its shiny golden armor, momentarily blinding her as she squeezed her eyes shut, muttering a string of curses under her breath. Her fingers began to slip, slick with sweat, and her heart erupted in fear. Letting go with one hand, she reached higher, trying to climb. Her feet dangled beneath her, scrambling to find purchase so she could hoist herself up. Every muscle in her body protested, begging her to stop, but she forced them to keep moving; to be still would mean death.

Thump. Thump. Thump. Her heart roared in her chest, hammering against her ribcage in a fury.

I am dead. I am going to die here. She shook the thought from her head, refusing to accept this as her end. *There is always a way out.*

Bracing herself for the piercing light of gold, she cracked her eyes open, wasting no time as she locked her eyes on a new handhold. Just as she made contact with the golden scale she was reaching for, the dragon whipped its head back in a great roar. The beast below her trembled with fury, and her heart crept into her throat. Kicking her feet, Adeline felt her left foot catch on a lip in the dragon's side. Not giving herself time to think, she used it to her advantage and began her ascent up the neck of the creature. Apparently, she would be battling a dragon tonight after all.

Adeline's knuckles turned white as she tightened her grip, her fingers aching with each new spot she latched onto. Chest screaming in protest to her movements, she felt impossibly limited in her mobility. The leathers alone were hard enough to move freely in.

This damn corset is going to be the death of me.

Regardless of the thought, she could not stop moving. Adeline lifted her right hand, feeling blood drip down her palm as she found purchase on the next scale, but she ignored it, filing it away to worry about later. She kept moving, unable to currently feel the pain that she was certain would later find her. Raising her other hand, she reached for the next hold, quickly regretting letting go at all when the dragon beneath her began to whip its head furiously in an attempt to buck her off. Her feet lost their hold, dangling beneath her once again as her body swung with each buck of the dragon. Adeline held on for dear life with her right hand, reaching aimlessly with her left trying to grab hold of something, *anything* that she could. It took several swings before her fingers made contact with the dragon's scales once more, but before she could curl her fingers in and use it to her advantage, they slipped from their hold entirely and she began her descent to the earth below with an ear-splitting scream.

It felt as though she had been falling forever, her limbs splayed out around her as if trying to brace her fall, yet it was eerie how peaceful falling was, how calm she suddenly felt with the wind whipping against her back and her gaze pinned to the sky above; she almost felt as if she was flying. Almost.

A victorious screech from the gleaming dragon drew her attention back to reality only a second too late, the world around her seeming to zoom back into motion. Her back made contact with the hard earth of the forest floor first, knocking any ounce of air she had managed to gather into her already restrained lungs out. As Adeline's skull bounced off the dirt-packed ground, her ears rang with such volume that she could no longer hear anything around her.

Several moments passed where she tried, unsuccessfully, to draw in a breath, even a molecule of oxygen. Adeline could no longer feel her limbs, her face, anything, all that existed was the burning in her lungs as she tried to suck in air.

Her eyes began to grow heavy, and the world around her became increasingly harder to see. With a cough, she managed to draw in a tiny breath and soon she was gasping, gulping in as much oxygen as she could muster. As she filled her starving lungs, she could suddenly feel every nerve in her body come to life with roaring pain.

Adeline felt herself scream out in agony, her throat raw, but she could not hear it over the ringing in her ears. A figure raced into her periphery, squatting down in front of her. The shadow dropped down to her level, scouring her body for the site of the injury. She tried to make out who was standing over her but her spotty vision hid the individual's features. She still wasn't getting enough oxygen.

"Can't...fucking...*breathe...*" she finally managed between gasps. Adeline lifted her hand to her midsection, weakly pulling her top up the few inches she could muster in an attempt to expose the white of the corset suffocating her beneath the leather.

Strong, firm hands lifted her shoulders off the ground, the figure reaching for a weapon on his hip before pressing something cold and sharp firmly against her back. Her body went taught with fear at the feeling of the dagger digging into her. Was this supposed stranger going to put an end to her? That was the last thought Adeline had before she felt her corset fall away, the ribbons sliced clean through, and her bare skin prickled with goosebumps as she was enveloped in the cold midnight air.

"Who the *hell* wears a corset to slay a dragon?" the shadow growled down at her as she lost consciousness.

CHAPTER EIGHT

*T*HUD. *THUD. THUD.*

Adeline's long brown hair nearly kissed the ground with every soft thud of her head against the solid muscle of a firm back. Her temples throbbed furiously and it took her several moments to gather the courage to open her eyes.

As the first rays of sunlight crept into her vision, she was blinded. The bright daylight was a stark opposite to the darkness she had been enveloped in mere moments before. Blinking her eyes quickly, she silently begged them to adjust to the light so she could take in her surroundings.

When her eyes finally came into focus, no longer bewildered by the harsh sunlight seeping in, she noticed two things very quickly. One, everything within eyesight appeared to be...*upside down?* Looking to her left and right, she noted the trees that hung from the earthy, moss-covered skyline, their roots gripping into the dirt to hold them in their place on the horizon. And two, her abdomen rested on someone's firm shoulder; she was being carried.

What the hell is going on?

Adeline's mind felt clouded, still groggy and heavy with sleep, and it took her several minutes to recall the events that landed her hanging off of this mysterious shoulder, staring at the plump rear of a man she did not know—not that she minded the view. The flash of a memory played in her mind, the dark-haired shadow of a man kneeling before her on the forest floor and just before she lost consciousness, the glint of a silver scar.

The man from the garden...Could he truly be my savior?

As her mind cleared, she realized what was going on. She was being carried back to the castle, this man was saving her. Though she was lost as to who this man was or why he treated her with such kindness, she felt *safe* being wrapped in his strong arms.

That realization shook her. *I do not know this man. I do not know this man. I do not know this man.* She echoed it over and over, seeming to have to try to remind her body to respond to the statement, but it felt useless.

Her arms still hung limply by her head, her fingers occasionally making contact with strong thighs, and she hated the way her cheeks heated with every brush against them. Pleading with her body, she strained her mind to move her fingers, wiggle her toes, something. Defeat had taken over when she noticed a twitch in the fingers on her right hand. She spent the next several moments testing her limits, each time finding she could move her hand just slightly further than the last. It took some trial and error, and a lot of biting back frustrated sighs, so as not to alert the man that she was awake, but after some time she could open and close her hand again. Now, she just had to wait.

Her eyes caught sight of a dagger hilt sticking out of a sheath on the man's thick brown leather belt, and her lips curled up in response. Listening carefully to each footfall on the hard forest floor, she waited for her arms to swing back toward his belt. Adeline counted her breaths between every few steps he took, her only way of measuring the passing of time. As she waited, she began to regain feeling in other parts of her body, first her toes, which she wiggled victoriously within her leather boots, then her arms. With a newfound confidence in her ability to escape, she swung her arm forward, wrapping her fingers around the hilt of the dagger poking out of the man's belt as they made contact with the cool steel. She counted a few more breaths, droplets of sweat sliding down her palm as she gripped the dagger tighter, willing herself to be patient.

One...two...

On three, she unsheathed the dagger and pressed it against his thigh, unwavering. Pushing with all the strength she could muster, she felt the dagger slice through the layers of hard black leather.

"Ow! What the fu—" the man gritted through his teeth, his hold on her loosening ever so slightly.

"Put. Me. Down." Adeline did not let him finish.

"I can't just *put you down*. You will—"

"Put. Me. Down!" she demanded, pressing the dagger deeper and watching as blood beaded on the surface of his skin where it was kissed by the blade.

"Fine!" He bit out, clearly frustrated with her antics. "You're a dangerous little thing, aren't you?"

She could hear the smirk in his voice even without seeing his face.

He hinged at the waist, dragging her body down the front of himself until her leather boots met the earth with a soft thud, a small cloud of dirt scattering around her feet. Adeline gasped at their close contact, as she'd felt each corded muscle of him as she slid over his front.

Her eyes roved up his body, scanning his broad chest covered in what appeared to be some sort of leather armor. The man wore a sleeveless tunic, his thick biceps free for onlookers to gawk at. And gawk she did, though she told herself it was only due to the winding black ribbons of ink that swirled up his arms, and not his considerable muscles.

A series of straps and buckles splayed across his chest, appearing to adjust the armor to his body as though they were fitted to his very build. At the center of his chest, Adeline noticed an embroidered set of wings, each spreading over his pecs and coming to an end at his sides. *Dragon wings.* They were intricately detailed, with veins crawling across each one. They were intimidating in their beauty.

From her time spent dangling over his shoulder, she knew the bottom half of this man extremely well, having committed the sight of his round ass to memory. Black cloth pants under what appeared to be the same style of armor wrapped around his legs, fastening around and protecting his thighs, knees, and shins. If the leather tunic he wore had fit his body perfectly, then these pants must have been simply an extension of his skin. The way the midnight fabric clung to his muscular thighs was nearly debilitating, but it was the tight fit of the fabric on his ass that was truly *sinful.*

Adeline forced her gaze up, her chin tilting higher as she searched for his eyes, needing a distraction from his body. She had known from the sheer fact that her eyes were level with his impressive pecs that he would be tall, but it wasn't until she was craning her neck to meet his gaze that she understood just how much he towered over her.

When her gaze finally met his piercing emerald eyes, she felt as if the air was knocked from her lungs once again. The man's eyes were like glittering pools of green staring back at her and as he held her gaze, she couldn't help but think that his eyes reminded her of the Emerald Lake at dusk, when the last glimpses of summer sun were dancing off the ripples of the water. The lake had always been a comforting place for her, hosting some of her favorite childhood memories. If he was the Emerald Lake, then she decided she was perfectly content with drowning.

His hair was a deep chocolate brown, cropped short on the sides with some length left on top, which fell parted in the middle and crested over his forehead, framing his face. A few unruly waves hung down over his forehead, curling at his thick, full brow that was currently beading with sweat. Adeline looked to his left eyebrow, unsurprised to find the jagged silver scar that cut through the hair there, yet her breaths still caught as her eyes locked on it.

This was the man from the garden. She was sure of it.

He glared down at her, his chiseled jaw clenched and frustration written all over his face. The dusting of a five o'clock shadow played across his jawline, which made him just that much more pleasing to look at.

Several beats passed between the two of them with Adeline still pressed firmly against his body. Her hand still grasped the dagger as she steadyed herself on his shoulder, while the other palm splayed across his chest, perfectly placed between the set of dragon wings there. Although he was still glaring down at her, his gaze seemed to soften ever so slightly, as he drank her in. He seemed to allow himself one moment to bask in her beauty before taking a quick step back, forcing her hands to fall from his body.

Adeline felt cold from the sudden lack of contact, and her muscles shook with fatigue.

"You were at—" her sentence was cut off by her abrupt collapse onto the dirt below.

"I tried to tell you that I couldn't set you down. But you were *oh so stubborn* in your demands to stand on your own two feet." The man looked down at her with his arms crossed, a smirk playing on his full lips.

"You could have mentioned that my legs no longer work, smartass. Did you drug me?" She bit back, annoyed at how amused he was with the situation.

"I tried to warn you, but you didn't give me the chance, remember? So, I figured you needed to figure it out the hard way." He motioned a hand toward where she lay in a heap on the forest floor, insinuating that her current state was *the hard way*. "And yes, I sedated you to ensure you were easier to transport."

Adeline managed to bring herself to a seat, but she didn't risk any further movement toward standing. She would need to allow the feeling to fully return to her legs before she tried that again. Her head throbbed and she was unsure if it was from the sudden contact with the forest floor just now, her fall the night before, or whatever the man had used to sedate her, but that did not stop her from prodding him for answers.

"You were at the ball last night. You were watching me from the gardens." She couldn't get the words out fast enough, her heart quickening as the accusation hung between them.

He looked momentarily stunned, as if shocked she had recognized him.

"Who are you and why were you there?" she questioned before he could reply to her first statement.

"Wouldn't you like to know, Princess."

The nickname turned her mouth sour. "Yes. I would like to know, *jackass*," she spit at him.

Adeline glared up at him now. Whoever this man was, clearly his appearance was the only good thing about him.

A tan, calloused hand cut into her line of sight, reaching for her. Reluctant to accept, but all too excited at the idea of no longer sitting on the cold ground while he towered over her, she groaned as she placed her hand in his. It was not lost on her just how small her hand appeared when enveloped by his as he pulled her upright.

Adeline felt dizzy as she transitioned from sitting to standing in what felt like the blink of an eye, and her head whirred with the sudden motion. The man planted his big hands around her waist, holding her upright, her hands naturally falling to his burly arms and she clung to him, desperate for any amount of added stability.

He stared down at her curiously, his eyes piercing her in a way that she knew was him peering through her eyes and into her soul. They were close again, their thighs pressed against each other as he held her securely.

"You want to know who I am, Princess?" he asked, his voice low as he stared into her, "then you have to earn it. Tell me your name and you can have mine."

Adeline's knees wobbled as she stared back at him.

"A—Adeline. My name is Adeline," she finally got out in a whisper.

"Good girl, Adeline. My name is Roman, and *I* was at the castle to kidnap you, not that you made it very difficult by running off on your own and incapacitating yourself."

"Kidnap me?!" she finally managed to gasp out, breathless.

"Yes. Kidnap you. Though judging by how poor a time you seemed to be having at the ball last night, I feel as though I have done you a favor by removing you from the castle. Is that true, darling?" he replied coolly, as though this was any normal interaction, and he hadn't just taken her captive and then proudly admitted it.

"You can't just *kidnap* me! I am the *Princess* of Scalebreak! They will send people to come find me! My father will be furious!" Her face grew red with anger.

"That's the goal, Princess. If it's any consolation, I am sorry you ended up in the middle of it." He looked down at her, genuine apology and regret in his expression.

"What is that even supposed to mean?! Why are you *kidnapping* me?" Adeline spit at him, her anger no longer suppressed.

"To get the king's attention. We know exactly what he has been up to and we will not stand for it any longer. *You* are being taken to send a message."

"I—a message? What has my father been up to? What are you talking *abo*—"

Before she could finish her demand for further explanation, Adeline felt a prick in her side, and suddenly, Roman lifted her into his strong, corded arms. She wanted desperately to thrash against his hold, to put up a fight, but she was seemingly no longer in control of her limbs or actions.

He sedated me again, she thought to herself as a frustrated yawn escaped her lips. Though she hated this man for taking her from her home, her mind and body seemed to forget that she was being kidnapped by a stranger as she snuggled into his chest and let the world fade away as her heavy eyes drifted closed once more.

CHAPTER NINE

ADELINE LAY IN THE center of a giant four-poster bed, tucked gently into the middle within a nest of blankets. Her cheeks were flushed pink, and brown curls fanned out around her, framing her head on the white silk pillow beneath it. Laying there in the center of the plush mattress, curled up in the mass of thick blankets she looked so small and gentle.

Roman had taken his spot in the highback green velvet armchair by the window, where he had a perfect line of sight to the beautiful girl in his bed. He had been watching her sleep for several hours, counting her breaths as she snored softly. He admired the rise and fall of her chest, each breath bringing him a sense of calm while he sat beside her. The dull glow of moonlight cast shadows across her face. Even still, he could not tear his eyes from her. She was captivating.

Roman had always had an affinity for night time; he loved the soft glow of the moon, the twinkle of stars in the sky overhead. There were many nights he had spent lying under a blanket of stars and bathing in the midnight moon. The shadows of the night were his peace, his serenity and the one place he could always go to quiet his mind, but sitting here watching her sleep, Roman felt for the first time like maybe the midnight sky was *not* the most beautiful thing he had seen in his life.; if the night was beautiful, then the princess was absolutely *breathtaking*.

He soaked in every minute detail of her face, from the curve of her deep black lashes resting so gently upon the pink flush of her cheeks, to the unguarded way she allowed sleep to envelope her fully, he found himself breathless at the softness of her beauty.

Several times, Roman had found himself reaching out involuntarily to tuck a stray hair behind her ear or softly cup her cheek with his calloused hand, a soft smile playing on his lips. He admired her in her slumber, desperately trying to memorize every piece of this moment, of this stunning woman strewn across his bed, because he knew it would be the last. It had to be. Once Adeline awoke, she was going to loathe him for bringing her here, for kidnapping her from the life she had known. Even if she never understood why he had taken her, he would accept her hatred for the rest of his life if it meant knowing his fight had been for her to know the truth.

Adeline stirred, stretching against the airy pool of silk surrounding her and rubbing her eyes with the heel of her hands before sitting up slowly. She looked dazed as she took in her surroundings with a crinkle in her brow.

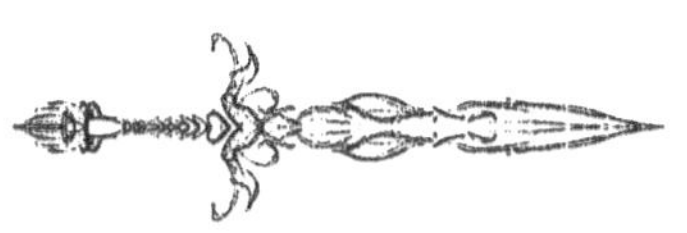

What time is it? I must have slept all day?!

Adeline's eyes began to adjust to the darkness, and she quickly real-ized she was in a foreign place. Her heart thundered in her chest. The bedroom she was in wasn't small by any means, but compared to the castle rooms she had grown up in, it wasn't large. Considering the oak paneling lining the walls around her, and the crackling fire in the brick hearth next to the bed, she believed this was a cabin of some sorts. There was a high-back green armchair poised next to the bed with a knit blanket haphazardly strewn across the seat.

What an odd spot for a chair, she thought to herself as she continued scanning her surroundings.

To her right were floor-to-ceiling windows that spanned across the entire wall, drawing her attention to the twinkling lights of a small gath-ering of cottages lining dirt roads in what she assumed was a small town below. On the horizon, a range of snow-dotted mountains stretched as far as the naked eye could see, and it was clear from the view out the expanse of windows that the house she was currently in was perched on a tree-lined hill.

It hit her all at once that she had no idea where she was, and her brows furrowed in confusion, her guard going up.

What the hell is going on..? Where am—

Her train of thought came to an abrupt halt when her eyes caught on the shadows of a bookcase on the wall opposite the foot of the bed. No, not on the shadows, but on *who* lurked within them. Emerald eyes stared back at her from the dark, unwavering as they absorbed her with intent.

She drank in the scene, the tall, muscular man enveloped in shadows. He wore a pair of gray cotton drawers, the white drawstring hanging between his brawny thighs. His chest was bare, his impressive physique on display for her to drool over. His chest and arms were covered in swirling black ink, tattoos that were difficult to make out in the darkness he stood within.

Adeline's face heated with desire, which quickly mixed with embarrassment when she realized she had been caught ogling the man shrouded in black. Both feelings fled, and were replaced immediately with frustration as she recalled that the man she was eyeing with desperate want had *kidnapped* her. Even as she tried to rationalize with herself, to beg herself to fight against this, her body stayed still, her eyes locked on him.

He stepped forward and as he did the shadows shrank back to the corners of the room, no longer casting out as far as they had moments before. It was almost as if he had *commanded* the shadows to reveal him to her. As he stepped toward her, his bare feet padding on the cool floors, Adeline sucked in a breath; in the light of the fire, this man was *gorgeous*.

With the moonlight shining in through the windows, she could make out some of the tattoos decorating the contours of his tense muscles. Across his left arm were endless swirls of black shadow, pooling across his peck before coming to an abrupt end. She could see each and every detail from where she sat and soaked it all in, unable to tear her eyes away. Adeline had seen tattoos before, but these were no ordinary tattoos, they seemed to come alive, the shadows moving against his tan skin with every inhale.

All that man and all that muscle and all that dark ink clouded Adeline's mind with thoughts not at all suited for one's kidnapper, almost making her forget she was in a foreign place. *Almost.*

"Taking in the view, Princess?" he smirked at her before lifting his arms behind his head to display the muscles rippling there.

His words drew her from her yearning, reminding her once again that he was *dangerous*. Adeline reached for her right thigh, grunting in frustration when she did not find the dagger that was normally strapped there.

"You *disarmed* me?!" She spat at him. "Seems like quite the length to go through for a *princess* don't you think?"

He lowered his arms and took a step toward her, closing the distance between them. His firm hand reached out and gripped her by the chin, turning her head so that Adeline was looking right at him.

"You and I both know that you're not *just* a princess, darling." He stared down at her almost hungrily, and Adeline felt butterflies come to life in her stomach, the color draining from her face. She didn't know this man, yet he had such a strange effect on her. It was as if her body was not in her own control when she was near him and she desperately wished she could rid herself of the odd sense of peace that his presence brought her. He had *kidnapped* her, and for some reason, she was swooning over him instead of trying to escape.

Roman. His name is Roman, she reminded herself as the events that brought her here washed over her. She tentatively reached her hand up toward his, letting him think her demure, before quickly curling her fingers around his wrist and flinging his hand away from her.

"I don't think you know a damn thing about me, Shadow," she said before shrinking back into the bed, and gathering the blankets around her exposed body. The chill reminded her just how vulnerable she was in the soft black cotton shirt that hung off one of her shoulders.

"I know a lot more about you than you want to allow yourself to believe, Sunshine." Roman's calm voice brought her attention back to him, seemingly unphased by her hostility.

"And to answer your question, yes, I did disarm you—to prevent you from holding a dagger to my throat in my own home."

Adeline's eyes widened at his statement. *Okay...maybe he does know me.* The thought was almost jarring.

"And how exactly, do you know so much about me, when I have never even heard your name before?" she asked, goading him.

Much to her dismay her pulse had slowed slightly, her body no longer interpreting this man as an immediate threat to her safety. Though he may be frustrating in nature, something about the mountain of a man was so...calming.

"Because, my dear, you are the very thing I grew up knowing would be my undoing."

He stared at her, letting the words hang between them. His eyes were laced with something akin to passion.

His undoing? Who talks like that? What does that even mean? Gods, men are so infuriating.

Adeline glared back at him, fighting to keep her gaze on his eyes instead of the exposed stretch of bare skin and muscle. Just because he kidnapped her, didn't mean she was blind.

"Oh please, do go on, Roman," her voice dripped with sarcasm, as she fought to keep her gaze locked on him while her hands searched in the sheets for something, anything, to put him in his place.

She had assumed a man like Roman likely did not sleep unarmed, as any good warrior. And as her fingers closed around cool steel, gripping the hilt of what she could only hope was a dagger tucked under the pillow, she felt a smile threatening to break free.

Roman smirked, clearly mistaking her violence for flirting. "You are a feisty little thing, aren't you, princess?"

As soon as the words left his lips, she lunged toward him, snaking an arm around his neck to use as leverage and flipping him. She shoved him backwards onto the plush mattress she had been sitting on mere moments before. Roman grunted with surprise at how quickly she had moved; it had all happened in the blink of an eye. One moment he was staring down at her, the next she had pinned him to the bed, her hips straddling his, that silver rose necklace swinging between them. She was leaning forward, her delicate frame pressed against his, and both of them seemed to flush with heat at the contact, but that did not stop Adeline from pushing firmly against his throat with the blade he had forgotten was stowed under his pillow.

Fuck, Roman thought to himself.

He couldn't think straight with the delicious feeling of her body pressing into his. His mind, normally sure and calculating, was occupied only by her, this infuriating, gorgeous woman straddling him in his bed, wearing *his* shirt. And fuck, did she look hot as hell in it. The cool blade bit into his skin, reminding him of the looming threat. And still, he couldn't make himself care. He tried desperately to convince himself that his quickening pulse was due to the dagger being held to his throat and not the proximity of the woman above him, but even he knew that was a lie. The princess was already his undoing, poised over him with a look of determination on her face, loose brown curls cascading down around her head, unruly from a good day's rest.

"You have no fucking idea," she hissed back at him.

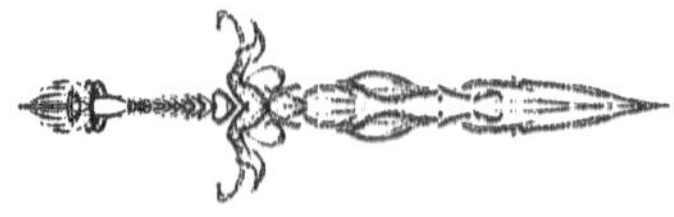

If there was one thing Adeline Ambrose had loved about being princess, it was that she knew just how often people tended to underestimate her. It was something she learned to use to her advantage years ago. And she had no doubt that it would work on Roman. What she had not considered, however, was how feeling her body pressed against his would affect *her*. This broody, solid mass of a man was arguably the most frustrating creature she had ever met, not to mention he was her *captor*, but that did not stop the desire blooming in the pit of her stomach from making itself known.

She fought to keep her focus. She had him right where she wanted him, yet she couldn't help but feel *guilty* for attacking him in the first place.

Guilty? Why should I feel guilty when he KIDNAPPED me?!

Tightening her grip on the hilt of the dagger and refusing to tear her eyes from his, she pushed the dagger further, watching his skin dimple where the blade made contact. Roman swallowed, bit his bottom lip, and started laughing. Adeline bounced on top of him with each exhale of laughter. Confused and distracted, her hand loosened ever so slightly on the dagger, but that was all he needed.

Roman's laughter came to an abrupt end when he grabbed hold of both Adeline's wrists and twisted his ankles with hers before flipping their position. He was now hovering over her, and the dagger was nowhere to be found. His hands firmly pushed her wrists down into the mattress, his legs pinning hers with his thighs on either side of her own. Her pulse raced, and she hoped that he could not feel her hammering heart with his chest pressed against hers. He brought his face down, his full lips hovering just above hers as he stared directly into her eyes.

"Or maybe, I do, Princess. Maybe I know *exactly* who you are and what you are capable of," Roman practically whispered between them, as if the words were meant just for her to hear, no one else.

CHAPTER TEN

A KNOCK CUT THROUGH the thick silence like a knife, and Roman went rigid with the unexpected disruption, untangling his limbs from Adeline's. She sat up, pressing her back into the cool wood of the headboard, and stared toward the door expectantly, her heart still thundering in her ears. Roman let out a deep sigh that sent goosebumps scattering over her entire body; clearly, he was irritated by the disruption. Rising from the bed, he stalked toward the door, throwing a sidelong glance and a tilted smirk at Adeline over his shoulder. Roman pulled the door open with force, showcasing his annoyance, but was calculated in his movements, ensuring to only crack the door wide enough to speak to the person on the other side and not expose the woman in his bed. She noticed he seemed to have to fight the urge to turn and look at her, as if she would steal his attention entirely.

"Sir, uh…I have just come to tell you that your mother has request-ed your presence at dinner tonight…Well, you and your, uh…guest," a squirrely sounding voice squeaked from the hallway.

Roman stood still, a look of shock washing over his features for only a moment. The reaction made Adeline wonder if anyone else was supposed to know she was here at all. Perhaps his plan had been to lock her away.

Shit, she thought to herself, feeling suddenly like this room was too small, the walls closing in on her.

"Reggie, kindly tell my mother that we will be there, per her request," Roman growled before slamming the door in his face.

Gods, this guy is a dick, Adeline thought to herself as she watched the exchange.

"You know, you could be kinder to…Reggie, was it? He is simply doing his job." Adeline glared at Roman, making sure her annoyance at his behavior was clear by her expression.

"Yes, *Princess*. I will apologize to Reggie later about my behavior." He stared back at her, the corners of his mouth curling up in a smile. It appeared he was almost enjoying her frustration with him, which just angered her more. What she hated the most, however, was that the moment he had turned his attention back to her, the anxiety bolted from her body, replaced instantly by a state of serenity.

"So, what exactly was your plan, *Shadow*? Sneak me in here with-out anyone seeing and keep me locked away for your own pleasure?" She spat the words at Roman, hoping they stung with the venom she laced into them.

Roman took slow, calculated steps toward her, the grin still plas-tered on his face, though his eyes darkened in response to her state-ment.

"Maybe that is *exactly* what my plan was, darling. Perhaps I intend to keep you locked away in my bedroom for no one else to gaze upon for the rest of eternity. After all, I do tend to get a bit...*possessive* when it comes to perfectly crafted art pieces."

He was standing at the edge of the bed now, staring down at Adeline. A breath passed between them before Roman reached a hand down, gripping her chin and tilting her face up so she was looking into his eyes. He let out a sigh so quiet that Adeline barely heard it herself.

"And you, Addie...*you* are the most gorgeous work of art I have ever laid my eyes upon."

"I—" Adeline tried to reply, but the words caught in her throat.

No one, besides Greta, had ever called her Addie before now. And, as much as she wished she hated the way the syllables rolled off his tongue and into the space between them, no matter how hard she tried she couldn't make herself hate the sound. She wasn't even sure she didn't want him to say it again, and again.

This stranger, this man—who had taken her captive and stolen her away from the life she had known, from her family—made her breathless without even trying, and no matter how hard she tried, she couldn't bring herself to hate him. As she stared up into his piercing green eyes, a small part of her couldn't help but think, maybe Roman stealing her away wasn't all that bad.

At the very least, he had rescued her from being courted by a line of horrible suitors, while her entire family stood aside and watched. Not to mention whatever was going on with Calum. If for nothing else, she was grateful to Roman for that. The more she thought about her situation, the more she recognized there was something intrinsic in him that soothed her. In fact, she found that she was less afraid of her captor, and more intrigued.

Roman dropped his hand from her chin, taking a few measured steps away from her, seeming suddenly distraught and uncomfortable. Glancing down at his hands, he shook his head in frustration, deep brown locks, disrupted by the movement, tumbling loosely around the crown of his head. He cleared his throat.

"I—uh, I should be going. I have some things to attend to before dinner. The bathroom is just through there." He pointed toward an open door frame on the wall to the left of the bed. "Please wash up, and I will have appropriate attire sent to your room for dinner."

He did not give her a chance to reply before he was pulling a black t-shirt, identical to the one Adeline wore, over his tan skin and slipping through the door. Even now, when he was so quickly trying to escape her, Adeline couldn't help but notice that he was the human personification of shadows, even down to his clothing choice, and she could not think of anything more beautiful.

As the heavy door clicked shut, her mind roared to life, beginning to craft an escape plan. She had absolutely no idea the layout of the building she was currently in, let alone where she was, which would make her getaway far more difficult. Adeline stayed in bed for several long minutes, turning over all the possibilities for escape as she slumped back down into the warm embrace of the soft blankets and plush mattress as if in a trance.

What am I doing? I should be running for my life, not getting cozy in my captor's bed. But just as quickly as the thought came to her, it fled. She was unable to coax herself up. While she let her body relax into the plush down comforter, her eyes caught on the expanse of windows next to the bed, her heart picking up as she stared out, taking in the beauty of the town below. Although she had no idea where she was, an odd sense of familiarity and *home* crept up on her while looking out into a place that felt like *her* somehow. She took a deep breath, allowing a feeling of peace to wash over her. Drawing in another inhale, she paused mid-breath, stunned by the scent that enveloped her and unsure how she had not noticed it before. Citrus, cedar, and jasmine flooded her senses, consuming her so wholly that Adeline found herself unable to move. Drawing the blankets up to her nose she breathed in deeply, inhaling as much of the smell as she could in a single breath. It was almost euphoric, the effect the smell had on her. Her body relaxed near instantaneously and goosebumps danced across her skin, covering the entirety of her body. It was only fair to assume that since she was currently snuggled up into Roman's bed, inhaling the scent clinging to his blankets like a mad-woman, that the lingering aroma had to belong to him. How had she not noticed it before? Now that she had lost herself to it, she wasn't sure she could ever ignore it again. Never in her life had she felt so encapsulated by something as simple as *a smell.*

It took several moments of convincing to pry herself out of the lush bed and into the bathroom to freshen up. All prior thoughts of an escape plan now gone from her mind, she found herself delighted that she had pulled herself from the safety and warmth of the sheets.

As her bare feet met the cool stone of the floor, Adeline embraced the cold creeping up her body, leaving goosebumps in its wake, while she took in her surroundings.

At the end of the bathroom stood a floor-to-ceiling window, spanning from one wall to the other. It was clear even from the doorway that due to the position on the mountain, there was no way anyone could see in. But looking out at the view was another thing entirely. Outside, a smattering of trees dotted the edge of the terrain, snow dusting their branches. On the horizon, mountain ranges spanned as far as the eye could see, all capped with snow and standing sure. In front of the considerable window sat a white porcelain tub that Adeline presumed was big enough for at least three people; her cheeks blushed at the improper thought, embarrassed to be wondering such a thing. Shaking the thought from her mind, she looked to her right where a white marble sink and faucet stood, next to which was a toilet. The bathroom was nothing grand—having grown up in a castle, Adeline had seen her fair share of grandeur—but she still couldn't help but feel overcome with awe as she stood in the doorway and took in the artistry that had gone into designing the space. Every miniscule detail felt so *intentional*.

A quiet thought skittered into the edges of her mind as she made work of filling the basin with steaming hot water. *I should be trying to escape.* But even as the words sunk in, she could not bring herself to care, instead stripping off the cotton tee hanging from her frame. Adeline gathered her hair into a messy brown knot atop her head before she stepped into the tub, welcoming the idea of cleanliness. The hot water was jarring at first, but as she sank into the basin it quickly became comforting, calming. Tendrils of steam curled up from the water, rising to the wood beams of the ceiling above.

She had added some mysterious oils from the counter to the tub before climbing in, which she now recognized as lavender and jasmine tickling her nose. Lavender had always been one of her favorite scents and now mingling with the jasmine, she recognized it as the foundation of Roman's aroma as it wrapped around her like a comforting embrace, soothing her very soul.

A part of her felt achingly *empty* as she sank into the water, having never gone this long without hunting; there was a part of her that yearned for the itch of power dancing beneath her skin again. Adeline drew her knees to her chest, letting a few tears spill from her eyes as she sat with the feeling of emptiness for a moment, letting herself become familiar with the foreign emotion. This was new, but that did not mean it was bad. Although she had grown used to the feeling of power surging through her, she was still Adeline even without it. Swiping at the tears that had spilled down her cheeks, she took a deep breath.

I am still powerful even without enchantment running through my veins, Adeline reminded herself, trying to convince herself of the words.

With another deep breath, she leaned back, settling into the water, and looked out the window, hoping to distract her mind with the breathtaking view. Snowflakes were gently falling from a cloudy sky now, dancing in the soft breeze before kissing the treetops. It was as if they had danced this same dance a million times before, only going through the motions now while Adeline gazed out in awe. As she watched the scene out the window, and her body submerged in the warm water of the tub, she felt herself finally relax. It had been so long since she had truly felt at peace the way she did in that moment. It had crept up on her, sank into her bones and muscles until her body felt loose, her mind empty, and she couldn't stop the content smile that crept across her lips.

I will figure out a plan for my escape later, she decided.

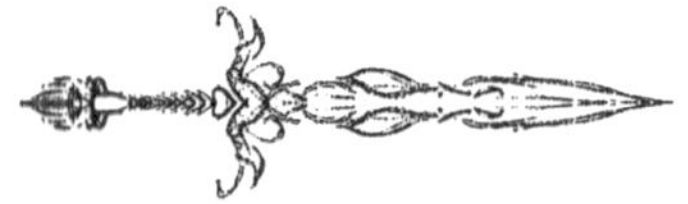

Adeline was not sure how long she had stayed submerged in the tub, lost in a euphoric daze of relaxation, only it had been long enough that steam was no longer curling from the water. It hadn't been until she had heard the door to the bedroom open, followed by some quick shuffling and the door closing again, that she finally shook herself from the serenity and made haste of scrubbing her skin clean, unsure of who had come into the room and if they were a threat.

When she had finally felt clean again, her skin supple and rosy from the temperature of the water and her thorough scrubbing, she stepped out of the tub, wrapped a soft white towel around herself, and made her way back through the doorway into the bedroom. With each step, the little voice in the back of her mind begging her to escape fell quieter and quieter until it fell silent as she met the edge of the bed. She was not surprised to find garments laid across the bed, waiting for her just as Roman had promised. It was not lost on her that he had said he would have the garments sent to *her room,* when this was very obviously his own private chambers. What caught her off guard was the allure of the clothing he'd sent for her.

Entranced by the almost silk gown, Adeline gathered the midnight fabric into her hand, taking note of how the soft material slipped out of her grasp; it was all the encouragement she needed to pull the dress over her head. After making sure that the seams were all sitting comfortably against her skin, she stared down at the gown and took in its beauty. The garment was simple, but achingly beautiful, the kind of dress that needed no help to catch the eye of a room.

Black fabric spilled down her waist, flowing loosely around her legs. She smiled to herself as she swished the skirts and realized how unrestricted her movements were, a detail she was grateful for. The bodice hugged her middle, accenting her waistline while still allowing her room to breathe freely and without difficulty, unlike the corsets she was used to wearing. Her favorite part was the way the neckline sat just below the shoulders, leaving them exposed, with loose, long sleeves that flowed down to a delicate cuff at the wrist. Silver dustings of what appeared to be stars grouped in tiny constellations played across the fabric, adding a celestial element to the already gorgeous garment. As she shifted her legs, swishing the skirts, the stars seemed to twinkle back up at her as if they were at home among the night sky. Silently, she wondered where Roman had procured a gown so beautiful on such short notice.

The craftsmanship of the gown had her mind wandering to Greta and her heart panged; Greta was the only thing she missed about Scalebreak, though she would never admit that outside the confines of her mind. Her hand wandered up to the silver necklace that still hung from her neck, her fingers closing around the rose pendant as she allowed herself only a moment to be homesick.

Adeline noticed a glimmer on the bed where the dress had just been, drawing her from her sadness. Her brows knit together in curiosity as she reached down and picked up the object that was carefully placed there. As she brought it closer to her, she realized that it was a satin bow in the same silver as the stars that dusted her dress. Bringing the bow behind her head, she gathered half of her loose brown curls, securing them in a simple twist with the satin, letting a few chocolate strands fall free to frame her face perfectly. Adeline did not need to look at her reflection to know that she looked absolutely ethereal. Although she had donned some of the finest gowns one could own, in every color imaginable, for balls and other events, she never felt as beautiful as she did in the celestial black dress.

CHAPTER ELEVEN

A FTER SEVERAL LONG MINUTES spent pacing back and forth, black skirts of her gown swishing around her legs, and trying to convince herself to leave the room and find her way to the dining room alone, the silence was broken by a firm knock at the door. It seemed her time for leaving alone had passed. Adeline took a step toward the entryway, reaching for the cool metal of the knob and closing her fingers around it, pausing to draw in a deep breath through her nose.

"I can hear you in there, Princess. Open the door for me." Roman's deep voice echoed through the wood door, pleading.

His words startled her. How had he known she was standing on the other side of the door, trying to convince herself to face him? How had he heard her through the thick wood? Adeline tightened her grip on the doorknob before throwing the door open with fervor, a huff escaping her lips and causing the loose strands of hair in front of her face to blow upwards.

"Just who exactly do you think you—"

"Wow. You look...there are no words in *any language* to describe your beauty. You look absolutely breathtaking, Addie," Roman cut her off, seeming truly breathless as he stared at her.

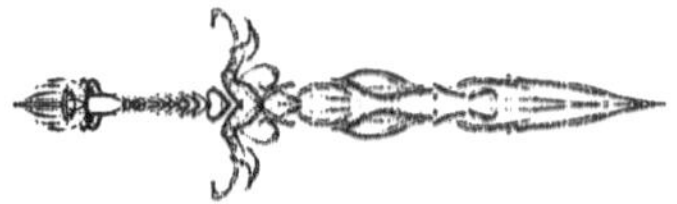

His pulse quickened as he took her in, standing before him in the gorgeous dress he'd had sent up for her. Breathtaking didn't even begin to describe how she looked. Roman may have barely known this woman, but he would crawl to the ends of the world for even the chance to look at her one last time, especially in that dress.

"I—um. Thank you," Adeline stumbled over her words, surprised by the sudden compliment.

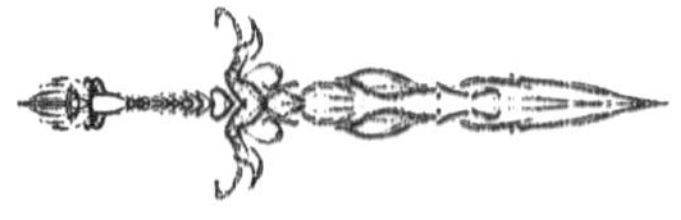

There was something about Roman that felt so...*comforting,* and she hated it. She wished she could bring herself to hate him the way she knew she should.

He kidnapped me for Gods' sake, she thought, her frustration with herself growing.

"Well, we better not keep my mother waiting. She can get quite impatient, to say the least." He stopped for a moment, seeming to choose his next words carefully, "And don't bother trying to gain her sympathy; my mother knows exactly *who* you are and why you're here, Princess."

Roman stuck out his arm, offering it to Adeline. She looked at him, taking in his attire for the first time and feeling a flush creep over her cheeks in response.

He wore a black silk dress shirt that looked almost liquid the way it clung to him in all the right places. His legs were clad in a pair of dark gray slacks that hugged his impressive thighs, secured with a simple black belt. Roman was already a handsome man, but he did clean up nice.

Adeline's heart rate quickened in her chest. He was striking. She glanced at his extended arm once more and decided that if she couldn't force herself to hate him, she could at least pretend she did, for both of their sakes. With the decision made up in her mind, she tilted her head upward ever so slightly and looked into his piercing green eyes, not allowing herself to drown in them the way she truly wanted, before breaking their stare and taking a step into the hallway and past Roman. Though she had been unable to convince herself to concoct a getaway scheme, that didn't stop her from gathering information while she was here. Besides, there was no way that her father wouldn't be sending someone to retrieve her, so why should she waste her energy on escaping in the first place. She tried hard to reason with herself as she became more and more comfortable in her supposed prison.

"For the record *Prince Charming*, I don't *need* you to guide me anywhere. I am perfectly capable of getting places on my own, *without* dangling off your arm like some pretty plaything," Adeline spat over her shoulder as she continued past him and down the hallway.

Sure, she had absolutely no idea where she was, let alone how to get to the dining room, but she refused to give Roman the satisfaction of leading her there. She was perfectly capable of finding it on her own no matter how long it took. Judging by the short hallway with only a hand full of doors in either direction, she presumed the dining room was down the wooden staircase that branched out to her right. Adeline continued to hold her head high, not letting her eyes wander so as to give away her feeling of disorientation.

As her foot made contact with the first step, she suddenly felt a presence behind her. *There is no way that Roman could have made it to me that quickly, that silently.*

Before she could turn around, she felt a cool whisper of contact on the back of her neck and a shiver raced through her. It felt as though a large hand had wrapped itself around the back of her neck, holding her there, but there was no warmth of skin on skin, only a chilling ghost-like presence. It was dominating, commanding, and yet ever so gentle so as not to hurt her. Adeline turned her eyes slightly over her right shoulder in an attempt to look behind her at who, or what, was pressing into her, but all she saw were black tendrils curling around her neck in the shape of a hand. Her breath caught in her throat and her fingers found hold on the railing that lined the staircase, tightening around the grooves in the wood as she tried to hold herself upright on suddenly weak legs.

What the hell is that??

She didn't have time to react before she felt the warm tickle of breath on her ear followed by a deep, low whisper.

"For the *record,* Princess, I do not doubt you are capable of anything. You could bring the world to its knees if you so wished," Roman's voice in her ear did nothing to calm her racing pulse.

Adeline craned her neck, trying to look further down the hall at the space Roman had occupied moments before, a part of her was unsurprised to find him standing there, exactly where she had left him.

He stared back at her, meeting her gaze as a smirk danced on his lips, spreading into a teasing smile when he winked.

But his voice? He had sounded so close?

Adeline once again wished she could be angry at him, or at least have some sort of quip to throw back at him, but instead she couldn't help but frown at the feeling of emptiness that came over her as the presence drew away from her, the shadows swirling and curling on their way back to Roman.

It seemed as though they were eager to reach him, to settle back into his skin and await their next mission, his next command. The interaction confirmed for her that Roman was a dragon slayer; that was the only explanation for his ability to command darkness.

She stood there on the top step for a moment, trying to collect her thoughts and regain control of her mind before continuing down the stairs. That moment was all it took for Roman to be across the hallway, standing right next to her with his arm extended in an offering to her once again, and this time, Adeline did not protest. Instead, she intertwined their arms and grabbed hold of Roman's impressive bicep, letting him lead her to the ends of the earth if he so pleased.

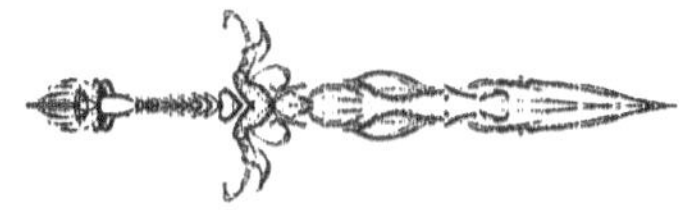

The dining room in the cabin was quaint compared to the castle Adeline had grown up in, but in a way that she found charming. The wood-panelled walls rose into a high-beamed ceiling. Large paneled windows adorned two of the walls, taking up most of them. From the middle of the ceiling hung a metal chandelier that twisted in delicate swirls, swaying gently above the dining area, which was composed of a long rectangular table with enough chairs and place settings for eight people. The table was much smaller than what Adeline was used to, but it was cozy. Everything about the space felt inviting and homey.

Through the spacious windows, Adeline caught a glimpse of the town below once again. The sun was going down, the horizon painted with hues of pink and purple, and the small mountain village was cast in an orangey glow. Everything in it seemed to emit its own light, even the inhabitants that were bustling through the streets, likely heading home from a day of work. Adeline watched as people laughed and smiled, shaking hands or waving at one another as they passed by. She had never seen so many people who looked so *happy*. Growing up, the people around her were always stiff and thought much too highly of themselves to bother with shaking the hands of people on the street. She couldn't help but let out an involuntary sigh of contentment as she took in the scene below. A part of her had always ached to belong to a community like that.

Somehow, even with his claims regarding his mother's impatience, they had beat her to the dining room. Adeline and Roman had just taken their seats across the long wooden table from one another when she walked in. As she made her way to the head of the table, Adeline couldn't stop herself from watching every move as she took in the woman. His mother was shorter than Adeline by a few inches, but her silhouette was etched in muscle. She wore her hair in a simple braid down her back, brown strands intertwining with silver in a way that made her hair appear to shimmer when it caught the light. The woman had the same piercing green eyes that Adeline had already become accustomed to drowning in, but hers had a twinkle of sadness behind them. She had some wrinkles that hinted at her age, but they were all the kind of wrinkles you get from a life well lived. Smile lines carved into the corners of her mouth and eyes, laugh lines across her forehead. Although she had a calming pres-ence, the way she carried herself commanded respect; her spine was ramrod straight as she walked with her shoulders back and chin tilted ever so slightly upward. Adeline sat in awe, trying not to let it paint her features.

This was the kind of woman who should be running a kingdom. She had always thought that her mother, while terrifying in her own right, was just not quite fit to be queen, but this woman, who com-manded respect in every room she entered and still had a tenderness in her gaze, she would have made a great queen. She was wearing fighting leathers that appeared to be a slightly more feminine version of the ones Adeline had seen Roman don before, the dragon wings at the center a familiar sight.

"I apologize for my tardiness. I had some business matters to attend to. Roman, kindly introduce your guest," his mother said, her voice somehow stern but caring all at once.

"As if you don't already know who she is, Ma," Roman quipped back.

"*Roman*. Introduce the young lady for crying out loud!" she responded, biting back a smile.

"*Fine. Fine.* Mother, this is Adeline Ambrose, Princess of Scale-break. Princess, this is my mother, Amira Drache," Roman said playfully as if he knew something that she did not.

The name knocked the air from Adeline. *Drache.* Where had she heard that before? And why did it sound so...*important*?

"Nice to meet you, Miss Ambrose. I hope that you have found your time here thus far to be comfortable, and that my son has not been too unbearable to be around," Amira teased, throwing a loving look in Roman's direction as she reached for her wine glass.

"Nice to meet you as well, ma'am. Roman has only been *somewhat* unbearable to be around, I can assure you that I am keeping him on his toes," Adeline responded, though her head still swam with questions of who this woman was and why she recognized her name.

Amira swirled the wine in her glass, crimson liquid sloshing up the sides as she made eye contact with Adeline. Her mouth tilted up at the corners in a soft smile. Much like Roman, something about Amira felt oddly comforting to Adeline, like she had known the woman her entire life and not a mere five minutes.

A tall, burly man with graying hair, whom Adeline presumed to be the chef, entered the room and began setting dishes overflowing with food in the center of the table. Bowls of creamy mashed potatoes, decadent looking pastas, and steaming piles of vegetables filled the space between her and Roman. Adeline told herself that the aching feeling of hunger that came over her was due to the delicious array of food before her and not the man sitting across the table, but she wasn't entirely sure that she didn't need both.

Roman and Amira filled their plates, piling mountains of mashed potatoes high on the white china place settings, but Adeline hesitated, unsure where to begin. In the castle, their plates were served by staff; they were never to serve themselves. After a moment she reached forward, deciding to serve herself anyway, not wanting to stick out.

"So, Adeline, has my dear son told you just where you are yet?" Amira asked, looking at Adeline with wonder dancing in her eyes.

"Uh, no ma'am, he has not," Adeline muttered, intimidated by the woman at the head of the table.

"Please, call me Amira! Ro, I will chastise you later for keeping this lovely lady in the dark. Kindly enlighten her as to where she has been held captive."

Roman let out a sigh, glancing at his mother with a tender annoyance. "Well, Princess, welcome to Drakmoor."

Chapter Twelve

A DELINE CHOKED ON HER wine, somehow managing not to spew the red liquid from her mouth like a fountain.

Drakmoor? Did he just say Drakmoor? Like the Drakmoor from the fairy tales read to me as a child? The ones that told of a clan of dragon sympathizers? That Drakmoor?

She took a deep breath, steeling herself to ease the now rapid pulse that thundered in her ears like a war drum.

"I'm sorry, did you just say *Drakmoor?*" she questioned, glancing between Roman and his mother with wide eyes.

"Yes. You are in Drakmoor...Is there a problem?" Roman's mother stared at her from her spot at the head of the table, her green eyes felt as though they were looking right through Adeline.

"I—um no. No problem. It's only that I grew up believing Drakmoor to be a fictional place," Adeline mumbled, embarrassed to be making the admission.

Roman laughed. It was a full belly laugh that caught Adeline completely off guard. Her attention was entirely on him as she took in this rare moment. She may loathe how drawn to him she felt, but hearing him laugh, seeing his face light up with that damn smile—it felt like she had forgotten how to breathe altogether. Though she reminded herself that they had only just met, and she hardly knew Roman, the air was entirely knocked from her lungs as she watched the tall mountain of a man keel over in *giggles*. This was only the second time she had seen him laugh, and was not yet accustomed to the intoxicating feeling that overcame her as she took it in. She could watch him like this forever and never grow tired of it. Adeline shook herself from the trance, hoping that no one else had noticed her gawking at Roman.

HE KIDNAPPED ME! Why can't I seem to make myself remember that?

"Is something funny, *Shadow?*" she spit at Roman through gritted teeth, narrowing her eyes in his direction.

His laughter continued for several short moments, and Adeline looked up to his mother with confusion in her eyes, silently asking her if maybe he always behaved this way and his mother's eyes softened, a smile spreading across her lips as she finally spoke up.

"Ro! That is quite enough. The poor girl is already confused; she does not need to be laughed at too." His mother had such a calming presence about her that even listening to her chastise her son felt like being wrapped in a warm blanket.

Roman's laughter cut off abruptly at his mother's statement and he looked at Adeline, a silent apology passing between the two of them.

Adeline felt herself soften at that. It was hard to be mad at him when he was so damn attractive.

Oh Gods, did I actually just admit to myself that I find him attractive.

"Apologies, Princess. It is only—did you just say that Drakmoor was fictitious? Our clan has been around far longer than your family has been ruling over Scalebreak, so I find it hard to believe that you were entirely unaware of us," Roman said, his face gentle as he delivered the statement.

Adeline let out a near silent gasp. *Longer than my family has been ruling over the kingdom...but that is not possible. We have been governing Scalebound for centuries....*

"It seems that you have much to catch up on, Adeline. Roman will happily get you familiar with the town and assist you in relearning history as you have known it. But for now, I would like to formally introduce myself. My name is Amira Drache, Matron of Drakmoor."

Adeline's jaw surely had to be on the floor at this point. *Amira Drache.* Now, paired with the last name, recognition and shock washed over Adeline.

Amira was clearly amused with Adeline's surprise, evident by the mirth dancing in her green eyes, but she was kind enough not to outwardly laugh at the princess.

"Judging by your reaction, I am going to go out on a limb and assume that I, too, was relayed as a fictional character and not a true piece of history?" Amira asked.

All Adeline could manage in response was a slight nod. Her entire world felt like it had just been dropped on its head. The fairy tales she had been told by Greta as she grew up were actually not fairy tales at all, but rather real places and people that had been disguised as fantasy her entire life. At the thought of her nursemaid, Adeline felt her hand wrap around the necklace resting at her chest, calling on it for comfort.

"But that means—" Adeline couldn't finish the sentence, breathless at the new information.

"That I am a dragon rider. Correct," Amira's response was gentle despite the weight of the truth she uttered.

It had taken nearly thirty minutes of questioning before Adeline was able to let any of the shock wear off. It was truly world shattering, hearing that the stories she was told as a child were a lie. *What else had been a lie?* Could she trust anything she knew to be true? *What has my father been up to that landed me in a clan of dragon riders? Does that mean Roman is a rider and not a dragon slayer?* She was not entirely sure that she was prepared for the answers to any of the questions that plagued her mind.

Amira had willingly answered anything Adeline threw her way, but excused herself from dinner to deal with an important clan matter after someone, dressed in the same battle gear that Roman had worn just hours ago, burst into the room declaring that she was needed urgently. They had spoken in hushed tones as Amira was ushered out of the dining room, but after years of listening to whispered conversations in the castle, Adeline had a keen sense of hearing, which meant it was not lost on her that they had captured someone, someone who had come here looking for *her.* Suddenly she found herself thankful that she had not tried to escape after all, and instead had stayed to gather information.

I knew my father would send someone to bring me home, she thought to herself, though the only feeling that overcame her as the realization sank in was despair—she did not want to leave, no matter how wrong she knew her being here was, this place intrigued her. It called to her in a way that made her skin itch, like the need to hunt. *I must stay to gather as much knowledge as I can,* she thought, though she knew that was not the true reason behind her not wanting to leave.

Adeline didn't wear the knowledge on her face, refusing to let Amira or Roman know that she was aware of the situation at hand. If they knew she had been listening, who knew what they would do to her? She had been brought here as a captive after all. It dawned on her that while her reaction to *being kidnapped* hadn't been what one would expect, she was experiencing those emotions instead at the thought of being returned home.

After they finished eating, Roman promised to take Adeline on a tour of the large cabin and further explain the history. Well, cabin was one word for it. Roman and Amira's home was more like a castle made of wood with the way it towered over everything else, dwarfing the entire town on the mountainside.

As they left the dining room, Roman made quick work of showing her where things like staff sleeping quarters, the sitting room, and the kitchens were, knowing she would not find them to be interesting and therefore likely would not find herself in those places often. While they moved through the lower floor, he began explaining in more detail what made Drakmoor so unique. It turned out that the Drache family truly had established this clan of dragon riders and sympathisers centuries ago. It had been over a hundred and fifty years since Amira herself had taken the role of matron in Drakmoor, having inherited leadership of the clan after the previous elder passed.

Adeline had reeled at that detail, but did not let herself prod. *Amira has been matron of the clan for a hundred and fifty years...that is far longer than any human should be able to live. She looks as though she is only in her early fifties, the only sign of her age the silver strands woven through her braid. How old is she, truly? How has she been alive this long? How old does that make Roman?*

It had taken a tremendous effort to tune back into Roman's story telling with all of the questions that spun through her mind.

"—Use dragon scales as currency, but that is something we have worked hard to abolish in Drakmoor. Instead we use the shed scales to reinforce our armor and occasionally craft weapons," he had continued on, not noticing how stunned Adeline had been by the information he so casually mentioned.

"You truly have never heard any of this before?" Roman questioned, his brow raised.

"Some of it is familiar, yes. Much of it aligns with the stories I was told as a child," Adeline replied. She could not muster any sarcastic quips when her head was reeling this way.

Roman shook his head, his face darkening in anger. A deep brown curl came loose from the top of his head, falling just above his brow. Adeline reached up and tucked the curl back into place atop his head gently, not pausing to think about the intimacy of the act.

Roman stared down at her; they were only a breath apart now. He had not expected such a gentle touch from the princess who constantly approached him with her guard up. Adeline dropped her hand back to her side, returning his stare as heat crept into her cheeks. Before she could manage an apology or retort to mask the tension in the air between them, Roman spoke up.

"Careful, Princess, wouldn't want me thinking you actually have a heart somewhere in there," he said, smirking down at her as he pressed a finger gently into her chest.

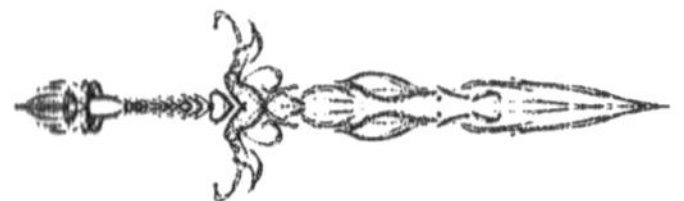

Knowing that she was overwhelmed with the unraveling of history as she had known it, Roman did not let himself give in to the desire to lean down and kiss her soft, pink lips, even though the idea was all consuming. When he was near her, he felt as though a flame ignited in his belly, and touching her, being close to her, was the only way to satiate it. He had to remind himself several times already that they had only just met, though he felt as if he'd loved her all his life with the way she enamoured him so entirely. Instead, he brought a large, calloused hand up to gently tuck a chocolate curl behind her ear. Just as she had done to him, stopping only for a moment to memorize the way her skin felt under his touch, the way she smelled, lavender and jasmine hanging in the air around them. He knew that these little moments were all he would ever get of her, all he could ever allow himself to have of her. Maybe she was meant to be his undoing, but he refused to be hers.

Finally shaking himself from the haze, he dropped his hand and began leading her up the staircase to the second level of the cabin. He watched her steps carefully, making sure that if she so much as faltered in her step he could catch her. Roman did not allow himself to touch her as he led the way toward the library. Large, arched double doors stood at the entrance to the grand room, ornate details carved into the oak. He wrapped his hands around the cool black metal handles of the doors and threw them open. It was impossible to bite back his smile at Adeline's sharp intake of breath.

The double doors gave way to an impossibly large room with high ceilings clad with wood beams. Each wall was lined with oak shelves holding hundreds of cloth and leather bound books. It was a miracle that the shelves were not audibly groaning under such weight. Adeline took a deep breath, seeming to try to absorb the scent of old paper and pine from the air. Roman noticed that as soon as they'd stepped into the library, she lightened, as if a weight had been lifted from her shoulders in the presence of the books.

Tucked into the center of the back wall was a beautiful fireplace, warmth radiating off of the crackling flames within and casting the room in a gentle aura. Just in front of the stone hearth lay a large plush rug and Adeline seemed to be hesitating just in front of it.

"What're you doing, Addie?" Roman spoke in a hushed tone so as not to startle her from her daze.

"Currently? I am resisting the urge to kick these damned heels off and bury my toes in the fibers of this rug." Her response was nearly a whisper, as if she could barely force the words out while she continued to take in the room around her.

On either side of the fireplace sat two overstuffed, forest-green armchairs that looked suspiciously similar to the one Roman had been sitting in when Adeline had awoken in his room earlier. Between the two chairs sat a circular table of the same oak as the shelves. Its surface was graced by a single open book, the pages of which turned themselves softly, seemingly enchanted by magic.

Not caring that Roman stood behind her in the doorway, Adeline made her way to the table, unable to tear her attention away from the book that sat atop it. She perched on her knees before the low surface, bringing her hands up to hold the book open on either side. The worn yellow paper was faded and tattered from age and as she looked down at the open pages before her, she stifled a gasp.

Startled, Roman looked to the book in her hands and had to withhold a gasp of his own. Right there, on the worn pages of a book open upon the table, as if in hopes it would be her who found it, was a delicately drawn dragon tucked neatly around text outlining the history of Drakmoor.

"Th—these dragons. They look nearly identical to the ones drawn in the storybooks I was told as a child," she said, the realization seeming to leave her breathless.

CHAPTER THIRTEEN

"**P**RINCESS...PRINCESS." A ROUGH HAND grasped her shoulder, shaking her awake. Adeline cracked open her eyes, wincing as light flooded her vision. It took several moments for her to gather her consciousness and take note of her surroundings.

She was curled up on the plush gray rug in front of the crackling fireplace in the library, a pile of books laid out in front of her and a thick blanket draped over her that looked suspiciously similar to the comforter that had been on Roman's bed. He had left her in the library last night without a word, understanding her need to absolve herself in the knowledge and stories that made up this room without her even having to speak a word. It was not lost on her how strangely well Roman seemed to know her already.

Adeline sat up, reaching her arms over her head in a stretch, before finally looking up at the person who had awoken her from her slumber. The man standing over her was quite tall, only an inch or two shorter than Roman if she had to guess. He had dirty blond hair cropped close to his head on the top, and shaven down even further on the sides. His eyes were a shocking gray color and he had a hint of mustache and beard, both of which were neatly trimmed close to the skin, making them appear as just barely more than a five o' clock shadow. He had a muscular build and was clad in the now familiar black leathers that she had been seeing all over since arriving in Drakmoor.

"Good morning sleepy—"

"Who the hell are you?" Adeline cut him off, her hand sneakily reaching toward her right thigh, for her dagger. She let out a frustrated huff when her hand met nothing but bare skin instead of cool steel, remembering that Roman had so kindly disarmed her upon her arrival.

"Disappointed at the loss of your weapons, are ya?" the man teased with a soft chuckle as he reached out a hand between them, a peace offering.

Adeline begrudgingly took his hand, letting him help her to her feet.

"Falrin," he said, now shaking the hand he'd used to pull her up from the ground.

"Sorry?" Adeline replied, her brows knitting together in confusion.

"Falrin. My name is Falrin, Princess." He chuckled again, flashing his white teeth in a cheeky smile.

"Uh, right. Falrin. Why the hell did you wake me up with the sun?" she stared out the windows on either side of the hearth, softening as she took in the familiar pinks and oranges that painted the horizon at the peak of sunrise.

At least the sunrise still feels like home.

"Roman said you could be a bit prickly, but I didn't think it would be *this* bad." Falrin sighed. "I'm here to take you to training. Did Roman not inform you that I would be assisting in your training while you're here?"

Training? He thinks I need training???

Adeline let out a laugh.

"I can assure you that I do not need any *training*. Regardless of what Roman may think, I am perfectly capable of handling myself."

Falrin only sighed in response before grabbing her arm and dragging her out of the library and down the hall. He pulled her to a stop in front of one of the closed doors.

"You have five minutes. There is fighting gear laid out for you. Get dressed or I will dress you myself and drag your ass down to the training gym," Falrin said, punctuating his statement with a saccharine sweet smile.

The only reply he got was Adeline letting out a loud groan before ripping open the door to what was apparently her new room, and slamming it in his face. He couldn't help but chuckle at the strange girl. *Prickly* was certainly an understatement.

It was only a few minutes before the heavy wood door flew open again and Adeline stalked out dressed in the black sleeveless fighting leathers, her long brown waves braided neatly down her back. She did not speak to Falrin as he led her down the stairs and into the dining room. Instead, she simply sat in the same chair she had occupied the night before and glared down into her bowl of porridge.

"Who am I? I am *so* glad you asked, Princess! Well, let's see here. I'm Roman's best friend. We have known each other since we were babies, practically grew up as brothers. And now, I fight as his second hand. Pretty cool, I know," Falrin broke the silence, winking at her.

"If you know him so well, then perhaps you can tell me why the hell he brought me here," Adeline bit back.

"No can do, Princess. Sharing secrets with the enemy is a war crime and all," he laughed.

Adeline let out another groan. *This man might be more of a sarcastic pain in my ass than Roman, and I didn't think that was possible.*

Deciding she was quite done with his sarcasm, Adeline chose to continue on eating in silence while Falrin busied himself chattering away with the cooks.

The training gym was nothing like Adeline had expected it to be. Falrin led her out of the house and down a path to another large wooden building a few hundred yards away. They entered through a small door, tucked away on the side of the facility. Adeline assumed that the structure would pale in comparison to the training gym she was used to at the palace, but her eyes lit with delight when she realized how wrong she had been.

The entire building was actually only one room, padded walls and floors cushioning the entire space. The ceilings were impossibly high, with a skylight directly in the center that allowed most of the light in the room to be natural. It was almost eerie how similar the structure was to the gym she had trained in at the castle. The back wall was lined with weapons: maces, swords, daggers, throwing stars, spears, all glinting in the rays of the early morning sun.

As she caught sight of the array of weaponry splayed out in front of her, Adeline had not hesitated before breaking into a sprint. This was her chance for escape. Her fingers itched with the need to feel the familiar curve of a dagger in her hands again. Her boots connected with the padded floors as she pushed through the balls of her feet, propelling herself forward. Faster, she had to move faster.

Her heart roared to life in her chest, her pulse hammering as she came within a few feet of the wall, she was so close. She reached out a hand, fingers brushing the hilt of a dagger and practically cried with delight as she closed in, stretching further until suddenly her fingers were no longer making contact with the hilt of the dagger. Instead, she found her feet leaving the ground as she was lifted up and away from the wall, a chilling breeze tickling her neck as her hair whipped around her, caught in a windstorm. *What the hell.*

Adeline did not have time to wrap her mind around what was happening before she was propelled to the left, her body colliding with the wall with a heavy thud. She fell to the ground with a groan and pain exploded in her lungs as the wind was knocked out of her. She tried helplessly for several minutes to draw in a breath, gasping hungrily when she finally felt her lungs expand. Several moments passed while she lay there in a heap on the ground waiting for the pain to leave her body.

An outstretched hand came into view above her, reaching down to help her up. The hand, unfortunately, was attached to Falrin, whom she had forgotten was there. Judging by the smug look painting his features, he had been responsible for throwing her against the wall, though how he did so, she was not sure.

Of course, she was familiar with the power one inherited from slaying dragons, as she herself had felt that power seep into her body time and time again. *But if Falrin is slaying dragons, then why the hell was he living with dragon riders?* Her mind wandered to Roman and his ability to harness shadows, *And what of Roman? How can he call upon the shadows?*

She couldn't, she realized, recall a single historical report of dragons slain by anyone in Drakmoor from her reading the night before.

She swatted his hand away, refusing to accept his help after he had thrown her into the wall with a gust of wind and kept her from the weapons that were necessary for her escape.

In the split second that she had felt her fingers brush the hilt of the dagger, she had no longer felt powerless. No longer did she feel that empty gnawing feeling in the pit of her stomach that she associated with the need to spill dragon blood. When her hand had made contact with the weapon on the wall, something in her had ignited to life, the flame quickly suffocated by her body slamming into the cold wall. Without weapons or the power she craved from killing dragons, she truly was *powerless,* a harsh reality for her to face.

Adeline stood in front of Falrin with her hands on her hips, staring at him with loathing. "Does Roman know that you have been slaying dragons, *sidekick?*" Adeline spat at him.

Falrin doubled over in a fit of laughter and Adeline decided that she was quite sick of being laughed at, so she took the opportunity to swing her leg out and kick his feet from underneath him. As his back made contact with the floor she pressed her left boot into his chest, pinning him to the mat beneath him. His laughter quieted at that, amusement playing in his eyes.

"I asked you a question," she growled.

"Damn, you're a feisty one. I like you." Falrin chuckled again before replying, "No, Princess. Roman does not know I have been slaying dragons because I have *not* been slaying dragons. Clearly you have some studying to do on how dragon riders tap into our power."

He wrapped his fingers around Adeline's ankle as he spoke, moving slowly and quietly. Once he had a good hold, he yanked her leg out from under her, sending her sprawling out on the floor right next to him in a flurry of tangled limbs.

"Oh, and call me *sidekick* again, *Princess,* and I will skin you alive and feed you to my dragon for breakfast."

His dragon? He's a rider?

He rose to his feet and reached down to grab hold of Adeline's arm, yanking her up without giving her any choice in accepting his help. She let out a defeated sigh before saying, "Addie. You can call me Addie."

She wasn't sure why, but something about their interactions had made Adeline feel as though she was safe with Falrin, like they could maybe be friends eventually. Maybe that is why she told him to call her Addie, a nickname that used to be reserved only for Greta.

"Alright, Addie. Now that we got that out of the way, today we are training in hand to hand combat. It is clear through the little tussle we just had that you are severely lacking in that area."

As Falrin spoke, a gentle wind blew through Adeline's hair, tidying the braid that it had previously tousled, and she fought back a smile knowing that the warrior had commanded the wind to right his wrong. *So he does harness the power of the wind,* she smiled to herself.

"Lacking? Oh I'll show you who is lacking, asshole, " she threw back at him with a full blown grin.

It turned out Falrin was right about her lacking in hand to hand combat. They had been exchanging blows for several hours. The afternoon sun now beamed down on them through the skylight, and she had yet to best him a single time. He, however, had sent her tumbling to the ground several times now, each one making her grow more and more frustrated at her lack of strength against him. Falrin was kind enough not to use his wind against her anymore, which she was grateful for. Her muscles were already aching from the previous impact of the wall but after hours of training they were now burning in protest.

Her back made contact with the floor once again and she groaned in frustration, raking her hands over her face to wipe away the sweat that beaded against her skin. Falrin reached out a hand, helping her to her feet just as he had every other time he took her down. She had to give him that, even through his gruff, sarcastic exterior his kind heart shone through.

"Alright, we're gonna call that a wrap for the day. I want you to work on building up your strength. That means eating more at meal times and doing some strength training on your own. For now, head back to your room and wash up. You are to meet Roman in the library in thirty minutes," Falrin wiggled his eyebrows at her suggestively.

Oh great. People are already getting ideas in their heads about Roman and I, she thought to herself as she made her way back to her room, refusing to acknowledge that she had her own ideas about what was going on between them.

CHAPTER FOURTEEN

H OT WATER LICKED HER collarbones as Adeline sunk deeper into the impossibly large claw foot tub. Tendrils of steam danced together, rising off the water into the cool air of the washroom. She had been surprised to learn she was being trusted with her own room, and was even more shocked at the luxury of an ensuite bathroom. It was almost identical to the one in Roman's bedroom, except there were pink accents throughout—as if the room had been personally designed for her specifically.

Her body was sore and tired after the long morning spent training with Falrin. A few bruises were scattered across her legs but she was unsure if they came from sparring with Falrin or the flight she had taken into the wall, though she supposed it didn't quite matter now.

Her brown waves were piled in a messy bun atop her head, out of the way of the water. Adeline knew herself well enough to know that she would be soaking in this tub again later tonight and that she would rather wash her hair then.

If she had to guess, it had been about twenty minutes since she'd gotten into the bath. With that realization, Adeline let out a deep sigh, *I guess that means I had better get out and get ready to meet Roman.* Her pulse quickened at the thought but she did her best to ignore it, refusing to admit that he had any sort of effect on her at all. *He took me as a hostage,* she reminded herself once more, though at this point she knew it was useless.

Wrapping herself in the plush white towel she had laid out before her bath, she stepped back into the bedroom. She knew the cabin well enough by now to realize that the room she was given was directly next to Roman's. She even knew it well enough to know that their beds faced each other, separated by one thin wall. The furniture in her room was similar to that in Roman's, with a wardrobe and bed frame crafted of light colored wood. She, too, had a large floor to ceiling window that overlooked the town below and she once again stared, yearning, down into the lives of the people bustling around.

Nothing else about her room seemed that similar to his. Actually, everything else in the room seemed as though it had been curated specifically for *her.* Adeline did not let herself think too long about who may have been responsible for that.

The bed was already made up with a plush comforter and throw pillows, all in a beautiful shade of light pink with matching shades curtaining the window. Aside from the walls themselves being a cool blue, the entire space was decorated in the familiar shades of her favorite color.

The vanity in the corner of the room held a vase full of delicate baby pink roses. There was no note with them, but she knew exactly who they had come from, the thoughtful gesture making her heart skitter in her chest. Adeline had never liked roses. With the last name Ambrose, the castle had seemed to be suffocatingly full of roses at any given time, even in the gardens she so loved. In some weird way, they felt like a constant reminder of the name she was meant to live up to. She couldn't help but soften as she admired the roses in the white ceramic vase atop the vanity; they were quite beautiful.

She had once again gotten so lost in her thoughts that if she didn't hurry she'd be late. She stood, pulling a white cotton dress and a pink corset embroidered with florals from the wardrobe. She couldn't help but smile as she got dressed, sliding her hands down the soft cotton and tracing the flowers of her corset. Adeline was not a woman who shied away from wearing a tunic and pants, but she *loved* dresses. Maybe it was the princess in her, but she quite preferred the femininity—it made her feel beautiful.

Pulling her hair into a loose four-strand braid, she let a few waves fall free to frame her face like Greta would have. She spared only a moment for the pang in her chest before she tied the ends of her hair and padded toward the library.

Once she threw open the doors to the library, Adeline did not bother to look for Roman, instead practically running to the plush rug in front of the fireplace. She had foregone shoes for this specific reason. As she stepped onto the carpet, she felt the fibers envelop her feet and had to stop herself from letting a moan slip past her lips. It felt heavenly. Her toes curled into the shag of the rug and she let out a satisfied sigh; this was even better than she remembered.

"Enjoying yourself, Your Highness?" Roman's voice cut through the silence with a chuckle.

Adeline let herself giggle in response, "Oh, I am *very* much enjoying myself, Ro." She continued wiggling her feet around, soaking in the sensation of the plush wool against her bare feet. She never would have been allowed to do something like this in the castle; it was too unladylike.

She watched him stare at her, noting his soft smile and how he seemingly couldn't tear his eyes from her. Adeline had felt confident when she'd donned the corset earlier, but seeing Roman notice how it hugged her in all the right places had a blush rising to her cheeks. She knew she was pretty, but he made her feel truly ineffable as he watched her giggle and dig her feet in the rug like a child. In the short time they had known each other, Adeline had never let herself be so *carefree* with someone. It didn't go unnoticed, the fact that each time she let herself go he was there. He kept his eyes on her, like he always did, and she eyed him curiously—trying to parse where his mind had gone.

"So, what are we doing in the library?" Adeline finally questioned.

"You are going to learn about where we derive our power from here in Drakmoor." He smirked at her.

"Ah, so you *did* hear about what happened with Falrin?"

"You mean how you face planted into a wall and then accused him of killing dragons? Yeah I heard *all* about that, Princess." His eyes met hers.

She wasn't sure why, but hearing him call her princess never quite angered her the way hearing others use the name had. Coming from Roman's lips, it felt almost sacred. She couldn't live with the idea of never hearing that word roll off his tongue again, so she didn't bother correcting him.

Adeline let out a dramatic sigh before plopping into the deep emerald armchair across from his. She draped her legs over one of the arms, crossing them at the ankles and causing her dress to slide up her legs, exposing the skin of her calves which Roman noticed were covered in bruises. Anger flared red-hot on his face.

He stood from his chair, stalking over to hers and grabbing her legs in his rough hands. Roman met her eyes. "Who the fuck did this to you?"

"Feeling protective, are we?" Adeline teased, not wanting him to stop touching her.

"Who the *fuck* did this to you?" He seemed to cut himself off at the end of the question, as if he had more to say still trapped behind his lips.

"They're just bruises from training with Falrin. Relax, Shadow."

He visibly relaxed at that, though his frustrated expression told her that he was likely going to have a talk with Falrin about going easier on her.

Roman knew that the training was necessary to keep Adeline safe, he couldn't be with her all the time, but that did not stop the rage that flared to life in his chest when he caught sight of the bruises dotting her legs. He'd be damned if *anyone*, even Falrin, laid a hand on his girl.

Did I just think of her as my girl? I am so fucked.

Roman raked his hands over his face, clearing his head. He needed a distraction and he needed one quickly. It took all of his self control to sit back down in the chair opposite Adeline and look over at her. She was staring at him with desire in her eyes. No, it couldn't be desire, she would never want him the way he yearned for her.

Several beats passed, the tension between them so thick it could be cut with a knife. It hung in the air and left them both feeling momentarily debilitated. Roman was the first to break the silence.

He cleared his throat. "Okay, so you are clearly unaware that you can wield power without spilling dragon blood. It is obvious you've experienced the power transfer that comes with slaying a dragon, and I am sure you also are aware that power is temporary. Typically, one can only wield the power of a fallen dragon for a few weeks before they must slay another, right?"

Adeline sat up, giving him her full attention now. "Correct."

"Well, as dragon riders, before we can actually ride or train with our dragons we must first establish a bond. That bond is best described as a mutual trust in one another. Ideally, we bond with dragons when they are still young and build that trust with them as they grow. That is what gives us our power without having to kill the dragons. However, due to the declining dragon population, our clan has been bonding with adult dragons for several years now." Roman looked up at her to ensure she was still paying attention.

Adeline seemed to shrink in on herself with his every word. Roman did not blame her for the decreasing population, or even to fault her for her actions in slaying the dragons, he just couldn't find the words to tell her that. Instead, he looked at her with gentle eyes that seemed to say *it's not your fault*. That did not stop the self loathing that painted itself across her face. Judging by her reaction, she had likely never felt guilt for killing the creatures before, it is just what they did in Scalebreak. Perhaps it was Roman's obvious adoration of the gentle beasts in the way he spoke that had filled her with guilt now. Though it pained him to see her so visibly upset, he continued on; she needed to know the truth of Drakmoor.

"When your dragon begins to trust you, they provide you with pieces of themselves. Once you are fully bonded to a dragon and they have the utmost trust in you, they will slowly begin to share their power with you. With that comes an extended life span, which explains how my mother has been matron of Drakmoor for a hundred and fifty years, yet doesn't look a day over fifty. Some riders live as long as three hundred years right alongside their dragons, however, most of us have died much more prematurely in an attempt to fight to save the dragons—but don't worry, Princess, I'm not a day over nineteen," he finished with a wink.

The words hung between them, and Roman watched as Adeline's somber expression turned angry, but he was not yet sure if her ire was directed at herself, her kingdom, or the other dragon slayers. It was unlikely she'd ever stopped to consider the gravity of her actions before, believing them to be normal and necessary. She was fed so many lies, raised in a place where killing dragons was a coveted skill. Anger bubbled within him at the thought.

"I pulled out a couple of books that go more into detail on the subject. In Drakmoor, we study magic and bonding with dragons as part of our schooling from childhood." Roman gestured to the pile of books he'd placed on the table. "It's not too late for you to learn."
Adeline looked at him, a silent thank you passing between them.

"I'll leave you to it then," He rose to his feet, seeming to hesitate.

"Can...can you stay?" Adeline asked, looking up at him with hopeful eyes. His heart roared to life as he took a seat once again.

"Just in case I have questions, or...something," Adeline mumbled.

The two of them sat together in the library in comfortable silence for several hours while they read. Adeline poured over the texts Roman provided, stopping to ask questions every so often. He leaned back in the chair, legs draped over the armrest as he read something titled *Embers of the Wild Heart,* which Adeline suspected was a romance novel, though she did not dare ask.

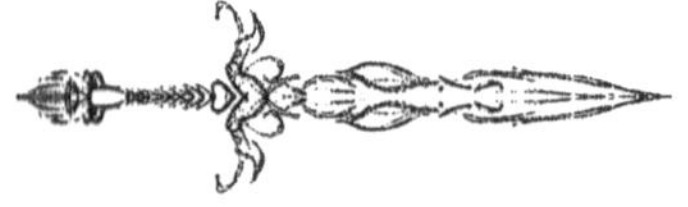

She wasn't sure if it was the comfort of the books and their endless knowledge surrounding her or Roman's presence in the room, but it was not lost on Adeline that she had never felt more at home than here in these stolen moments surrounded by tattered pages.

"Hey, Roman?" Adeline mumbled, breaking the silence.

His eyes found hers over the book he held in his hands, brows furrowed in question.

She took a deep breath, readying herself for the conversation she was about to open up. "You said you brought me here as a message to my father that Drakmoor knows what he is doing...what exactly has he been doing?"

"You don't know?" Roman's eyes filled with an apology as the realization struck him. "Oh, Princess. It's been a long day and you have enough to process already—"

"I want to know. Please, Roman," she begged.

"I'm sorry, Addie. I promise I will tell you, but not today. Give yourself time to absorb everything you've already learned first."

She knew she should have been frustrated at his lack of answers, yet relief flooded her body at his refusal—she wasn't sure she would ever be ready to hear the whole truth.

CHAPTER FIFTEEN

Adeline had awoken before sunrise the next day, unable to sleep with all the questions running through her head. A familiar empty feeling crept back up into her chest, her body itching for the euphoric release of power. She wanted to kill, needed to feel the power surging through her again, but those thoughts now came with twice as many feelings of guilt. How could she bring down a dragon with the knowledge she had gained?

Making her way to the large window, she found herself staring down at the village longingly. The sun was rising over the peaks of the surrounding mountains, and the first glimpses of daylight were kissing the center of town, slowly creeping outward. The sky was dusted with hues of pink and orange, making the normally stark white clouds appear in glowing pastels instead.

As she watched the sun rise and the colors change, movement among the clouds caught her attention. *Was that? No, it can't be.* She squinted her eyes, trying to get a better look, and let out a gasp. A black dragon zipped through the pastel morning sky. Even from a distance, Adeline could tell the creature was massive, its wingspan stretching an impressive distance as it coasted against the morning breeze. It was a breathtaking sight, the onyx scales reflecting the warm hues of the sunrise as the dragon cut through the clouds.

The dragon's obsidian silhouette was a stark contrast to the gentle colors lighting the horizon, and Adeline watched in awe as the dragon and its rider expertly dove and spun. She couldn't stifle her sense of wonder as she stood at the window watching in astonishment at the two creatures, so different in size and strength, moved as one. Adeline didn't dare move until they both landed, disappearing beyond her view, leaving her enamoured.

Unsure how much time she had lost to that moment, Adeline tried to quiet the excitement and adoration that had bubbled to life in her chest. Her heart squeezed, and it felt as if everything she knew herself to be was collapsing; she felt lost. She was supposed to be Princess Adeline Ambrose of Scalebreak, slaying dragons in secret to protect her kingdom and her people, but that could not have felt further from the girl in the window. No, that girl's heart was practically bursting with the need to feel a connection like the bond Roman had described to her yesterday. The girl in the window wanted to *ride* dragons, not slay them.

Adeline wiped at a silent tear, interrupting its path down her cheek. She felt so unsure of who she was supposed to be, who she wanted to be, who everyone else wanted her to be. No decision felt like the *right* decision, and the turmoil of trying to sort through them was plaguing her. The more she sat with it the sharper the tears gathering behind her eyes burned. She gathered herself, needing to stop the flood. Wiping her watery blue eyes, she made her way to the wardrobe on the other side of her room.

She rifled around the closet for a few moments, taking note of the fact that its contents seemed to inexplicably multiply, new dresses and corsets appearing every day. The familiar off-the-shoulder dresses of soft, white cotton greeted her among a sea of intricate gowns, and a small smile spread across her lips as she pulled one out of the wardrobe and over her head. Something about the loose cotton pooling around her legs made her feel free, her movements fluid and unrestricted.

Satisfied with the dress that now hugged her body, she went back to rifling through the wardrobe. It was several minutes of digging through the array of gowns and fighting leathers before she began to grow frustrated at the lack of casual wear. Just as she was about to step away and accept that the white dress was the only garment she would be wearing that day, her fingers came to a stop on a crimson corset near the back of the wardrobe.

The deep red cotton was soft to the touch, accented along the edges and the boning with thread of a dark pink. As Adeline's eyes fell on the side panels of the corset, she felt her breath hitch in her throat. Delicately embroidered into the side panels in the same thick pink thread were roses with vines of forest green, branching out from beneath them and swirling in every direction. She had detested the hints of roses that seemed to grace her entire wardrobe at the castle, a constant reminder to others that she was an Ambrose, but as she stared down at the intricate flowers that lay across the side panels of the corset in her hands, she felt a sense of comfort—of home.

Adeline stood there for several moments admiring the handiwork of the garment before she finally pulled on the corset and drew the red laces in the front together to cinch her waist. She noted how much more comfortable they were than anything she'd had back home as her fingers made quick work of tying the laces into a bow at her back. She smiled to herself as she smoothed down the fabric, the memory of a familiar voice in her mind grumbling, *"Who the hell slays a dragon in a corset?"*

She spent a few moments tying her hair in a single bubble braid down her back, the brown strands curling up at the ends. Today, she had decided she was going to ask Roman to take her down to the village. She steeled herself, preparing not to take no for an answer. She was growing antsy, yearning to be with the people she so often observed from her window.

The kitchen was small, cozy in a way that felt homey, not cramped. Although it was much smaller than Adeline was used to, it still felt open and airy thanks to the high ceilings and the comfortable heat that radiated from the stone hearth tucked into one of the walls. Wood crackled in the fire within, adding to the soundtrack of the early morning. Cooks were bustling throughout the kitchen preparing breakfast, cookware clinking together between the shuffling of feet across the floor. Unlike the castle that had more cooks than one could count, the cabin only had three cooks whom Adeline had quickly come to know as Milo, Thistle, and Seraphina: an unlikely bunch to say the least.

Thistle was an old man who walked with a slight hunch in his spine and had sprinkles of salt and pepper throughout his graying hair. Adeline instantly recognized him as the cook who had served their dinner the night before. He had warm eyes, weathered with age but shining with a timeless sort of joy. He wore a content smile on his face as he prepared breakfast, as if there was nowhere else he would rather be than in the kitchens. He had calloused hands that told stories of years upon years of slaving over stoves. A soft tune filled the kitchen as he hummed while he worked. It did not take much observation to know that he had spent his life in the kitchen and that he took great pride in his work. Everything about the man was inviting and comforting.

He made his way straight to Adeline as she entered the kitchen, pausing his prep work to introduce himself.

"Good morning! My name is Thistle, and you are?" Thistle held out his calloused hand in invitation.

"Good morning, Thistle. I'm Adeline. I'm so sorry to interrupt! I'll get out of your way."

"Oh, nonsense! You are welcome in these kitchens any time you please. Whatever it is that drew you here must've known we could use an extra set of hands," he exclaimed.

"The smell of fresh bread," Adeline's cheeks colored with the admission.

Thistle's only response was a soft smile before he began escorting her through the kitchen, making introductions.

Milo looked to be around fourteen years old, all awkward, lanky limbs. He had a head of thick, untamed auburn curls that fell into his eyes more often than not. His bright green eyes had a sparkle of youth, the promise of a life not yet touched by hurt. Freckles dotted his face and cheeks below a pair of round silver-rimmed glasses that he had to constantly push up the bridge of his nose. When Adeline had entered the kitchens, he had paid her no mind, not even looking up from the peppers that he was chopping with expert precision, only coming to introduce himself when Thistle had chastised him for ignoring their guest. Upon coming to greet her he had pulled her wordlessly into a hug, more an awkward tangle of limbs than anything, before going back to his cutting with laser focus.

Seraphina had been the most peculiar towards Adeline. She was short, but they appeared to be about the same age. She had her jet-black hair pulled back into a neat braid behind her, keeping it out of the way of her work. Her eyes were such a bright blue it was almost jarring, how intense her stare could be. Seraphina had been kneading dough when Thistle was making introductions, and had not even bothered to utter a hello. Instead, she simply nodded her head in acknowledgement to Adeline. Though most people would have likely found the gesture to be cold, Adeline saw much of herself in the girl standing there. There was something broken hiding behind her distant gaze, something that called to the broken parts within Adeline. So rather than be offended, she had offered the girl a soft smile and continued through the kitchen with Thistle.

The cabin hummed to life with the sounds of everyone waking up and preparing for their work days, Adeline found herself offering to help. Before she could register the words she had spoken—or remember that she'd never worked a day in her life—an apron was tied around her waist and she was ushered to a station. Thistle's smile was wide as he led her to an empty counter space where he laid out several balls of dough. He spent several minutes explaining how to roll it out in an even rectangle and to brush the butter on before sprinkling a sugary cinnamon mixture across the top. Thistle was patient as he demonstrated how to roll the pastry into a neat tube, silently showing Adeline how to properly wield the pastry cutter to produce perfect little coils of dough.

After walking her through the process, he left her to her own devices to transform the remaining balls of dough into rolls. She took her time neatly rolling out the dough just as she had been shown. Almost expertly, as if she had been doing this her entire life, she brushed the melted butter over the dough and sprinkled the cinnamon mixture over top. The dough was perfectly proofed and easy to work with, almost eager to cooperate as she rolled it in on itself, as if it had a mind of its own. She lost herself in the comfort of the movements and the satisfaction of the work, and it wasn't long before she too was humming through her task, a soft smile plastered across her lips. Adeline followed Thistle's direction and placed the finished cinnamon rolls into the oven before making her way back to her workspace. He had set out a recipe for frosting on the stone countertop, as well as all the ingredients she would need, and she was determined to figure it out on her own.

Surprisingly, she did not have difficulty following the handwritten recipe card, and once she finished the concoction, she sneaked a taste. She was instantly bathed in delight as the sweetness coated her tongue. A sense of pride bloomed in her chest as she savored the smooth frosting, the warm aroma of the cinnamon rolls curling into her nostrils.

An overwhelming sense of peace overcame her as she looked around the kitchens and took it all in, the laughter, the humming, the heavenly scents. All of it enveloped her like a warm hug from the cabin itself, and for the first time, Adeline felt the homeliness that she often had yearned for within the cold walls of the castle.

After a few minutes, the now finished rolls were ready to be dressed with the icing. Clutching the bowl of delicious cream cheese frosting in one hand and a spoon in the other, she delicately dripped white peaks onto each pastry. She lost herself in the movements, feeling more than content to stay in the comfort of the kitchens forever.

Her thoughts were interrupted by a deep voice.

"And here I was thinking that you were incapable of smiling, Princess," Roman teased, sticking his finger into the bowl of frosting before sucking gently on the tip.

He moaned in delight as the sweet taste met his tongue.

"Holy shit, Addie. This is amazing."

"Tsk. Tsk. Paws off, Ro. You can wait until they are done like everyone else," Adeline swatted his hand away.

"Well, even if it pains me to say it, we are going to need to take the rolls to go."

"Wha—" Adeline was interrupted by Falrin, who had materialized out of thin air behind her, dipping his finger into the bowl in her arms just as Roman had.

"You heard the man. We have places to b—*oh my Gods this is so GOOD!*" Falrin interrupted himself, reaching back into the bowl for another taste.

She swatted him away. "Where are we going?" She cocked an eyebrow at the two standing in front of her, both of them smirking like mad-men.

"We are going down to the village. It's time you saw Drakmoor." Roman grinned at her.

CHAPTER SIXTEEN

A DELINE HADN'T PUT MUCH thought into how they would get all the way down to the village, but on the back of a dragon had definitely *not* been something she considered. When the three of them had walked out of the cabin they were met by two dragons, one with scales of a familiar gold and the other a deep forest green. Her heart leapt into her throat.

They aren't seriously considering having me ride on these beasts, are they?

Upon catching sight of the creatures towering high over her head, her feet had promptly planted themselves in place—not allowing her to move from where she stood, gawking. Her pulse quickened beneath her skin, her heart skittering with excitement and fear. Instinctively, her hand reached down to her thigh where she always kept a dagger sheathed.

The old Adeline would've considered this a situation that called for its use, but her breath caught when her fingers once again brushed against bare skin. She had forgotten that she was no longer allowed to be armed outside of the training gym, a silent reminder of the lack of trust between her and Roman.

The moment it took her to realize she was unarmed was enough to give her pause, and looking up at the creatures, her body hummed to life—itching for the kill, yet her mind felt conflicted as she took them in. They were breathtaking, the midmorning sun glinting off of their scales made them appear almost iridescent, and it made her heart swell with something that felt like pride. There was an unfamiliar part of her that now protested against the urge to kill, but the feeling dissipated quickly when she realized that the dragons were staring back at her with contempt. She watched as they sized her up, as if they knew she was a threat, as if they knew their loved ones had fallen at her hand.

Fear took hold of her. *Surely these dragons are going to kill me for what I have done.*

A large hand tugged her forward, breaking the trance that she had been stuck in. Citrus and jasmine flooded her senses as she was crushed against a broad chest, and she did not need to look up to know that it was Roman she was now pressed against. Roman reached up, calluses brushing against the soft skin of her face as he gripped her chin and tilted her face until their eyes met. He did not drop his hand when her eyes finally met his, seeming to savor every second of his skin on hers. A breath passed between them, and Roman seemed lost in thought as he stared into her eyes.

"Ground rules first, Princess. The first one is the most important: You *will not* try to kill my dragon again. It was hard enough to convince Aurelius to even allow you to ride with me down to the village after your last attempt on his life, and you will not help your case with any more feeble attacks."

Adeline cast her eyes down, embarrassed to learn that the golden dragon who had bested her in the forest the night of the ball had been Roman's. Of course it had.

"Eyes on me, Addie," he tugged her chin gently, "we all have a past, you don't need to hide from me."

All she could manage was a gentle nod of her head.

"Good girl."

The nickname made her knees wobble.

"Rule number two: keep your seat." Roman paused for a long moment, his brow furrowing in thought. "Well, I guess those are the only two rules I've got. Fal, you got anything?" He threw a glance over his shoulder to where Falrin stood leaning against one of the large stocky legs of the emerald green dragon.

"You could always ride with me, Princess. Raegorath and I don't have any rules," he said with a wink, sending a warm gust of wind in Adeline's direction in invitation.

"No. She will ride with me. End of story." Roman said through gritted teeth.

"What's wrong, boss? Jealous?" Falrin quipped.

That remark, coupled with the deep sigh that came from Roman in response, earned a giggle from Adeline.

Roman dropped his hand from her face, and an all-too-familiar emptiness flooded her following their separation. He spun on his heel and stalked toward Aurelius.

"I guess that's my cue," Adeline muttered to herself as she followed hesitantly. She was not completely convinced that Aurelius had forgiven her for attempting to kill him only a few nights prior, and she didn't entirely blame him.

When they reached Aurelius' feet, Adeline felt her stomach growl in protest, or maybe it was hunger? Even though she had pleaded with Thistle to let her take some of the rolls to-go—Roman and Falrin making puppy-dog eyes behind her the entire time—he had refused. He did, however, promise to have some of her cinnamon rolls waiting in her room when they got back. That declaration had earned twin sighs from the men behind her, sending a smile tugging at the corners of Adeline's lips. It was nice to see someone else refuse to give the boys what they wanted.

However, as she now stood below Aurelius' massive body, all of the happiness she felt in the kitchen that morning was nowhere to be found. In fact, the feelings flooding her body could be better described as sheer terror.

"What's wrong, Princess? You scared?" Falrin chuckled as he took his seat in the worn leather saddle atop Raegorath. His taunt had shaken her from her fear, but she threw a glare in his direction anyway.

It seemed rather silly to her that she was so anxious at the thought of riding the very creatures she used to slay without flinching, but the scariest part was that she was about to put her own life in the hands a dragon she had tried to *kill*, and she wasn't yet convinced that he would not return the favor. The golden beast let out a huff, tendrils of smoke curling from his nostrils before dissipating into the air around them, and Adeline was sure by the timing of his display that he had to have been listening in on her thoughts.

Aurelius growled in annoyance and tilted his wing down until the gleaming scales kissed the grass. Roman reached for Adeline's hand and tugged her behind him as he climbed up the massive wing, making his way to the saddle secured atop the dragon's back. He stopped to usher Adeline in front of him, letting her take her seat just behind the pommel before taking his own behind her.

Strong arms corded with muscle wrapped around her waist, holding her in place on the saddle before Roman let out a long, low whistle. The dragons responded almost immediately to his call, beginning to beat their wings in preparation for launching them into the sky. Adeline looked down, locking her gaze on the white-knuckle grip she had on the pommel. Fingers squeezing even tighter, she startled when she felt the soft skin of lips brush against the outside of her ear. "Be afraid, but do it anyway, Addie," Roman whispered for her and her alone to hear.

That was the only warning she had before they were launching into the sky; her only sense of comfort was the cool feeling of Roman's shadows around her body. They pressed her firmly into the saddle beneath her, tying her and Roman together in thick black ribbons with the warmth of his body grounding her as they ascended into the waiting clouds.

Wind whipped around her as they made the journey up into the clouds, and Adeline felt as if it was cutting into her skin. Her face burned from the cold air and she gritted her teeth, trying to steel herself against the bite. Her stomach felt like it had taken up permanent residence in her throat and though she had not eaten anything for breakfast, she felt bile crawling its way up the back of her mouth. The scales beneath her bit into her thighs as she squeezed her legs around the beast, but she would *not* lose her seat. Hands aching from how tightly she held onto the leather pommel, she winced, but refused to loosen her grip even slightly.

All she could hear was her heart beating furiously in her ears. The wind pressed into her with so much pressure that she was sure she would be ripped from the saddle at any moment if it weren't for Roman's solid arms and cool shadows holding her in place.

Her body lurched as they suddenly leveled out. Roman's arms tightened against her in a reassuring squeeze. The hard part was over.

Now that they were soaring, the wind was no longer biting, but instead dancing through her hair and nipping gently at her cheeks.

Adeline looked down and felt her heart skip a beat. From this high up, the village and cabin seemed minuscule; she could no longer make out the people bustling around between buildings. It was captivating. Something about being among the clouds made everything else seem so insignificant. All that existed in that moment was her, and Roman's arms around her, and she felt more powerful than she ever had. She threw her arms out and let loose a shaky laugh as she let the beauty of her new favorite memory consume her, refusing to let her fear ruin the experience.

As if he had been waiting for the moment she felt comfortable, Aurelius tucked his massive wings into his body and started leaning to the side.

Oh Gods. Please no, Adeline thought to herself as she squeezed her eyes shut.

And suddenly they were spinning, a golden spiral streaking across the sky. Adeline and Roman were flipped upside down so many times she felt as though her head was going to burst from the pressure as she screamed. Roman had tightened his knees around her body and pulled her onto his lap where he held her securely, safely, his shadows still wrapped tightly around her.

With each twist and turn, Adeline's stomach lurched, and if she wasn't sick before, she was certain she would be after this. The world whirled around them in streaks of motion that blurred into one another until she could no longer discern the sky from the mountain below. The pressure of the wind felt like it was pressing into her from all sides, consuming her entirely and making her body feel as though it was moments from starting to break apart. She didn't know how many times she was flipped, only that she would pray fervently to whatever god would listen if she never had to experience that again. As Aurelius shot his wings back out at his sides and they leveled out once again, he let out a noise that sounded almost like—

"Is he *laughing* at me?!"

Roman let out a chuckle of his own. "Sure is. Seems Aurelius wasn't entirely over the assassination attempt, Princess."

She grumbled, huffing out a breath to blow a loose strand of her braid out of her face. Uncontrollable laughter rang out beside them.

"You should have seen your face! That was hilarious!!" Falrin was consumed by another fit of laughter, keeling over until his forehead pressed against Raegorath.

Maybe I should have ridden with Falrin after all.

Adeline tried to maintain the scowl on her face, but failed miserably watching the two massive warriors dissolve in a fit of childish giggles. There was no fighting the smile that crept across her lips as her heart swelled, getting swept up in their joy and laughter, even if it was at her own expense.

Falrin's smile was familiar and comforting, but Roman's was a rarity in and of itself. She would endure a thousand more rides on Aurelius if it meant getting to witness the way his face lit up when he laughed. It was intoxicating and all-consuming, almost enough to forget that she should not be feeling the way she did about the man pressed against her. Almost.

Due to the close proximity of the village, they were not airborne for long, Adeline did not know if she was sad or grateful for that fact, but the aching feeling that filled her as they made their way to the land below did not go unnoticed.

The rest of the flight had been relatively uneventful, and she was itching to get to the village, to experience the community of people she had spent days watching from the cabin above.

As sharp talons met the dirt and the dragons landed just outside the bustling village, Adeline forgot how to breathe entirely. The village had been gorgeous to gaze upon from above, but from within it was truly ineffable.

CHAPTER SEVENTEEN

T ucked into the folds of the snow-capped mountains, the
village of Drakmoor was nearly indiscernible from the base of the
peaks. Expertly built into the mountainous terrain were stone houses
with thatched roofs and chimneys exuding thick puffs of smoke into the
crisp mountain air. From here, Adeline could just barely make out the
vines of ivy that adorned so many of the houses and buildings throughout the village, claiming the brick homes. People bustled through cobblestone streets, and the soft murmur of a thousand conversations kissed
her ears. It was both elegant and cozy, nestled away from the rest of the
world like it belonged in a storybook.

Although she fought it, she could feel the smile proudly plastered to
her face as she watched. She had never been allowed to see any of the
villages in Scalebreak because it was *not the role of a princess,* as her

father had reminded her each time she begged. Something within her had always yearned for that experience, to build a connection to the town and speak with the villagers she was meant to one day govern. Adeline had spent years begging and pleading to be allowed to visit even just once, but after being denied over and over again she eventually gave up her pleading and took to daydreaming of what would never be. Maybe that was why her heart felt so complete as she admired the town just a few steps ahead of her, a promise of a dream finally coming to life.

Roman watched with wonder as Adeline took in the quaint mountain town before her, and he couldn't stop his heart from swelling at the way her expression took on a sense of awe as she looked out over the people and buildings. It was as if she had never seen anything so breathtaking. His heart beat against his chest as he realized that even this couldn't rival the way she looked at *him.* Not allowing himself to read into it, he shook the thought from his head and closed the distance between himself and Adeline. As he reached her, he did not speak out of fear of shattering her bubble of fascination. Instead, he let himself give in to the need for physical contact and wrapped her hand in his, their fingers intertwining wordlessly. His hand dwarfed hers and was rough and calloused where hers were soft and gentle, yet another silent reminder of how different they were. Adeline did not look up or utter a sound, but he knew the touch was a comfort when she gently squeezed his hand in thanks.

"Come on, Sunshine. Lets go mingle," Roman finally broke the silence as he began walking toward the bustling village, gently tugging Adeline behind him, leaving Aurelius and Raegorath on the mountainside. They would likely fly off to go hunt once Roman and Falrin left their line of sight.

"Gods, you two are *insufferable*!" Falrin chuckled as he walked in line with them.

Truthfully, Roman had forgotten Falrin was with them entirely and was not impressed with the interruption to what felt like an intimate moment between him and Addie. His frustration did not help the heat from rising to his cheeks.

"Awe, are you embar—" Falrin did not get the chance to finish his retort before Roman threw his shadows out on the ground in front of him, causing him to trip.

"Alright, alright, I get it! Watch out, Princess, he can get kinda broody sometimes," Falrin said with a wink.

Adeline bit back a laugh. Broody didn't even begin to describe Roman and his attitude. It was no secret that he could be gruff, but she had seemed to enjoy toying with that very same attitude more than once over the last few days.

As they made their way into the village over weathered cobblestone streets, Adeline quickly noticed how *friendly* everyone here was, and whispered her surprise to Roman. Every person they passed met her eyes with a smile lighting their own, and several made a point to greet Roman as well. He was the heir to all that these people loved, and rather than cower in fear from him, they were clapping him on the back, offering handshakes and hugs with bright smiles as if delighted by his presence.

Adeline watched as strangers embraced Roman with bright smiles, and it was a bit jarring to say the least. Back in Scalebreak, any subjects that came to the castle shrank away from King Thorian and Queen Eloise, cowering in fear of even Adeline and Briar. It was a feeling she had never been able to accept, one that made a part of her recoil in disgust at her title. Watching the villagers light up with excitement as they saw Roman made her heart both sink and skip a beat. Clearly, his attempts at being gruff on the exterior had been futile if even the people in this town welcomed him joyously. There was a good heart and pure intentions behind his shadows, and it made Adeline wonder who or what had hurt him so badly that he felt the need to shield the tender parts of himself behind darkness.

Falrin had branched off on his own to join a group of children who were kicking a ball around the town square ahead of them, but Adeline could still hear his whoops of laughter echoing through the air. It tugged on her heartstrings and made her start to imagine Roman and Falrin as boys, stirring up trouble throughout the village. She could see the pair of them tearing through the streets, bumping into vendors and snatching treats from their carts only to be met with soft laughter from the victims of their sticky fingers. The two of them had likely played the very game that Falrin was now playing with the children on these streets. Knowing how they tousled like brothers, she could only imagine the kind of havoc they caused as boys. Even just the thought sent her heart ablaze with both love and envy for the younger versions of the men she now knew, the versions of them she would never get to know.

A young girl with a long silver braid bouncing off her back stopped in front of Adeline, tearing her from her thoughts. She had the brightest blue eyes, and it was clear with the way they glimmered that they were untouched by harm, a detail Adeline was grateful for. People were *safe* here.

The girl wore a lilac cotton dress with a white, waist-length apron tied across the front, but the plainness of her clothing did not take away from her beauty. She looked up at Adeline with a smile that revealed the gaps of her missing baby teeth and held out a pretty pink lily in offering. Adeline's heart squeezed as she briefly saw Briar in the girl's face, the combination of silver hair and striking blue eyes making her think of her baby sister. Slowly, she crouched down and accepted the flower, her heart feeling as if it would burst as she tucked a loose silver strand behind the girl's ear.

"This is beautiful. Thank you, honey," she said before wrapping the girl in a tight hug. Tears tumbled down her cheeks silently as she absorbed the feeling of peace in the air. Here she was not Princess Adeline; she was just Addie.

As soon as the embrace ended, the girl ran off toward her friends in a fit of giggles. Adeline lingered for several moments before she finally stood, feeling Roman's gaze on her as she wiped a stray tear from its path down her cheek. She waited for his teasing, but it never came. Instead, he simply intertwined their fingers once more and began leading her through the streets.

They passed through several clusters of stone homes before they made their way to the center of the village. The town square was vibrant, brimming with merchants and market stalls offering handcrafted goods—wool blankets, shiny trinkets, handmade jewelry—and fresh foods. Worn wooden crates overflowed with a colorful array of fruits and vegetables, the smell of fresh-baked bread wafting through the air from the little bakery nestled in the corner, its deep red awning boasting the name *The Bread Basket* in white hand-painted lettering. Pine from the surrounding forest mingled with the scent of freshly baked bread in the crisp mountain air, wrapping Adeline in a warm embrace.

In the center of the square stood a stone fountain that made the breath die in her throat as her attention caught on it. The sculpture was eerily similar to the one that stood in the gardens of Scalebreak, the one where she had first seen Roman, but instead of the depiction telling of a man slaying a creature, it showed a great warrior *riding* on the back of a mighty dragon. The two fountains looked so much alike that they had to have been handcrafted by the same artist. It was just another reminder of the history she thought she knew. How different it was from the version she learned more and more truths of every day in Drakmoor. Roman noticed her staring at the statue with a furrowed brow and stepped in front of her, cutting off her line of sight. He reached up and tucked a loose, brown wave behind her ear with a gentle smile.

"You don't have to rewrite history as you have known it all at once, Princess," he said softly. "It's a lot to take in, so take your time."

Roman had shown her his soft side on a few occasions, unintentionally revealing his weakness when it came to her, but never like this. Down in the village, among his people, it was like the sarcastic and broody Roman she had come to know was gone. Replaced by the tender bleeding heart she knew he kept buried deep within himself, the version that he knew she needed in these moments.

She nodded gently and only tore her gaze from his when she heard wing beats mingling with the soft murmurs around her. Adeline turned her face toward the sky, and when she did, her jaw dropped in wonder. Dozens of dragons dotted the clouds high above, an array of colors and sizes all flying in a cluster together, the smallest ones tucked safely into the center of the pack.

"Are those—"

"Hatchlings, yes, they are. They just learned to fly a few months ago and only recently have been welcomed to join the elders in the hunt," Roman responded before she could even get the words out.

"The hunt?" Adeline asked, her forehead wrinkling in question.

"Yes, they go out in packs for safety against...well, against Scalebreak armies." He seemed to regret the honesty when Adeline's face fell. "—to go hunt mountain goats in the area," he finished quietly.

"Oh, I see." Her tone was cold.

Hearing that the reason they flew in packs was to protect themselves against her kingdom—her *family*—had made something in Adeline break. She felt nauseous as her head once again began to spin, overwhelmed with realizations and questions. It felt as though she didn't know which way was up anymore, what was right or wrong. It was exhausting.

Roman closed the distance between them as he wrapped her in a hug, once again knowing exactly what she needed, and she let herself be broken from the endless chasm of thoughts. It was difficult to think at all when his warm, solid body was pressed into hers. Her mind seemed to melt along with every muscle in her body as she relaxed and just let herself be *held*. For someone so corded in muscle, his embrace was gentle and soft, safe.

"Hey guys I brought you some—oh...am I, uh...interrupting something?" Falrin's steps toward them slowed as he took in the sight of them wrapped around one another.

"No, not at all," Adeline said with a laugh as she pulled her protesting body from Roman's, fighting the flush that crept onto her cheeks.

"Uh, *okay then.* I brought you guys some bread from The Bread Basket. Ivy just pulled it out as I was getting there!" Falrin tossed each of them a chunk off of the perfectly browned loaf.

Adeline wasted no time biting off a piece, pleasantly surprised to find that the flavor was a rival to even the delicious aroma it gave off. Her taste buds exploded in gratitude with each bite she took. As she stood there breaking bread with Falrin and Roman in the town square, people bustling around them busily, she felt a piece of the cold dragon slayer she had been fracture, falling away.

CHAPTER EIGHTEEN

T HEY SPENT THE REST of the morning and all of the afternoon in the village mingling with the residents and enjoying the delicious food. Adeline made sure to look at every single item being offered by the vendors and was more than delighted when Roman tossed her a velvet bag full of coins and told her to buy anything her heart desired. Adeline warned him that he would regret his decision. Yet, after watching her make her way through the market stalls with Falrin—his arms completely full of various items and trinkets—Roman was only sure of one thing: he didn't.

He would hand over his life savings if it meant watching her face light up the way it had as she made small talk with the vendors, browsing the entire array of goods before her. Roman decided while watching her that he would give everything he had just to see her smile the way she had in the village. This woman made him weak, but he was beginning to think that maybe being weak wasn't such a bad thing. He already felt as though he had known her his entire life, even though they had only truly met a few days ago. His soul knew hers as if it were a piece of his own.

Maybe it was the smile she wore so proudly, or maybe it was the way she looked in that corset he'd had made for her, but something about her had him completely entranced. So much so, that when the street performers came out with violins and cellos and began playing music that was almost as enchanting as Adeline was, he pulled her into the open area around the fountain and began leading her in a dance without a care in the world. She had let him drag her out into the square and pull her close to him without protest.

Bodies flush, Roman could feel her pulse race beneath her chest as he intertwined their fingers and pulled her closer. The steps he led them in were elegant but playful, the perfect match to the music that flowed between the stone buildings around them. He led her effortlessly, and she followed, trusting him entirely to avoid the obstacles around them. As the music picked up in pace, so did their steps. They moved like they were one with the notes, as if they had danced with one another a million times before. Their bodies were fluid, the music pushing and pulling them like the tide.

Roman stepped back from her, lifting their still connected hands over their heads as he spun her. The white cotton of her dress fanned out around her legs, and she spun, turning her face to the sky and letting the sun kiss her skin. Adeline let out a string of delighted giggles as she twirled until her body connected with his again, and Roman relished the contact of his body against hers.

They were drunk on each other's touch, intoxicated by the music enveloping them, and before long the people were joining them in the square, finding partners of their own to dance with. A flurry of moving bodies surrounded them, but he felt as if they were the only two people in the square as they stepped in turn with one another, gazes locked. Nothing and no one else existed but them and the music that paved their dance as they fully gave themselves away to it.

Adeline had danced plenty in her time at the castle, at balls and lessons, but *never* had she danced like this. She had never felt so overcome by the movements and the music while following her partner, but with Roman it didn't even feel like an effort to follow his lead. He helped her move, gliding across the dirt, and it felt as though they were one entity, not two bodies moving together. It was a glorious feeling to dance, to lose herself in the flurry of movement, anchored only by Roman's steady gaze locked with hers. The air between them was electric, so many unspoken words released while they danced; apologies and confessions exchanged without either of them opening their mouths at all.

It wasn't clear how long they had been dancing, only that they had been in the center of the square long enough that everyone else had fallen away, now silently watching in awe as the couple moved with an elegance they had never seen before. The steps were the perfect combination of Adeline's grace and Roman's playfulness. They only fell away from one another when a throat cleared next to them, Falrin.

"Sorry to interrupt, but I—" his words ebbed into silence as Roman covered him in shadows, muffling his words.

Adeline didn't want this to end. She would happily dance with Roman until their feet ached and their muscles screamed in protest, but she still shot a look of disapproval at him while fighting back a smile. She could've spent forever tucked under his chin, but his efforts to stop the interruption had been in vain; she wanted to hear what Falrin had to say.

"Ro, let the man speak." Adeline swatted his chest playfully.

"Fine." He called his shadows back to him and Falrin was visible in front of them once again.

"Oh, thank *Gods!* Roman, your shadows are creepy as fuck," Falrin said with a shiver.

Roman chuckled at his friend. Falrin always spoke exactly what was on his mind.

"As I was *saying.* We have to get going. The sun is setting, and if we don't leave now, we're going to miss dinner." Falrin wiped his hands on his trousers as if trying to clear away any lingering darkness that might cling to him.

Adeline felt herself go heavy with disappointment at the idea of leaving. She had never felt as at home as she had among these people on the mountain side.

As if sensing her disappointment, Roman brushed his lips against the shell of her ear. "Don't worry, Princess, I'll bring you back here as often as you like," he whispered.

Gods, I am utterly hopeless when it comes to this man, she groaned internally. She had long since given up trying to remind herself that Roman had brought her here as a captive.

Adeline's reply came in a soft nod of her head as she let herself be led out of the village, her heart swelling at the warm golden light glowing in the windows of the homes they passed. Even though she was sad to be leaving so soon, she felt grateful that she had gotten to spend any time in the village at all, as it was something she was never afforded in Scalebreak.

Aurelius and Raegorath stood like beacons just outside the village, waiting dutifully for their riders. Adeline noticed a large wooden chest strapped onto Raegorath just behind the saddle and smiled to herself, knowing that Falrin had taken extra care to ensure all the things she had bought in the village made it back to the cabin safely.

The way the setting sun cast a variety of colors onto the gold and green scales of the dragons was incredible to witness, but what was truly breathtaking was the way the colors were reflected off of them. It made the dragons appear almost transparent the way their scales *became* the shades painting the skyline behind them. It was so beautiful that it loosened some of the fear that had built in Adeline's chest at the idea of mounting the massive creatures for the journey home.

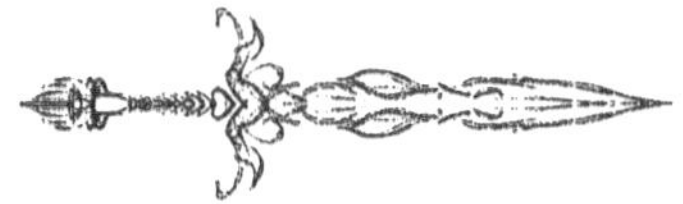

The next week passed relatively uneventfully. Adeline quickly fell into a pattern of familiarity and comfort in Drakmoor. Every morning she met Falrin in the training gym, learning how to move her body in ways she had never known possible and honing her skills with various weapons. The training sessions were filled with equal amounts of sparring and laughter as she became truly acquainted with Falrin. He had carved out a spot in her heart that was now especially soft for the blond-haired goofball she spent her mornings with.

After they trained until their muscles ached, they made their way to the kitchens where Adeline would help Thistle, Seraphina and Milo to prepare cinnamon rolls and bread for the day. She would knead the thick dough until she lost herself in the motions, humming along with Thistle, who always greeted her with his comforting smile. He had made good on his promise to leave Adeline cinnamon rolls in her room when they'd returned from the village that first time and had even made a habit of doing so every afternoon. He didn't know it, but it was the one thing Adeline could look forward to at the end of every day.

It had taken quite a bit of effort but Adeline even managed to crack Seraphina's defenses a bit, enough that she too now offered a smile when Adeline came into the kitchens. Adeline's time in the kitchens was the perfect balance after training to her body's limit with Falrin, and she had found immense comfort among the trio in the warm glow of the hearth. It quickly became her safe space in the cabin, not that she truly needed a *safe* space when all of Drakmoor felt so secure.

After she assisted with the baking, she would eat breakfast as quickly as she could before racing upstairs to change into a dress, another of her favorite parts of the day. The clothes in the wardrobe seemed to replace themselves constantly, and she had still yet to wear the same outfit twice—except for her leathers and the red corset she had worn to the village. For some reason, the corset remained the only constant among the ever-changing clothing, as if the cabin itself knew it was her favorite.

Once she was dressed, Adeline would head to the library and immerse herself in the texts there, attempting to learn as much as she could as fast as she could. It felt as if she was making up for lost time. Most days her head still felt like it was spinning, a war between all the new information and what she grew up believing to be true.

Seraphina, slowly softening to her, had started bringing her lunch in the library and after some convincing had even joined Adeline for the meal. She would often spend the rest of the afternoon helping Adeline work through the texts and was more than willing to answer any questions she had. Adeline made an effort to throw jokes around often and had earned a smile from Seraphina only a handful of times, but she cherished each one. Something about the girl called to Adeline, and even though she wasn't certain why, she refused to let that go.

It was among those too short afternoons in the library with Seraphina that she learned of the girl's ability to manipulate water. Adeline had been delighted to watch as Seraphina pulled the water from a glass on the table and formed shapes with it above their heads, all without breaking a sweat. If she was able to do something like that with so minimal effort, Adeline could only imagine how deadly the woman would be near a whole body of water. She filed the information away in her brain as a reminder not to get on her bad side. The unlikely friendship had been one of her favorite parts of being in Drakmoor, and Adeline wished desperately to hold onto it.

Afternoons in the library were followed by dinner and late night rides with Roman, who had made a habit of dragging her onto the back of Aurelius and taking her to fly among the stars. The first flight had been full of protests from Adeline, still hesitant to mount the dragon after he had sent them into a death spiral the first time, but Roman never took no for an answer. It quickly became a part of her day that she treasured above all else. Something in her had eased toward Roman the day they had danced in the village square, and she was aching for *more*, though she had yet to work up the courage to ask him to take her back to the little town.

Most nights not a single word passed between them, not needing to fill the comfortable silence that surrounded them as they soared through the clouds so high up Adeline felt like if she were to reach out her arms she could touch the stars; not that she had worked up the courage to try.

Although she had become more akin to riding on the back of a dragon, Aurelius clearly still had some level of disdain for her. He would wait until he knew she was letting go of some of her fear before he would bank right or left, spin in tight spirals or tuck his wings tightly against himself until they were plummeting toward the earth, only to throw his wings back open at the last second. Aurelius reminded her an awful lot of Roman most days, and it made sense to her why the two had bonded with one another.

The two of them would sometimes spend hours just taking in the beauty of the stars and the forest, enjoying each other's company. Once they headed back to the cabin, it had become routine for Roman to walk her to her room and say goodnight, watching in what Adeline recognized as disappointment night after night as she closed the door between them. What she didn't let him know was that on the other side of the door, her heart was heavy with the same feeling. Both of them were far too afraid of hurting the other to break the routine they had fallen into.

Even in the short time that Adeline had been in Drakmoor, she found herself becoming addicted to the freedoms that she had here. Sure, Roman still did not trust her with weapons outside of the gym, but that was a small price to pay for the happiness she felt. She no longer felt as if she lived here as a hostage; instead, she found herself hoping that no one would ever come for her. That she could simply slip away from Scalebreak entirely, her existence forgotten.

And so, in an attempt to quiet her thoughts, Adeline would soak in the bathtub, coaxing her muscles to relax before making her way to bed and slipping into dreams of a world where she could be with Roman the way she wanted—praying they would keep the nightmares of home from plaguing her mind.

CHAPTER NINETEEN

ADELINE AWOKE BEFORE THE sun, groaning as she looked out the large expanse of windows and realized daylight was just barely kissing the tops of the snow-capped mountains around the cabin. It was far too early to be awake, but she knew she would not fall back asleep if she rolled over. So she forced herself out of bed, her body still heavy with sleep as she padded toward the bathroom. Still clean from last night's bath, she did not need to wash, but the water would help wake her for training.

Making quick work of filling the tub with cold water, she stripped off the silk nightdress she had worn to bed and stepped in. Her skin protested as the cold bit into her, but her aching muscles thanked her as she forced herself into a sitting position. The water was cold enough that goosebumps rose on her flesh, and she could only convince herself to stay in for a few minutes, but it was all she needed. As she stepped out of the bath and wrapped her wet body in a towel, feeling much more awake than she had only a few minutes prior.

Adeline made her way to the wardrobe and pulled out the deep black leather training clothes that she had donned yesterday, slipping them on before pulling her hair into a messy ponytail, letting the brown waves cascade down her back.

Adeline made her way through the cabin, passing by a few people who were busy with cleaning, before stepping outside into the first glimpse of morning light. As she crossed the path to the training gym, she threw several glances over her shoulder, unable to shake the feeling that someone was watching her. She paid extra attention to her surroundings, scanning the treeline and bushes until she finally made it to the gym. *I'm probably just paranoid,* she thought as she stepped inside the safety of the building.

The first thing she noticed as the door slammed shut behind her was that the training gym was significantly darker in the early morning light than with the afternoon sun she had grown accustomed to. The skylight overhead barely illuminated the room with the light of the rising sun, and the entire room was shrouded in shadow.

It took several minutes for her eyes to adjust to the darkness, but when they did, she had to fight to contain her gasp, letting only a barely audible, sharp inhale pass her lips. Just to the left of the door, she could barely make out the shape of a body pressed against the wall, very obviously trying to conceal their presence. Judging by the sheer height and build of the figure, Adeline assumed it was a man tucking himself into the shadows, trying futilely to disappear within them.

Who the hell is trying to ambush me? Her mind raced trying to figure out who would be in the gym this early, an attempt to find a rational explanation.

Adeline stood in place for several heartbeats to formulate a plan. She had two options: continue standing there and wait for the man to make his move, or pretend she had not caught sight of him and "begin her training." It took only a moment for her to settle on a decision.

Steeling herself against the growing nerves, she took two breaths before casually beginning her journey to the back wall. Each muffled step on the padded floor felt like it took an eternity, her muscles taut and ready to pounce at any moment, but she could not move any quicker without alerting the intruder that she knew of his presence. *Thud...thud...thud...*

Adeline's heart was thundering furiously in her chest the closer she drew to the wall, her saving grace. It took every bit of willpower she had left in her body not to sigh in relief as she finally made it to the wall and no longer had to draw her steps out slowly. A sly smile spread across her lips as the fingers of her left hand closed around the hilt of a steel blade, the cool metal biting into her skin. She took a step away, pivoting on her foot and grabbing a second dagger in her right hand before she exploded in a flurry of movement toward the shadowed man.

Adeline could not remember the last time she felt so predatory, so dangerous; it was intoxicating. An eerie calm settled over her, not disrupted even by the figure pushing off the wall to meet her on the mat.

Pushing through the balls of her feet, Adeline exploded into a leap as she threw her body forward, tucking her upper half in on itself as her legs splayed out in a split. She cartwheeled just above the man's head, watching as the world around her turned upside down. Landing perfectly on her feet with a muffled *thud* behind the man, she let out the breath that she had been holding.

Before he could react, Adeline wrapped her arm around his front, poising one of her daggers expertly at his neck. She heard a quiet gasp escape the intruder as she pushed the dagger into his throat, sure it was biting into his skin. A quiet laugh escaped her lips; she did not need power to be a force to be reckoned with.

"What the hell do you want?" she spat through gritted teeth.

There was no response, only deafening silence before Adeline felt her feet disappear out from under her as the man delivered a sweeping kick to knock her away from him. She began tumbling forward, her chest pressing into him as strong hands wrapped around her, grasping her shoulders as the man threw her over his shoulder.

SMACK.

Her body connected with the mat in a flurry of movement, and stars danced across her vision as she tried to regain her breath. The daggers she had been wielding were now just barely out of reach, so close that if she strained against her protesting muscles, she could just brush her fingertips against the hilt. By the time she managed to draw in a full breath again, the man was looming over her, the early sun glinting behind him. Adeline squinted her eyes, unable to make out any distinguishing features of the man above her against the morning rays that now rained down through the skylight.

Frustrated, she moved her arms ever so slightly, making sure to disguise her movements so the man wouldn't see her reaching for her dagger. Having noted her slight shift, he threw himself down onto her, his knees pressed between hers and his calloused hands gripped her wrists. Adeline let out a grunt of disappointment and anger at her compromised position.

"I—*OOF*" the man hadn't seen her movements this time, judging by his surprise as Adeline hooked her legs through his and threw his body to the side, rolling them so she was straddling him. In the chaos of the maneuver, she had just barely managed to slip one of the daggers into her palm and was now pressing it against his throat once again. Her left hand stretched between them, pinning both of his arms above his head. She had him exactly where she wanted him, and she would not let him—

"Calum?!" She stared down at the man pinned beneath her, mouth agape as shock flooded her body.

"Hey Addie," he chuckled beneath her, as if it had all been some kind of joke.

"Do *NOT* call me Addie! What the fuck are you doing here? And why were you trying to attack me?" Adeline applied more pressure to the blade at his throat. She did not care if the man pinned beneath her was Calum, her childhood best friend; she was going to get answers.

"Woah there! I um...I was sent by your father. We all were." He swallowed thickly, glancing down nervously toward the blood that had begun beading against the glint of silver at his neck.

Adeline felt her head spin with the words Calum said. She had far more questions than answers lately, and it was getting old. *By my father? Why would my father send Calum after me?*

"How did he know where I was?" She spoke her last question aloud, shaking her head to clear room for his answer. "And what do you mean 'we *all* were'? *Who* else is hunting me?" she managed to say through gritted teeth.

She knew she was looking down at him with hatred written all over her face, but she could not bring herself to care. At that moment, she *did* hate him. Her mind spun with the conflict of hurting her best friend, but she wasn't so sure that he *was* her best friend anymore.

Calum flinched, clearly not prepared for the reaction he was receiving, and continued to glance down toward the dagger at his throat as if unsure whether Adeline would truly use it or not. He took several moments to answer her question, which only added to her growing frustration.

"Th-the other suitors. Your father sent us all to rescue you, to bring you back safely. H-he said that whoever brought you back would win your hand in marriage." He winced as his words hit their mark, as if hearing them aloud had made him understand their weight.

WHAT THE FUCK? MY HAND IN MARRIAGE? Part of her was not surprised at his admission. Her father was a ruthless man and he would stop at no end to steal back things that were of value to him. It seemed Adeline was just that, something valuable that had slipped through King Thorian's fingers.

Adeline pressed harder, watching with something that felt eerily similar to delight as more drops of crimson bubbled onto the blade. The little voice in the back of her mind roared to life the harder she pressed into his skin. He is *your best friend!* The rational side of her screamed.

But the deeper she pushed the blade into his skin, the quieter the voice got. Calum was *not* the best friend she had grown up with, not anymore.

A gash was beginning to form along his neck where she held her weapon, and his face had gone white, every ounce of color drained from him as if he truly feared Adeline would end his life. She would not kill him, but he did not need to know that; she needed to send a message.

"I am *not* some *damsel in distress!* You do *not* just get to swoop in, decide I need saving, and claim me as your *prize!*"

"I—"

"I am not done speaking! And frankly, I do not care what you have to say. You being here tells me *everything* I need to know about you, Calum." She took a breath, preparing herself for what was to come.

Whatever may have remained of their friendship was about to be shattered, and though she knew it was best for the both of them, she could not avoid the hurt radiating in her chest at the thought.

"Here is what is going to happen. You are going to get up from this floor, and you are going to *leave*. Head straight back to the castle and inform my father that I am exactly where I was always meant to be and that he can call off his dogs. And then, Calum, I never want to see your fucking face again." Even though she meant the words that rolled off her tongue, she felt as if a piece of her broke as she heard herself speak them. It was a hard pill to swallow, knowing that Calum had grown to be someone she hated.

"I—Addie...Plea—"

"I believe the lady told you not to call her Addie. And judging by the dagger she has pressed to your throat, you may want to follow her directions. Calum, was it?" A gruff voice cut through the shadows.

Adeline did not need to turn her head to know that Roman was now standing behind her. Shadows peeled away from the walls and wrapped around Calum's wrists, tying them together and confirming her suspicions. Not that she needed the confirmation; she would recognize the sweet melody of his voice in any room.

"Though, now that I think of it, I don't take well to people harming the people I love, Calum. So before you go back to the castle to be King Thorian's little *bitch*, you and I are going to have a quick chat."

Love? Butterflies danced in Adeline's stomach as she lingered on that little detail.

Before she could protest, she was lifted off of Calum and hauled to her feet with her arms pinned at her sides.

"Sorry, Princess, gotta do what the boss man says," Falrin said from behind her with a smirk.

CHAPTER TWENTY

A DELINE FOUGHT AGAINST FALRIN'S hold furiously, desperately throwing her body weight around to break free of him, but her efforts were futile. No matter how hard she struggled against him, Falrin held tightly, refusing to loosen his grip. Roman did not need to watch to know that every attempt she made was countered; Falrin knew exactly what she was going to do before she actually did it. Judging by the brunette waves flying wildly around her face, Falrin's wind was pushing against her, adding extra force to keep her exactly where she was. It only made her attempts at escape even more useless, though Roman knew she would not stop trying.

While she fought against Falrin tirelessly, Roman hauled Calum out of the training gym, his hands and feet both shackled with thick black bands of shadow. He had heard everything he needed to know about the man when he threatened Adeline's safety, and now Roman was seething with anger. With every step he took toward the cabin, dragging Calum behind him with his shadows, his blood boiled. Initially, he had planned to only interrogate Calum and send him back to Scalebreak as a messenger to the king, but now he was itching to make him pay for ever laying a finger on *his* girl.

Roman led Calum through the cabin, earning curious glances from the staff as he dragged him up the stairs. There had been one place in the home he had intentionally kept from Adeline when he gave her the tour, and that was exactly where he planned to take Calum. Though the guilt at his dirty secret now gnawed at him, he pushed his feelings down. This was not the time to deal with them.

The heavy wood door to his bedroom slammed shut behind them, having been thrown closed by the dark ribbons he tossed out. Roman's shadows often felt more like a sentient part of him than something he had to harness control over; he never had to work at keeping them tamed. The darkness was just as much a part of him as he was of it. He never had to consciously send the shadows to do simple things like shutting doors or even shackling Calum, they simply sensed his wishes and behaved as such—shooting out of his fingertips as if eager to cause mischief.

Roman stalked over to the fireplace mantel and pulled a dagger from his belt, sliding the cool blade over the palm of his hand and watching as blood trickled to the surface. He turned his hand, letting several drops of dark blood land in the ash of the fire he had smothered before bed the night before. Calum, who had gone pale as a ghost and deigned not to speak after being wrapped in shadows, cleared his throat at the sight, clearly disturbed.

"So, uh...what exactly is the blood—"

"You will speak when I give you permission to do so." Roman's shadows, once again feeding off of his disgust with Calum, extended out and tied themselves dutifully around Calum's mouth, gagging him.

Looking up from the fireplace that separated from the wall with a groan, Roman caught sight of the gag in place on Calum's mouth and bit out a laugh; his shadows really did know him best. Turning back to the fireplace, Roman closed his calloused hands around the rough stone, pulling until it swung open like a door to reveal a dimly lit stone staircase. A mischievous grin splayed across his lips as he turned to Calum, who looked like he had stopped breathing altogether.

"After you, *Duke Windford.*" Roman's words may as well have been poison with the way he spat them.

Calum must have decided it was in his best interest not to reply and swallowed thickly before taking the first step. Roman's hand pushed impatiently at Calum's back, telling him that he was not moving fast enough. Roman could practically hear the way Calum's heart hammered in his throat as the distinctive *bang* of the stone door slamming into place echoed around them. They were locked away in the cellar with no way for Calum to escape.

Roman let Calum make it down only about ten steps before he pushed firmly against his back, sending him flying face first toward the bottom of the staircase. Calum screamed through the gag, and the sound was delicious as it met Roman's ears. He was afraid for his life. He let Calum soar toward the hard stone landing for long enough to believe he was about to meet his end. At the absolute last second, he sent his shadows spiraling down until they caught Calum in a not so gentle embrace, lifting him gruffly before depositing him upright on the bottom stair. Calum sucked in several shaky breaths, clearly disheveled from his haphazard flight down the stairs.

Knowing they were deep in the cellar of the cabin, solid walls surrounding them, Roman removed the shadow gag from Calum's mouth. Much to his dismay, the idiot had wasted no time in speaking once it was gone.

"Very funny, *Roman,*" Calum gritted through his teeth, spitting Roman's name out as if it burned his mouth. No matter how tough he tried to appear he could not hide the breathlessness that came with the statement. The fear gripping him was very apparent.

They stood in the center of an empty room, dark gray stone walls boxing them in save for the iron chains hanging from the ceiling and the crimson stains that stared up from the rough concrete floor. Calum's heart ceased beating in his chest as his eyes fell to those dark stains, he had known he was in for some sort of interrogation when Roman hauled him off, but staring into the permanent blood spatter on the floor he realized an interrogation was only the beginning of what he might face in the cellar.

Roman was walking around the room now, his boot-clad feet echoed almost menacingly with each calculated step he took. Several moments of silence passed between the men, the only sounds the click of Roman's heeled boots and the loud thumps of Calum's heart against his ribcage. The monster that was Roman stalked his prey, circling Calum with eyes that dripped in a thirst for bloodshed.

"Are you gonn—" Calum's question was cut off as his body was hauled upward by an unexpected curl of shadow, lifting him up until his feet dangled above the ground. Calum barely had time to realize what was happening before he felt the cold bite of iron against his bare wrists.

Chains. He was chained in this dungeon below the cabin with Roman Drache staring down at him, murder in his eyes.

Gods help me, he thought.

"You are only going to speak if it is in direct response to my questions. You will be honest in your answers, and if you are not, you will face the consequences. Are we clear, Calum?"

"Ye-yes," Calum stammered in response, frustrated by his inability to hide his growing fear. He was the general of Scalebreak's army for Gods' sake, he should not be cowering in submission this easily.

Roman flicked a dagger from his sleeve, an inconspicuous hiding place, and looked down at the polished silver of the blade as he pretended to inspect the metal for blemishes before he spoke again.

"What did you come here for?" The question hung in the air between them for several moments, Calum looking between Roman and the blade he held before speaking.

"I came to bring Addie home. To rescue her," he said through gritted teeth. Already the iron manacles were cutting into his skin, and his wrists ached.

Roman clicked his tongue in reply.

"Tsk tsk. I thought we agreed to be honest with each other." Roman was in front of him now and slowly dragged the tip of his dagger across the bare skin of Calum's lower stomach, left exposed by the way his body stretched against the shackles. A sinister grin played on Roman's lips as he applied pressure to the blade and stared at the deep red droplets that beaded against the clean metal.

"Your first mistake, *General,* was thinking that Adeline needs saving. Your second, was referring to her as *Addie.*" He moved the blade to Calum's throat. "She is *not* your friend anymore. You lost the privilege of calling her your friend after you failed to believe she could protect herself. Now, let's try answering that question again."

Calum trembled as pain bloomed at the fresh wound on his abdomen, and he gritted his teeth as he replied, "I came to bring her back to Scalebreak. King Thorian sent all the suitors to find her and bring her home. He promised the victor would win his daughter's hand." Calum's eyes scanned Roman's face for the poor reaction he was sure would follow.

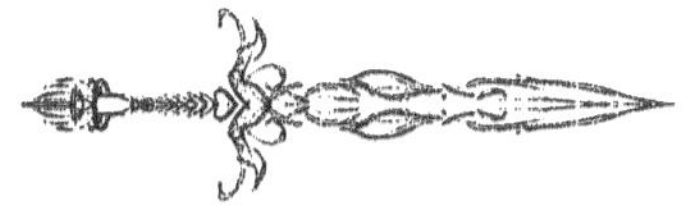

Her hand?! Gods, who does that man think he is? Addie is not a bargaining chip. Roman reeled his thoughts back in, turning his focus back to where Calum kneeled on the cool stone floor, his chained arms hanging above his head.

"Ah." An eerie calm settled over him as he spoke, "So you thought you could play her knight in shining armor, come scoop the princess up, and take her home to make her your bride?" Roman let out a menacing laugh, any blood remaining in Calum's face drained as he turned a ghostly shade of white. "I know exactly the kind of man you are, Calum Windford. And you will never deserve Adeline."

He removed the blade from Calum's neck, but not before slicing gently, just enough to break the skin. Calum winced at the cut.

"How did you find her?" Roman asked, twirling the blade between his fingers. Calum only stared back, silently glaring at Roman and refusing to budge.

It seems I'll have to be more specific in my questioning, Roman thought to himself.

In a flash of movement, the dagger was no longer poised between his fingers but instead hung in the air just in front of Calum, poised over his face, black tendrils of shadow curling around the hilt.

"No! Please. I—"

"I asked you a question," Roman cut him off.

"I—" he let out a deep sigh before continuing, "I followed her into the forest that night. She would never tell me what she was doing leaving the castle that late and I-I just wanted to make sure she wasn't in danger. I watched her get wounded, and when I saw you move for her, I ran for help. By the time I returned with soldiers you were both gone, the only proof she had ever been there was her tattered corset lying in the moss. I-I brought it back to the castle and had my hound scent her. The dog led me a few miles outside of your town only a few days ago, but I lost him trying to evade one of your oversized watchdogs in the forest. I barely escaped the dragon myself. I managed to make it the rest of the way by using the tracking skills I picked up while hunting as a boy. I only found her this morning by chance. I hid out in the gym last night because it was the most sheltered place I could find to rest and regroup. I was more than shocked when I woke up to footsteps and in walked Addi-Adeline." Calum hung his head, cowering away from his own words as they hung in the air.

Roman growled, "She is not some animal for you to hunt. You are lucky that I need you to send a message to the king or I would kill you for ever laying a fucking *finger* on her."

The manacles around Calum's wrists popped open, and he fell to the floor with a loud thud. His hands immediately went to his stomach, where blood was trickling from the wound Roman had delivered there. It wouldn't be fatal, but it would make getting home a hell of a lot more difficult—just as Roman had intended.

"Is that all? You're just going to let me go?" Calum said, looking up from where he knelt on the ground to meet Roman's eyes.

Roman stared back with a blood-thirsty grin. "Oh, we are just getting started, *General*."

That was all the warning he gave before he was a flurry of fists and kicks flying at Calum. With his first punch, his fist connected with the side of Calum's face, causing his lip to split open wide. The sight only fed his desire to watch Calum bleed.

Roman lost himself in the rhythm of the quick, calculated movements, throwing himself at Calum and making him pay for underestimating Adeline. His fists flew through the air, delivering sharp blows. Punches collided with the wound on the general's stomach, throwing him back, but Calum barely fought back—only attempting to shield himself from the rain of blows coming down on him. Blood trickled from his nose, but he did not move to wipe it, clearly accepting that he was no match for the man above him.

Calum connected with the wall behind him and let out an ear-splitting groan as his face contorted in pain, trying to gather his breath. Roman pulled him up from the floor by the collar of his shirt, pushing him against the wall and holding him there roughly. His eyes were dark as he glared down at Calum, a storm of dark shadows raging within them.

"Tell the fucking *king* that Addie is not his to offer as a prize, and that the Drache family will consider this an act of war," Roman spat at him.

He waited until Calum's eyes lit with understanding before slamming his head against the wall with a *bang* and watching in delight as he lost consciousness.

CHAPTER TWENTY-ONE

C ALUM'S HEAD FELT HEAVY as he stirred, finally waking. His legs rustled against fallen leaves on the forest floor as he tried to lift himself to a seat, his body screaming in protest and aching in places he didn't even know could hurt.

Somehow finding the strength, he cracked his eyes open. The first thing he noted was the dirt that clung to his skin and clothes; the second was that he was in the forest. He wasn't sure how long he had been unconscious out here, only that it was now dark and the sun no longer shone overhead to light his journey home.

He reached up to wipe his face, his hands coming away with crusted blood, and as if on cue, his head began to throb violently against his skull. Finally hauling himself into a sitting position, Calum ignored the protests of his muscles and leaned against a tree to lessen the strain on his body. Looking down, he took inventory of the countless bruises and wounds that now marred his tan skin and tried desperately to recall where they had come from.

His memory felt hazy, but if he rallied all of his focus, he could just barely make out flashes of a girl, *Adeline*, and a man who commanded the shadows. He shivered, chilled to the bone as one memory made itself clear.

Tell the fucking king that Addie is not his to offer as a prize and that the Drache family will consider this an act of war.

Oh Gods. I am so fucked, he thought.

Chapter Twenty-Two

R OMAN'S MIND WHIRLED. AFTER depositing Calum's uncon-scious body at Falrin's feet and ordering for him to be taken far the fuck away, he hadn't wasted a second in getting back to *her*. Adrenaline fading, his head spun with all the possibilities of what could have been. Adeline's safety had been at risk, and he wasn't there. She had held her own just fine before he arrived, but that wasn't the point. She deserved someone who would be there to watch her fight for herself, to be there to protect her when she couldn't.

What if it had been someone with a higher skill set? What if I lost her? He could barely stand the thoughts raging in his mind.

Despite all the new information he had just learned regarding King Thorian's plans for Adeline, and the fact that he had just encited a whole fucking war on perhaps the most powerful kingdom known to man, his only focus was getting to Adeline. People whirred by as he stalked up the stairs, paying them no mind. He needed to see her, to *touch her*, to prove to himself that she was okay and nothing and no one would come in the way of that. He would not allow anyone to put her at risk again, even if his very life depended on it.

Before he could rationalize with himself, he was knocking fervently on the solid wood of her bedroom door without ceasing, silently pleading with Adeline to open it. His knuckles—now purple and black with bruises from the punishment he had dealt Calum in the cellar—screamed in protest with every knock, but he did not stop. He would not until he at least heard her voice.

The door flew open on its hinges, revealing a very disheveled Adeline. Her brown hair, normally tidy and pulled back out of her face, was a wild, unkempt mess of curls piled haphazardly atop her head in a bun.

"What the hell, Ro? What are you doing here? It's the middle of the night." She pulled at the lace edges of the black silk nightdress, and he felt himself hardening at the sight. Adeline appeared suddenly self-conscious at the lack of material covering her skin, but Roman reveled in it.

His only response to her question was a deep growl in the back of his throat as he looked her up and down, drinking in every inch of her exposed skin; committing it to memory. As his eyes scanned her, he couldn't help but notice the way her nipples hardened beneath the midnight fabric as she watched him drink her in, hunger written all over his expression.

"I thought—" the words died in her throat as Roman stepped toward her, wrapping his hand around her delicate wrist and pushing her backward, further into the bedroom. His shadows curled out to slam the heavy door behind them, not slowing him at all. He stalked, backing her up until finally the bare skin of her exposed back met the solid oak wall.

His every move was calculated, a predator hungrily stalking its prey. The animalistic way he felt must have been displayed on his face judging by the way Adeline eyed him curiously.

Roman dropped her wrist, moving his hand up to her chin where he gripped her face firmly. "I can't stop fucking thinking about you, Princess. What are you doing to me?" He stared into her blue eyes with an unrelenting desire playing behind his pleading gaze.

Her pulse roared to life under his touch.

"Did he hurt you, Addie?" His eyes never left hers.

"N-no he didn't hurt me," she finally managed, her reply breathless.

It was as if she had stolen all the oxygen in the room. Roman couldn't think clearly anymore; he was drunk on her touch. His every word ignited the tension between them. Adeline stared back at him with the same hunger reflected in her eyes. She tugged at the edges of Roman's shirt and pulled it over his head quickly, as if she was trying to act before her mind could tell her to stop. Her breath caught in her throat as she drank in his bare skin, the swirls of black ink that snaked up his arms stole all of her attention—watching the way she eyed him with hunger had Roman's mind filling with thoughts of what his bare skin might feel like pressed against her own.

A breath passed between them, and before either of them had a moment to speak, Roman reached up and pulled at the ribbon that Adeline had used to tie her hair atop her head, sending her brown waves tumbling down her back. A low growl sounded in the back of his throat at the sight, and he reached up, twirling a chocolate wave around his finger.

"Have I ever told you how much I love your hair, Addie?" He sounded just as breathless as she did. "These brown locks alone could bring me to my knees," Roman finished, letting his hand fall from her hair as he turned his gaze back to hers.

She looked as if she was disappointed by the sudden lack of contact between them, and it had him letting go of whatever self-control he had convinced himself he still held onto. He grabbed hold of both of her wrists, pressing his body into hers as he held her arms against the wall above her head. A flicker of surprise flashed across Adeline's features, gone just as fast as it had come. In its place was a look of complete and utter desire as her eyes bore into his in a silent plea.

"I know you can handle your own, Princess, but I'd be lying if I didn't tell you that I hate the idea of him touching you, of him possibly knowing your body in ways I don't," his eyes darkened as the truth slipped from his lips.

"I—we never. He never—It was never like that between us. Calum tried to force himself on me once. He kissed me, and I rejected his advances." The admission hung in the air between them. "I've never, um, I've never kissed anyone else. He stole that from me." Her cheeks heated in embarrassment.

Roman's face transformed into the epitome of disgust as her words landed. *That son of a bitch touched her without her permission.* His mind cleared of any other thoughts. The only thing combating his anger was the need to remedy the hurt she had faced, even if not at his own hand.

"He can't have stolen what wasn't his to take, Addie. Only *you* get to decide who gets to touch you." Roman took a step back, dropping her wrists as he realized that he had been no better than Calum, forcing himself on her without knowing if she wanted it. He turned his back to her, raking his hands through his hair.

"Fuck, Addie. I'm sorry. I wasn't thinking." The thought of turning around and being met with her disdain was too much, and it had nausea curling in his stomach.

Gentle hands wrapped around his bicep, pulling him from his anguish as she tugged him to turn toward her, to look at her.

"Hey, Ro. Look at me. You aren't him. Even just the fact that you are reacting the way you are right now shows me that you are *nothing* like Calum."

He softened a bit as the words sank in. "I should never have laid a finger on you without being sure that you were okay with it, Princess." He stared down at her, afraid that at any moment she might choose to look away.

"I *want* you to touch me, Shadow." Her cheeks heated as she continued on, "I want you to do a lot *more* than just touch me." The words were almost a whisper with how quietly she murmured them into the heavy silence.

Roman's eyes darted to hers, scanning her face for any sliver of uncertainty. It felt too good to be true. *There is no way this is real.*

All of his willpower had been used up when he put the distance between them, and now he was itching to feel her skin on his. He met her eyes again and saw the plea written in her gaze.

Fuck it.

He closed the space between them, bringing his hand up to cup her cheek gently. Emerald eyes met hers, still searching for any amount of apprehension.

"Are you sure that is what you want, Princess? You want to feel my hands on you?" His words were dripping with desire, and Adeline's knees wobbled in response.

She nodded her head gently. "Please, Ro," she begged.

That was all the confirmation he needed. He lowered his mouth to hers, their lips crashing feverishly. The hand that had been so gently cupping her cheek now snaked behind her, grasping the back of her neck to pull her to him. A small moan escaped Adeline, barely a sigh between her lips, but it only fueled the growing fire between them. Shadows swirled around them in response, wrapping them in ribbons as if his darkness were dancing for her. His free hand wrapped around the curve of her waist, pulling her body flush against his. Even the thin fabric of her nightdress was too much separating them.

Closer, he needed her closer.

Without breaking their kiss, he wrapped his arms under her thighs and scooped her up, settling her on his hips. Adeline wrapped her legs around his torso, and tightened the arms that had made themselves at home around his neck, helping him to hold her up. His erection pressed into her as he grinded his hips into hers, unable to restrain himself. Even through the layers of his training leathers, she could feel the hard length of him straining to be let free, and suddenly nerves came to life within her. As if sensing exactly where her mind had gone, Roman pulled back from her mouth with a soft chuckle.

"What's wrong, Princess? Scared?"

Though he was sure in his words, he knew Adeline was aware that all she had to do was utter a single word of discomfort, and he would stop. Maybe that was why she felt comfortable letting him explore now, even though Roman could practically feel the nervousness that radiated from her. She was safe with him; he just hoped she knew it. Rather than respond, she lowered her mouth to his again, reaching between her legs to wrap her hand around his arousal.

Roman moaned at her touch, bucking his hips in a silent plea for her to keep going. The sound seemed to ignite a confidence in her.

Holding her against him, he carried her to the bed and laid her down. Taking a moment to admire her, his eyes traced her body, lingering on the outline of her peaked nipples. His gaze roamed down to the lace trim of the nightgown now just barely covering her ass. Every curve of her body was committed to his memory as he stared down at her. Feeling his gaze on her, Adeline looked up at him as she bit her lip, eyes darting over every inch of his skin and drinking him in just as he had her. She was breathless, and Roman wasn't sure if it was from how turned on she was watching him stand over her hungrily or the nervousness that she felt experiencing his hands on her in places she never had before.

"Gods, you haven't even undressed me yet and I'm already letting anxiety creep in," she whispered, a blush rising to her cheeks.

"Tell me what you want, Princess," Roman demanded between them as he unbuckled his belt and slid it free of his waist before discarding it on the floor. He was giving her the control.

Any words she may have said died in her throat as she took in the impossibly large bulge of his leather pants.

Roman leaned down over her, wrapping his hand around her chin and bringing her eyes back to his.

"It's okay, don't be scared, Addie. Tell me what you want," he practically whispered, trying to ease her nerves.

She swallowed thickly, gathering the courage to speak.

"I want to feel you. I want to feel your touch everywhere," she finally admitted.

A devilish grin spread across Roman's lips. "Good girl, Addie."

His hand dropped from her throat, skimming across her chest until it cupped her full breast. A groan escaped him as he slid his touch to her nipple, rolling it between his fingers with delight as she arched into him with a whimper. Ribbons of his shadows began twining up her legs, slipping over her skin in response to her moans. As many fantasies as he'd had about using his shadows on Adeline, he called them back. Tonight it would just be the two of them, giving into something that had been burning between them since the very first night she saw him from her balcony.

"Please," she whispered, pleading for more. She sounded desperate for him.

"Fuck, Princess. I like hearing you beg."

Roman dropped to his knees and pulled her hips toward the edge of the bed until his head was between her thighs.

"Wait, I-I want *you,*" she protested, feeling self-conscious at how close his face was to her.

"Don't worry, love. You'll get plenty, but first I want you dripping for me, and I need to make sure you're ready. Now, I want to hear you beg again."

"Please, Ro. Please," she whimpered, her voice shaky.

"That's my girl," he pressed two fingers to her clit, circling gently as he teased. "Gods, you're already so wet for me, Addie," he pushed his fingers more firmly against her, watching in delight as she writhed with pleasure at his touch.

"Gods, Roman!" Adeline moaned, grinding her hips into his fingers.

"Use your words, Princess. Tell me exactly what you want."

"More, I-I want more," Adeline begged, and his cock twitched in response.

Roman let his fingers slide down until he was gently pressing the tip of just one against her entrance.

"Please, please don't stop." Her hands gripped the sheets as she pushed her hips down into him, and any nerves she had been feeling before were gone now, replaced by a desperate need.

Slowly, he let his finger slide into her, making sure to be gentle with her, knowing it was the first time she was being touched like this. Adeline arched her back in response and that was all the encouragement he needed to begin pumping his finger in and out, only gently adding a second when he was sure she had adjusted.

As he slid his second finger in, Adeline seemed to let herself go, relishing entirely in how he felt. The feeling of his fingers driving in and out of her was enough to have her hands fisting the sheets. She arched into his every movement, sounds of desire escaping her lips. There was no shame in the pleasure she found as Roman worshiped her body.

"Roman, oh Gods," she moaned, and it was enough to have him letting go of the single thread of control he had left. He lowered his mouth to her clit, lapping at the tight bundle of nerves with his tongue.

Adeline cried out, pulling at the fabric between her fingers in a desperate need to take hold of something. She ground her hips against his tongue, wanting more, needing more of him as the pressure built inside of her.

Roman knew she was close, knew that it wouldn't take much more to send her over the edge in a poetic fall from grace. He yearned to see the polished princess come undone beneath him, moaning into her at the thought. Adeline squirmed beneath him, eager.

"Tsk tsk, Princess," Roman withdrew his fingers, kissing his way back up her stomach and breasts before closing his mouth over hers in a soft, sensual kiss that swallowed the gasp she breathed in. She whimpered against his lips, frustrated by the sudden emptiness she felt and the way it seemed to amuse Roman.

Roman was anything but amused, dragging out their kiss in an attempt to give himself time to gain some composure. This was about Adeline, and he wasn't entirely sure how far they should take it. She pulled away, breathing heavily with her palms splayed across his bare chest.

"Did you... change your mind?" she asked breathlessly, her tone laced with humor.

Roman chuckled, bringing a hand up to her throat in a gesture that made her heart beat in her ears. "Princess, if I spend one more minute between your thighs, I'll spend all night there. We don't have to—"

Adeline reached down, gripping his cock in her hand and squeezing hard, cutting him off. "If I wanted a man to tell me when I was ready to get married, when I was ready to be fucked, when *I* was ready to do anything, I would've gone home with Calum." She pulled at the laces of his pants, not giving him a chance to protest. Roman blinked the shock from his eyes, kicking his pants off and claiming her in another kiss with a gruff moan of desire.

Adeline met the fervor in his kiss, biting his bottom lip as she wrapped her hand around the length of him. She let her fingers roam from the base to the tip, trying not to let his size distract her from their kiss.

"Tell me again, Addie." His warm lips brushed hers as he spoke against her mouth.

"I *need* you. Please."

That was all the confirmation he needed before he grabbed her hips, lifting her legs until they hung off his shoulders. Guiding Adeline's hand below his own, they lined the head of his cock up with her entrance. He braced his knees against the curve of the mattress, pressing into her. Adeline gasped in response, and he stopped immediately, giving her a moment to adjust.

"Don't. Fucking. Stop," she moaned.

His movements were slow and languid as he slid into her, knowing it would be uncomfortable but understanding she'd adjust. In moments,

Adeline was pushing her hips up in a plea for him to keep going, whispering her need for more of him.

Roman held her gaze as he pushed his hips against hers, sliding into her and delighting in how quickly her body welcomed him. Almost instantly, they were moving in sync, grinding against one another as their moans intertwined in the air between them. Roman knew they were likely causing a commotion, but he couldn't bring himself to care as he thrust deeper into her, his rough hands gripping her hips and sliding her back onto him to meet every thrust. They lost themselves in the pleasure, both of them so close to release.

"Roman, I'm—"

"I know angel, let go." He gave himself permission too, taking the fall from grace at her side as they gave into their pleasure in a euphoric release of shaking limbs and heavy breaths.

CHAPTER TWENTY-THREE

ROMAN AND ADELINE HAD spent nearly two hours in a pile of tangled limbs as they relished in the comfortable feeling of skin on skin, both of them stroking lazy circles on the other. It was only when Roman had begun to nod off, his lashes fluttering in an effort to keep his eyes open that Adeline broke the contact, standing and pulling Roman behind her and into the bathroom while he protested.

"Can't we just go to bed?" he groaned, though a smirk played on his lips.

"I'll be damned to hell before I'd let you sleep in my bed covered in blood, Shadow," Adeline teased as she turned on the faucet and steaming water began to fill the basin.

"If you insist, Princess," Roman sighed, pulling her toward him until her back was pressed against his chest.

He wrapped his arms around her waist and burrowed his head into the crook of her neck, drawing in a deep breath of lavender and jasmine as he did so. Roman let out a sigh. This time it sounded of contentment as he trailed gentle kisses up Adeline's neck, grinning at the soft moan that escaped her in response. Though they stood naked, bodies flush with one another in the cool air of the bathroom, nothing about his touch was sexual. Instead, she felt the comfortable passion that was laced into every kiss he pressed against her skin, leaving goosebumps in its wake.

The tub filled with water far faster than Adeline would have liked, and she bit back a groan as Roman dropped his hold on her. Now cold without the feeling of him pressed against her, she stepped forward, turning off the running water before stepping carefully into the basin.

She relaxed into the tub, letting the water gently lap at her collarbones as Roman followed, settling behind her. He leaned back, letting his back rest against the edge of the tub, and pulled Adeline to him, tucking her under his chin.

Relaxed sighs escaped both of them as they soaked in the hot water, letting the comfortable silence envelope them as the tension in their muscles slowly dissipated. Every so often, Roman pressed a gentle kiss to her hair, as if he couldn't stop himself from having his lips *somewhere* on her body. Adeline's smile grew each time he did, and she relished in the perfect moment, their bubble of peace. Where she wasn't being promised as anyone's bride, where there weren't expectations or political agendas. She would allow herself this moment, in the middle of the night, bare skin and naked emotion with Roman in the bathtub.

It was only when the water no longer had tendrils of steam rising from it that she finally sat forward, reaching for a cloth that had been draped over the edge of the tub. Wordlessly, she wrapped a bar of soap in the rag and made work of scrubbing away the dried blood from Roman's skin.

Adeline took extra care to be slow and gentle in her movements, rubbing tenderly at his tan skin. When she reached his arms, she began mindlessly tracing over the shadows etched in ink on his skin, mesmerized. Her fingers trailed over his arms until they met his wrists, where the ribbons of black ink came to an end. It was only then that her eyes caught on his bruised and bloodied knuckles.

"Ro...your hand!" Her voice was heavy with worry.

"It's nothing. I'm alright, Addie."

"It is *not* nothing, Roman! I don't even want to know what Calum looks like if this is the condition your hand is in! I can't imagine that it doesn't hurt." She turned his hand in hers, inspecting the wounds on his knuckles with wide eyes.

"Hey, look at me," Roman pleaded, and she obeyed. "I am *okay*, Princess. Calum got everything he deserved for ever putting a hand on you, and selfishly, I'd deal him the same punishment a thousand times over to protect you. Any pain I feel is dulled by the knowledge that I left him in far worse a state."

Adeline pressed a kiss to his battered knuckles in response, not speaking as she gathered the cloth into her hands once more and went back to cleaning his body of any remaining blood.

Only when she was satisfied with her work did she let Roman grab the cloth from her and take his turn at tenderly cleaning her body. Neither of them wanted this perfect moment to end and it was only when Adeline had begun softly snoring that Roman roused her, drained the tub and gathered her damp body into his arms. He carried her to the bed and tucked her gently next to him in the sheets, where they both fell into a deep slumber.

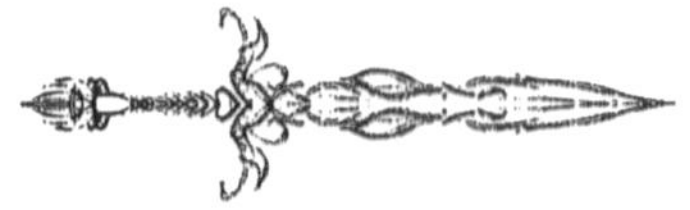

Adeline awoke to the sound of birds chirping the next morning. In a tired haze she rolled over, her bare skin caressing the silk sheets, causing her nipples to peak in anticipation for the man on the other side of her bed. A sleepy smile spread across her lips as the events of the night prior replayed in her mind. Something in her felt lighter knowing that she no longer had to hold herself back around Roman, even if she was unsure of where they stood.

Her joy, however, was short lived once she rolled over to find the other half of the bed cold and bare—save for a slip of paper.

I hate to leave you lonely after the beautiful night we shared together, but know that I do not do so lightly. Don't miss me too much, Princess.

—Roman

P.S. There is a fresh cup of willowbark tea on the vanity for you.

Adeline let out a groan of frustration, her brown waves blowing up and out of her face with the exasperated exhale. Though he had afforded her the courtesy of leaving a note and willowbark tea for contraception, she could not stop the gnawing pit of anger that grew in her belly; he had left her alone. Her blood boiled in her veins, making her sure she could not fall back asleep, so instead she threw back the blankets and made her way to the bathtub. If she couldn't wake up with him she would at least soothe her anger in the comfort of last night's memories.

As she lowered her body into the steaming water she couldn't help but notice the lingering scent of jasmine and cedar stuck to her skin—*Roman's scent.* Although she was unhappy with him, she couldn't stop her body from softening at the familiar comfort that was being enveloped in his smell.

The hot water stung her skin in a delightfully painful but welcome distraction. The memory of her sitting in a too-hot basin and scrubbing her skin until it was bright red and irritated to erase the feeling of Calum's unwelcome kiss flashed across her mind. All at once she recalled how *dirty* she had felt in that moment, and a shiver went through her as the memory passed. It was not lost on her how different she felt in those two moments. Where Calum had been demanding and forceful in his advances back in Scalebreak, Roman had been gentle, patient even, using every ounce of control he could muster to make sure she felt safe. She had known the entire time they lay together that all she had to do was hesitate and he would have stopped. Maybe that was why rather than scrubbing furiously at her skin now, she was mindlessly gliding her hands across her breasts, the curve of her hips, everywhere that Roman's hands had been the night before—as if she could satiate his phantom touch that lingered on her skin.

Her anger dissipated little by little as she took her time gently cleaning herself, even taking an extra moment to slip some jasmine oils into the water in hopes that she could cling to even a fraction of Roman on her today. She was angry, but the thought of him still brought her comfort.

By the time she raised herself from the bath, she felt calm, her seething anger having faded to a mere frustration. She was hurt, but some part of her knew that he truly would have only left if it was of great importance.

Was last night really so bad for him that he needed to get away from me?

Not wanting to think of it any longer, she tugged on a simple cotton dress of blood red before slipping on a cream-colored corset to accent it. Pulling her hair behind her head, her fingers made quick work of weaving with one another as she tied the loose brown waves into a braid down her back.

Her mind wandered back to the incident with Calum in the training gym as she fell into the motions of readying herself for the day. *The king sent the suitors to come hunt for me, as if I am some prize to be won.* Fury rose to the surface with the thought. *I am quite sick of letting the men of Scalebreak behave as if they own me. I need to send a message.* Rage roared back to life within her as she thought of the way the men in her life had become so comfortable with walking all over her. Adeline's eyes caught on a tablet of paper and a pen perched on the vanity where Roman must have left them after writing the note he'd left on the bed. The reminder of the note caused her rage to boil over.

"Gods, men are *useless* creatures," she huffed under her breath as she stomped over to the vanity, feeling herself soften slightly at the sight of the pink roses still poised there. Even in her rage, Roman brought her a strange comfort.

Before she had even fully come to a seat, she took up the pen in her hand and began writing furiously.

Father,

As I am certain this letter will reach you after Calum does, it is surely no surprise to you that I have been taken captive by the dragon sympathizers.

What surprises me, however, is the unwavering kindness that I have been shown by the people here and the courage that each and everyone one of them holds. I have spoken with tenderhearted men and women who have faced travesties that you could never hope to understand. While I hate that it has come to you now sending people to come fetch me like some prize, I refuse to continue to sit idly by and allow you to dictate the course of my life. I am happy where I am, and am not in need of saving. Call off the search for me, because I am not coming home. Ever.

—Adeline

Feeling satisfied that she had gotten her message across, Adeline rose from the vanity, folded the parchment neatly, and began running her fingers anxiously over the creases. She had hoped that writing the letter to her father would quell the raging emotions she felt, only to be disappointed to find that they still tightened her chest. A defeated sigh escaped her lips. Regardless of whether she felt better or not, she knew that she owed it to herself to send the letter anyway.

CHAPTER TWENTY-FOUR

R OMAN WOKE UP DREAMING that morning as memories consumed him, coming through in flashes; him pressing Adeline against the wall, making her beg for him, the way she took control, the way she came undone. Even now, the kiss of her cool satin sheets and the warmth of her body tucked gently into his drove him mad with want. He could feel himself hardening at the thought and silently cursed the Gods as a near-silent knock on Adeline's bedroom door drew him from the perfect morning. Roman considered pretending he didn't hear it, but the sleeping angel next to him called forth something primal and protective in him that he could not suppress. *No one should be at her door this early in the morning,* he thought. The only thing that could possibly be more important than getting to lie with Adeline for the rest of the day was keeping her safe.

Before he moved to stand, he gently tucked a stray chocolate wave behind her ear and pressed a soft kiss against her temple, being careful not to wake her. When he finally made it to the door, he made sure to slip out into the hallway to greet whoever it was waiting on the other side. He was met by a frantic-looking Reggie standing in the hallway, his unruly hair sticking out every which way as if he had only just rolled out of bed.

"Commander Drache. Sorry to wake you, sir. There are reports coming in from riders this morning. They say they caught sight of some men who appeared to be making their way toward the cabin. The last reports place them only about five miles outside of the ravine, heading toward the village." Reggie spoke quickly, as if expelling the words would ease him of the burden of their weight.

Any amount of bliss that still clung to him from the perfect night he had spent with Adeline immediately dissipated to make room for the fury that crept in. He knew exactly who was heading this way, and what they were after. He would sooner set the world ablaze than let them lay a finger on her.

Roman dismissed Reggie, thanking him for the information, and immediately returned to his room to ready himself. He dressed quickly in his sleeveless fighting leathers, making sure to tuck extra daggers into any open slots he could find; he would need to be heavily armed for the day he had ahead of him. Roman wasted no time in heading off to find Falrin. He needed to update him on the severity of their situation. As he stalked through the cabin, he realized just how little information he truly had—*How many of them are there? Do they have an army backing them up? How long do I have before they are here trying to take her from me?*

The last thought ignited a waking nightmare in his head. They were heading toward the cabin, which meant that if they somehow made it here before he could stop them, they would take Adeline. He needed to be sure she was not here for them to find without alerting her to what was happening, which would be no small feat.

So engrossed in formulating a plan to get Adeline away from the cabin, he nearly ran straight into Falrin. Judging by the mess of his best friend's blond bedhead and noticing he was already dressed as if ready for a fight, Roman knew the news had reached him too. Not speaking, the two of them walked to Roman's study, shutting the doors behind them as they began to devise a scheme, a plan of attack.

They were hidden away in the study for all of thirty minutes before they heard the signs of people waking for the day. Roman, knowing Adeline would be waking soon to head down to the kitchens, scribbled down a quick note and tenderly placed it next to her, where he had been less than an hour before. Though he had things to prepare, he couldn't help but stop to take her in, lying on her stomach peacefully as she slept. He allowed himself only a moment to memorize how angelic she looked before chaos ensued. The early morning sun cast a gentle light on the brown waves of her hair, which had spread across her back and frizzed at the crown from sleep. She was the picture of grace, with the soft curve of her slightly parted lips and her sleep-heavy breaths escaping through them.

Roman had seen her in many different forms during their time together, but he always found her slumbering state to be the loveliest. It tugged on his heartstrings to see how serene and calm she looked lying there, as if she was truly heaven sent. As if sensing his presence, Adeline stirred slightly, nuzzling into the mass of blankets. Roman took that as his cue to leave, though he would be lying to say that his heart did not cleave in two as he stepped out of the room, leaving her alone after the night they had spent together.

He clung to the memory of her sprawled across the bed snoring peacefully as he and Falrin quickly prepared their dragons for flight and warmed up their bodies in the training gym before leaving. It had been decided that Falrin would leave first, scope out the area and figure out what they were dealing with while Roman took Adeline to the ravine, placing her somewhere the suitors would *hopefully* never find her.

"Be safe, Fal. Do not make a move on them without me being there to back you up." Roman's voice was stern, yet endearing. Falrin was like a brother to him, one he would lay his life on the line to protect with no questions asked.

"Yes, sir," Falrin gave him a mock salute, throwing him a signature eye-roll before he mounted Raegorath and the two of them disappeared into the sunrise in a flurry of green. It was so like Falrin to make such a stupid joke at such an inappropriate time.

CHAPTER TWENTY-FIVE

FIVE DEEP BREATHS WAS all she allowed herself before she made her way out the door and down to the kitchen. If there was anything that would calm her racing mind, it would be falling into the peaceful motions of helping make sticky buns with Thistle, Milo, and Seraphina. While she made her way through the halls, her eyes scanned for someone she could entrust the letter with. She was delighted when the first man she stopped introduced himself as Reggie.

The man was tall and lanky, all skin and bones, but his eyes were full of kindness behind the wire frames of his glasses. Adeline trusted him immediately, comforted by the gentleness he carried. She explained where the letter needed to go and that it was urgent. Reggie wasted no time in turning on his heel, letter in hand, and rushing to complete the task she had assigned him. Watching him walk away, Adeline felt the anxiety creep in on her once again. She stood there in the hallway for a few minutes, trying desperately to calm her mind, before remembering where she was going.

Adeline softened immediately when she stepped foot through the kitchen doors and took in the familiar hustle and bustle of the people within. Thistle stood over the stove, his round cheeks rosy from the heat radiating off the fire, looking up as she walked in and throwing her one of those famous smiles that made his eyes crinkle at the corners. They did not speak as Adeline tied a well-loved white apron around her waist and gathered her ingredients.

Milo noticed her and his face lit up instantly as he abandoned his chopping and made a beeline straight to Adeline, wrapping his arms around her middle. Adeline ruffled the mop of red curls atop his head and murmured, "Missed you too, kid," with a soft smile.

Milo always greeted her with a childlike excitement, in an embrace of awkward limbs that had become one of her favorite parts of the day. No matter where she may come from, he never failed to treat her like she was one of his favorite people.

After a gentle prodding from Thistle, mentioning his need for the ingredients that Milo had been chopping, he pried himself off of Adeline and went back to his work. Adeline made her way over to what she had fondly begun to refer to as *her* station next to Seraphina, who did not so much as look up at her. It wasn't unusual for the quiet, dark-haired beauty, but the scowl that played on her lips was a surprise.

She must be in a mood today, too, Adeline thought to herself.

Deciding to leave Seraphina be, she fell into the motion of rolling out the dough Thistle had already prepared for her. Her mind went silent as her hands led the way, flattening the balls of dough before brushing them in butter and sprinkling them with the cinnamon mixture. It was so comfortable, so familiar, and just what she needed that morning to soothe her anger.

What she failed to realize, however, was that rather than just leaving her, the anger had bubbled to the surface and she began mumbling about everything that was plaguing her mind lately. Ramblings about *stupid men* and *egotistical dragon riders* snuck past her lips. Her thoughts had been so focused on the task of preparing the buns that she didn't notice she was speaking aloud. That is, until she looked up—her eyes scanning for a spare baking tray on which to place the rolls that were now ready to go into the oven—finding Seraphina's scowl now trained on her. Adeline stilled as her gaze met ocean eyes glaring at her in pure disgust. She was unsure how long the girl had been glowering at her, only that the sour mood that she had scented on Seraphina earlier was apparently now directed at her.

Oh, Gods.

"You know, you should really watch where you say those things. Not everyone takes so kindly to the mistreatment of their people, myself included. If that is how you truly feel, then you know where to find the door," Seraphina spat at her through gritted teeth.

What is she talking about? What did I say?

"Uh...I'm sorry. I'm not quite sure what I said that offended you so greatly," Adeline replied softly, her tone careful, calculating her next steps.

"Yeah. Right. Like I am supposed to believe that you magically *don't remember* muttering to yourself about how much you've always loathed dragons and that you don't feel like you will ever belong here. Trust me, *Princess*, I wish I could pretend as easily as you to forget you ever said you can feel yourself 'itching for the kill'."

Shit, Adeline thought to herself. It seems the thoughts she had fought so hard to bury deep within herself had all come tumbling out of her mouth the moment she lost herself in the warmth of the kitchen.

"Woah. Seraphina, I am so sorry. I didn't even realize I had been speaking aloud and I—"

Seraphina cut her off. "*Sorry?* You think *sorry* is just going to fix everything? *Sorry* doesn't mend the pain from the words you so carelessly tossed around as if they meant nothing. These *dragon sympathisers*, as you called them, are my *family*, Adeline. And they are the only family I have left, so count your lucky stars that you even have living parents to consider, loving or not. I would give anything for just one more day with mine." A small sniffle escaped her, and she quickly wiped her eyes with the back of her hand before continuing, "You need a serious reality check if you are more worried about insulting my *people* than you are realizing just how fortunate you are to have ended up in Drakmoor."

She did not stick around to hear Adeline's response. Before there was even a moment for Adeline to wipe away the shock and embarrassment that colored her cheeks, Seraphina had turned on her heel and stalked out of the kitchen.

As the door slammed shut, rattling the dishes on the shelves around the room, Adeline looked up as her gaze met Thistle's, who stared back with an apologetic but unforgiving look on his face. Adeline's heart shattered in her chest. Never had she felt such guilt as she did looking at the clear disappointment written in Thistle's features, hurt that had come from her own words. How she wished she could pluck the words straight from the air and stuff them back inside her, shoving them further down to be sure they never got out.

"Seraphina has a bit of a hot temper when it comes to people mistreating those she loves. While I am still hurt by your words, I do not believe that you deserved to face the aggression she threw at you," Thistle explained.

If there was more left of her heart to break, it would have fallen to pieces in her chest. Gods, how could she have been so careless? She had been an expert in swallowing her feelings her entire life, and she wasn't sure what had changed when she walked into the kitchen this morning.

Thistle waved a hand in dismissal, as if he could feel the guilt rolling off of her.

"Well, nevermind that. Let me make us some tea, and we can sit and talk about where those feelings you were muttering about came from."

Adeline winced.

"I am not taking no for an answer, young lady." He set about grabbing a pair of well-worn earthenware mugs and preparing their tea. He was not humming to himself the way he normally did, and a heavy weight seemed to have settled over him, but still, he moved with gentle grace throughout the kitchen. Adeline hadn't even had time to process what was going on before a hot cup of tea was pressed into her hands, tendrils of steam curling up from the darkening liquid within. The warmth of the cup against her palms had her relaxing ever so slightly.

"So, tell me what is plaguing you, dear," Thistle looked at her, his eyes soft once again.

"Um—well, where do I even start?" she asked, hoping for some guidance. Adeline was far from used to speaking of her feelings aloud, let alone for another to hear.

Well, I've already done it once today, so what's another? she thought as she steeled herself to say the hard part out loud.

"I just feel so lost lately. Everything I have known for the past eighteen years has been called into question, and I don't know which way is up anymore. All that I thought I was and wanted to be now feels so distant from who I am becoming, and I don't quite know that I like her either. I fear I have lost sight of who I am entirely, and I don't know that I will ever find her again." Adeline took a long breath, slowing herself down. "But no matter what confusion or frustration I feel about everything going on, a part of me feels at home here, and it scares the shit out of me, Thistle."

"Do you feel safe here?" he questioned.

She let the question linger in the air for a long moment, turning it over in her mind. Was she safe here? Yes, she was. Even if she had been kidnapped and brought here in the first place, since she awoke dangling over Roman's back she had not felt unsafe for even a moment. But it wasn't just Roman; her mind turned to the day she spent in the village eating, laughing, and dancing among the people of Drakmoor. The mornings she spent laughing with the three people she had begun to call her friends in the kitchens, and her heart swelled. These people, all of them, had welcomed her with open arms from the very beginning.

"I have never felt more safe and protected in my life," Adeline answered thoughtfully.

Thistle nodded gently before asking, "And are you happy here?"

This question caught her by surprise. She had not ever in her life stopped to think about her own happiness; simply doing what was expected of her was all she had ever known. Sure, she'd had moments of delight while in Scalebreak, but happiness was not quite the word for that; content was more like it. Scalebreak had made her feel *small*. She constantly had to shove down who she wanted to be to fit into the mold expected of her by her parents, her kingdom, and she realized now that she had never been happy there.

"I do not believe I had known happiness before coming here." The words were barely a whisper between them.

"Then that is all that matters, Addie. If you are protected and happy, then you can figure out the rest later. There is no timeline on finding yourself. In fact, what would life be without an eternal journey of self discovery? That is the beauty of this existence; it is always changing to make room for us to continue to grow." Thistle placed a weathered hand over hers, squeezing it in a gesture of comfort. "Give yourself some grace. Everything you thought you knew has been unraveled, and it will take time for you to find the truth, to accept it as your own."

Adeline swiped at her cheeks with her free hand, wiping away the tears that had gathered in the corners of her eyes. Thistle had spoken words she never knew she needed to hear before today, and she felt the broken pieces of herself slowly come together in her first step toward healing.

"Now, I believe you already know that you owe Seraphina an apology, as she does you, but I would first like to tell you a bit more about her story—so that you might better understand why she behaved the way she did today."

Thistle took a long sip from his mug before continuing.

"Seraphina has been in Drakmoor since she was six years old, after she was brought here by Amira herself. She had been out in the forest with her dragon, hunting for wild game for the clan when our matron found her. Amira had wandered away to relieve her full bladder, and when she returned, she found a small girl in singed clothing with a tear-stained face trembling with fear and hiding behind a tree trunk. Seraphina was terrified, attempting to disguise herself from the threat she assumed Amira's dragon to be. Amira approached the girl and asked her name and where her parents were, which only sent the small child into a fit of hysterics. She didn't think twice before she wrapped Seraphina in her cloak and held her until her tiny body stopped trembling. The girl eventually told her that her name was Seraphina and she was from Scalebreak."

Adeline could not disguise the look of shock that etched itself onto her face.

Seraphina was from Scalebreak? From my kingdom? Her stomach dropped to her feet as she turned the revelation over in her mind.

Thistle continued, "She explained to Amira that her family had been killed in a dragon attack on her village, every single one of them reduced to nothing but ashes. She had only made it out safely because she was playing out in the woods when she should not have been. Knowing that she had nowhere to go and no one to turn to for safety, Amira brought her home to Drakmoor. You can imagine how difficult it was for Seraphina to adjust to life here, among the dragons. At first, she went mute, refusing to speak to anyone. She spent years full of hate for Amira and for the creatures that had destroyed her family. It took three years before she softened to us, rarely even speaking, and imagine my surprise when her first words were spent asking *me* for a sticky bun. She has spent every day since in these kitchens. Most days she is quiet, but if you are lucky enough to earn even so much as a laugh from her, it is worth its weight in gold."

Adeline felt sorrow bury itself in her belly. She had treated Seraphina so poorly today, and after all the hurt she had faced, how hard she had to fight to even be comfortable here...Adeline felt terrible. The people of Drakmoor were even more so Seraphina's people than those of Scalebreak had been Adeline's; at least Seraphina had earned the right to call them that—*her* people. Adeline could not say the same for herself.

She lingered in the kitchen for several more minutes, apologizing to Thistle again for her earlier words and thanking him for his patience and kindness. As she made her way out of the kitchens, she had only one thing on her mind.

She owed Seraphina quite the apology.

Chapter Twenty-Six

A DELINE HAD ALL BUT run out of the kitchens. Normally, her hustle was to prepare herself to go train with Falrin, but today he was occupied elsewhere with Roman—wherever it was those two had gone off to. It was only mid-morning and already she felt emotionally exhausted, but that was not an excuse large enough to avoid finding Seraphina to apologize. She was unsure of where exactly to find Seraphina. Typically, Adeline only crossed paths with her in the kitchen or the library. Not knowing where to start, she decided she would willingly search every room of the cabin if she had to.

Much to Adeline's surprise, it had not taken much effort to search for Seraphina at all, as she practically collided with the girl as she made her way up the stairs after failing to notice Seraphina making her descent down them. She only stopped in time thanks to the abrupt "*oof*" that escaped Seraphina when she halted, ripping her from her concentration.

Adeline's eyes met the familiar blue gaze, and her stomach sank to her feet when she noticed the whisper of gray that streaked down her cheeks, the only evidence remaining that Seraphina had been crying. The two girls stood there for several moments just staring at one another, guilt and apologies written on both of their faces.

Seraphina moved first, and much to Adeline's surprise, she stepped forward and wrapped her arms around Adeline in a comforting embrace. The deep red fabric of Adeline's dress mingled with the deep blue of Seraphina's until even their skirts looked to be entangled in a hug. No words were spoken between them as they stood in the middle of the staircase, exchanging silent apologies while wrapped in each other's arms. Tears slipped down Adeline's cheeks, her guilt bubbling to the surface.

"I'm so sorry, Adeline. I never should have spoken to you the way I did earlier. While I may still have some problems with the things you said, there were definitely better ways for me to approach you," Seraphina practically whispered the words.

Adeline pulled away and placed her hands loosely on Seraphina's shoulders, leveling her gaze with the sad, blue eyes staring back at her.

"Seraphina, *I'm* sorry! I lost myself in the familiarity and comfort of the kitchens and let my subconscious thoughts slip through the cracks, perhaps because I myself was not yet ready to confront them. I did not mean any of the horrible things I said about Drakmoor or its people, and I sincerely apologize for speaking them aloud at all. I hadn't realized I'd been feeling so lost and *confused* since being here, or rather, I didn't want to face those feelings. And when Thistle told me about how you came to be here, I—I'm just so sorry."

"That's the thing though, Addie. I, of all people, should have understood that. I spent so many years here trying to sort through my feelings toward these people and their dragons. I resented everything that Drakmoor was because I couldn't understand how they could love and respect the same creatures who stole my family from me. It took me *years* to sort through those things, and here I am expecting you to have it all figured out in a matter of a few short weeks. I only hope you can forgive me for my brashness and that we can turn over a new leaf, one where maybe we could be friends?"

Seraphina lowered her gaze to the ground as if embarrassed to have even suggested it. Adeline did not give the girl the chance to regret her bravery in extending an offer of friendship and again wrapped her in a tight embrace.

"We've always been friends, Phina."

Adeline tightened her arms around Seraphina, feeling her thin body slowly relax with the words. After a long second, Seraphina squeezed back, returning the gesture as if in silent confirmation that they indeed had been friends since the moment they met.

The sadness within her calls to the broken parts of me in a way I have never known, as if calling me home, Adeline thought to herself.

Seraphina broke the embrace first, taking a minuscule step backward and casting her watery gaze toward the ground as she swiped away the wetness clinging to her cheeks. She let out an uneasy laugh.

"So, now that we've got that out of the way, I heard a certain dark and broody man was looking for you, too." She smirked as she watched the color rise to Adeline's cheeks at the mention of Roman.

"Oh, really...uh..." Adeline frantically tried to search for the right words before parting with her friend.

"Well, before I go find Ro, would you maybe want to come train with Falrin and me tomorrow? I would love to have you there and I thought maybe it would help you clear your mind." She was rambling now, feeling the heavy silence as if it was crawling down her throat, begging her to shut up. "Not that you needed help with that, I ju—"

"Yes, Addie. I would be happy to join you in your training. I only ask that you don't poke fun at me since I tend to be a tangle of awkward limbs more than the picture of grace and poise." Seraphina's face heated with the admission as if she were embarrassed.

Relief flooded Adeline's body at the acceptance, it seemed that things might be a bit strange between her and Seraphina for a little while, but this was the perfect opportunity for them to grow in their friendship as they overcame it.

Before she could give Seraphina a proper goodbye, she felt the soft, familiar tickle of shadows against her bare skin, brushing against her as if they couldn't help themselves. Adeline's breath caught in her throat at the intimacy of the touch as dark ribbons slid across the skin of her wrists and fingers in a silent promise of the very real touches that would follow later.

"Hate to interrupt, ladies, but I have need of the princess," a deep voice called out from behind Adeline.

Seraphina let a not-so-subtle smirk paint her lips as Adeline looked over her shoulder, down to where the voice was coming from, and her eyes fell upon Roman standing at the bottom of the staircase. Not that she had expected anyone else there after feeling the way he had been caressing her with his shadows before he ever spoke.

"Gods, these two are going to damn each other to hell," Seraphina muttered so quietly that Adeline had barely caught the words.

"Well, I better get back to the kitchens; wouldn't want Thistle to have to pick up *both* of our slack!" She said it so quickly that Adeline barely had time to register being spoken to before Seraphina was running down the stairs, her deep blue skirts gathered in her hands so they would not trip her.

She let out a deep sigh, trying to appear as annoyed as she could muster, which unfortunately for her was not nearly enough in the presence of Roman Drache. Adeline made a show of turning around slowly; *he can wait.*

"And what exactly was so important that you needed to interrupt?" It took all the energy she had to coat her words in venom as she spat them at him. Much to her dismay, Roman smirked back up at her, and she couldn't stop her body from softening at the sight. A smile from him was like being bathed in sunlight, ironic given that darkness was the very thing he harnessed.

"Well, Sunshine, I am so glad you asked. *I,* the ever so kind man that I am, have decided to take you...wait for it...to see the dragons." The smile clung to his face as he spoke, only now it seemed to be in amusement with himself.

There was no stopping her jaw in its path to the floor as she stood in a state of open-mouthed shock at the declaration. She had been convinced it would take ages, possibly years, before he would fully trust her around any dragons other than Aurelius and Raegorath. It was not lost on her how much trust it had taken for him to allow her to even be near those two magnificent beasts, and now he was *willingly* taking her to go see more dragons? Adeline felt like she must be dreaming.

"Close your mouth, Princess." His words were somehow laced with desire despite the non-sensual nature of their conversation, and it made goosebumps prickle up across her skin. It was a dangerous game they played with one another. They'd yet to speak to each other about the night they had shared or her waking up alone. Yet, here they were, falling into the old habit of poking fun at one another—bordering on verbal foreplay for anyone to overhear.

She obeyed, mentally cursing at herself for giving in so easily to him. He made her weak, and lately she wasn't even sure if being weak was a bad thing.

"Are you just gonna stand there or..." Roman drew out the last word, stretching it out between them until she finally seemed to shake from her stupor. It was her turn to toy with him now.

"Unfortunately, Shadow, a princess cannot descend a staircase without being bowed to."

"Oh, is that so?" Again his words were heavy, his eyes hooded in lust as they greedily swept over her figure.

That was all the protesting he did before he hinged at the waist and leaned his impressive upper body forward in a bow. He even went as far as to extend a calloused hand in waiting, inviting her delicate one to meet his grasp.

Though he was leaning forward, Roman seemed unable to help himself as his gaze lingered on her figure, watching her descend the stairs. Even in what would be considered a simple dress, he looked at her as if she was breathtaking. Adeline had almost chosen a different outfit that morning, shying away from the blood-red color that only served as a reminder of her family name, but something in her had resisted—a fact she now found herself grateful for thanks to the way Roman eyed her hungrily. He started to speak, but stopped before a single sound could escape him, as if there were no words to adequately capture what he wanted to say to her.

The cool kiss of Roman's shadows met the barely exposed skin on her shins when she stepped down, and she smiled. Adeline wasn't entirely convinced anymore that Roman had complete control over them. She was starting to believe them to be more of a sentient extension of him than something he commanded.

The thought was jostled from her as the rope of shadows that had been weaving in and out of her legs, as if playing with her, went suddenly taut in front of her. Not having enough time to react, Adeline let out a squeal as she jolted, losing her footing on the stairs and falling forward. The deep-red skirts of her dress fanned out behind her, and for a brief moment, she felt as if she was flying down the staircase rather than tripping. She squeezed her eyes shut tightly as if that would ease the hurt that was inevitably going to meet her at the bottom.

Roman jumped into action, immediately running up the few stairs separating them to get to her before she could make contact with the hard wood below. Adeline felt her body make contact with something firm and was immediately confused. It was not quite as hard as she had expected the floor to be. Strong, sure arms hooked under her knees and behind her back, cradling her in a safe embrace.

Roman.

Her eyes flew open, scanning him to make sure that she had not hurt him in her oh-so-graceful fall, but she was met with a smolder.

"Careful, Princess. Wouldn't want you to hurt that pretty face of yours." He winked. Adeline wasn't sure anymore if her breathlessness was from her near-death experience with the set of stairs or the proximity to the man now cradling her against his muscled chest.

CHAPTER TWENTY-SEVEN

The wind whipped Adeline's once neatly braided hair violently around her face as she and Roman stepped outside the cabin. If it weren't for the relentless intensity of the wind, it would have been a perfect day with clear skies, but the addition of the sharp air biting their skin made her stomach lurch with fear for the coming flight.

As if knowing exactly when they were ready for him, Aurelius landed on the patch of grass just outside the cabin in a flash of gold that would make anyone's breath catch—he was the definition of magnificent. The way the sun glinted off of his golden scales made him appear to be shining with every movement he made. Even though the shine of the sun reflecting off of scales was, at times, near blinding, Adeline always found herself unable to look away from the gorgeous creature.

She was still not entirely convinced that Aurelius liked her very much at all. Night rides spent on his back with Roman's arms and shadows wrapped around her firmly, holding her tightly, were almost always interrupted by the golden dragon deciding he was going to bank left or send them into a spiral toward the forest below with no warning. It was a behavior that always resulted in a fit of laughter from Roman, and that fact alone had made Adeline withhold her protests.

A huff from Aurelius shook her from her daydream, and she couldn't help but smirk as she took note of the tendrils of smoke curling out of his nostrils and into the air around them, whisked away by the wind. He was an awfully sassy creature, as Adeline had come to learn very quickly.

Roman and Adeline moved wordlessly, not needing to speak as they fell into the very familiar steps of mounting Aurelius and taking their places in his saddle. Adeline took her seat just behind the pommel and felt her heart stutter at the thought of Roman's touch. Even though this morning had been weird, he still had the same effect on her. When she had woken that morning to find her bed cold and empty all she had craved was the warmth of his touch, but now she was unsure if it was excitement or anxiety bubbling in her chest as she anticipated the press of his body against her own. They had yet to speak of last night, and given the closed-off nature that Roman was presenting with today, she doubted that they would. The thought made her heart sink.

Roman plopped into the saddle just behind her, and she felt her breath catch as his thighs brushed the outside of her own. Every touch felt so sensual yet so tense, the atmosphere around them charged with unspoken words.

He leaned forward, his lips brushing the shell of her ear as he whispered, "Hold on tight, Princess, Aurelius is in a mood today."

When is he not? she thought to herself, bracing for takeoff.

Roman's whisper was all the warning she had before his shadows slipped over her waist and thighs, pinning her to her seat in the saddle. Each dark ribbon sent shivers through her body as they grazed her skin, and she wished that she hated the familiarity of their touch.

Aurelius lurched toward the sky, forcing Adeline to tighten her grip on the pommel as her knuckles went white. If it wasn't for the hold of Roman's shadows, she was sure she would have fallen from her seat. The unrelenting push of the wind was much worse with the added force of their ascent into the sky, and Adeline felt as if her skin was moments from peeling off her bones. The pressure did not let up as they climbed higher and higher. Adeline could feel a scream rising in her throat with the unbearable weight. Aurelius shifted suddenly, leveling out to coast just below the clouds where the unrelenting wind was little more than a gentle breeze against them.

Silence settled over them once again, but this was nothing like the comfortable quiet they had slipped into earlier. What surrounded them now was thick and taut with tension, and Adeline made no move to speak. If he wanted to pretend that last night had never happened, fine. She would pretend too—but that did not stop the heavy dread that pooled in her stomach, or the lone tear that slipped past her eyes and down her cheek at the hurt she felt.

All of the men in my life have done nothing but disappoint me, so why did I ever think he would be different? She felt stupid for falling victim to whatever game she had unintentionally become a part of.

Their trip to the cliffside, though short in distance, felt as if it took ages. Adeline spent the entire ride trying desperately to think of anything other than the man behind her. By the time they were approaching the clearing on the mountainside, her head was swimming, unspoken words and broken promises eclipsing every other thought.

Gods, if this hasn't been the most emotionally exhausting day.

Time felt as if it moved in slow motion as they made their dismount from Aurelius, Roman taking more space from her than he normally did. His behavior had shifted drastically since their encounter on the stairs. Earlier he had been his usual playful and sarcastic self, practically throwing himself onto the stairs to catch her; he was now cold and distant. It made Adeline's chest ache.

Apparently, I didn't mean nearly as much to him as I thought I did, she thought, holding back more tears as they made their way through a tangle of oak tree branches. It did not matter how broken she felt at the thought of not being good enough; she would not give him the satisfaction of seeing her cry because of it.

All thoughts of Roman's lack of interest died in her mind when they stepped between the last two trees. Long, twisted branches curved into one another overhead, the forest creating a grandiose archway to welcome people in. Adeline felt as if her heart had stopped beating in her chest as she looked down into the small cluster of buildings tucked against the rocks on one side, quaint homes lining the ravine. She was snapped out of her reverence as her eyes caught on a great orange dragon, then darted to a green, a group of reds, a blue. She blinked hard, trying to refocus her eyes. Surely she had to be miscounting. There was no way there could be *this* many dragons just tucked away here. She wasn't even sure that many dragons even *existed* anymore.

"Do you want to stand here gawking all day, or would you like to go down there?" Roman's deep voice cut through the silence like a knife. There was a hint of annoyance lacing his tone, and it made anger heat in Adeline's stomach.

She spun around, turning to find him casually leaning against the trunk of one of the trees that made up the archway, his arms crossed over his chest. Adeline wished she did not immediately notice how deliciously the fabric clung to the muscles in his arms, detailing his impressive biceps. She hated even more that he had any effect on her at all. He had chosen the route of giving her the cold shoulder, and she could do the same.

"Have somewhere more important to be?" She spat the words at him with false bravado, determined to care as little as he did.

"Matter of fact, yes, Princess, I *do* have somewhere better to be." His eyes were dark, a storm raging behind the normally bright flecks of green.

With that, he pushed off the tree and began stalking down the dirt footpath and into the ravine, seemingly choosing that he would not dedicate any further energy into conversing with her.

Adeline trailed him at a distance, more than annoyed to be forced to follow him after that exchange. If nothing else, she had no idea where she was going, and there was more than one dragon lurking around. The sight of his ass in those sinfully tight pants was a bit of a consolation, but she would never give him the satisfaction of knowing that. When they were only a few steps from the valley, Adeline's eye was caught by a deep red dragon breaking through the clouds overhead, seemingly about to make its landing in a clearing just off to the side of the ravine. Even from a distance, the dragon was the most intimidating she had ever seen; its yellow eyes narrow and full of disdain as if angry at everything around it for simply existing. It seemed to be stalking every breathing creature in the clearing, watching its prey. A shiver snuck its way down Adeline's spine and she made a mental note not to get on the bad side of the blood-red dragon and whomever its rider was. Brows knit together in confusion, she watched as the creature expertly lowered itself onto the earth with a huff.

If the dragons can land so close to the others, to the village here, why did Aurelius drop us off so far from here? And why is he not down with the other dragons…mingling? Or doing whatever it is that dragons do with one another. She realized she truly had no idea what it was the dragons did when they weren't flying.

She mulled over the thought as she kept walking, following Roman deeper and deeper into the cluster of buildings until they were just outside of any structures, and into the clearing. Adeline kept her focus on her feet, avoiding both the brooding man ahead of her and any stray roots in her path—a decision she quickly came to regret when she felt her face connect with the hard, solid muscle of Roman's back. She let out a soft "*oof.*" Apparently, he had stopped only a moment before, and she had failed to notice. Her cheeks heated in embarrassment, and she took a quick step back, hoping that Roman would fill the silence with his usual sarcasm. Disappointment and jealousy curled in on her when instead, the first word that left his lips was another woman's name.

"Xandria."

"Ro!" The woman threw her arms around Roman's neck and pulled him into a tight embrace. There was something intimate about the way his name rolled off of the woman's tongue, and it took all of Adeline's self-control not to lunge at this woman and strangle her. If her anger with him earlier had been hot, then the feeling that bubbled in her now was better described as an inferno. As Xandria pulled herself off of Roman, Adeline got a better look at her and immediately wished she hadn't.

She was around the same height as Adeline, but that was where their similarities ended. Where Adeline was muscular and lean, Xandria was slim in all the right places yet filled out her clothes as if they had been made specifically to fit her every curve. Long blonde hair, so bright it was almost devoid of pigment altogether, coiled into tight curls that cascaded down her back. Her eyes, a deep forest green, were perfectly accented by full, black lashes that curled up neatly at the corners. A smattering of freckles played across the bridge of her nose, fading across her cheeks. Xandria was fucking breathtaking, and that fact alone drove Adeline into a rage.

"So, Ro, what brings you down to the nesting grounds? We haven't seen you around here in months!" Xandria questioned playfully, her every word sultry and flirtatious, dripping with desire.

"You know Aurelius doesn't like it down here, Dria."

Dria. The familiarity between the two of them made Adeline sick to her stomach.

How could I have been so stupid? So naïve. He is in love with Xandria. It was never going to be me. She needed to get out of here.

Adeline's blood boiled beneath her skin, jealousy and rage consuming her wholly. She could no longer hear anything other than the thundering of her heart in her ears. Half-moons formed on her palms as she clenched her fists so tightly that her knuckles turned white and red clouded her vision.

"And who is this?" Xandria threw her a half-hearted sideways glance full of disinterest, and Adeline was not entirely convinced that she cared who she was at all.

"This is Adeline. She's, uh...." he hesitated, as if unsure what title to give her, "new to Drakmoor and has shown an interest in the dragons." Roman's eyes found hers, searching her face for something.

Adeline was not sure what he hoped to find there, but did not fail to notice the edge of disappointment that momentarily flickered in his eyes. She took a deep breath, steeling herself against the emotions she couldn't sort through until later. She swallowed her anger and plastered on a fake smile. Her entire life had been about playing pretend; it was one thing she was far too good at.

"It's nice to meet you." Her words were stiff, but polite, given her feelings toward the woman.

"I was actually hoping that you would show her around a bit, I have some business to attend to." Roman did not give Xandria a chance to respond before he was walking away from the women, leaving them standing together in a heavy silence.

I am going to kick his ass for this later.

Chapter Twenty-Eight

A FTER SEVERAL HOURS TOGETHER, it was clear to Adeline that Xandria did not like her at all, not even enough to fake it. Every bit of kindness had been sapped out of the woman as soon as Roman walked away and now she was very clearly disinterested. Adeline assumed Xandria still wanted to appease Roman, since she showed her around the ravine and explained that it was the dragon's nesting place.

This is where they came when they were not with their riders. This was their home, and frankly, it was stunning. The buildings, which were few and far between, Adeline learned were actually shops. They sold dragonscale armor, weapons, saddles, everything a dragon rider would need, all made from shed dragon scales. Everyone else that they had come in contact with had been much more friendly than Xandria, even so kind as to offer Adeline their services, should she ever need them. Much like the village she had come to fall in love with, this place was cozy and felt strangely like *home,* a word she felt like she was coming to know more and more about every day.

By the time they finally made their way through the shops and over to the cluster of dragons that were nestled in the open land, Adeline was sure that she was one word away from biting Xandria's head off. It was near impossible for her to keep her composure around the woman who had a very clear attitude problem, and she was not entirely sure that the Gods weren't testing her when they left her with *'Dria.'*

Without even being spoken aloud, the nickname made her saliva turn sour. There was obviously history between the two of them if Roman had felt comfortable enough to award her a nickname the way he had Adeline.

"So, how do you and *Ro* know each other?" Adeline finally threw the words she had been holding carefully inside into the space between them, immediately cursing herself for letting the question free.

Xandria stopped walking and stared at her, cocking an eyebrow inquisitively. They stood there, staring each other down for what felt like several minutes. If looks could kill, the ones being so carelessly cast between the women would be lethal. It was Xandria that finally broke the heavy silence with a sharp laugh.

"Jealous, are we? If you must know, *Ro* and I grew up together." She spat the words at Adeline with contempt, as if she found her unworthy of the answer but gave it anyway.

"Ah." It was all Adeline could manage in response, feeling herself deflate as the words hit their mark.

Xandria's green eyes lit up with mischief momentarily before she continued, "You know," she drew the words out, "Roman was my first kiss."

Adeline felt her heart plummet into her stomach. *Roman was her first kiss. No wonder they're so familiar with one another.* Envy was all she could feel as the confession sunk in, playing over and over in her mind as if stuck on repeat. *He was her first kiss. Her first. Had she been his first too?*

"I mean, if you ask anyone around here," she gestured to the buildings now behind them, "Roman and I are practically meant for each other. Our mothers have been planning our wedding since we were in diapers," Xandria's words were salt in the already festering wound. *Amira approved of Xandria? Worse, she wants her son to marry her?*

Adeline felt as if she was going to be sick to her stomach, but she refused to give Xandria the reaction she so clearly wanted from her. Swallowing her ever-growing jealousy and anger, a habit she was getting much too comfortable with lately, she took a breath to regain her composure before speaking again.

"Is that so?" Adeline painted a smirk across her face and looked right at Xandria. "I suppose that means it is *you* who I should thank for how good he is with his tongue then?" She finished with a wink, watching with delight as Xandria's pretty face contorted with unfiltered rage.

Though she still felt immense envy, Adeline's face was the picture of composed arrogance as she let out a little laugh and walked past Xandria, who stood with her mouth slightly agape in shock. Soft billows of dust curled around Adeline's boots with each step and she paid them extra attention, trying to divert her focus to anything but the feelings that she did not have the time to feel. She refused to let anyone see her as weak or less than, like the way they had in the castle. Here, she would be calm and collected, even if it killed her to do so.

The open field came into view, and suddenly Adeline no longer felt as though she needed to focus all her attention on shoving her emotions down, instead finding herself unsure where to let her eyes wander first. Everywhere she looked there were more dragons, and with each one she counted, her heartbeat quickened, though it wasn't clear to her if her body's response was in awe or fear.

Adeline was not entirely sure how she felt about coming face to face with so many of them at once; she had only just barely grown accustomed to being around Aurelius and Raegorath. She had never even seen more than two dragons together at any given time. Until today, she wasn't entirely sure how many of the great creatures still lived after the centuries spent at war with Scalebreak. Her heart broke at the thought. Every moment she spent away from Scalebreak, Adeline questioned what had been real and what was simply ingrained in her as truth. The longer she was among the dragon riders, the less she was sure she ever wanted to go back to the kingdom she had once loved and fiercely protected. Quietly, she wondered which of these dragons was bonded with Seraphina and if she would ever get the pleasure of meeting the creature. In her time spent in the clan, she had still yet to learn if any of her other friends carried power from their bonded dragons. Though she had been slowly weaseling her way into the hearts of many people in Drakmoor, many of them still held their guards up when it came to their dragons, and Adeline could not blame them for doing so.

A flicker of silver flitted across her line of sight, drawing her from her daze. Sure she had to be mistaken; her blue eyes darted to and fro in search of whatever it was that created the metallic glint she had seen. *It must have been a blade. It can't be-*

Her jaw dropped when her eyes landed on the very thing she had refused to believe was truly there. Blinking hard, she tried to refocus her sight, sure that the midnight-black eyes staring back at her must be her mind playing tricks. No matter how many times she tried to shake herself from the daydream, the silver dragon still eyed her curiously from across the rolling green field that separated them.

Adeline was fully enraptured in the silver beast, its reflective scales casting the space between them in the shimmering gold light of the day and the earthy green tones of the surrounding forest. She felt the creature call to her before her mind could catch up, and her body moved on its own accord in a beeline path toward the dragon. Their gazes stayed locked, Adeline afraid that if she looked away, it might disappear altogether.

The only sound that filled her ears as she moved was the soft, melodic hum of a tune that felt so eerily *familiar*, as if she had heard it in a far-off dream. The music wafted through the valley, and Adeline could all but see the notes curving up and around the other dragons as it moved to her. It seemed to pull taut, like a thread, as it dragged her closer to the source; the dragon. A smile melted into the curve of her lips as she got closer, something in her certain that she had known this creature her entire life—as if she was being called *home*.

She had made it halfway across the expanse of grass, standing just next to a cluster of red dragons. Adeline felt her body hesitate with the next step, not understanding what was to blame for the sudden urge to stop.

"Adeline!" Xandria's voice cut through the symphony that had enveloped her in a daze. She felt slender fingers wrap around her bicep, pulling her backward.

The abruptness of the movement brought her back to the present, but it took her a moment to regain her sense of direction. Adeline shook her head, trying to clear the fog away so that she could figure out why Xandria had so frantically yelled her name and how she had reached her so quickly.

"Wha—" Adeline finally started.

"I don't know what happened. You were staring off into the distance one second and the next you were marching your ass toward Synacthdris like you had a death wish. If I can give you *any* advice, it is to stay the hell away from the silver dragon. Syn hasn't borne a rider for over a century, and that is *not* by coincidence." Xandria sounded breathless, as though she had run across the length of the field to get to Adeline, to stop her. It struck Adeline as odd, that after being so cold to her, Xandria had not hesitated to run after her.

Confusion swam in her mind as she tried to make sense of what the hell had just happened. *Silver Dragon. There is a silver dragon here.*

Adeline had spent her entire life being taught that silver dragons were both nearly extinct and the most deadly to encounter; they were to be avoided at all costs. If it weren't for Xandria's warning just a moment before, she was not entirely sure that she wouldn't have walked headfirst into that danger. *At least not everything I grew up knowing was a complete lie,* she thought to herself, though it did not bring her much comfort at all.

If the silver creatures truly were as ruthless as they were made out to be, why had she felt so *at home* the closer she had gotten? Why had it called to her like a long-lost friend? A missing piece of herself? As was becoming her new normal, Adeline found that she had more questions than answers, but nothing could deny the way her heart still yearned desperately to get nearer the silver beast. As Xandria tugged her away, each step drawing them further from the curious dragon, everything inside of her felt so painfully empty.

She had been so focused on trying to understand what had just happened that Adeline *almost* did not notice the woman standing in the distance, watching her and Xandria approach. She was too far out to make out too many details of her face, but the closer they got to her, the more the unmistakable blonde curls began to take form. The woman looked far too similar to Xandria to be a coincidence.

"Um, do you have a twin or something?" Adeline asked, unable to tame the curiosity.

Xandria nearly doubled over with laughter in response.

"A twin? Gods, you are hopeless. No, I have the ability to clone myself. It is one of the most rare forms of power that a rider can get. I am one of only two living riders known to be able to do it," she finally responded after her laughter died down.

"There's more than *one* of you? Gods help us all."

CHAPTER TWENTY-NINE

R OMAN HAD GONE BACK inside earlier just in time to witness the tail end of an apology between Seraphina and Adeline. Deciding not to pry about what had prompted the exchange, he had whisked Adeline away as fast as he could. He had to get her out of the cabin soon.

It had just been the Gods smiling in both his favor and demise when Xandria had been in the ravine, so eager to insert herself into the situation. Adeline was sure to be furious with him for it later, but Xandria was the perfect person to distract her while he went to stop the so-called suitors. Roman had all but sprinted away when he had delivered the news that they would be spending the day together, as if trying to outrun a soon-to-detonate bomb.

Aurelius had been waiting for him to return and his body hummed with nervous excitement as he mounted the gold dragon and they made their assent—hanging lower in the sky than normal so that Roman could scope out the land below for Falrin and Raegorath, who would be waiting with a report. His heart flooded with relief as he spotted a flicker of green motion below, and they made their way to meet them, knowing even if he had been annoyed, Falrin had heeded his request to wait for him.

Few words were exchanged once they landed. Falrin told him that there were only three men, all seemingly ill-prepared for a true battle, and that they were only about a half a mile away. A devilish smirk turned up the corner of Roman's mouth as the excitement built—he was about to go suitor hunting.

Darkness enveloped Roman, crawling up his limbs and wrapping around him like the embrace of a friend, and he couldn't help the menacing grin that spread across his lips as he moved, one with the shadows. Even at midday with the sun high in the sky, he had no trouble cloaking himself in darkness, sticking to the naturally shaded patches of earth. To the untrained eye, he was practically invisible, a ghost in the trees. Every inch of shadow on the forest floor was simply an extension of him, his to command at will.

He'd been vague with Xandria and Adeline about where he was going, stating only that he had business to attend to, though now he felt guilty for doing so. Adeline had seemed so hurt by him today, and even though his cold nature had been calculated, his chest still panged at how wrong it felt. His distant persona had been intentional, because he needed her to focus on anything other than what he might be doing, even if the thing she was focusing on happened to be her seething anger for him. His heart ached, but right now, his focus needed to be honed in on the men he could hear approaching in the distance. Tucking himself behind a nearby tree, he listened intently to the chatter that grew nearer.

"I can't wait to get my hands on the royal *bitch* and make her pay for forcing us to come out here and find her." The voice was squirrely and Roman cringed as it rang in his ears.

"Not if I get my hands on her first, *Blake*. She might be a royal pain in the ass, but she will make for quite the arm candy." This statement was followed by chuckles from all three men, and Roman felt his blood boil.

"If Thorian is making us go to so much trouble to find her, her innocence had better be intact when we get our hands on her."

The words ignited a fury unlike anything Roman had ever felt before. Anger seared him like a burning flame, burrowing itself in his chest. He could not stop himself from stepping out from behind the tree, walking with a confident swagger as he flipped his dagger twice and caught it in a calloused hand.

"Actually gentlemen, you will not be laying a finger on the princess." He smirked as the trio stopped walking, terror creeping into their gazes as they assessed the situation they'd walked right into.

Looking at the group of them now, Roman had to bite back a laugh at the thought of Addie even so much as entertaining any of these men. Before him stood a too thin, balding man, a man with a disgustingly large nose and hair that seemed devoid of color entirely, and a red haired man who seemed to be corded with muscle across his entire body. For the life of him, Roman could not figure out what the handsome redhead was doing with the other two suitors, though he suspected that they had pleaded with him to come along as the muscle of their operation. The laugh he had held back escaped him in an almost menacing chuckle as he thought of Adeline marrying one of them. He knew she had put up a fight in Scalebreak, making all of them exceedingly frustrated with her, and pride bloomed in his chest at the thought.

"And just who exactly do you think you are? Do you know who you are talking t—"

"Silverdawn, Blake, Fike," Roman pointed at each man as he announced their names. "I know exactly who you are, though I suppose no one around here will recognize those names in history once I am done with you. You lot seem awfully," he lifted his dagger, pretending to inspect its blade in disinterest, "*forgettable.*"

He'd spoken only a single sentence, and the chorus of offended stammering had already begun. Roman rolled his eyes; these men were so predictable it was disappointing. He took a breath, letting them stammer like idiots for another moment, before moving. His shadows curled around the group, not that they noticed—too busy trying to defend their pride. Dark ribbons wrapped around their waists and with a whip of wind from behind him, courtesy of Falrin, the three men were thrown into the air, their bodies bound by dark ribbons of shadow and suspended from an overhead branch.

The stammering promptly stopped, replaced instead by terrified whimpers, and Roman let out a low laugh as he noticed a wet stain spreading across the front of Anthony Blake's trousers. The bloke had pissed himself.

Unfortunately for Blake, their visible fear only made Roman's sinister side snap into place, his eyes darkening. He let his shadows lower the man, now trembling, to the forest floor. Blake didn't bother to stand; he simply cowered away from Roman, curling in on himself until he lay in a ball of awkward limbs in the dirt at Roman's feet.

"P-p-please don't kill me," Anthony Blake pleaded.

"Oh, I won't." Roman paused, watching as relief washed over the man on the floor. "I'm leaving you to Falrin." As soon as the words left his lips, Blake began sobbing, pleading for his life once more.

Falrin moved quickly, one with the wind. In the blink of an eye, he had his hand wrapped around Anthony Blake's scrawny neck, hauling him into the air and staring at the man with disgust in his eyes.

"You're going to regret ever so much as *speaking* Adeline Ambrose's name, an honor you did not earn."

Roman watched proudly as Falrin defended the princess before finally turning toward the other two men, still suspended from the tree. He did not speak as his shadows loosened on Feron Fike, the tall, muscular man landing with a *thud* as his pristine leather boots kissed the earth. Green eyes narrowed on Roman, and the man wasted no time in charging at him, freeing a blade from his belt as he ran.

With nothing but a flick of his wrist, Roman's shadows reached out and snapped the blade from Feron's grasp. He watched in delight as it flew through the air wildly before getting lodged in the trunk of a nearby tree. Shock colored Fike's features, but he continued to run toward Roman. *One, two, three.* Roman counted the seconds that passed, waiting for the perfect time to strike. On three he lunged forward, hinging at the waist as he grabbed Feron at the hips and threw him over his shoulder. He threw his own body backward with the motion, landing on top of the man and knocking the wind from him. Roman moved quickly, his shadows pinning Fike to the earth as he pressed the sharp tip of his dagger into the man's throat.

"Adeline is *not* just arm candy for you to pine after. She is a force to be *reckoned* with, and you should count your lucky stars that you're on the other end of my blade and not hers."

Roman sliced with his dagger, watching as the light left Feron's eyes and his body went limp. He was off the man in an instant, barely taking note of the now purple face of Anthony Blake as he lay slumped against a tree. It seemed that Falrin had already tired of the man and wasted no time in handing him into the waiting arms of death.

Roman had decided that Silverdawn's death would be anything but quick after the disgusting remark he had made about Adeline's *innocence,* and it seemed Falrin had the same mindset, as he was already on the man and raining down blows. Silverdawn already had a split lip, blood leaking down his chin, and a black eye by the time Roman reached them, but it wasn't enough punishment for his heinous thoughts.

"He's mine, Fal."

Roman stepped forward as he let his words hang in the air, giving Falrin a few moments to get some more blows in before he stepped away. He let go of his hold on Jared's shirt, and the man dropped like a sack of potatoes to the dirt. As Roman took slow, measured steps in his direction, Jared Silverdawn stood from the ground. Glancing between the two men, his eyes filled with fear. He somehow managed to hold a dagger in his trembling left hand, not backing down.

Roman, tired of the foreplay and ready to put an end to the man, was on him in a breath. He kicked Silverdawn's feet out from under him and threw his body to the ground. His back thudded against the earth as he let out a loud exhale, bringing a smirk to Roman's lips. The momentary distraction of his mirth allowed Silverdawn to move quickly in retaliation, with Roman not expecting his speed.

It seemed he had calculated Roman's movements and took the chance to slice with his dagger, cutting a slash into the skin of Roman's chest just over his ribs. He winced in pain, but did not let it distract him as Silverdawn had hoped it would. Instead, Roman grabbed the sides of Jared's head tightly, let out an animalistic grunt, and slammed it forcefully into the ground.

"Rot in hell, you perverted fuck," Roman spat at him through gritted teeth.

He threw punch after punch at Silverdawn's face, not reacting as the man landed a few of his own. Roman could feel blood leaking from his own split lip now, but he didn't care. His body seemed to move on its own as he continued swinging his fists, curses and obscenities escaping his lips with each blow at the man beneath him until he stopped moving altogether.

It wasn't until he was sure the man was dead that Roman stood, wiping the blood from his lip with the back of his hand as he grinned devilishly at Falrin, who had a grin of his own already playing on his lips. The pair of them were quite the sight covered in blood, both their own and the suitors', and they were drunk on it.

"You know Addie is gonna kick your ass when she finds out you hid her away with your ex-girlfriend while you came out here to fight her battles for her, right?" Falrin said with a chuckle, seeming to find Roman's impending demise comical.

Roman's only response was his shadows snaking out and kicking Falrin's feet out from under him, resulting in him falling onto his backside in the dirt. The two of them doubled over in laughter at the absurdity of everything that had just happened in the forest, letting themselves delight in the joy before Adeline surely berated them for keeping her in the dark.

CHAPTER THIRTY

B Y THE TIME ADELINE had made it to the cabin on the back of
the terrifying red dragon she'd spotted earlier that day, the one she
had come to learn was Xandria's, she felt so tired she thought she might
collapse before she made it to her bed. The thought alone was enough to
have her body sagging in relief as she dismounted Cidynth, though she
still watched her back in fear that the dragon might change its mind and
choose to eat her after all. Cidynth seemed to hate Adeline as much as
Xandria did, which was absolutely no surprise to her.

As her boots thumped into the dirt, she looked up at the glowing
windows of the cabin, only a few yards in front of her, and felt tears well
up in her eyes. *Home.* She was *home.* A tear rolled down her cheek, but
she did not give Xandria the satisfaction of seeing her cry. Instead, she
walked as fast as her tired feet could carry her until she met the wood of

the front steps. It took all her strength to keep from weeping there, her every bone aching as the exhausting emotions of the day caught up with her. It was a miracle she had made it this far without releasing the tears that had hung heavily behind her eyes, threatening to fall since she and Seraphina had fought in the kitchens that morning.

She was almost there, almost to her room. She just had to make it a bit further and then she could rest her body and her heart. Adeline felt made of lead as she took the stairs up to her bedroom. *Just a bit further,* she kept reminding herself with each step, and when her fingers finally closed around the cold metal of the doorknob to her bedroom; she felt the tears she had been fighting begin to silently fall. Adeline made quick work of shutting the door behind her, letting a sob escape her as the latch finally closed with a *click*.

She had been thinking all afternoon that as soon as she laid eyes on Roman she was going to give him a piece of her mind for leaving her with Xandria, for being so cold with her, for breaking her heart and acting as if she meant nothing to him, but when her eyes caught on him standing in the middle of her bedroom, she felt a cold sense of dread. Roman crossed the room and was on her in an instant, her back meeting the wood of the door as he pressed himself against her.

"Addie? Who hurt you, Princess? Who made you cry like this?" His hand cupped her chin, his fingers twining with her hair as he stared into her eyes, and she let out a harsh, clipped laugh.

"*You* did, Roman." Her words were laced with venom as she spat them at him.

"I? Ad—" He dropped his hand from her face, shaking his head as if in disbelief.

"No, *I* get to talk right now, *not* you," she pressed her pointed finger into his hard chest and took a breath, trying to calm the tears that now flowed freely. This conversation had come far sooner than she had been prepared for.

"We shared what *I* thought was a beautiful night together last night. I gave you *all* of me, every piece of me that I have been afraid to bare for anyone I *gave to you, Roman.* And today? Today, you have barely looked at me. You have treated me like it was nothing more than just one night. Was it all a mistake to you? Was I just the most readily available to satiate your desires? Gods know you could have gone and found *Dria* to get you off in a meaningless *fuck* if you wanted. Did it even fucking matter to you, Roman?"

He reached a hand up and swiped away the tears falling from her blue eyes, but something behind his green ones seemed to shatter as he stared down at her.

"Did it matter to me?" He grabbed her chin, forcing her eyes to his. "Princess, your mouth on mine is the only Gods-damned thing I could think about today, the only thing that I think about *every* day, even before I ever touched you. The feeling of your skin on mine, your breath mingling with my own, every lingering touch has consumed my mind, my every *breath* today. I can't get you out of my head, and frankly I don't *want* to, Adeline. *Nothing* about the way I touched you last night was a mistake, nor will it ever be. I will worship at the altar of your body for the rest of my life, even if only in my mind." He leaned down, only a breath above her mouth now. "But I will not kiss you again, will not *touch* you again, until I am sure that you want it, Angel."

As if the words made him realize their close proximity, he took a step back, raking his hands through his thick, brown hair, now matted with blood. *Blood. Is he hurt?* Adeline sucked in a sharp breath as she took him in, dark blood coating his skin and crusting his clothes. The realization drew her from the moment and immediately stopped her flow of tears.

She closed the space between them and began intently inspecting him, trying to find the source of the blood.

"Are you hurt, Shadow?" she frowned as her eyes landed on the gash across his ribs. Taking inventory of the blood he was covered in, she no longer cared about her own hurt.

"Just some scrapes and bruises. Most of the blood isn't even my own." He met her eyes. "I'm okay, Princess."

Relief flooded her body as the words soaked in, quickly followed by white hot rage. She had a feeling she knew where he had gone, and there were not many things that could've landed him in such a state. There had been murmurs around the cabin for days about a group of men making their way here, seemingly on the hunt for someone. Adeline had dismissed them as rumors, sure that Roman or Falrin would have told her if that was the truth. Clearly she had been wrong.

"Good, because I am going to kick your *ass* for not keeping me informed that there were *suitors* on their way here to attempt to kidnap me and take me back to Scalebreak! What the hell, Roman! I can handle myself, and at the very least I deserve to know what's going on! Why do you underestimate me? Why does *everyone* underestimate me?!" She was jamming her finger into his sternum again, backing him against the wall while he raised his hands in defeat.

"Woah there, Princess, easy! I do *not* underestimate you. I am fully aware that you are formidable all on your own, but as someone who loves you—"

Even while he was still speaking, the words slammed into Adeline like a wall. *Love. He loves me?*

"—I don't want you to *have* to hold your own anymore. I need to protect you, Addie. Everything within me *commands* me to protect you."

"If you truly," she paused, unsure what word to use next, "*care* about me, then you would *include* me in decisions. Especially when they concern *me!* I want to be a *team,* Roman, and we can't do that if you are constantly leaving me confused and uninformed."

Roman hung his head in disappointment, and she knew her words had hit their mark.

"You're right, Princess. I'm so sorry I hurt you." Roman looked up at her with sadness written all over his face.

"I'll forgive you, Shadow," Adeline stepped forward and wrapped her arms around him, pulling him into a tight embrace. She was exhausted, and if she was being honest with herself she craved his touch. He nuzzled his head into her hair, tightening his arms on her as if he was scared she might slip away altogether.

Adeline pulled back slightly. "I do not, however, forgive you for leaving me with Xandria today. That woman is awful. I don't know what you ever saw in her."

Roman chuckled, pulling her back into his chest before he spoke.

"I have a feeling you may *never* forgive me for that. For the record, Xandria has never been anything more than a friend to me. It was our mothers' friendship that clouded their sanity when they dreamt of setting us up as adults, though my mother gave up on the idea when she saw how much I detested their plans."

"But, she said you were her first kiss?" Adeline wished she could take the words back. She cursed herself for sounding so jealous.

"She said that?" He barked out a laugh. "Addie, she kissed *me* when we were all of seven years old. I didn't even know what she was doing before it was over. I hardly think that counts as a kiss." Relief flooded her body with his words. "In fact, Princess." He tilted her eyes up to meet his own. "*No kisses* before you meant anything at all. They could never compare." He practically whispered the words to her.

That admission alone had her standing on her tiptoes and pressing her lips gently to him. "And don't you forget it, Shadow." She winked at him.

"Wouldn't dream of it, Princess." He kissed the top of her head. "Wouldn't dream of it."

"On the note of that nasty woman, she showed me today that she has the ability to *clone* herself. Did you not find it important to tell me that the soulless bitch could create *several* soulless bitches? Just when I thought she couldn't get any worse," Adeline joked.

"Showed you? Xandria hasn't had control over her clones for years. I am truly shocked that she even had the strength to summon one in the first place."

"Unsurprisingly, she failed to mention that detail, but she did brag about how she was one of only two riders with that magic." She rolled her eyes.

"Easy, Princess. Xandria is just jealous of you, as she should be." Roman chuckled, tucking her head under his chin.

They stood there embracing one another for several minutes, soaking in the feeling of each other's warmth.

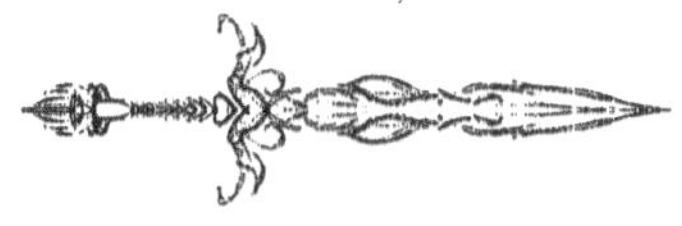

When Adeline had begun to slouch into his body, clearly exhausted, Roman scooped her up—his arms hooking under her knees as he cradled her—carrying her to the mattress before gently laying her down. He dropped to his knees on the side of the bed and began making quick work of pulling the boots off of her aching feet, taking a moment to massage their soles. Continuing on, he peeled her clothes off, admiring the curves of her naked body for only a second before pulling her back into his arms, showering her in kisses as he did. Her giggles filled the room, and it was the most angelic sound he had ever heard.

Roman left her there for just a moment, slipping into the bathroom to fill the tub. He had been desperate to relive the tender moments they had spent washing each other the night before, and being covered in the blood of her enemies made the perfect excuse.

When the tub was full and steaming, he returned to Adeline, gently carrying her into the room and setting her down next to the basin. He watched hungrily as she stepped over the side and sank into the reprieve of the water. He wasted no time in following her in, taking his seat behind her and letting the hot water seep into his aching muscles, soothing them. The two of them fell into the motions of using a cloth to gently wash the day off of one another, both of them moving slowly as exhaustion crept in. As much as he was enjoying the feeling of Adeline's hands on his body, he did not hesitate to scoop her right back up once they were both properly clean, carrying her out of the draining tub.

Roman used a plush white towel to dry both of them off before he lifted Adeline back into his arms, carrying her to the bed. There was still so much he had to tell her, but it could wait until tomorrow because right now she needed to rest. Rather than speaking, he lowered Adeline gently into the bed and crawled beneath the sheets, curling his body around hers as he held her until sleep found them both.

Chapter Thirty-One

WARMTH FLOODED EVERY ONE of Adeline's senses as she awoke, delighted to find Roman awake and still tucked cozily into the bed beside her. A soft smile found its way onto his lips as he watched Adeline stretch, waking up her body from its slumber. Dawn was just kissing the morning sky, painting everything in a pale orange hue. They both knew that the rising sun meant that they would need to drag themselves from the comfort of the bed and each other's embrace soon, but until then, they were determined to soak up every second they spent tangled up in one another.

Roman reached up a hand and gently intertwined his fingers with Adeline's mess of brown waves. Lazily, he stroked her hair and watched in what seemed to be satisfaction as her eyelids fluttered in ecstasy with his every movement. She nuzzled her head into his touch, a silent plea for him to continue the motion, and Roman's gaze filled with adoration for the woman lying on his chest. With a chuckle still heavy with sleep, he halted the movements, for only a second, taking the time to sit up against the headboard and pull Adeline into his lap. As soon as her head settled comfortably on his chest, he resumed stroking her hair and watching her relax into him. Adeline knew her hair was still mussed with sleep, but Roman was gazing at her as if she were the most beautiful thing he had ever seen, like it was a sight he could never grow tired of—but just below the surface, just for a second, Adeline saw the flash of guilt in his eyes. Though she had forgiven him for his cold tone yesterday, it seemed he had yet to forgive himself for the way he had behaved, leaving her entirely alone after she gave herself to him. Though he had thought it necessary for ensuring her safety, leaving her had been the worst thing he could have done, and then, to add insult to injury, he had gotten so in his head and zoned into the task of finding the suitors that he had been distracted and distant, coming off as far more disinterested than he ever intended. Adeline hated that he had behaved the way he did, but knowing that he felt remorse for his actions made her less angry. Besides, with how upset he had been seeing her cry, Adeline was sure he was going to spend the rest of his life making it up to her. Maybe Roman wasn't entirely convinced that he was worthy of her, but she would spend the rest of her life *showing* him just how worthy he was.

A comfortable silence had enveloped the two of them as they lay there watching through the large window adjacent to the bed as the sun rose over the mountains.

I could live in this moment for the rest of my days and be perfectly happy, Adeline thought to herself. In her bed, wrapped in Roman's strong, safe embrace, and watching the sunrise paint the sky—she felt all the thoughts that typically buzzed through her mind uncontrollably go quiet, as if finally soothed. Adeline was sure that she had never experienced the true meaning of peace before this moment. As she glanced around the room, the question she had held in the back of her mind crept past her lips.

"Why blue? I far prefer pink."

Roman chuckled softly before speaking, "Because as soon as I caught sight of your beautiful blue eyes, they became the only color that existed. Never before meeting you had I felt so at peace with the idea of drowning, not until I looked into your blue eyes, then suddenly I was welcoming the fate. Blue makes me think of you, because you are my favorite shade of it. It only seemed fitting that your bedroom be made up in the very color that drew me to you in the first place."

He pressed another kiss into her hair as he finished explaining, and Adeline could not find the words to respond, feeling breathless as a tear slid down her face. She had never felt so *seen*.

A sharp knock drew them both out of the blissful peace that had settled around them.

"Maybe if we just stay quiet, they'll think we aren't in here," Roman whispered into the crown of Adeline's head with a smile, earning a soft giggle from her lips.

"I know you guys are in there." Falrin's tone was somehow playful even through the heavy door. "You have five seconds to acknowledge my presence on the other side of this door or I am coming in."

They knew he wasn't bluffing.

"Five, four—"

"Okay! Okay! Jeez, Fal. Give us five minutes to get dressed." Roman's reply was laced with annoyance, clearly unhappy to be disturbed once again from a blissful morning.

"Five. If it is even a second more, I am coming in there and dragging the princess out myself, even if I have to take her kicking and screaming. We have training to do, and it would be rude to keep our new student waiting."

Adeline could practically hear the smirk in his voice and silently prayed that he would behave himself today, if only for Seraphina's sake. Roman and Adeline peeled themselves out of the warm comfort of the bed, and she tried desperately to ignore the sudden chill that crept across her skin and the dull ache that had buried itself in her chest now that she was no longer pressed against him. They moved in silence, both of them pulling on their fighting leathers in preparation for the day, letting them cover their bodies like a second skin.

As she tugged her shirt over her head, Adeline was surprised to find Roman right behind her, as if waiting. Wordlessly, he leaned down and planted a kiss on the curve of her shoulder before reaching around her and grabbing the brush that sat in its place atop the vanity. Roman still did not speak, letting a comfortable silence settle around them once more as he gently brushed her hair, taming her mess of bedhead. Once he was finally satisfied with the lack of knots in her long, chocolate waves, he set the brush down and made quick work of tying her hair into a braid down her back. Adeline took note of how expertly his fingers danced with the strands of her hair and filed it away in her mind to ask him where he had learned to braid later—not wanting to ruin the last few moments they had together that morning and secretly fearing that Xandria's name might be included in his answer. He tied the ends and pressed another kiss to her skin, this time on the shell of her ear.

"I hope you're planning on handing Falrin his ass for pulling us from this perfect morning," he whispered, causing goosebumps to scatter across her skin.

Adeline's only response was a wink before she pressed herself up on her tiptoes and planted a gentle kiss on the stubble that dusted his jaw. Falrin chose that exact moment to throw open the heavy wood door and let out a groan loud enough to wake anyone who may still have been sleeping.

"Gods, you two are *insufferable*," was all he said before he stomped over to Adeline, closed his fingers around her wrist, and as promised, dragged her behind him and out of the room as a gust of his wind slammed the door shut behind them.

"You sure are in a hurry to get to the gym this morning...would that happen to have anything to do with the lovely lady awaiting our arrival?" Adeline teased. Falrin's steps faltered for only a moment before he spoke again.

"Yeah, right." His tone was dripping with sarcasm so thick that Adeline was sure it had taken an immense effort to coat the words. She giggled, knowing that training was going to be quite entertaining this morning as Falrin tugged her down the hall and out into the cool morning air.

By the time they made their way into the training gym, Seraphina had already begun stretching, likely in an attempt to pass the time as she had awaited their arrival. Seraphina, who was usually found wearing plain cotton or linen dresses, looked absolutely lethal in her current ensemble. Like Adeline and Falrin, she wore a tight-fitting pair of fighting leathers that hugged every soft curve of her body. Her long, jet-black hair was pulled into a neat four-strand braid over her shoulder, coming to a stop at her ribs where it was tied off with a thin, dark piece of blue ribbon carefully fastened into a bow. The deep blue of the ribbon accented the bright blue of her eyes just enough to draw attention to them. Adeline had thought Seraphina was pretty before, but now she saw how cunningly beautiful the woman truly was, and judging by the way Falrin hadn't looked away from her since they stepped inside, he noticed it too.

"Close your mouth, Fal, or you'll get drool on the mat." Adeline threw him a wink before making her way over to where Seraphina was now sitting in a full middle split, curving her body to one side in a deep stretch.

The two girls fell into a comfortable chatter, talking about nothing in particular, but glad for each other's presence. They spent several minutes warming up their bodies, Adeline occasionally throwing Falrin a knowing glance when she caught him staring at Seraphina, who seemed to be entirely oblivious to his gaze.

"Alright, ladies, time to get moving. Each of you grab a weapon of your choice and then you will take turns sparring with me," Falrin said with a smirk as if he couldn't wait another second to begin training.

Adeline went straight for the daggers, the weapon she had been most comfortable with even before coming to Drakmoor, feeling as if they called her to them. She slid two of them into the open slots in her pants before palming a third, letting the cool bite of the steel hone her focus. As she made her way back to the center of the mats, she noticed that Seraphina had chosen to wield a simple steel sword. An interesting choice for someone who, as far as she knew, had little to no experience with weapons at all. Adeline kept the thought to herself and simply fell into her place on the mat across from Falrin. As much as she wanted to watch him make a fool of himself with Seraphina, she was itching to pay him back for the interruption he had provided this morning.

Heavy silence hung in the air as the two of them circled one another, each waiting for the other to make the first move. After several full circles, Falrin finally lunged, aiming for her wrists in a move that, unfortunately for him, Adeline had anticipated. As he lunged, she slid out of his path and spun around, kicking her leg out right in front of his. Falrin gasped before he flew forward and collided with the mat with a *thud*, his cheeks coloring pink.

"Alright, alright, I see how it's going to be," he finally said, taking Adeline's outstretched hand and pulling her to the ground with him where the two of them collapsed into a fit of giggles.

Seraphina pushed off from the wall where she had been watching with a grin, clearly amused by the spectacle of the two of them, and helped them both to their feet before taking her place in the center of the mat. She squared up against Falrin, appearing almost giddy to spar, and he dusted his hands on his pants before crouching into his fighting stance.

"Is it always that easy to take you down? I thought you were supposed to be the teacher here?" Seraphina asked sweetly, her eyes portraying her true intentions with the question.

"Why don't you come over here and find out, Sweet Cheeks." Falrin winked, falling into her carefully laid trap. The momentary distraction of answering her question had been all she needed, and she took advantage of every second. Lunging forward, Seraphina unsheathed the sword that hung at her hip and raised it to chest level where she thrust it at Falrin. He did not react fast enough and stumbled backward in surprise as the dull, rounded tip of the training sword pressed into his chest. Again seizing the moment, Seraphina drew back only a fraction of a step before swinging the sword out between them once more, this time watching in delight as the blunt edge of the steel connected with Falrin's legs and threw them out from under his body.

Adeline stifled a giggle as she watched the look of shock that was quickly replaced with pure admiration on Falrin's face. He was looking up at Seraphina as if she had done him the kindest service of his life by knocking his ass on the mat, and she was gazing back down at him with a smirk, silently gloating.

Resheathing her sword at her side, Seraphina stepped forward, sticking out a hand to help Falrin up. He accepted, slowly scrambling to his feet, only for Seraphina to slide her leg out and bring him to the mat as soon as he was mostly upright. In a move so fast Adeline almost missed it, Seraphina flipped a surprised Falrin onto his stomach, twisting his arm behind his back.

"*That* is for calling me *Sweet Cheeks*," she said through gritted teeth, though something about it felt playful.

"I think I just fell in love with you, Sweet Cheeks," Falrin said with a love-struck gaze in Seraphina's direction.

After a long day spent training, followed by a long afternoon in the warmth of the kitchens helping to prepare dinner, Adeline heard her stomach growling eagerly as she took her seat at the table across from Roman. Falrin, Seraphina, Roman, and Amira all found their places around the table, and Adeline felt her heart swell as the space filled with conversation. These family dinners had once been her least favorite thing at the castle, but here surrounded by people she had come to love, it was slowly becoming one of her favorite parts of the day.

They all fell into a chatter as they piled their plates high with mounds of mashed potatoes, gravy, and meatballs. The pleasant aroma of the food curled into the air and wrapped around them as if in a warm embrace. Adeline locked eyes with Roman from across the table, and they softly smiled at each other.

"Don't let her fool you with the sweet facade. Phina took my ass down *seven* times while training today! She is ruthless!" Falrin's words sounded more adoring than frustrated, and Amira let out a laugh. It seemed she had noticed his sudden tenderness for Seraphina as well, and felt fond of the two of them together. Adeline let out a giggle of her own as she watched Seraphina's cheeks heat with Falrin's admission of her strength.

Conversations continued around the table as Adeline sat quietly eating, content to be listening to the happy chatter of everyone around her recounting their afternoons. It wasn't long before she found herself daydreaming, remembering the strange experience with the silver dragon in the ravine. It felt as if her chest suddenly ached with a need to be near the creature, and she was unsure how she had managed to go nearly an entire day without thinking about it. Unable to shake the intense need to find the magnificent beast again, she finally spoke.

"So, Ro. When can we go see the dragons again?" She tried to hide her desperation.

Roman lit up at the question, beaming with pride.

"Soon, Princess. Soon."

CHAPTER THIRTY-TWO

ADELINE DIDN'T KNOW WHAT she had thought Roman meant by 'soon,' so she was pleasantly surprised to find herself strapped to Aurelius' saddle the very next morning. Dark ribbons of shadow held her in her seat, tucked under Roman's chin as they flew just below the clouds. He had one muscled arm wrapped around her middle, as if securing her with his magic was not enough contact and he needed to feel their skin touching too. Roman craved her touch all the time lately, finding himself yearning for even a brush of her skin against his to get him through the day; it was like a drug. He took every chance he got to soak in the feeling of her body pressed against his, to memorize how perfectly the curves fit into the divots of his own, and these stolen moments soaring in the early morning sky were no exception to that. His eyes roved over every minute detail of the beautiful woman in front of him with such focus that he was sure he could map every strand of hair on her head if asked to do so. Every little thing about her captivated him, drawing him to her until he was drunk on the weight of her presence alone. It was lost on him how he ever managed to keep his hands off her before, because now he couldn't keep them away if he tried.

Before he knew it, they had landed and were walking hand in hand through the same arched trees she had followed him through the day before yesterday. Though he was frustrated with how quickly the flight had come to an end, Roman still found himself smiling contentedly as he threw a sidelong glance at Adeline. His gaze lowered to where their hands were joined, swinging between them. The connection had been unspoken, something that did not require a conscious effort on either part, both of them desperate for any amount of shared contact.

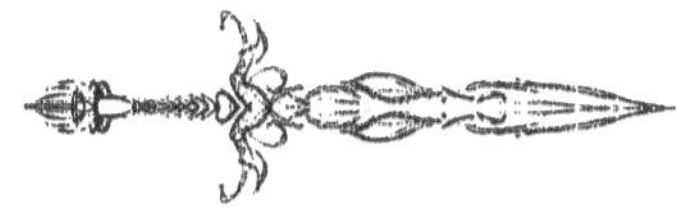

Though Adeline was practically jumping out of her skin to get to the silver dragon that had left such an impact on her, they walked leisurely, taking in the smell of the fresh mountain air curling through the valley and the familiar chatter of people as they passed between shops. The village was Adeline's favorite place in Drakmoor, its only competition being the ravine they now stood in. Looking out over the creatures she had once feared, had once slain, Adeline felt as if her heart had never been capable of holding such admiration as it did now. The great beasts were no longer a threat, but instead had become a challenge. Adeline was familiar with the aching desire to be flooded with the power that came from slaying a dragon, but the way she felt now was new. Something in her yearned to ride among them, to witness that power rather than harness it for herself.

She took a deep breath, letting the crisp morning air fill every inch of her lungs before she finally exhaled, dropping Roman's hand. Adeline took a step forward, scanning the gathering dragons in the ravine for the familiar glint of silver scales. Her blue eyes darting to and fro, she felt desperate to locate the mysterious creature that had begun to plague her mind.

"Ro! I am *so* happy to see you!" The familiar screech of Xandria's voice flooded Adeline's ears, pulling her focus away from the field of dragons as she spun on her heel, turning and finding that—much to her dismay—Xandria had wrapped herself entirely around Roman.

What quickly squashed that growing bud of anger, however, was the fact that Roman's face displayed nothing but discomfort and his hands hung by his sides as if he were afraid to touch her. A mischievous smile curled Adeline's lips as she watched with delight while Xandria continued to hug him, refusing to budge until Roman finally reached up a hand and practically peeled her off of him. It took every bit of control Adeline had in her body to hold back the laugh that had bubbled up at the uncomfortable exchange.

"Dria!" Adeline forced her voice much higher than its normal pitch as she continued, "I am *so* glad you're here! I was *so* hoping we would run into you." Her words were thick with sarcasm, and it seemed Xandria felt their sting, judging by how she winced as they hit their mark.

She blew a stray blonde curl away from her face before looking back at Adeline, leveling her green eyes at her as if sizing her up. "Oh, Adeline! I didn't realize Ro had brought company with him!"

"I imagine it must've been so hard to notice me here with your head so far up *Ro's* ass," Adeline quipped, no longer wishing to play nice, and sending Roman into a fit of laughter.

Xandria, on the other hand, did not appear to be nearly as amused as Roman. Her cheeks heated with embarrassment, and her face contorted with anger as she stammered for the witty reply that never found its way to her tongue. She waited for Roman to calm his giggling before she finally replied.

"Well. Aren't you just a *delight*."

"What can I say, Dria, play with fire and get burned," Roman said with a wink, pushing past Xandria and throwing his arm around Adeline's shoulders, guiding her with him as he walked.

"Oh! And Xandria?" Adeline looked over her shoulder at the woman, a smirk playing on her lips. "Thanks again for teaching Roman that tongue trick."

"Easy, Princess. Put the claws away, you've already got me," Roman chuckled, pressing a kiss into the top of her head. "You're somehow even sexier when you get territorial," he whispered for only her to hear as they retreated, leaving Xandria standing alone with her arms crossed in a jealous rage.

As soon as they were away from the distraction of Xandria, Adeline began scanning the surrounding field for the silver dragon once more. Her heart sunk in her chest when after several passes she did not see the creature anywhere in the ravine. Her defeat must have been apparent because Roman was watching her curiously.

"Why the long face, Princess?" He finally asked.

"I was just...looking for someone, I guess. I was hoping they would be here."

"Well, you were looking in the wrong place. I'm standing right here, Addie," Roman joked with a smolder, earning a small laugh from Adeline. He tilted his head. "Okay, I'll bite. Who are you looking for?"

"I don't know who she is, just that I feel drawn to her. The silver dragon—she was here the last time and I just hoped she would be here again." A weight she hadn't realized she'd been carrying began to lose its hold on her as the words tumbled out.

"Sorry, did you just say *silver* dragon?" Roman's eyes widened as he mulled the words over, as if he was hoping he had simply misheard her.

"Yeah, I'm surprised *Dria* didn't tell you all about it. I figured she'd be jumping out of her skin to tattle on me for going after it last time. I was completely entranced by the entire moment. I didn't notice what I was doing until Xandria came to rescue me."

"Entranced? Princess. Please tell me you don't mean what I think you mean," Roman replied, looking at her as if she had three heads. "Silver dragons are not only rare, but extremely deadly. If it is the particular beast I am thinking of, she has not bonded with a rider in over two hundred years, not since she lost her last rider in battle. I am begging you, please do not engage with her again. You can bond with *any* other dragon here, hell you can bond with Aureluis if it keeps you away from the silver one, just *please, please* do not interact with Synacthdris again." Roman's eyes were full of a pleading sort of fear.

"What happened to being able to 'bring the world to its knees if I so wished?' You don't think I can handle myself?" She felt frustration beginning to come to life inside her.

"I have never and *will* never doubt you, Princess. I am only asking that you don't walk into certain death."

Adeline, however, did not hear his last plea to stay away from the silver one, her senses now clouded by a familiar music that was beginning to burrow its way right to her heart.

Before she could register her feet moving in the dirt, she was walking away from Roman towards the rocky cluster of caves tucked into the side of the ravine. The notes felt as if they became the very air she breathed as she drew closer, coiling their way into her body and finding their way home as they meshed with her soul. She thought she heard someone calling out to her from behind, but she couldn't convince her body to pay the voice any mind at all and instead felt herself beginning to run. She could hear nothing, feel nothing but the music calling her to the creature, to Synacthdris.

Shadows suddenly crept into her vision until she was entirely surrounded by darkness. She felt her body slow, unsure of where to go next as the music quieted, but only slightly. Warmth flooded her body as a calloused hand wrapped around her wrist, pulling her against Roman's familiar broad chest.

"Addie. Princess. Please stop," Roman begged her, wrapping his arms more tightly around her, scared that if he let go of his grip that she would sprint straight for the caves.

His words just barely crept in, almost intertwining with the music as if he were a part of the symphony, but it was enough to draw her attention to him. He stroked small circles in her hair while they stood pressed together in the midst of ribbons of shadow, his darkness encircling them like an impenetrable shield. Slowly, the music faded, and with it went the trance she had been in.

Roman and Adeline stood there for several minutes, both of them regaining their composure little by little, only snapping out of it when Xandria's voice cut through the thick darkness around them.

"Oh great. She did the creepy possessed-by-the-silver-dragon thing again, didn't she?"

"Go. The. Fuck. Away." Roman growled at her, unwilling to deal with her petty games when he had just nearly watched Adeline walk into a violent death. Clearly jarred by his sudden aggressive nature, Xandria conceded, walking away with her head down as if hurt by the words he had spat at her.

It felt like an eternity passed before Adeline finally looked up at Roman, and his body sagged with relief when her blue eyes met his. She suddenly felt so tired, so fragile. Whatever force had been pulling her seemed to have taken all of her energy with it.

"Why does it call to me?" Adeline practically whispered the words, as if she were asking herself the question as well.

"I don't know, Princess. I promise to help you figure it out, but first let me take you home." It was more of a demand than a question, and he did not wait for a reply before he hooked his arm under the crook of her knees, the other wrapping around her back as he pulled her against his body and carried her out of the ravine. Adeline did not protest, instead nuzzling her head into his pecs and letting her eyes flutter closed.

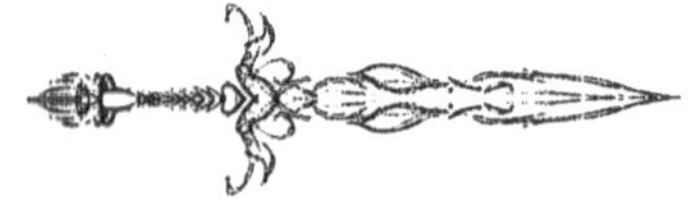

Though his heart still felt as if it were about to hammer out of his chest at any moment in fear for the princess' life, Roman couldn't help but admire the way she looked in his arms. Even the way her eyelashes lay against the pink flush of her cheeks had him thanking every God he could think of for putting this woman in his life. He craned his neck, pressing a gentle kiss to her forehead. As he walked into the clearing where Aurelius sat waiting to take them home, he couldn't help but feel that by stopping Adeline from going to the silver dragon he had somehow stood in the way of fate.

Chapter Thirty-Three

A DELINE'S BODY WAS HEAVY with exhaustion as she awoke the next morning, feeling as though she had exerted her every muscle to its fullest extent. Even coming to in the warm embrace of Roman's arms had not been enough to soothe the aches that seeped all the way down to her bones. She had slept for Gods knew how long but still felt drowsy, as if her head were underwater. She stretched deeply in a desperate hope that it would ease the pain even just a little.

Realizing without her having to utter a single word just how fatigued she truly was, Roman had risen without speaking and gone into the washroom. It was only a second before a squeak sounded and the euphoric sound of running water echoed off the walls. His dark brown hair was still mussed from sleep, and as he walked out of the bathroom and leaned on the doorframe, Adeline felt her heart rate quicken. The familiar gray drawers from her first night in Drakmoor once again hung off his hips, drawing her eyes to the deep V etched just above the waistband. Each and every muscle in his crossed arms seemed to be competing with his tattooed chest for her attention.

Gods, he is so infuriatingly handsome, she thought to herself.

She found his eyes, unsurprised to find them heavy—she had known he likely did not sleep until he knew she was okay. It seemed that he was not as oblivious to her gawking as she had hoped; the way he smirked at her ignited his tired eyes with an almost sultry sort of mischief.

"Careful, Princess. Keep eyeing me like that and I might be inclined to let you explore whatever you're fantasizing about over there," Roman teased.

"Unfortunately, I don't think I could even get myself out of this bed right now, let alone do any of the dirty things I'm imagining right now." Her cheeks heated with the admission, embarrassed at both her current weakened state and that fact she couldn't deny wanting to take advantage of his half-nakedness.

The mischief in Roman's eyes immediately died, quickly replaced by concern. He made his way to her and, as gently as he could, gathered her body into his arms. Though she did not protest, she winced at his touch. He watched her face twist, as if even the soft hold he had on her caused a great deal of pain, and fear found its way across his expression. As he carried her into the bathroom, he seemed to mull over the events of the day before, trying to discern what exactly had caused her to hurt this badly. Adeline, equally confused, was having similar thoughts herself. *We didn't train yesterday. I didn't attempt to mount a dragon other than Aurelius. I didn't fall or suffer any injuries, so what is causing me such pain?* Roman's concern for her current condition was written all over his face, and it made Adeline's heart pang with guilt for causing him such worry.

Lowering her into the steaming tub of water, Roman watched her every breath with rapt attention. Adeline finally let out a moan of relief and the tension that had coiled into his body eased slightly. He was grateful the solace of the bath eased her aches, but he needed to discern why she was so weak to begin with.

Adeline's eyes had fluttered closed in ecstasy, and Roman took the opportunity to gather the rest of the supplies he needed: lavender oil, a bar of a cream-colored soap, and a cloth. He moved quietly so as not to disturb the peace she was finally feeling. Gently, he grabbed the bottle of lavender oil and added a few drops to the bath water in hopes the oils would help ease her discomfort. The earthy scent filled the air, and his eyes did not leave her as Adeline relaxed just a little more, letting the aroma calm her.

He dunked the cloth into the hot water, letting it soak in the warmth for a long moment before he pulled it up, wrung it out, and folded it into a long strip. Pushing any stray strands of hair off of her forehead, Roman placed the warm cloth over her eyes to block out any light that shone through the large window. A soft smile found its way to Adeline's lips as the warmth of the cloth and the water she was submerged in slowly chipped away at her suffering, bit by bit.

Still not satisfied, Roman lowered himself to his knees at the end of the bathtub where Adeline's feet stuck out over the porcelain. He wet his hands, taking a moment to rub the bar of soap onto them until it began to bubble on his skin. Once they were coated in a slick layer, he tenderly grabbed one of her feet in both of hands, beginning to rub the arch. Another moan escaped her as he worked his thumbs into the ball of her foot, kneading away the aches. He spent Gods knew how long on his knees, soothing the pains in her feet and legs, letting his hands fall into a rhythm with her sighs of pleasure—all Adeline knew was that she didn't want it to end.

"*Gods,* Shadow. Your touch is heavenly," she whimpered.

"Do you think you can sit up?" he asked.

"Um, I think so."

Roman let her move on her own, not wanting to infringe too much on her independence when he knew she was already feeling fragile. Adeline eyed him as she moved, suddenly hearing the echo of the words he had spoken two nights before; *as someone who loves you.* He scooted his way to the edge of the tub so her back was facing him and gathered her hair in his hands, making quick work of braiding the strands.

"Where did you learn to do that?" The question she had tucked away finally bubbled out.

"My mom…" he hesitated, as if gathering the strength to continue, "when I was nine, she got really sick. It took over her body, and she was unable to move from her bed for days. All the healers had told me to prepare myself for the worst, but I didn't know how; she was all I had. There was a particularly bad day…I thought I was going to lose her, so I lay by her bedside crying while I held her hand, begging her to stay. Talking took all her effort at that point, but instead of letting me be scared, she started speaking softly, using all of her energy to teach me how to braid her hair. Gods forbid the woman go out with an unkempt head of hair. Really, I think it was just to distract me from how badly she was truly doing, and it worked. I braided and unbraided her hair for hours until she finally fell asleep. I slept in the chair in her room that night, afraid that if I left her side, she would be gone when I awoke. Much to my surprise when I woke up the next day, she had improved drastically. To this day, I have no idea how or what happened to heal her, but if I ask she always says my act of service, my final act of love for her is what saved her in the end." He tied off the ends of the braid and pushed it over her shoulder so it hung in front of her.

Adeline swiped at her cheeks, brushing away the tears that had gathered there with a sniffle. "Ro, I had no idea. That had to have been so hard for you, to deal with that all on your own and at such a young age. I'm so sorry."

"Nothing to be sorry for, Princess. I still have my mom at the end of the day, and that is all that matters to me."

Silence settled over them again as Roman gathered more suds in his hands and began rubbing Adeline's shoulders. He seemed unwilling to rest until he had eased as much of her pain as possible, and she was beyond thankful for his care.

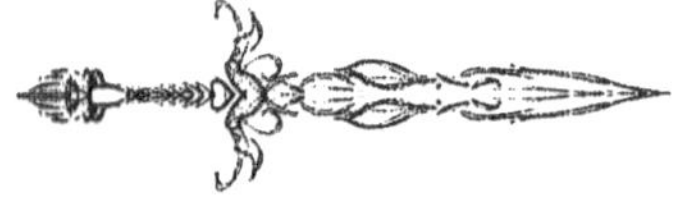

After Roman's attentive work on her every muscle, Adeline's pains had eased to more of a dull ache, though she still felt more tired than she ever had in her life. That did not stop her from escaping to the library the moment Roman had let her out of his sight to go ask Thistle for some cinnamon buns. The long morning spent soaking her body in the tub had not quite been enough to quiet her mind. She still had so many questions about the silver dragon and why she was so drawn to it, and she needed answers now.

Her bare feet padded with soft thuds on the hardwood as she made her way to the library. Roman had helped her dress in a pair of his loose drawers—which were rolled several times at the waistband to fit her properly—and one of his signature black shirts that fit her more like a dress, though her aching body thanked her for the loose fitting fabric.

Adeline was surprised to hear the familiar crackle of the fireplace, and even more surprised to step inside and find Amira sitting in one of the high-back chairs with a book in hand. She looked up as Adeline entered and gave her the kind of soft smile that made tears threaten to well in Adeline's eyes, thanks to the tender story Roman had shared with her still being heavy on her heart.

"Addie! I am so glad to see you. You look better than when I saw you last night. You were a little worse for wear, and Roman was so worried." She gestured to the chair opposite hers. "Please, come sit!"

Suddenly self-conscious about her clothing choice, her fingers knitted their way into the folds of the pants, gripping onto the extra fabric anxiously. Amira, though she had been nothing but kind, intimidated her in a way she had never experienced before—while her own mother had been cold and calculated, Amira felt warm, but powerful.

"What knowledge do you seek?" Amira asked as Adeline settled into the upholstered chair.

"I-I'm sorry?" Adeline asked, her brows knit together in confusion.

"What knowledge do you seek from the library? I thought maybe I could help you find a book on whatever it is you are searching for." She waited patiently for an answer, as if she had nothing but time.

"Oh, sorry, I guess my mind still feels a bit fuzzy. I was hoping to find something on silver dragons," Adeline admitted, still feeling embarrassed to utter the words aloud.

Amira's eyes lit up. "This wouldn't happen to have anything to do with the way you are drawn to the silver one, would it?" She smiled knowingly.

"I-uh, yeah it does." Her cheeks heated with shame at the fact that Amira knew she had practically death marched to a silver dragon not once, but twice.

"I had a feeling. Don't be embarrassed, dear; it is quite alright. I don't have any books on silver dragons here." She stood and made her way to a nearby shelf, "but I do have one on bonding with dragons that I think you may find particularly helpful."

Amira pulled down a thick leather-bound tome with markings on the spine so faded with age they were unreadable.

"Bonding with dragons? No, I-I wasn't bonding with it. I am just drawn to it," she responded as Amira pressed the book into Adeline's lap and took her seat again.

"Exactly! It feels as if it calls to you, doesn't it? As if you will stop breathing if you do not answer it?" Adeline was shocked at how well the words fit the exact feeling she had experienced in the ravine.

"Yeah, that's exactly it. When it happens, I hear this music...and every other sound ceases to exist; all that matters is me and the source of that music, the silver dragon."

"Music, you say?" Amira gave her a knowing smirk. "You know, they say only the strongest riders have unique bonding experiences, such as hearing music."

"Th-That can't be right. I can't bond with a dragon. They would never accept me as a rider after how many of them I have slain." Adeline looked down at the rug as the words tumbled out, humiliated by the person she was before she came to know the truth.

"There is nothing to be ashamed of, honey. I myself used to slay dragons before I understood who they truly were. It is not something I am proud of, but I refuse to hide from it. Own your past, Addie, or it will be your undoing." With that, Amira stood from her chair. "Well, I hope you find some answers in that book. I have to get going, but it was lovely seeing you again."

Adeline watched as the Matron of Drakmoor exited the library, feeling somehow worse now than before getting the answers to some of the questions that had been consuming her.

Chapter Thirty-Four

AFTER SPENDING SEVERAL HOURS in the library scouring over every sentence in the book Amira had handed to her, Adeline had found absolutely nothing that explained the pain and exhaustion that plagued her after the encounters with the silver dragon. Frustrated, she slammed the book closed and set it on the table with a groan.

"I don't think groaning at the pages is going to make them say what you want to hear, Princess," Roman quipped from where he had just materialized in the doorway.

In his hands he held two plates, each with their own sticky bun atop and if that sight alone wasn't enough to make her moan, she noticed that his pants were now covered in a thin layer of flour.

He must've helped Thistle make the cinnamon buns in my place today. The thought had her heart swelling.

"Nice buns, Shadow," Adeline teased with a soft smile.

Chuckling, Roman made his way to the table and presented her with the still-warm pastry, watching in admiration as she wasted no time shoving as much of it in her mouth as she could. Adeline couldn't bring herself to care for the manners she should have when it came to Thistle's cinnamon buns, not that the heavy look in Roman's eyes implied he cared either way.

"Well, if you have a problem with my groaning at books then find me one that explains why my body feels like it saw battle yesterday afternoon," Adeline sassed, knowing that if he knew where to find answers he would have given them to her already.

"Actually, I think I may have an idea of why that happens..." he rubbed the back of his neck nervously before continuing, "If I am right—which I hope I'm not—then the pain is a direct result of you *not* going to the dragon."

"Bu—" As she began to protest, she realized just how much sense it made. Amira had insinuated the dragon was trying to bond with her, and the pain she experienced must have been the consequence of not giving in to it.

"Then that means..." She couldn't find the words to finish the statement.

"That you need to face the silver one, yes," Roman finished for her, looking as if he might be sick.

Adeline knew it had taken a lot of courage for him to speak those words to her, but he was keeping his promise to not leave her in the dark any longer, which she appreciated.

"I need you to take me back," Adeline demanded, rising from where she sat on the floor as if she were ready to leave at that exact moment.

"Easy, Addie. As much as I hate the idea of it, I will take you back. Tomorrow. You need to rest and be at your strongest before you face her," Roman said gently, almost pleading.

As much as she hated it, he was right. She needed to be at her full strength, just in case. *Gods know what could happen tomorrow.*

"Tomorrow then," she nodded and sat back in her place on the floor, flipping open the crisp pages of the book on the table. Just because she had to rest her body did not mean she needed to rest her mind; she was still starving for any information she could find about the mysterious silver dragon.

Though she had practically begged Roman to take her to the ravine as soon as he awoke the next day, he made her sit through breakfast first. As she stood in the afternoon air, she felt a familiar tug, the beginnings of the sensation she knew would draw her to the silver one, and she felt her fear take hold. *Maybe this isn't a good idea*, she thought to herself, throwing a glance at Roman to see if he was hesitating as well.

Even though he had been extremely vocal about how much he hated the idea of her following the call, he looked at her now as if he had never been more confident in her abilities. There was so much pride in his gaze that it melted away the fear that had begun to burrow in her belly. If he was confident in her, then she had no doubt she could face this; Roman would never put her in harm's way.

"Go get her, Addie," Roman gave her a comforting pat on the butt and then stepped back, letting her focus on the task at hand. She took an unsteady step forward, and then another, and another, until soon her steps were sure and steady, her false confidence giving her the boost she needed.

It took only twelve paces before she heard it, that familiar series of notes curling through the valley and calling her home. This time, however, she followed it willingly, taking extra caution to maintain her control over her body. With every step she took, she repeated in her mind the comforting words Roman had once given her. *Be afraid, but do it anyway.*

Those words felt as if they were the only thing keeping her body moving as she approached the dragons clustered in the field, all of them watching her. Adeline was not yet sure if it was with curiosity or a desire to eat her for stepping foot on their nesting grounds that they eyed her with, and she did not plan to stick around to find out. Her pace quickened as she made her way through the valley, weaving between the massive creatures who stared down at her as she passed. The closer she got, the louder the music became. It became harder and harder to maintain her control on not only her body, but her mind. It felt as if one misstep would have her back in the trance she had slipped into twice before, a fate she was trying desperately to avoid for fear of facing the physical repercussions.

As if on their own accord, her feet began to move faster and faster until suddenly she was running, then sprinting. Blurs of red, blue, and green flashed in her vision as she blazed past the other dragons, her eyes catching on an unexpected silver glint tucked into the corner of the ravine.

Adeline's gaze darted to the movement immediately, her body following in response as her eyes locked on a pair of dark gray ones. She no longer felt her own chest rising and falling with breath; the pull of the music was the only thing that kept her body moving as if it carried her closer to the dragon.

Only a few yards separated them now, and Adeline felt as though her heart was about to take flight from her chest, yet still her feet moved her forward. She kept her focus locked on the dragon, afraid that if she looked away, it might seize the opportunity to attack her. Even though she feared the deadly creature in front of her, she could not ignore its beauty. After the few weeks she had spent in Drakmoor, she had learned to appreciate just how gorgeous the dragons truly were, but the one before her was an entirely different level of ethereal. The way the sunlight glinted off of her scales made her appear almost translucent in the right light, which explained why she was so difficult to see more often than not. Her midnight eyes were warm and cunning all at the same time, and something about them reminded Adeline of Amira in a strangely familiar way.

The silver creature had backed herself against the rocky cliffside, protecting her back while she called Adeline to her. It made Adeline's chest ache knowing that habit was something she'd likely had to learn the hard way. She was a bit smaller than the other dragons Adeline had interacted with, but that did not make her appear any less deadly. In fact, Adeline thought her smaller size might prove to be an advantage when needing to evade a dangerous situation.

Five paces was all that stood between them, and she found herself wishing she could remember the name that Xandria had referred to the creature by. She was both beautiful and deadly; she deserved the respect of being called by her name. *Syn? Syna?*

Synacthdris. The voice cut through her own thoughts, startling her. The familiar melodic tone in the words told her that it had been the dragon in front of her, somehow speaking directly into Adeline's mind.

The realization sent a shiver down her spine. *Be afraid, but do it anyway.* She took an unsteady step forward.

"Synacthdris. I answer your call!" she declared as she stepped forward again, leaving even less space between them.

Synacthdris eyed her curiously, allowing a moment to pass before she craned her neck, moving her head toward Adeline. Afraid of what the dragon was going to do, but trying to gather the courage to trust her, Adeline extended her hand with her palm facing the creature. Unsure of what the next move would be, and unable to convince herself to watch, she turned her head to the side and cast her eyes away.

It felt as if an entire lifetime passed before she felt it, the cool bite of scales against her hand. Adeline took a deep breath, trying to rally her remaining strength before she turned to find Synacthdris' nose pressed lovingly against her flattened palm. Her breath caught in her throat at the sight, and she felt tears starting to well in her eyes, blurring her vision.

With Aurelius and Raegorath, Adeline had learned that the dragons could sense the lives of their fallen that she carried with her in the echoes of their past power, but it seemed that they could also sense the immense guilt that she held for each and every one of them. With Synachtdris' nose pressed to her palm, it felt as if she had finally been accepted. It made her heart swell to realize that though she had never truly encountered this dragon before, Syn somehow saw her for who she was and the mistakes she had made and still chose to trust her. It was no small gesture, and it chipped away at a part of her that she didn't realize had been so afraid of being rejected here. As that little bit of her fear fell away, she caught a glimpse of a sudden flash of red.

Blinking quickly to clear the tears from her eyes, she gasped as she saw her hand enveloped in thick tendrils of red and orange flame. For a split second, she thought the flames had curled out of Synathdris' nostrils, but she quickly realized that they did not hurt her; instead, they felt more like an extension of her hand than an outside force.

Adeline bent her fingers, watching in awe as the flame followed the movement, shrinking ever so slightly before swelling up again. The fire was coming from *her*. Her heart skipped a beat as she tried to make herself believe what her eyes were seeing. It was coming from her; she was wielding fire. It was so comfortable and yet so foreign to feel the burn of flame itching to be released just beneath her skin. It felt like lifetimes had passed since she last felt the heat of this particular power.

Synacthdris withdrew her head suddenly, pulling back and letting out a low, menacing grumble that made Adeline stumble backward a step. It was only once she looked over her shoulder and saw Roman and Xandria approaching that she realized it had not been directed at her. Relief flooded her body. As the pair drew closer, Adeline watched Synacthris glower at them, seemingly awaiting a signal to attack. Roman eyed Synacthdris with fear in his eyes, making Adeline fight to bite back a laugh. Maybe the strong, dark man was not as fearless as she had once thought him to be.

"It seems that your power has manifested, Princess. I always knew you were hot, but flame was not my first guess." He threw her a wink before wrapping her in a tight hug, earning a growl from the silver dragon behind her. Synacthdris seemed to be protective over her already, and it made her heart swell with pride.

"Don't flatter her too much. It's just a boring old red flame after all," Xandria prodded, though no one had asked her to be here.

"And they aren't fully bonded yet. I'd watch who's bad side you put yourself on Xandria, the princess is already deadly without dragonfire in the palm of her hand," Roman bit back, glaring at Xandria with dark eyes. *It seems Syn isn't the only one feeling protective over me.*

"What is she talking about?" Adeline chimed in, her brow furrowing in curiosity.

"Your fire. Stronger riders who manifest fire tend to have flames of varying intensities. Most riders manifest with red or blue, but there is a rumor that there have been riders in history that harnessed flames far more powerful than that," Roman answered, keeping his eyes trained on Synacthdris as he spoke as if he was afraid she might change her mind and decide to eat him after all.

It seemed that though she had started to earn Synacthdris' trust, Adeline still had a lot to learn when it came to the dragons. Though it didn't quite feel so overwhelming anymore, she was eager to connect with her bonded.

CHAPTER THIRTY-FIVE

I T HAD TAKEN ROMAN far too long to convince Xandria to leave them, but when she finally did Adeline breathed a sigh of relief; that woman was the bane of her existence. With Xandria gone, Roman turned to Adeline and closed the distance between them, planting a passionate kiss on her lips as he held her tightly against his body. He had been adamant in telling her he believed she could handle herself, but sending her off to Synacthdris alone had seemed to genuinely terrify him. His entire body sagged with relief as he pulled Adeline in his arms, in one piece and still alive.

"Woah, you must've *really* missed me, Shadow. I should walk into danger more often if it earns me a greeting like that," Adeline said with an intoxicated smile.

"That is not exactly the opposite effect I was going for. You are going to be the death of me, Princess," he chuckled and took a step back, giving her space to breathe for a second. She had just experienced a life-altering moment and appreciated that he tried his best not to smother and overwhelm her in the midst of it. She was happy, but still had so much to process.

"I am so Gods damned proud of you, Addie," He looked at her with pride in his eyes and a pleased smile painted across his full lips.

His expression alone made her heart feel as though it might burst as tears began welling in her eyes. Unable to find the words to respond, she closed the space between them once more and wrapped her arms around his middle.

They held each other for several moments before she finally spoke, nearly whispering the words, "Thank you, Roman. Thank you for being afraid and letting me go anyway, for believing in me. I will be eternally grateful for your confidence in my ability to handle myself," the *unlike everyone else in my life* was implied, not needing to be spoken aloud for him to understand the gravity of the words she had just shared.

Adeline had spent the entirety of her life before him being doubted by everyone around her. Her father, mother, the kingdom, they all questioned her every move and she felt as if she was suffocating under the weight of all they expected her to be, but with Roman it was simple. He saw her for everything she was and never shied away from it, instead reveling in her ability to handle any enemy, to face any problem. With him, however, she knew that she would never have to face those things on her own, not ever again so long as he was by her side. As if hearing the sureness snap into place in her mind, he took her face in his hands.

"Thank *you,* Addie. For saving me from the darkness I thought to be my destiny. You are the light I have been searching for my entire life,"

Roman pressed a kiss to her forehead before tucking her under his chin, giving her another tight embrace.

They did not need to continue speaking to convey the feelings that passed between them. Something had shifted between them and in the silence Adeline again heard the quiet echoes of his declaration *as someone who loves you.* They just held on to one another, unmoving until Synacthdris, seemingly annoyed with their display of affection, glared at Roman with tendrils of smoke curling from her nostrils.

That sight alone was enough to have him taking several steps back, putting space between him and the massive beast. Even though Adeline had gotten on her good side, Roman did not seem to be entirely convinced Synacthdris was not going to eat him. His blatant fear earned a fit of laughter from Adeline.

"What's wrong, Shadow? Scared of a little ole dragon?" Adeline teased, walking over to Synacthdris and gently rubbing her snout. The dragon nuzzled into her palm and let its eyes close in delight at the touch, Roman just stared in disbelief.

"Synacthdris is a killing machine, thank you very much. And yes, I *am* afraid of her. You are insane not to be," he shivered as he uttered the words. "Frankly I don't know if I should be afraid of you or turned on by how fearlessly you handle her."

Adeline looked back to the dragon, the smile slipping from her face as she noticed that Synacthrdris was still backed against the cliffside, protecting herself. She knew that the habit was likely due to something she had faced in the past and the thought made her heart ache. She needed to know the truth about the dragon's past.

"Do you know why she does that?" Adeline asked quietly, afraid of the story that was likely coming.

"Does what?" Roman asked, clearly clueless as to what she was referring to.

"Covers her back the way she does. It seems like she's been attacked from behind before, it would explain why she refuses to leave herself open. Out of fear of another assault." Adeline continued rubbing Syn's nose gently, comforting both the dragon and herself with the movement.

"Oh, right. I guess I am just so used to seeing her tucked into corners it didn't stand out to me. Before she lost her bonded, Synacthdris was a sight to behold on the battlefield. Wherever there was battle, one was sure to find her at the forefront, making any enemy who faced her bend to her will. It was one of the many reasons that no one had even dared try to bond with her after she lost her rider in an attack; they all feared her and what she was capable of. After she lost Dean, Synachthdris went into mourning for years. She would go weeks at a time sometimes without leaving the caves. Between her already smaller size and her grief, the more ruthless dragons marked her as weak and started attacking her. Cydinth, Xandria's dragon, was among them," Adeline felt anger bubbling up in her chest, as if she had needed more reasons to hate the woman.

"The dragons would sneak into the cave while Synacthdris slept and wait for her to wake before they attacked. They knew just how dangerous she could be, so they always assaulted from behind to be sure their blows landed. She's done that ever since, protecting her back wherever she goes. They were wrong to count her out though, their attacks turned the already cunning nature she possessed into the cold, calculated one of a killer. Cydinth is the only dragon who attacked her that still lives, Syn has taken out all the others over the years, getting her revenge. I'm not entirely sure why Cydinth still stands, but I guess that is for Synacthdris to know, not us."

Romans heavy words had tears prickling the backs of her eyes once again. To Adeline, the story had been all too familiar, too similar to her own experience in Scalebreak. While she had not suffered physical blows, Calum and the other suitors had felt like an attack from behind from her own family—forcing her into a life she never wanted and not taking no for an answer.

A stray tear slid down her cheek as she pressed her forehead to Synacthrdis' snout, a silent exchange passed between them and Adeline hoped that Syn could hear the thought she uttered only for her to hear, *We will never again be mistaken for weak.* Though there was no response, Synacthdris ever so slightly nodded her head as if in understanding.

Synacthris had not borne a rider for nearly two hundred years, but she hadn't needed one; she was a ruthless killing machine. Adeline was determined that together they would be a force that the world was not yet ready to face. Roman watched the two of them from afar, unsure if he was more proud or afraid of the challenge painting Adeline's face.

"Teach me how to wield my flame," Adeline finally spoke, turning to Roman as she uttered the words. Roman didn't dare refuse her request, knowing she would not take no for an answer.

With the demand hanging in the air between them, Adeline stepped toward Roman leaving Syn tucked in the corner, not wanting to cause her any stress. They moved away until they were about ten yards from her before they began. She was tired of being told to wait, so she did not give Roman the chance to make her.

"First things first, you need to tie your hair up," Roman said, pulling free a leather strap that he'd had wrapped around his wrist. The gesture made Adeline's heart skip a beat, knowing that he had placed the strap there just for her, in case she needed it.

"I'd sooner die a fiery death than let you burn off a single one of those gorgeous chocolate strands," he teased as she gathered her hair into a ponytail, though judging from the careful attention he always paid her hair she wasn't entirely sure he was teasing at all.

"And here I thought you were asking me to tie my hair up for *other* activities," she winked.

A low growl sounded from the back of Roman's throat in response, "Easy, Princess. I have no problems with taking you into one of those caves, letting every dragon and rider in this ravine be our witness," he smirked as a blush rose to her cheeks.

Gods, I am hopeless when it comes to this man, she thought.

"Be serious, Ro. I need to learn how to wield my fire," Adeline chastised, drawing in her focus.

"Fine," he sighed, stepping behind her and wrapping one hand around her waist and the other around her bicep. Adeline felt her breath hitch at the contact.

"Truthfully, it's all about focus. You have to drown out everything around you and hone in on the feeling of the power buzzing in your veins, waiting for you to call on it."

"Focus, easy enough," Adeline closed her eyes and tried to close herself off to the world around her.

Slowly, the sounds faded out, but no matter how hard she tried, she could not stop thinking about the way Roman felt pressed against her, holding her. Hoping she could use the distraction to her advantage, she raised the arm that Roman was holding and willed flames to appear in her palm as they had earlier. Adeline cracked her eyes open slightly, disappointed to find that absolutely nothing had happened.

She let out a frustrated sigh. "It is not easy to focus with you pressed against me, Shadow," she grumbled at him.

"That's the point, Princess," he teased, pulling her closer to him. "You have to be able to wield *with* distractions."

"Focus, Addie," he whispered against the shell of her ear, causing goosebumps to come to life across her skin.

This is going to be harder than I thought.

Adeline looked over at Synacthdris, who was now laying down where she had been tucked against the rocks, watching curiously. She shifted her focus to the dragon, trying to forget that Roman was touching her at all, though that was a particularly difficult feat. She closed her eyes again and took a deep breath, focusing her mind on the tingling sensation that lingered just below her skin. *This is no different than the power I wielded before,* she reminded herself.

Slowly, she felt herself beginning to hone in on the sensation more and more, Roman and Synacthdris falling away until there was only her, the sound of her breathing, and the prickle of power waiting for her to unleash it. Raising her hand again, her palm facing the sky, she willed flames to come to life in her hand once more.

Throwing all of her focus into the power, she waited several moments before opening her eyes again and was delighted to see that this time, instead of nothing, there was a steady cluster of sparks smattering to life in her hand. It seemed that perhaps this power was quite different from what she had become accustomed to wielding after all and the realization caused defeat to take hold in her, killing her concentration and causing the sparks to die out once again.

"Hey," Roman spun her around to face him, "don't get discouraged, Princess. Half the battle is earning the wholehearted trust of your dragon, and you and Synacthdris only just met. It will take time, but you are already far ahead of most riders."

"Really?" She looked up at him, hope in her eyes.

"Really," he pressed a kiss to her forehead, "it took me two weeks before I could call on *any* of my power, let alone as much as you just did."

The admission soothed the growing doubt that had taken hold of her. Roman was right, she'd only just met Syn, it would take time for them to build trust with one another—she only hoped that time was something they had.

Roman may have taken care of the suitors but Adeline was still the heir to the throne of Scalebreak. She was valuable to her father, and she knew the trio of men he had sent to retrieve her was only scratching the surface of the lengths he would go to regain his control over her.

CHAPTER THIRTY-SIX

THE NEXT SEVERAL DAYS went by in a blur. Adeline awoke every morning and spent time in the kitchens with Thistle, Seraphina, and Milo, helping them to make the pastries for the day. It was the quiet in the chaos and one of the most treasured parts of life at the cabin, the warm embrace of the kitchen offering her solace.

Once Falrin was awake for the day, he would whisk her away from the kitchens and usher her to the training gym, where they would meet Seraphina. To her credit, Seraphina had somehow vastly improved her sparring skills in only a week of training, something that Falrin never failed to comment on during their sessions. Adeline would spar with Falrin and Seraphina until the early afternoon, letting the familiar movements empty her mind entirely and relying solely on memory to guide her body. She too had improved greatly in her combat style in the time she had been in Drakmoor, a fact that made her feel proud of herself. Though the lessons with Calum had made her a skilled warrior before, she was truly a cunning force after being trained by Falrin.

Afternoons were spent with Roman and Synacthdris in the ravine, an entirely different kind of training, one that Adeline grew more and more frustrated with her lack of skill in. But still, she carried on, excited every day to spend another afternoon working on wielding her fire no matter how difficult or exhausting it was.

Though they had spent several days with her, Synacthdris still disliked Roman's presence, never failing to make him aware of it with frequent grumbling. Roman still seemed to fear her because of it, always careful to keep his distance. Their distaste for one another never failed to send Adeline into a fit of giggles.

Today, Adeline had made some headway on finally summoning her flames, now able to call forth tiny buds of fire, which was much more than she had been capable of in the last several days. Synacthdris watched her from her place tucked into the cliffside, and her eyes seemed to light with approval as she saw the progress that Adeline made. It was all the encouragement she needed to keep working at it.

Roman refused to remove himself from behind her, swearing that the physical contact between them was the perfect distraction for her to work on focusing, and as much as she hated how much his touch affected her, Adeline agreed. When he was pressed against her, her mind and body turned to goo, and she had to use all of her mental strength to regain control of both, refusing to let his breath on her neck be the only thing standing between her and her power.

Focusing once more, she honed in on the tingling sensation just below the surface of her skin, begging to be set free, this time leaving her eyes open, wanting to watch her progress as it happened instead of hiding from her fear of failure like she had been the past several days.

Extending her palm out in front of her once more, Adeline took several deep breaths, filling her lungs entirely before she continued. She looked past her palm and felt a smile spread across her face as her eyes fell upon Synacthdris watching her intently. Adeline kept her eyes trained on the dragon, remembering the way she had felt when the call of her music filled her soul, the way it had guided her exactly where she needed to go. It had felt like home, like all she had needed to do was follow it and everything else would fall away. The memory sparked an idea, and Adeline began humming what she could remember of the notes under her breath, for only herself to hear. As she did so, she focused the rest of her attention on calling forth the power.

A surprised gasp escaped her as the tiny bud of flames that flickered in her palm grew in size until they were licking the air several inches above her hand. She laughed in disbelief before flexing her fingers, making the flames dance for her. The orange and red blaze moved at her will, and it had Adeline beaming in excitement. Unable to contain herself, she spun around to show Roman her accomplishment, finding him already beaming at her with pride.

"I knew you had it in you, Addie." His words were sure and confident, as if he had never doubted her for even a second. "I'm so proud of you."

There were those words again, the ones that rattled her to her core. He was the first and only person to utter those words to her, *I'm so proud of you*, and both times she'd heard them she felt as though she might burst into tears. Hearing him say it made her proud of *herself*, a feeling that was still so foreign to her.

It shook her enough to hear those words that the flames died in her hand and as soon as they did Roman closed the distance between them, picking her up and spinning her around with a smile plastered across his face, "I am so Gods damned proud of you, Princess."

Her white skirt fanned out around them as he spun her, creating a gentle breeze that kissed her bare legs. It was euphoric, twirling in the grass with Roman, and she felt as if every one of her senses was heightened because of it.

This time, she didn't try to hide the tear that slid down her cheek, instead letting it trail her face while she smiled bigger than she ever had. When Roman finally set her down, Adeline felt dizziness creeping in on her, making her giggle. Knowing he had been the cause of the slight wobble in her legs, Roman held her upright until the feeling faded.

"Well, now that you're starting to get the hang of that, I suppose it is time for you to tackle flying on Syn." Roman smiled at her.

Adeline felt all the air leave her lungs as she absorbed the words. *Fly. Oh Gods. I am going to have to fly alone. Synacthdris will never let Roman mount her,* she thought to herself, feeling any previous excitement flee her body.

Though she knew she would have to eventually, the idea of flying at all still made her nervous, let alone flying on her own. Her knees wobbled at the thought.

"Hey, eyes on me, Addie. I know you're scared. We will only do this at your pace, okay?" Roman's voice was calm and steady, squashing some of her fear, but even he couldn't extinguish the growing anxiety she felt.

She took several long breaths, her fingers reaching to grab hold of the silver rose pendant hanging from her neck, seeking the familiar comfort of Greta, before she finally let her feet move from where they rooted her to the earth. Roman followed beside her, walking hesitantly toward Synacthdris, who lifted her head as they drew closer, tilting it curiously.

She eyed Roman with distrust as they approached, standing with a grumble and lowering her head when only a few paces remained between them. Letting out a low growl, Syn narrowed her eyes in Roman's direction, clearly communicating a warning. Now knowing that if the two of them could not get along, she would have to fly alone, Synacthdris' distrust in Roman was no longer amusing to Adeline.

"Synacthdris. It's okay. He's okay. He won't hurt us," Adeline reassured her dragon, patting her silver snout gently.

Synacthdris looked Roman up and down, as if trying to decide whether or not she believed Adeline's claim that he was safe.

Craning her head forward, Synacthdris hovered right over Roman's head and sniffed him deeply, inspecting him. Roman squeezed his eyes shut, his body tensed as he waited to be reduced to ash. Only that moment did not come. Synacthdris instead lowered her head further and pressed her nose into his chest, nudging him. Roman opened his eyes, seeming to be in disbelief, and hesitantly brought a shaky hand to her snout.

It took him several seconds to gather the courage, but finally he gave her a gentle pat on the nose and she nuzzled into his touch. Realizing that she had finally accepted him, Roman smirked and looked over at Adeline, who was staring at him and the silver dragon as if they had hung the moon.

"See, nothing to be afraid of, Princess," he resumed patting the dragon's nose.

"*Right*," Adeline scoffed playfully, knowing that Roman was likely still terrified by the silver dragon.

Adeline was still nervous to take her first flight on Syn, but felt somewhat better knowing that Roman would be joining her. Giving herself no time to change her mind, she began approaching Synacthdris, careful to come at her from the side and not behind, ensuring that she felt safe.

Adeline ran her hand along the rough scales of the dragon's wings, staring down at them in awe as she walked. Synacthdris was truly a gorgeous creature, and she felt honored to be given the chance to mount her, even if the idea filled her with terror. Sensing Adeline's approach, Synacthdris moved her head from Roman and turned herself toward Adeline with a curious tilt, waiting for her to speak.

"Alright, Syn, here's the thing. We are gonna have to fly at some point. I, for one, am terrified of doing so, but I trust you." She reached her palm up and pressed it between Synacthdris' eyes. "Do you trust me?"

An answer came in the form of Synacthdris lowering her wing to the grassy earth and nudging her head toward it, as if telling Adeline to get on. Adeline had not expected it to go over so well and threw an uneasy look at Roman, still unsure that she had the courage necessary.

"Be afraid, but do it anyway, Princess," he reassured her with a smile, grabbing her hand to help her step onto the dragon.

"Don-Don't I need a saddle?" she asked, looking for any excuse not to climb onto Synacthdris' back.

"Not if she will allow me on with you, I can hold us in place with my shadows. What do you say, Syn? Help me help our girl here." *Our girl*, the words struck Adeline in the heart.

Synacthdris did not react at all, simply standing there waiting for Adeline to mount her. Taking a deep breath, Adeline took a step forward and onto the dragon's wing, hearing Roman mirror her movements right behind her.

When Synacthdris did not react, Adeline blew out a sigh of relief, glad that she was allowing Roman to accompany her. Knowing that he would be with her every step of the way made any remaining fear wither away as she found her seat on the dragon's back, feeling Roman settle in behind her, wrapping an arm around her middle. Adeline slid her fingers onto a notch at the top of one of Synacthdris' scales, the only thing she could find to hold on to.

Before she could speak the request, Roman's shadows curled out in ribbons around the both of them, securing themselves around their laps and holding both of them firmly in their seats. The familiar caress of his darkness against her skin made her shiver with excitement. They had been here before, she reminded herself. *This is no different than our nights spent flying atop Aurelius.* The thought calmed her racing pulse.

Hold on, the familiar lull of Synacthdris' voice cut through her mind and she wondered if Roman could hear it too, but she did not get the chance to ask before the dragon was launching into the sky.

The takeoff was more abrupt than Adeline was used to with Aurelius, and it made her hold her breath until they leveled out and began coasting through the sky. Once they were flying at a slightly less terrifying speed, Adeline let go of the breath that had caught in her throat and laughed maniacally. *This isn't half bad,* she thought.

"Look, Princess," Roman whispered to her, and she looked down at Synacthdris below her, too stunned to speak. Adeline had thought that the dragon was breathtaking to look at in the valley, but here in the clear blue sky she was entirely ineffable.

The normally silver glint of her scales was nearly gone, the sun reflecting off of her in a way that mirrored everything surrounding them. Every inch of the blue expanse, clouds and all, reflected off of her scales, making her appear one with the sky. If she could not feel Synacthdris beneath her, Adeline was not entirely sure that she would believe her to be there at all.

"I've never seen anything like it," Roman's voice was full of wonder, as if he too was encapsulated by the creature they rode atop, and it made Adeline's chest swell with pride. This was *her* dragon. Synacthdris had chosen *her*. A choice that she would be grateful for until her last breath.

Smiling wildly, Adeline threw her arms out at her sides, letting the wind wrap around every inch of her that wasn't dressed in Roman's touch. It almost seemed silly that she had ever been afraid of *this*. Never in her life had she seen such a breathtaking being.

Wondering if Roman felt the same, she turned her head and looked over her shoulder, surprised to find him staring at *her*. They were riding atop the most magnificent being she had ever laid eyes on, and he was watching *her* as if she had painted the very sky they soared through.

"You are truly a sight to behold when you come to life like this, Princess," he said with a smile, the faintest hint of tears growing in his eyes. "I've never seen you so *happy*, so *alive*."

He reached up and tucked a wave of hair that had come loose from her braid behind her ear with a gentle touch.

Adeline wasn't sure what the future held for them, but she knew one thing for sure: whatever future there may be, she wished to spend it with *him*. Whatever fate had in store for either of them, she hoped Roman shared her desire to face it together.

CHAPTER THIRTY-SEVEN

A DELINE WASN'T QUITE SURE how long they stayed atop Synacthdris, soaring through the clouds, but she knew she had never wanted it to end. Among the clouds with Roman and Synacthdris, she felt completely untouchable, and it intoxicated her. Roman, on the other hand, seemed to be drunk on *her* happiness. He had told her that watching her come to life the way she did that afternoon, whooping and laughing as if she had never felt even a glimpse of pain, had rivaled even his favorite moments spent in the sky. Over and over again he assured her that he could watch her like this—wrapped in his shadows and smiling like a madwoman—forever, never tiring of the sight.

Much to both of their dismay, Synacthdris did not seem to be as immersed in the moment and had begun preparing to land. With every inch closer they came to landing on the earth below, Adeline felt her excitement begin to die down little by little. She was not quite ready to be done yet, but would respect Synacthdris' choice to end the flight. There would be plenty more chances for her to fly atop the silver dragon.

Looking down, Adeline took in the scenery as they approached the dirt. Expecting to see nothing but the wide open space where they had taken off from, Adeline felt her heart stutter as her eyes fell upon Aurelius waiting patiently for their arrival. It struck her as odd; she had never seen him in the ravine or anywhere near the other dragons, something that had piqued her curiosity every time she had been in the valley. *Aurelius is a sassy dragon, but did that mean he truly detested the others so much that he refused to be anywhere in the vicinity of the nesting grounds, choosing instead to be isolated?* The thought broke Adeline's heart.

As Synacthdris' claws curled into the dirt, leaving plumes of dust in their wake, Adeline gained the courage to ask the question that she had been putting off for some time. "Hey, Ro?"

"Yes, Princess?" He grabbed her by the hips, lifting and spinning her around so that she was facing him with her legs wrapped around his waist.

The movement should not have surprised her, but his touch never failed to leave her more than a little breathless. Adeline looked over his shoulder at Aurelius; the setting sun reflected off of his gold scales, casting the earth around him in a golden hue and making it seem as if it had been kissed by the sun. He was beautiful, but there was something sad that lingered in his eyes, something Adeline had never noticed before that moment.

"Why doesn't Aurelius ever come with us to the ravine?" she asked quietly, as if trying to afford the gold dragon even a sliver of privacy.

Roman looked over at Aurelius, and it seemed as if a silent conversation passed between only the two of them before he finally spoke again.

"He lost a hatchling many years ago, stolen away by Scalebreak's army. Even ten years later, he does not know if the child lived or died. The ravine was her home, the only place the young dragon had been before the night of her capture. She loved it here. It is too painful for Aurelius to be here without her, so he tends to prefer to keep his distance." Roman's face was solemn as the words hung between them as if he too felt the pain of Aurelius' lost daughter, carrying it like it was his own.

Adeline looked over to Aurelius, staring at the great beast with far more understanding of his character than she had ever had prior. She didn't know if she hoped his daughter was alive or dead, knowing that if she had somehow survived that she was likely suffering. Silent tears slipped down her face as she climbed down from Synacthdris and approached Aurelius, wrapping herself in a tight embrace around his front leg, pressing a kiss to his golden scales.

"I will make them pay for what they did to her," she said under her breath, knowing that he could hear her regardless.

She did not wait for him to acknowledge her words, knowing that he knew she meant them. Adeline pushed off Aurelius' leg, approaching Roman, who was now leaning against Synacthdris with his arms crossed, watching her with wonder. Her tender heart, though it often left her frustrated, had become one of her favorite things about herself.

"So, what is he doing here?" Adeline asked finally.

"Well, we thought that maybe we could give you some solo flight lessons, me on Aurelius and you on Syn." He rubbed the back of his neck almost nervously, as if he were maybe asking for too much too fast.

Looking back at Aurelius, she noticed now that he had an extra saddle strapped to his back. The gesture had tears gleaming in her eyes but, knowing that Aureluis would likely grumble over her emotional display, she wiped them before she approached him once again, letting him lower himself to the ground before she began undoing the straps on one of the saddles. Roman, unable to stand watching his lady saddle her own dragon, grabbed the heavy leather from Adeline and carried it to Synacthdris, where he made quick work of using his shadows to help him secure it. Synacthdris, to her credit, only grumbled at him twice in the process, a display that had Adeline fighting back a laugh. The two of them had just flown together, and yet they were still at each other's throats.

Once he double-checked his work and was sure he had the saddle perfectly secured, Roman knelt on one knee, bending his head and extending a hand outward. "My lady," he teased, earning an eye roll from Adeline.

"I do love seeing you on your knees for me," she joked, knocking Roman speechless as she put her hand in his and mounted Synacthdris, who had extended her wing against the earth to allow her easy access.

Now that the seat was atop Synacthdris, Adeline noticed several straps and buckles poking out as extensions of the leather. It was then that it dawned on her that without Roman's shadows holding her in place she would need extra belts to make sure she didn't plummet to her death, a fact that it seemed Roman had already considered.

He had been extra attentive to her every possible need since the night she had told him how badly he hurt her, and it made her heart swell. Though she hated that it took her breaking down for him to realize the damage he'd caused, she was glad that when she made him face it that he had actually *listened*. It was yet another way that he so greatly differed from everything she was familiar with.

By the time she finished fiddling with the belts on the saddle, sure that she was securely in place, Roman had mounted Aurelius and was patiently waiting for her cue that she was ready to go. Adeline took a deep breath, rubbing a hand over the rough silver scales just in front of the saddle before giving them a gentle pat to signal that she was prepared for ascent.

Synacthdris bent down slightly, preparing to launch them into the sky, and Adeline took the moment to throw Roman a wink, watching a smirk paint itself across his face before the wind was whipping her hair and they were climbing. The near-vertical path that she had once feared now made her heart roar to life with excitement.

A blur of golden scales flashed in her periphery, and her smile widened, Roman. Aurelius and Synacthdris, seeming to read one another's next moves, began to weave into a spiral until they were intertwined with one another, curling in and out of where the other had just been as if braiding the clouds with flashes of gold and silver until finally they leveled out, flying side by side. Adeline, hair sticking out from her braid where the wind had whipped it free, looked over at Roman with wide eyes, surprised to see him mirroring her expression.

"Tha-The- I've never experienced anything like that before," he finally found the words.

"It was incredible!" Adeline sounded breathless.

"He's never done anything like that before," Roman repeated, still in shock.

There were no words that encompassed the feelings that passed between them as they stared one another down with wild eyes, laughing in disbelief of what had just happened. It took them several minutes to recover, finally calming their hysteria when Aurelius grumbled at them, a plea for them to focus.

"Right," Roman said, "Okay, so really, it isn't too much different from riding a horse, only the horse has wings and is flying hundreds of feet above the ground, the only thing standing between you and certain death...no pressure," he teased.

The joke had Adeline pulling on the leather straps and buckles of her saddle, ensuring that they were still secure.

"Not helping," she groaned at him.

"Okay, okay," he laughed, "lean to the right if you want to move right, left if you want to move left. You will learn quickly that you are really not in control at all, but you can still have some influence over the direction you are heading. Synacthdris will handle everything; you just have to tell her where you want to go."

Testing the advice Roman had just given her, Adeline leaned left, whooping in delight as Synacthdris veered slightly to the left, bringing her closer to where Aurelius and Roman flew beside them.

"That's my girl," Roman said proudly, his eyes full of light.

Excited by his praise, Adeline leaned right, hoping to lead Synacthdris in the same direction. Only this time she leaned further than before, and it seemed Synacthdris misinterpreted the request when instead of banking right she tucked her wings and began flying in tight spirals, only stopping when Adeline audibly gagged at the dizziness plaguing her.

As Synacthdris righted herself, Adeline clung to the pommel with white knuckles and blew a stray brown wave out of her eyes. Roman barked out a laugh to her left, clearly amused at her failed attempt, and Adeline glared daggers at him.

"This will be a lot easier once the bond has snapped into place and you can communicate with her without even speaking," Roman explained.

"Like, she can read my mind?" Adeline asked, though from her own interactions with Synacthdris, she thought she knew the answer.

"Only what you intend for her to hear. I am sure you have heard her speak to you through the trust you have already established, likely only a few words. Once the bond is in place, you'll be able to communicate freely with her."

Adeline felt herself sag with relief at his words. It would be much easier to communicate with Synacthdris once they were fully bonded but, taking more of Roman's advice, she leaned down and whispered to the dragon, "Take us home, Syn."

Roman continued giving her little tips as they flew in the direction of the cabin, the two of them moving side by side through the sky painted with the colors of the setting sun. Pinks and purples reflected off of Synacthdris' silver scales and onto Aurelius' gold ones that seemed to amplify the hues reflected at them. The creatures were beautiful alone, but together they were indescribable. It left both Adeline and Roman at a loss for words to watch the way the light bounced off of one and was almost absorbed by the other.

As they neared home, Adeline noticed the familiar faint orange glow of lights in the windows and smiled, excited to be back at the place she had grown to love. It was almost as if she could hear the people bustling around inside the cabin the closer they got, and it was music to her ears, calling her home.

As if seeing the cozy house tucked atop the mountain reminded her body of its need for sustenance, Adeline's stomach let out a long, low growl, breaking the silence that her and Roman had fallen into.

"We are just early enough that we should still make dinner," Roman said with a soft smile.

"Thank the Gods!" Adeline laughed.

Aurelius and Synacthdris moved in perfect sync as they made their landings in the patch of grass beside the cabin, each leaving just enough room for the other. Adeline had barely had the control to wait until claws met the earth before she started fumbling with the buckles, freeing herself from her place in the saddle.

Excited for the promise of a warm meal, Adeline dismounted Synacthdris, patting her bowed nose in thanks before she made her way over to Roman, who waited for her with a smile. It seemed that today had healed something in both of them. Roman reached for her hand, lacing their fingers and pulling her toward the front steps.

It was only once they reached the bottom stair that they finally noticed Falrin leaning against the railing with a deep frown etched into his face. He looked as if he had been awaiting their arrival, and the sight made any hunger Adeline had felt die immediately. Something was wrong.

"What is it, Fal?" Roman questioned, the smile having been wiped from his face. Falrin cast a questioning glance at Adeline, unsure if he should continue on.

"It's okay. She can know. I am done hiding things from her." Roman tightened his grip on her hand as he spoke.

"Thank the Gods," Falrin said, but it was devoid of the familiar playful tone his words always carried.

He cleared his throat before he continued speaking, "It seems your declaration of war struck King Thorian as the perfect challenge. There was a small army spotted heading this way today. They are two days out."

"How many?" Roman gritted through his teeth.

"At least five hundred strong."

Adeline fell to her knees.

CHAPTER THIRTY-EIGHT

ADELINE'S HEART FELT AS if it had cracked open and poured all of its contents on the front steps of the cabin as Falrin's words sank in. At least five hundred men from her father's army were on their way to Drakmoor, and it didn't take a genius to know that they were not coming for tea. A sob escaped her throat.

I was such a fool to think that I could simply be happy here, that he would allow me to do so. Gods. What are we going to do? She thought, feeling her chest heave in an effort to draw in a breath. *Everyone in Drakmoor has dedicated their entire lives to protecting the dragons, and it's all going to come crashing down because of me.*

Adeline felt as if her skin was crawling off her body with the way it itched so desperately. Her lungs ached, begging her to draw in even a fraction of a breath, but she couldn't. Instead, her breathing quickened until all she could manage were small gasps. Her head felt heavy and clouded with an array of thoughts, while what-ifs made her stomach churn. Nausea clawed at her empty stomach, and she was sure if there had been anything in it, it would have now been spilled across the wood slats in front of her. Everything about the world around her faded out until all she could hear was the thousands of thoughts fighting for their chance to be heard first, and she felt as if her skin was vibrating with nerves.

Somewhere distant she thought she could make out a whisper, maybe the sound of her name? It was difficult to tell with the blood rushing in her ears, making it sound as though she were submerged underwater.

A firm hand closed around her chin, drawing her eyes to a familiar set of piercing green ones. The gesture slowed her mind only slightly.

"Breathe for me, Addie," Roman whispered to her, trying desperately to get her to calm down, to *breathe*.

His words settled into her bones, and she felt her breaths begin to slow. Roman's eyes never left hers as he breathed with her, coaching her on slowing their pace. Bit by bit, the blurred edges of the world around her came into focus again, and the ringing in her ears was replaced by the soft chirp of crickets practicing for their nightly symphony.

"Good girl, deep breaths." He stayed kneeling in front of her, regulating her inhales until she began to take deeper breaths on her own, relishing in the feel of oxygen flooding her starving lungs. As she drew in breath after breath, her mind began to clear until only one thought remained: *I will make him pay for this. King Thorian is going to wish he never sent his men to Drakmoor.*

Once he was sure that she had regained her composure, Roman helped Adeline to her feet again, reaching down gently to brush away the dirt that had gathered on her shins where she had sunken to the earth. Even once she stood, he did not drop her hand, seeming to need to feel her touch to calm his own raging mind.

Looking up, Adeline realized that Seraphina had joined them on the front porch at some point while she had been panicking and though her body told her she should be embarrassed that Falrin, Seraphina, and Roman had all witnessed her breakdown, her heart inflated with gratitude that they had not shied away from her weakened state. Instead, they had chosen to stand by her side, trusting her to work through it on her own and knowing that they would step in if she could not, the way Roman had. Seraphina offered her a soft smile that melted away any sliver of self-consciousness Adeline may have clung to. These people were her friends, and she would go into battle right alongside them. She would die for them if it meant protecting their lives, their safety.

"What's the plan?" Adeline finally asked, her voice still shaky with fear.

"Well," Falrin glanced at Roman in a silent request for his permission, only continuing when Roman gently inclined his head. "We were kind of hoping you would help us figure that part out?"

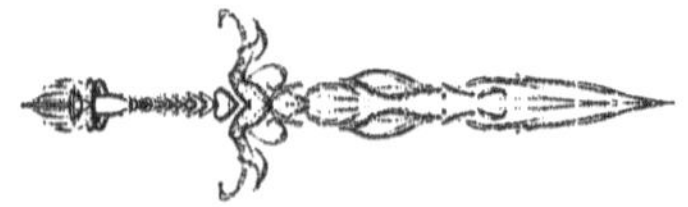

The four of them had locked themselves away in the library for several hours before anyone came up for air, only breaking when Milo shyly knocked on the heavy door and entered with plates piled high for each of them. They all offered him soft smiles and gleeful thanks, Seraphina and Adeline both stopping their scouring over maps to give him a hug.

Milo did not linger, not wanting to disrupt their plotting; he left just as abruptly as he had appeared—shutting the door softly behind him as if he had never been there.

"What if we came at them from the south and set up an ambush of men in the north, where they will be expecting us?" Falrin offered, his finger gliding across the tattered map as he spoke.

"That could work! They'd never be expecting us to come at them from behind," Seraphina agreed excitedly.

"That's what she said," Falrin winked at her. Even in the weight of the moment, he was cracking jokes, lightening the somber tone of the room and making Adeline feel all the more thankful to know him.

"No, but seriously, that is actually not a bad plan," Roman agreed, stepping up to the table to see exactly where Falrin was pointing, tracing the trajectory with his gaze and nodding.

"We could set up attack points here and here," he pointed to two places on the map, and Adeline tucked herself under his arm, using the excuse of needing a better view to be pressed against him.

"That won't work." Adeline shook her head, pointing to the last spot that Roman had indicated. "They will expect you to attack from here. They have *trained* for counter-attacks like the one you are suggesting. It is walking into certain death," she finished. The room filled with a thick silence, all of them deflating with her words.
It was exactly as it had been for the last several hours they had been locked away. One of them would call out a plan that *should* be flawless and then Adeline would step forward, the bearer of bad news, once again.

Though she was a princess, she had paid an immense amount of attention to the battle brief conversations that occurred throughout the castle, usually finding them far more interesting than any possible suitors. Between her unintentional spying and her conversations with

Calum about training with the guard, she knew a dangerous amount about Scalebreak's army. In this moment, however, it was all proving to only discourage them rather than bring them any sort of advantage.

"We have to face the truth," Adeline broke the silence, "they are prepared for any attack. They have trained for this exact scenario day in and day out, we can't take them by surprise here."

"You're right," Falrin sighed deeply, "it's hopeless. No matter which way you look at it, they are going to beat us."

"No matter which way you look at it," Seraphina mumbled to herself, suddenly deep in thought as she traced her finger along the map in front of her.

"You're gonna have to speak up, Sweet Cheeks."

"No matter which way you look at it, only we *haven't* looked at it from every angle. We have deliberated coming at them from all directions, except for one," Seraphina locked eyes with Falrin, hope sparkling in her gaze.

"You aren't suggesting..." Falrin trailed off.

"That we attack from the sky. They will be expecting us to *hide* our dragons, to protect them from harm. But what if we *used* them instead?" Adeline's heart thundered against her rib cage as she turned the plan over in her mind.

"No," Roman growled. "Absolutely not. Everything we have built here has been to *protect* the dragons from Scalebreak, from Thorian. We will *not* fly them directly into harm's way!" His tone was harsh, every bit the calculated leader he was destined to one day become.

"No, Ro, she's right. We haven't flown our dragons into battle in over a century. It is the *only* thing that they are not prepared for," Falrin said desperately. "It's brilliant really, I couldn't have come up with something better myself." He glanced at Seraphina like he was refraining from closing the space between them and kissing her for her brilliance.

"Just think about it. We have protected the dragons for so long, and for what? If we do not succeed in our attack, everything we have fought for will be gone. They will *capture and kill our dragons*, Roman," Seraphina's voice cracked with the words they had all been too afraid to speak aloud.

"She's right, Ro," Adeline wrapped her arm around Roman's bicep, a comforting touch amidst the chaos.

Roman was silent for several minutes, his eyes darting over the map again and again until he sighed. "Okay, and say we go with this *insane* plan, where would we start?"

They all jumped into a feverish discussion of details, including where they would launch their strikes from, what their attack strategy was, which dragons would be permitted into battle. The chatter of their planning filled every corner of the quiet library until they felt they had considered every last detail of what was to come.

In two days, they would be flying into battle with Scalebreak, but they had a plan. All of them bone-tired, they parted ways, Seraphina and Falrin excusing themselves to bed while Roman and Adeline collapsed into the pair of armchairs in front of the fireplace.

Adeline wasted absolutely no time, barely letting the door to the library latch behind Falrin and Seraphina before she spoke. "I want to go with you."

Roman looked at her as if she had two heads.

"Addie…"

"No, you don't get to do that. You promised me that we were a *team*, Roman. I am going to fight alongside you, Falrin, and Seraphina. It is not a question or a request. I will not stand idly by and watch the people that I *love* be slaughtered in a fight that is not their own," she spat at him, sensing his refusal before he even uttered a word.

"I agre—"

"I am not some damsel in distress that you need to swoop in and *save*! I can fight my own—wait...what?" She finally registered his response, realizing she had been arguing for nothing.

"I said I agree, Princess. You are perfectly capable of fighting your own battles, and you have proved that time and time again. I doubted you once before, and it caused you great pain. I will not make the same mistake again," he said softly.

"You-you're not going to argue with me?" Adeline questioned, sure she had to be mistaken.

"No, Addie. I am not going to argue. We have just over forty hours until we will be preparing our attacks, and I will be damned if I spend even a moment of that time arguing with you. We have had enough chaos to last us a lifetime already. Let's allow ourselves to live in ignorant bliss for a day." His voice was pleading.

All he wanted was just one day, one perfect day where they could pretend that they were not fated to hate one another, where they could hide from the life the fates crafted for them and finally lose themselves in one another, and Adeline would by lying to herself if she said she did not want the same.

"I will be damned to hell before I lose another moment by your side, Princess. Play pretend with me before it all goes to hell, just one day is all I ask," he begged, his gaze a desperate plea to her.

"I couldn't dream of a better way to spend our time," Adeline smiled at him softly.

"I'm glad we're in agreement," Roman said with a mischievous grin on his lips as he rose from his spot in the chair. "Because our time starts now."

He walked over to the door, ensuring it was closed securely, before turning the lock. When he turned to face Adeline again, any trace of fear for what was to come had vanished from his face, replaced by desire as he closed the distance between them, leaning down to press his mouth to hers in desperation.

His fingers traced along her bare calf, and the touch felt somehow more sensual than their open-mouthed embrace, causing her to arch into him. Roman moaned into their kiss as he watched her curve her body against him, any control he once had lost. He dropped to his knees in front of her, placing himself between her spread legs, where he pressed a gentle kiss against her inner thigh.

"Good girl."

She laced her fingers with his hair, gripping tightly as she stared into his wild eyes.

"Ruin me, Shadow."

Chapter Thirty-Nine

Having awoken before Roman the next morning, Adeline took the opportunity to sneak out of the warm embrace of the satin sheets and dress as quietly as possible to avoid waking him. Settling for the first thing her fingers caught on when she opened the wardrobe, she pulled out a pale lilac dress that hung off her shoulders elegantly, the cotton coming to her ankles before ending abruptly. It was one of the few she had not yet worn, and the kiss of the untouched fabric against her skin set a grin upon her lips.

Wanting to feel the freedom of the flowy fabric, she forewent a corset, instead opting for a white ribbon tied onto a long wavy ponytail as an accent to the beautiful sundress. Glancing at herself in the mirror before she exited the room, she decided she may never have looked as beautiful as she did in that moment. Happiness radiated off of her, even in the circumstances she tried to push to the back of her mind, bringing a glow to her face and a twinkle to her eyes, enough so that even she noticed it in her reflection.

Roman stirred slightly, a soft snore escaping his lips as he rolled over, causing Adeline to freeze, holding her breath for a moment. She wanted him to enjoy the rest as long as he could, unsure of what may face them the next day. Once his breathing deepened again, she let go of the breath she had been holding onto and tiptoed to the door. Turning the knob as quietly as possible, she slipped out into the hallway and shut the door with a near silent-click behind her.

Practically sprinting, Adeline made her way down the stairs and into the warm, familiar glow of the kitchen, feeling her smile grow as she stepped through the door and the scent of baking bread curled into her nostrils. Her mind went blank in the kitchen—something that she was now grateful for—as she did just what Roman had pleaded for her to do: play pretend.

Adeline took a deep breath, letting the sweet smells sink into her body until they loosened her every muscle. As she blew the air out through her nose, she looked up, unsurprised to find that Seraphina had managed to slip away this morning as well, seeking the familiar comfort of their shared space.

Smiling, she greeted Seraphina with a tight hug, holding back any tears that managed to find their way to her eyes at the gesture. Those bright blue eyes looked into hers, fighting tears of their own. The embrace was heavy with unspoken promises, and it was all the time they allowed themselves to think of the coming day before they returned to their work.

Adeline relied on memory to carry her through the room as she gathered her supplies, stopping at the glowing stove to bid Thistle a good morning. Despite the coming danger, Thistle seemed somehow *lighter* than before, a detail that Adeline did not have the strength to question. Instead, she found her place at the counter space she now called her own, setting out various bowls of ingredients. Before starting, she grabbed a spare white apron off the hook on the wall, tying it tightly around her waist.

No sooner had her fingers left the laces before she felt a gangly body collide with her own, seeing Milo through nothing but a flurry of red hair. Judging by the still-swinging door and his sleep-mussed auburn curls, he had only just entered the kitchens, not wasting a second before wrapping his arms around Adeline.

"Is it true?" Milo asked excitedly, beaming up at her. "Did you really bond to Syn?"

"Sort of," Adeline admitted, "though the bond is not fully intact just yet." She reached down and tousled his hair affectionately, smiling at him.

"I *knew* you could do it! I knew you were supposed to be here, to be one of us!" Milo's declaration made her heart flutter. She could not find the words to respond but did not need to, as Milo continued on after a pause.

"You know," his freckled cheeks colored pink, "I know you have not always been sure of your place here, but I am glad that you're sticking around to give us a chance."

Tears pricked her eyes with his words, burning with the tender words he spoke.

"Me too, kid. Me too." Adeline wrapped herself around him now, returning his tight embrace as she fought to hold back her tears.

"Milo! Good morning!" Thistle interrupted with a cheerful smile. "I could use some help chopping these vegetables."

Milo peeled himself off of Adeline and began preparing his station as if nothing had happened at all. Blinking away the moisture from her eyes, Adeline did the same.

As she always did, Adeline lost herself in the motions of baking, only coming up for air to pull the freshly baked buns from the hearth and set them on the counter to cool while she cleared away dishes to make room for preparing the frosting.

Roman, as if sensing there were fresh pastries that were nearly ready for him to devour, stepped through the door of the kitchen with a smile. The sight of him standing there so casually, in his usual gray drawers and black tee, made Adeline's heart stutter for several beats. Though he had taken the time to tame his hair, his features still hinted at sleep; he hadn't been awake for long.

Apparently unable to stand the distance between them, Roman crossed the kitchen. He placed himself behind Adeline, wrapping his arms around her waist and tucking his chin into the curve of her neck so he could watch her movements. She melted into his touch, stopping her tidying for only a moment; it was all he needed.

Roman spun her around so that she now faced him. Leaving one hand on her waist, he swiped the other across the countertop, the surface still dusted with flour. The white powder clung to his skin and his smile turned mischievous as he swiped his finger across her face, leaving behind a trail of flour on her cheek.

"Good morning, Princess," Roman laughed, his eyes crinkling shut.

"Good morning to you, too, Shadow," Adeline giggled, letting her hand slip behind her and onto the covered countertop until she was satisfied with the feeling of flour on her skin.

She waited until his eyes closed for only a moment before she swiped her finger across his jaw, leaving behind a gritty fingerprint identical to the one that now adorned her cheek. The two of them dissolved into a fit of laughter, pausing only to arm themselves with more of the flour that served as a weapon in their war. It wasn't long before they were both dusted in a layer of white and their bellies ached with laughter. They fell silent as they locked eyes, still smiling, and as the soft melody of Thistle's usual humming filled the air around them, Roman's smile widened.

Grabbing her hand, he pulled Adeline against him and began swaying them to the tune, pausing only to spin her while she giggled. He stared at her like it was his favorite sound, and as such he took every opportunity that the beat of Thistle's humming allowed to spin her again and again, his eyes never leaving her. When Thistle's melody finally slowed to an end, Roman pulled Adeline against him, his hands pressed into the curve of her back, and pressed a gentle kiss to her forehead.

"I will do whatever it takes to get us both out alive tomorrow, if only so I can live to see more moments like this one," he whispered into her hair, wrapping his arms around her in a tight hug.

"Promise me that you will live, Ro," Adeline pleaded.

"I'd live a hundred lives if you only asked," was his only response before he was tugging the apron from her waist and pulling her behind him and out of the kitchens.

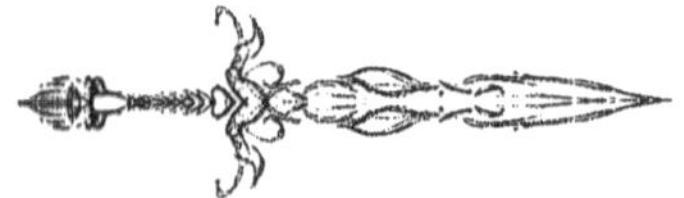

They spent the remainder of the daylight in the village, Roman wanting her to enjoy every moment she could in some of her favorite places, surrounded by her favorite people.

Adeline's face had been the epitome of pure delight when he finally told her where they were going to spend their afternoon, and she made the most of every second in the village. She tugged Roman with her through all the shops and crowds, stopping to talk with each and every person before continuing to the next. Her charm and joy were infectious, so much so that many of the shopkeepers had turned down her payment and given her the trinkets that she gaped at in awe free of charge. Arms overflowing with goods, Adeline dropped Roman's hand while she fell deep into conversation with a heavily pregnant shop owner, not noticing when he slipped away.

By the time Roman returned, someone had provided Adeline with a wooden basket to carry her shiny new things in, freeing her arms of the burden of carrying them all. She sat perched on the edge of the fountain in the town square with a little girl sitting cross-legged on the ground in front of her while she intertwined the child's bright blonde strands with one another into a braid. Roman stood back for a moment, watching her with adoration, admiring the way the golden hues of the late afternoon sun brought her into the light. *My sweet-souled Addie. She would have made an incredible queen,* he thought to himself.

After tying off the end of the young girl's braid, Adeline looked up, her eyes locking on Roman's. She pushed off the ledge she had been sitting on and walked toward him, both of them moving to close the distance between them.

"Where did you wander off to, Shadow?" she teased.

"I'm so glad you asked. Do you trust me, Princess?" he asked.

"With my life," she said seriously.

"Close your eyes and hold out your hands."

She obeyed, placing her hands out in front of her with the palms facing upward, waiting. Roman welcomed the cool bite of metal against the skin of his hands as he placed the object in her hands. When she opened her eyes to see the dagger lying in her palms, her face lit up.

Roughly twelve inches in length, the dagger was a sight to behold. The hilt was made of steel, but had somehow been turned a blush pink color, her favorite. Two strands of the pink metal twisted into one another, making the perfect grip, before branching out into the slight upward curve of the guard. The pink ended there, giving way to a silver that was nearly identical to Synacthdris' scales. Adeline seemed to stop breathing entirely, her lungs failing her as she took in the beautifully crafted blade in her hands.

"Roman, I—it's beautiful," she managed, still breathless.

"It is customary for a rider to be given a gift when they bond to their dragon. I know the bond isn't quite fully intact yet, but not knowing what tomorrow holds...I wanted you to have this now," the words came out coated in nerves.

"It's perfect. I love it. Thank you, Ro."

"Actually, there is more. I refuse to walk into the hands of death tomorrow without first telling you how I feel." His words seemed to come out in a rush, as if he would burst if he didn't get them out in that very moment. "Addie, you have made every hardship I have faced in this life feel somehow *worth it*. I would walk through the worst days of my life a thousand times if it meant meeting you on the other side. And even now, I feel robbed of time. No matter what tomorrow brings, I know that I would have loved you for a lifetime," he paused, taking a shaky breath. "But that's the thing, Princess; one lifetime with you could never possibly be enough time. *No* amount of time with you would ever be enough. I will love you long into any other lives that may find us, because you are it for me, Adeline Ambrose. My soul will find yours, always." Roman stared at her, his green eyes glistening with tears. "I am *yours* in every lifetime."

"Oh, Roman. I—"

"No, don't say anything, not yet. I know you love me, Addie, but don't utter the words yet. Give me something to live for tomorrow."

And with that he was pulling her behind him, dragging her back through the flurry of people and into the trees. Adeline looked shocked to find Aurelius standing there, waiting for the two of them with a look of annoyance, as if they were late.

"What are we doing?" She finally asked.

"I will not face tomorrow without ending our perfect day with a night ride spent holding you, tucked among the stars," he declared with a mixture of sadness and love dancing in his gaze.

Adeline seemed unable to find the words to respond, tears of her own prickling her eyes as she mounted Aurelius. When the familiar, cool kiss of Roman's shadows curled around them to secure them in place, she breathed out a sigh, relaxing against him in the saddle.

Aurelius was far gentler with his takeoff than normal, seeming as if he too was soaking in every moment before they faced their fate. Adeline whispered her thanks to the usually surly dragon, and Roman smiled like a fool.

As they leveled out in the sky, Aurelius' gold wings beating gently against the evening breeze, Adeline let herself relax a little more. The sun was almost entirely set, the last glimpses of light still clinging to the blue horizon, and Roman could see stars blinking to life around them. His arms were wrapped around her waist, his head tucked into the crook of her neck, and he watched blissfully as his every breath tickled her skin, leaving a trail of goosebumps behind. She leaned into him, seeming to give herself over entirely to the feeling of peace that overcame her.

"Even before I met you, night rides were always the only thing that could calm my mind. I used to spend almost every night out here, searching for *something,* but I never knew what. I always found the darkness to be a familiar comfort, something that was beautiful and endless, but now I realize that even the night sky can't rival your beauty, Addie. Seeing you among the stars that I spent so many nights scouring for answers, I finally understand that it was always *you*. You are what I have spent endless nights searching for, because up here with you, among the stars, I finally feel at *home.*" A tear slid down Roman's cheek as he finished, and he did not move to brush it away.

"Oh, Ro. I—" she hesitated, seeming to have to stop herself from uttering the words he had begged her to save for after they won the battle tomorrow. "You are home to me too."

They let the comfortable silence of the night sky envelop them, taking any thoughts of the coming day from their minds as they rode, tangled in one another atop Aurelius—one with the stars around them.

CHAPTER FORTY

THE DAY TO FACE their fate came all too quickly. Though Adeline and Roman had relished in every second of playing pretend, the time had come for them to walk into battle.

Nausea was heavy in Adeline's stomach as she and Roman dressed, both of them pulling on their fighting leathers, emblazoned with dragon wings across the chest, before slipping on heavy, black dragon scale armor to cover their vital organs. Even though the uncertainty of what lay ahead was heavy, Adeline couldn't help but admire the handiwork that went into crafting the pieces of armor she now wore. She knew it was made of previously shed, dead scales, hence the black color, but she couldn't quite figure out how they were all held together. Pondering the thought, she began tying her hair up behind her, twisting the waves into a dragon braid down her back before slipping the pink-hilted dagger that Roman had gifted her into the sheath strapped to her thigh.

"You look absolutely deadly." Roman broke the silence with a growl as if he was unable to help himself.

"I could say the same about you," Adeline said with a wink.

"Hate to interrupt, but we have a battle to go fight, so if you guys could wrap it up that would be great," Falrin interrupted from the doorway.

Gods, he is always interrupting, Adeline thought to herself, though she couldn't bring herself to be irritated by it.

Taking the hint, Roman pulled Adeline against him desperately, holding her as if his life depended on it. She held him back just as fervently, neither of them speaking for several moments. Roman pulled away first, pressing a passionate kiss to her lips and seeming not to care that Falrin was watching. They had agreed they would not say goodbye, nor would they wish each other luck. Instead, they would face this day as they would any other, hand in hand.

Finally separating, they followed Falrin out of the safety of Adeline's bedroom and into the arms of uncertainty. He led them outside to where Raegorath, Aurelius, and Synacthdris all stood awaiting their arrival, their saddles already secured. Several other dragons that Adeline recognized from the ravine stood proudly behind them.

There had to be at least twenty others, all with riders confidently seated and awaiting their orders to launch into the skies. Adeline felt her heart swell. Regardless of the weight of the moment, it was an honor to see so many riders with their dragons. She saw some familiar faces on the backs of the other creatures and felt worry coursing through her as her eyes fell upon Thistle and Milo among them. She would not stop them, would not ask them to stay behind; she just hoped that they made it out alive.

There was no further delaying this, and they all knew it. So rather than try to stop the people she loved from heading into battle, she joined them. She mounted Synacthdris proudly, securing herself tightly in the saddle upon her back. Adeline glanced to her right, finding Seraphina and Falrin astride Raegorath, and then to her left, her eyes meeting Roman's.

A million unspoken words passed between them, but they were out of time, so Adeline nodded her head, signaling that she was ready, and Falrin let out a long low whistle before they all took off. No one spared a glance back at what they left behind.

They flew in silence, no one daring to speak a word of what they were about to face. Both fortunately and unfortunately, they did not need to travel far before they spotted the progressing army below.

Adeline felt her heart drop to her stomach as her eyes fell upon the familiar red and gold armor of her father's troops. As her eyes caught on the glint of metal worn by the marching men, she couldn't help but feel guilt creeping in on her. These used to be *her people.* Her *army.* And here she was heading into battle on the opposing side, preparing to overtake them with whatever means necessary.

The closer they drew, the more the guilt grew until Adeline could all but feel it crawling up her throat. She felt as if she were barely breathing. Her lips parted slightly, as if begging her to utter the one word that would potentially put a stop to it all. *Stop.* But as the word echoed in her mind, never finding its way past her lips, it began to take on a new meaning. *Stop.* She repeated in her mind once more. *Stop it, Addie. These people are your enemy. They fight alongside your father proudly. These are the very people who stood idly by and watched you be oppressed more and more with every year that passed. These are the people who have taken pride in killing the very creatures you have come to love.*

With the last thought, Synacthdris turned her head back to look at Adeline, and as their eyes met, it felt as if Syn had heard her desperate pleading with herself and understood the exact feeling. Pride filled the silver dragon's eyes as she stared at Adeline for only a few seconds, not having time to waste, but it was all Adeline needed to shake the feeling of guilt, not wanting to let it distract her when it mattered most.

Falrin led the attack, sending Raegortath into a nosedive straight for the waiting army. As they neared the ground, Raegorath let out a blast of fire, not stopping until they pulled up into the sky again, readying for another attack. In perfect synchronicity, Falrin sent a blast of wind in the opposite direction, sending several men flying backward until they connected with the forest floor, dazed. Adeline watched as at least twenty men fell to the ground and before she could process the fact that the battle had begun, screams erupted around them.

Not giving Adeline a chance to react, Synacthdris began spiraling down, readying for an attack of her own. Though the situation they were in was grave, Synacthdris seemed to come alive at the challenge set before them. She tucked her wings, letting them spin toward the earth at a terrifying speed before she finally threw her wings out at the last second and let out a blast of fire of her own.

Dark ribbons of shadow shot out from behind them, curling down to wrap around the ankles of as many men as they could reach. Aurelius shot higher into the sky, pulling five men fighting to be released from the shadows that bound them. Once they were high above the clouds, Roman flicked his hand out, freeing the men from their binds and sending them plummeting to the earth where they landed with a sickening crunch.

Around them, dragons deposited their riders on the land below before soaring back into the skies to attack from above. As Synacthdris lowered them to the earth again, Adeline loosened the belt of her saddle and took the split second she had to tuck her head and roll to her feet.

Unsheathing the dagger at her thigh, she looked up with death dancing in her eyes and found three soldiers trying to overpower Falrin in front of her. The sight ignited a rage deep within Adeline, erasing any glimmer of guilt that lingered from before. *They will NOT hurt my friends,* she thought as she reached for the familiar hum of power lingering beneath her skin, calling it to her.

She raced forward with a battle cry, one hand out in front of her while the other gripped the dagger at her side. Flames of orange and red shot from her outstretched palm and collided with the men, knocking them off their feet. It was more than she had ever been able to summon in her training sessions, and it had been just as shocking to her as it had been to her victims. Not letting her surprise show, Adeline reached within herself again, calling on that same power as before. She delighted in the feeling of her second strike as the flames kissed her skin in their path to her target, this time melting the men's armor off their bodies and leaving the skin bubbling off their bones. Their screams filled the air as they clawed desperately at themselves, and it shocked her slightly at how delicious the sound of their screams was in her ears.

Falrin did not waste a second, taking the opportunity to slice in one solid motion with his sword across all three men. Deep crimson flooded the earth beneath them, and within seconds the men who had been writhing in pain were motionless in the dirt.

One breath of shock at the death that lay at her feet was all Adeline allowed herself before she was running again, this time straight at two soldiers who had begun to approach her, presumably thinking she would not notice. She tightened her grasp on the hilt of her dagger, the only piece of Roman she had in the chaos around her, and narrowed her eyes on the men closing in on her. They both carried heavy swords in their hands, and Adeline knew the added weight meant they would be just a fraction slower than she was, but it was all she needed.

At the last second possible, she tucked her body in on itself and rolled between the men, slicing at their heels with her blade. Blood sputtered from the wounds, and Adeline felt several droplets stick to her face, wiping them with the back of her hand as she stood. One of the men lay unable to move on the ground, moaning in pain from the wounds she had inflicted. His friend glanced between the man and Adeline, fear in his eyes.

The forest around her was bathed in blood, she was not sure just how much of it was their own. Though the thought made her sick, she refused to show it. A devilish grin painted itself across her face, masking the fear that was taking hold.

"Guess it's just you and me now," she eyed the man as if he were prey.

His sword wobbling in his grip, the man stared back at her for a long moment before turning on his heel and running in the opposite direction.

"Well, that's no fun," Roman appeared at her side, his armor covered in blood.

She scanned him with her eyes, desperately searching for any wounds that could have resulted in the amount of blood he wore. Several quick passes with her eyes told her that, luckily, none of it appeared to be his own. Adeline wasn't sure if the relief that filled her body was due to his lack of injury, or his impeccable timing.

Thank Gods he's here.

CHAPTER FORTY-ONE

BEFORE SHE COULD REPLY, a helpless scream filled the air, turning her blood to ice. *No.* Her eyes darted through the chaos, trying to pinpoint where the sound had come from, and her stomach plummeted as her eyes fell on a familiar head of red curls being hauled away by four soldiers, Milo. Terror washed over her at the sight.

Wasting no time, Roman raced past her, running toward where the men held Milo thrashing against them, pulling Adeline from the daze. She watched in horror as Milo's wire-framed glasses fell from his face and onto the dirt below. *Not his glasses,* Adeline stepped forward, reaching desperately forward with her hands as if she could somehow snatch the glasses from where they lay in the dirt several yards in front of her and place them back in their rightful home atop the freckled nose she loved.

All restraint she had managed to keep hold of was set free when one of the men restraining Milo stepped on his glasses, shattering them with a crunch that snapped something within her. Adeline's feet moved on their own, carrying her as fast as she could run to Milo. *Gods, please not Milo.* Everything around her felt as if it moved in slow motion as she ran as fast as her body could carry her, begging her muscles to let her move just a little faster.

Roman got to Milo first, his shadows shooting out to grab hold of the two men, whom Adeline now realized had been using their blades to carve into Milo's skin. The sight of blood pouring freely from the wounds they had created made her sick, nausea bubbling to life in her stomach. There was no time for anything other than saving Milo, so she pushed the feelings down.

Black ribbons curled around the men, fully enveloping them as they cried out in surprise. Roman's shadows seized the opportunity, their black tendrils diving down their throats and choking them from the inside out while they hung suspended in a cloud of darkness.

Several seconds passed while the men clawed at the shadows, trying to grab hold of them and pull them from their throats if only to draw in one last, hopeless breath. Unfortunately for them, the more they struggled, the more force Roman pushed his shadows with. It wasn't until they stopped moving altogether that he finally called his shadows back to him, letting the two men fall lifeless to the ground—discarded without a second thought.

Adeline surged forward, reaching for the electric hum beneath her skin once more, but was quickly stopped by fingers roughly closing around her wrist and hauling her backward. Confused, she looked over her shoulder, her breath catching as she found Calum staring back at her.

Her body softened slightly as she met the familiar pair of blue eyes and she cursed her body for its response. Of all the people she should have expected to be here Calum was at the top of the list, but she would be lying if she didn't admit that a small part of her had hoped he would somehow change his mind, choose to be better. No matter how many times he *showed* her the person he had become, she still found herself hoping that he would appear before her as the boy she had once known.

"Addie. You shouldn't be here." His voice was desperate, pleading as he tried to pull her with him.

She shook her arm out of his grasp aggressively, staring daggers at him.

"No, Calum. *You* shouldn't be here. Are you *proud* of the army you've walked straight into the hands of death?" she spat at him, not giving him time to reply before she turned and started running back in the direction of Roman and Milo. But as her eyes met the two of them ahead, her feet stopped moving entirely, as if the life had been sucked from her body. Everything faded away except for the scene unfolding before her.

Roman had been able to bring down one of the other men, who was now lying motionless next to the other two, but he had been attacked from behind before he could get to the fourth soldier. She looked to where their enemy now stood with a trembling Milo tucked against his chest, a dagger poised at the boy's throat, and gasped in horror. A pair of wire-framed glasses perched on Reggie's nose as he glared back at her. Any kindness she had once seen in his eyes was now replaced with hatred and disgust.

Suddenly everything about her stay at Drakmoor and her father's ability to track her down with ease made sense. Reggie had been lurking in the background feeding him information. *Did he even deliver my letter?* Adeline couldn't bring herself to look at him anymore and instead let her gaze slip down to where he held the boy in his arms, desperately wishing she could turn back time and tell Roman not to trust Reggie, but it was too late.

Tears were sliding down Milo's cheeks as he drew in shaking breaths, his green eyes that had once been so full of life now filled with terror and defeat. Adeline took a shaky breath, her heart crumbling in her chest for the boy who had trusted her so wholeheartedly.

It's going to be okay, she mouthed to Milo before letting her gaze shift to Roman as she desperately tried to come up with a plan.

Directly across from Milo, Roman was being held by three soldiers with his arms hanging in heavy iron shackles in front of him. Despite his hands being tied, Roman still bucked wildly against the men restraining him, trying to free himself of their hold. It was useless; he was outnumbered.

Chapter Forty-Two

A DELINE'S BREATH WAVERED AS she took in the scene playing out in front of her, and she willed her body to move, but found herself frozen, unable to advance and staring helplessly. Her body felt heavy, and no matter how hard she fought her mind to get it to move even a little, it did not budge.

Reggie looked up from where he was holding the blade to Milo's neck and laughed harshly. "Not so fun facing the consequences of running from fate now, is it, Princess?" He stared directly into her eyes as he slid the dagger across the pale expanse of Milo's throat, slicing the skin open in a deep gash.

Blood oozed out of the wound immediately and began to pour down Milo's chest in a cascade of crimson. A helpless gurgle escaped Milo as

Reggie let him go, pressing his boot against the boy's back and kicking him into the dirt.

His body hit the earth with a thud that felt as if it echoed throughout the forest, and ringing filled Adeline's ears as she watched, still unable to move from where she stood. Milo's skin was already a sickly pale white by the time he connected with the ground, and she knew that if there was any chance to save him, it was quickly escaping them.

As if he could hear her frantic thoughts, Milo looked up at her from where he lay in a growing puddle of his own life force. The fear that had previously been written on his face was gone now, replaced by a peaceful smile. He had stopped trying to fight the fate that awaited him, and instead used his last moments of life to reassure Adeline.

I love you, Milo mouthed as the last glimpse of light faded from his green eyes, the very same light that had made Adeline feel so at home in Drakmoor. A scream escaped her body as she watched his bright eyes flutter closed for the last time. The innocent young boy who had just hugged her so tightly in the kitchens the day prior, lifeless at the hands of her father's army. Her heart shattered in her chest, and she felt nothing but rage as she turned back to where her lover was being held.

Roman fought against his chains, yelling out in agony for the life they had just taken. His muscles strained with every move, his body trying desperately to help him escape.

Adeline again willed her body to move, even an inch, but again found herself unable to feel a thing—as if she were frozen in time. Sobs wracked her body as she watched in desperation at Roman trying to free himself, his tear-filled eyes never leaving Milo's crumpled body in the dirt. She had never felt so *hopeless.*

Calum let out a laugh in response to the scene that had unfolded and walked around Adeline, closing the distance between her and Roman in only a few paces. When he reached the men restraining Roman, he inclined his head in permission with a devilish grin upon his face. Dropping only one hand from where he was gripping Roman, one of the soldiers unsheathed the sword at his hip, raising it high into the air before slamming it down onto the top of Roman's head, knocking him unconscious.

"I really hoped it wouldn't have to come to this," Calum said, feigning sympathy through the smirk that splayed across his lips.

Adeline felt something inside her crack as she watched Roman crumple to the floor, unconscious, and a desperate scream loosed itself from her throat. She fought her mind, begging her body to move, to get to Roman. No matter how much she willed it to be, she could not move and was forced to watch in despair as they grabbed Roman under the arms and drug him, wrapped in iron chains, away from her. It was the last thing she saw before she felt something heavy connect with her head as she, too, lost consciousness.

Chapter Forty-Three

E VERY MUSCLE IN ADELINE'S body screamed in pain as she came to and tried to sit up. The memories of the battle came flooding back to her, the life fading from Milo's eyes as his throat was slit, Roman being dragged away from her in chains, and despair buried itself in her stomach. She opened her eyes, hoping to find that it had all been nothing but a nightmare, and instead found Amira leaning over her, her graying braid dotted with specks of drying blood.

"Easy, Addie. Sit up slowly, I'll help you," she said, helping Adeline sit up and lean against the sturdy trunk of a tree, the bark biting into the skin on her back.

"Milo," Adeline spoke his name in a muffled cry, tears spilling from her blue eyes uncontrollably.

"I know, honey." Amira stroked her hair, tears of her own slipping down her cheeks.

"R-Roman, they have Roman," she sobbed. All Amira could muster was a solemn nod in response.

Adeline looked around them, her eyes scanning the blood-soaked earth and too many bodies, both human and dragon, surrounded them. Her stomach churned, and she forced her eyes back to Amira, who was now staring blankly, and she took a deep breath before she spoke.

"And when the rose draws forth the darkness,
Reminding him the beauty of fate
She'll lure him into her caress
And he will realize all too late
For his destruction lies in wait."

The words struck Adeline like a blow. The prophecy that Amira had just uttered had been what Roman was referring to when he said she was meant to be his undoing.

They had been *fated* to love one another, and now he was gone without ever hearing her utter the words aloud. Something deep within Adeline snapped into place, sobering her, and she stood. Power hummed under her skin, unable to be contained, and silver flames licked up her arm as she began walking into the forest.

I am his in every lifetime was the only thought echoing in her mind as her feet crunched in the dirt. She was going to get her prince.

THE END.

Acknowledgements

First and foremost, I would like to thank *you,* dear reader. My story is nothing without friends to share it with. Thank you to my team of ARC, Alpha, and Beta readers; there are too many of you to name individually, which is something that never fails to bring me to tears. Thank you for believing in my story, and taking a chance on an indie author; your endless love and support truly means the world.

To my OG street team: Alex, Alexandra, Kier, Micca, Mychailia, Ray, Cheese, Alyssa, Jazzy, Skyla, Morgan, Haeli, Sarah H., Rae, Sarah D., Hannah, Katelyn, Kendra, Sam, Steph, Laura, I love each and every one of you with my entire heart. *Blade of Broken Scales* would not be what it is today without all of you! You took a chance on a weirdo with a baja blast addiction and a dream and never looked back, and for that I am eternally thankful.

Alex, there are no words for the endless gratitude I have for you. Not only have you carried me through this journey, never failing to be there when I needed you, but you have loved it as if it were your own. Walking this road together and getting to watch you become a published author has filled me with so much pride. I could truly go on forever expressing how thankful I am for you, so I'll leave you with this: *whatever our souls are made of, yours and mine are the same.*

Kier, I truly feel as if we were sisters in another lifetime. You understand me on a level that I sometimes cannot comprehend myself. Throughout this insane journey, you have shown up for me on countless occasions with open arms and a helping hand. Thank you for your endless love and for being one of my biggest cheerleaders from day one. Your soul is one of the kindest I have ever met, and I am forever thankful to bear witness to it.

Sarah H., where do I even begin? I will forever thank my lucky stars that I get to know and love you! Not only are you one of the greatest friends I have ever known, but you never fail to show up for everyone around you. Your generous heart and kind spirit radiate into those around you. Thank you for loving *Blade of Broken Scales* as much as I do.

Skyla, my sweet sweet Skyla. You truly are my soul sister. I don't know how I ever survived so many years without you by my side, but I hope I never have to face another. You welcomed me with open arms from the very first day and never looked back. Not once did you complain when I asked for help; instead you jumped in head first with me. I am humbled by your love. You truly feel like a missing piece of my soul and I would not have survived any of this without you. Your help and support has truly kept me sane through all of this.

Jazzy, you have guided me through this journey with a gentle hand and a kind heart, never once steering me in the wrong direction. You are always there with no complaints, whether I need to crash out or needed your help. I truly believe we were meant to find one another, and I am so thankful we did.

Sarah D., you are one of the very first people who I ever entrusted to read *Blade of Broken Scales* and from that very first night, I knew we would be fast friends. You have shown up for me in more ways than I can count, even when it has meant staying up until 3am to do emergency line editing for me. I have been brought to tears by your kindness and generosity on numerous occasions, but especially during the chaos we have been thriving in this last month before release. Thank you for being an incredible friend and showing up with a village when I needed it most.

Mychaila, you came back to me at what could not have been a more perfect time. It has been so heart-warming and healing having you join me on this journey and support me without wavering. I am so thankful that we found each other again and have gotten to heal side-by-side. You are the best friend a girl could ask for, and I am so beyond blessed to have you in my life again.

Amanda, you have supported me in my journey from the very beginning, jumping for joy when Sarah pointed you my way. Your endless excitement for my story has fueled my passion. Thank you for jumping into the fire without hesitation.

Sarah E., thank you for having one of the gentlest souls I have ever met and for never having been a stranger. The moment we met, you welcomed me like a lifelong friend. Thank you for letting me crash out in your DMs and for offering your help when I needed it most. I am so thankful to have you in my corner.

Alyssa, there is no way I could ever encapsulate my gratitude into a few short sentences, but I am going to try. You have been in my corner through every era of life, sometimes silently and others right by my side. When I have lost myself and felt like there was no way back, you've guided me back to the girl you never once stopped believing in. You are my best friend, my soul sister, my ride or die, and I am so honored to have gotten to share this journey with you. It is so crazy to think that what started as two young girls writing One Direction fan fiction on Wattpad at 1am has turned into something so big and beautiful. I am so proud of us and the worlds we have created. We were girls together, and now I get the joy of growing into a woman by your side. I love you endlessly.

To every single person who dropped everything when my timeline fell to pieces: Sarah D., Alex, Kier, Jazzy, Alyssa, Skyla, Sarah H., Amanda, Sarah E.; it is because of you that this book is in the hands of all these readers right now. When it felt like everything I had built was falling around me, not a single one of you hesitated to help me pick up the pieces. I have cried endless tears of gratitude for your sacrifices. Because of all of you, there is girlhood among these pages and that is something I wouldn't trade for the world.

And lastly, to Jordan, my love. Without you, there would be no Roman. You waltzed into my life just when I needed you and made a hopelessly romantic girl believe that maybe her hope had not been misplaced. Thank you for believing in me when I could not do it myself, for carrying me through the dark and teaching me to embrace it, and for igniting my passion for life again. You make it easy to write swoonworthy book boyfriends. In this life and the next, my love.

CINNAMON BUNS

Ingredients:

DOUGH:

- 1 cup warm milk (110 degrees F/45 degrees C)
- 2 eggs, room temperature
- ⅓ cup margarine, melted
- 4 ½ cups bread flour
- 1 teaspoon salt
- ½ cup white sugar
- 2 ½ teaspoons instant yeast

FILLING:

- 1 cup brown sugar, packed
- 2 ½ tablespoons ground cinnamon
- ⅓ cup butter, softened

ICING:

- 1 ½ cups confectioners' sugar
- ¼ cup butter, softened
- 1 (3 ounce) package cream cheese, softened
- ½ teaspoon vanilla extract
- ⅛ teaspoon salt

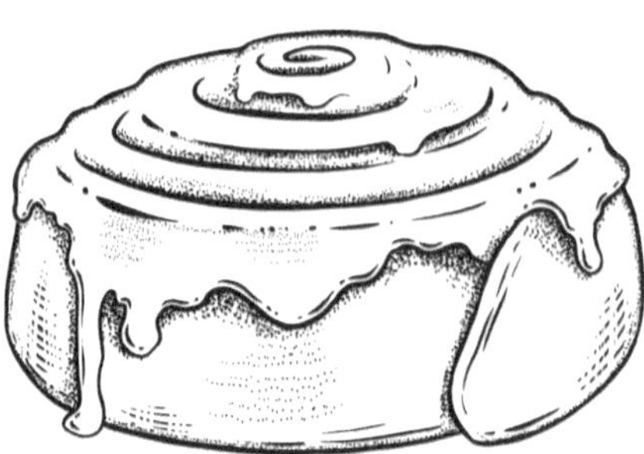

Instructions:

1. Prepare dough: Mix by hand the milk, eggs, margarine, flour, salt, white sugar, and yeast and set aside in a covered bowl.
2. When dough has doubled in size, turn it out onto a lightly floured surface. Cover it with a kitchen towel or plastic wrap and let it rest for 10 minutes.
3. Roll dough on a lightly floured surface to a 16x21-inch rectangle.
4. Prepare filling: Combine brown sugar and cinnamon in a small bowl. Spread softened butter over the dough, then sprinkle cinnamon-sugar mixture evenly over top.
5. Starting at the longer end, roll up the dough; cut into 12 rolls. Place rolls in a lightly greased 9x13-inch baking pan. Cover and let rise until nearly doubled, about 30 minutes.
6. Meanwhile, preheat the oven to 400 degrees F (200 degrees C).
7. Bake rolls in the preheated oven until golden brown, about 15 minutes.
8. While rolls are baking, prepare icing: Beat confectioners' sugar, butter, cream cheese, confectioners' sugar, vanilla, and salt until creamy.
9. Spread icing on warm rolls before serving.

Addie says enjoy!

Makayla is a self proclaimed poetry and romantasy author. Growing up, she always found herself daydreaming up extravagant stories and found most of her happiness in playing pretend (who doesn't love playing mermaids). When she found herself struggling to enjoy working in a corporate environment she decided what better to cure that than a little daydreaming. When she isn't found dreaming up her next literary adventures, Makayla can be found crafting, doodling art pieces for other authors, cozy on the couch with her dog Lilo and her boyfriend, or snuggled up with a good book and a cup of coffee enjoying the beautiful Wyoming sunsets.

Keep up with future projects!

: @makaylamariewrites

: @makaylamariewrites

www.ingramcontent.com/pod-product-compliance
Lightning Source LLC
Chambersburg PA
CBHW030044130726
47901CB00007BA/1958